*Eleni Beach*
An Adult Novel

Elizabeth Slater

Bloomington, IN — Milton Keynes, UK

*AuthorHouse™*
*1663 Liberty Drive, Suite 200*
*Bloomington, IN 47403*
*www.authorhouse.com*
*Phone: 1-800-839-8640*

*AuthorHouse™ UK Ltd.*
*500 Avebury Boulevard*
*Central Milton Keynes, MK9 2BE*
*www.authorhouse.co.uk*
*Phone: 08001974150*

*© 2006 Elizabeth Slater. All rights reserved.*

*No part of this book may be reproduced, stored in a retrieval system, or transmitted by any means without the written permission of the author.*

*First published by AuthorHouse 7/7/2006*

*ISBN: 1-4259-3647-4 (sc)*

*Printed in the United States of America*
*Bloomington, Indiana*

*This book is printed on acid-free paper.*

## Author's Note

It is obvious that many of the settings used in this book are real but I would like to point out that while the taverna at Eleni beach does exist I have no knowledge of it's owners and I have used the setting purely because of it's stunning beauty.

D Force Royal Engineers operated in the Singapore area during the Second World War.

Throughout this story any reference to persons living or dead is purely coincidental.

## Chapter 1

She watched as the ground quickly rose to meet them, thinking of her beloved father she closed her eyes tightly. Had he sat by the window looking? Was he watching as the sea got nearer, knowing that in seconds he was going to die? Tears fell down her cheeks and she began to tremble.

"Hold my hand love. I don't like this bit either. We can comfort each other." She felt a warm hand take hold and opened her eyes. The lady in the seat next to hers, the one she had ignored all the way from New York was smiling.

"Now isn't that better?" she inquired. Both hands now holding tightly on to the girl. "That's it we're down."

They both let go of deep breaths when they felt the bump as the plane hit the tarmac and heard the roar of the engines, confirming the woman's words.

"Thank you." was all she could mutter; still in shock from her thoughts whilst landing. "Thank you so much" She mustered a weak smile and wiped her face with her hands.

She felt slightly silly needing the comfort of a stranger, but she was so grateful to the woman.

Eleni was 27 years old, although today she looked much younger. Only minimal make up on her lovely face, her long black hair held back by a red band, her tiny frame dressed in jeans and t shirt emphasizing her slim figure. She could have passed for a teenager.

"I hope you enjoy Athens," the woman almost shouted as other passengers making their way towards the steps now in place parted them. "We love it. All the old things. Its great." Her strong Yankee accent making it sound irreverent to describe the wonderful antiquities as "old things".

"Yes. I'm sure I will" Eleni replied thinking that she probably wouldn't see any of it.

Athens was just the first stop on her journey, one more plane trip, a ferry to Skiathos, and then after that a few days on to Kefalonia. This was going to be one hell of a tiring journey, but hopefully, eventually, it would prove worth it.

After collecting her large rucksack from the carousel, she checked in at the Olympic desk for the next leg. Luggage gone and ticket safely stowed she went in search of a café.

Eleni walked slowly through the busy airport, desperately in need of fresh air, but with only a very short stop over, dare not risk going outside.

Spotting a ladies loo she went in to freshen up, anything to pass a little time. The heat from the hand dryers hit her as soon as she opened the door; it made her feel quite queasy. She splashed cool water on her face and let the tap run over her wrists and hands. Using a paper towel she dried off and re applied her face cream and sparse make up. Only lipstick and mascara for now. After a quick brush of her hair, which she let fall free, and a long squirt of body spray she did in fact feel slightly better. Now for a coffee.

The meals on the plane had been bland, and mostly she had declined, but now all of a sudden she felt hungry. Picking a delicious chicken salad baguette to go with the strongest coffee they made, she found a table and sat people watching, waiting for her flight to be called.

It was just under an hour before she heard her number come over the crackling speakers. She picked up her handbag and made her way quickly to the departure gate mentioned. Other passengers coming the opposite way made the short walk quite stressful and by the time she had reached her gate she felt shattered, hot, and once again quite grubby.

The plane on the tarmac looked so small compared to the huge Boeing that had flown her from New York, she thought, but then it did only have a short way to go in comparison. Athens to Thessalonica.

Safely strapped in her seat she waited for the engines to kick in and felt the pull on her body as they gathered speed. It seemed that no sooner had they taken off, than the descent into Thessalonica had begun. Only drinks and snacks had been offered this time, nothing like the constant stream of refreshments on the previous flight. Eleni settled for water.

Once again the ground rushed to meet them as they landed, but this time, closing her eyes she tried to remember the soft hands of the woman on the Boeing. It worked; she kept control of her feelings, and stopped the tears from falling. Just.

With her rucksack safely on her back, she made her way out into the heat of the Greek afternoon. The sunshine hit the minute she stepped outside. The smell of fresh, but hot air, the sudden sounds of cars hooting, the weight on her back, and the time difference all played a part in her fainting there and then on the spot.

Coming round slowly she could see a sea of faces peering down at her. Babbling Greek ladies enquiring of each other if she was all right and a young English couple who had been on her flight, just standing watching.

Luckily having a Greek father she was fluent in their language and sitting up slowly reassured the women that she was indeed OK. She asked if they could direct her to the taxi rank and accepted their assistance in standing up. Cold water was offered and accepted gratefully as the ladies took her to the nearest vacant car. She thanked her helpers in their native language and was pleased to see their reaction. It was obvious from her accent that she was American, but they acknowledged her speaking their tongue with hugs and kisses.

After asking for the port she sank into the dark leather seats of the taxi. The driver had put the air conditioning on full and soon the cold air began to work on her tired body. She watched as they made their way quickly through the cities suburbs and out into the almost barren countryside. The heat of the Greek summer scorching any crops left in the ground, only fig and olive trees seemed to thrive at this time of year. She stretched out her tired legs and at last began to relax.

It seemed all too soon that the driver steered the car into the harbor side road and stopped at the side of a huge building.

The ferry terminal was large, very busy, hot and noisy, and quite a shock after the lovely car ride she had just had. Once again she felt the stress and tiredness of her long journey creeping into her body as she made her way through the huge green doors of the entrance.

Inside the building many people were making their way to an assortment of different islands and a loud piercing voice was unceasingly announcing the departure times through huge speakers on the walls. The noise made it feel exciting. The smells even more so, all mixed with the shouting of many languages and people, people everywhere. Her head began to throb.

Lorries laden with marble, some with live animals and chickens, others with fruit, all fought their way on to the boats. Their exhaust fumes tainting the air in the confines of the crowded terminal. It was exciting, but a little frightening. She watched as they inched their way towards the ferry, cars and little vans taking up any space that came available. How they would manage to fit them all in was a mystery to her.

She stopped by the only shop, which seemed to sell almost everything you could imagine, now desperate for some water and headache tablets, and surprisingly spotted a display of pretty flowers. They gave her an idea. Being unable to decide between red or yellow rose buds, she bought two bunches, one of each. They looked so lovely in their cellophane wrapper, their colours so bright, it almost seemed a shame that they were soon to be destroyed.

Making her way on to the ferry and through the throng of people she managed to find a seat on the top deck. It was hot there in the sunshine, but it was where she wanted to be. She wanted to see Skiathos as the ferry neared but mostly she wanted to see the sea.

An hour into the trip she stood up, and taking her flowers leant as far as she could over the railings. Muttering a prayer she threw the roses into the sea and watched as the wake from the ferry gently took them below the surface.

She sat looking at her entwined fingers and felt the familiar trickle of tears. This time there was no one to comfort her. How she would have liked the lady on the plane to be there now. How she would have loved to have her wrap her arms around her and hold her close. But no. She was on her own now, and forever.

Managing to pull herself together she turned and watched as the island came into view, at first a dark lump in the horizon, but slowly she could make out the buildings and trees. It was as if everyone on board wanted to see it and very quickly the top deck was packed. Using her elbows she stood her ground and managed to keep her place at the front, Eleni watched in silence as the harbor came slowly closer.

The ferry's horn blew a long hoot announcing their arrival, and as it docked gave a couple more. Everyone began to collect their belongings and make their way to the quaint quayside to haggle with the owners of vacant rooms, or to jump into waiting taxis. The noise was tremendous, people jostling everywhere, car horns hooting, and voices shouting, suddenly she needed space.

She found an empty spot on the pavement and stopped. She stood and looked around at the lovely tavernas with their fresh fish tanks outside, at the little red kiosks selling cigarettes and newspapers, the pretty white buildings with blue shutters, the tubs of large red geraniums and took a deep breath of the strong garlicky air.

It was as if she had come home. She felt so close to her father at that minute it was incredible.

"Rooms for rent" she heard a man shout "Rooms for rent" he repeated. She looked around and saw an old man holding a placard. Eleni Beach Rooms it read. Deciding it must be a good omen she made her way over and asked, once again speaking Greek, for details. The man took out a photo album and began to show her pictures of a lovely bright, spotlessly clean, bedroom, a splash room, and outside breakfast table. He chattered away telling her how beautiful it was, how peaceful, and gave her a price so cheap she found it impossible to turn down.

She asked to stay for one week and he agreed reluctantly

"You are welcome to stay longer if you wish. I am sure you will find a week is not long enough on this lovely island" His voice was deep and calming.

He helped her climb into the front of his battered little Fiat van and threw her rucksack into the open space behind.

"Are all your rooms full then?" she asked as they dodged the town traffic on their way from the port.

"No little one. I only have one room to rent, but when I first started, no one came. No one wanted to be on their own, so now I shout rooms, it works well you see. When I saw you I felt you needed some peace, I can see it in your eyes. That is why I called out to you." He smiled down at her and she smelt the slight hint of garlic in his breath. "You will love it trust me"

Soon out of the town they found themselves on the only road of the island. He explained as they went, how it ran from the town to a wonderful beach right at the tip of the island, not far in fact from where she would be staying. It only went down one side, as the other was far too rocky and dangerous for a road to be built. He told her about the frequent bus service that ran virtually 24 hours a day, and pointed out places of interest that hopefully she would visit during her stay.

He asked a little about her journey and was surprised to learn she had not stopped traveling since she had left New York.

"You will be so tired later little one. But do not worry we will look after you" he said comfortingly.

They had traveled for almost the whole length of the road before he turned off on to a dirt track and up a steep hillside. She wondered if this was wise. What did she know of this man, yet here she was in his van, going into what seemed a small forest.

She looked across and studied him. Typical Greek she thought. Loose grey trousers held close with a large brown belt, his gleaming white shirt, the sleeves rolled up and open at the neck. Thick stubble on his chin, and his flat cap firmly upon his head. He looked 60ish, but who could tell? He turned to see her staring.

"Don't worry little one. We will soon be there" Once again he smiled. It was such a lovely soft smile that she relaxed again immediately.

Her first view of the beach took her breath away. Never before had she seen anything so beautiful. A small crescent of golden sand littered with ragged raffia sun umbrellas and brightly coloured loungers. The sea a wonderful bright blue, moved lazily in the heat of the afternoon, seemingly beckoning her to bathe.

"It's wonderful." She gasped.

"You see," he said bringing the van to a stop "I knew you would love it. Welcome, little one, to Eleni Beach. Here let me help you."

They walked down towards the water and turned along the sand. A large white house built so close to the beach that the sand reached almost up to the front door, with only a few marble slabs stopping it, stood before them.

"This is my home and where you will hopefully stay for many days" He opened the blue wooden door and ushered her inside. "I will show you your room and then I think you would like to swim. Am I right?"

"Oh you bet. I can hardly wait to jump into that lovely sea" For the first time in weeks her eyes shone. All of a sudden she felt so lucky to have met this man at the harbor; it was as if someone was looking after her from above.

It didn't take long for her to unpack; the rucksack held only shorts and tops, a couple of dresses and two pairs of sandals, and, of course her toiletries. She threw them all on the bed in her search for her swimming things. The clothes could wait, her body could not, it needed the sea this minute.

She stripped off her clothes dropping them on the floor, promising herself to wash them later, slipped into her black costume and headed for the sea.

Remembering to take her passport she stopped on the way and gave it to the old man. He needed it to register her as a visitor to the island he had told her, and would give it back as soon as he could.

He saw as she ran down the sand, dropping her towel as she went. She carried on running straight into the waves until the sea proved to strong to lift her legs. Momentarily she disappeared under the water, coming up brushing her hair from her face. He watched as she swam, on her front, then rolling over and floating on her back. He could almost feel the tension being released from her body.

He turned and looked at the passport still in his wrinkled hands and tapped it on his thumb. There was no need for him to open it. He knew who she was. He had known the second he laid eyes on her.

Eleni Russos. The daughter of his childhood best friend.

## • CHAPTER • 2

The old man looked on as she swam, bobbing up and down so smoothly, just like a dolphin, just like her father used to do.

He watched as she left the water and flopped full stretch on an empty sun bed. He turned to his wife and smiled.

"Our new guest Sofia, Eleni Russos" he looked over to the girl again and sighed.

Back to work he thought and began to busy himself in the kitchen. He occasionally stopped and thought of those days so long ago. He must tell her before she left. But when? When would be the right time to tell her it was because of him her father had died? How do you tell someone that?

Eleni too was thinking. Her mind still in a whirl from traveling. She had left New York on the 10am flight to Athens, but now what day was it? She had no idea of the time, but did time really matter. Here she was, lying in the sun after a wonderful swim. She turned over slowly feeling the warmth soak into her back, her head pillowed on her crossed arms.

Who cares about the time she thought, or for that matter what day. She drifted off into a lovely sleep.

"Eleni, Eleni, wake up" The voice that crept into her mind was her fathers. "Eleni you have been in the sun long enough for today" She felt a hand on her shoulder gently move. Opening her eyes slowly she focused on the old man and jumped.

"I'm sorry to startle you little one, but you have been her for quite some time. The sun is very hot today and I do not want you to burn" He looked concerned. "Come into the shade. Please"

"Yes" she replied still sleepy "I think I will" She stood shakily and stretch her arms high above her head as she gave a long yawn. "You know you sounded just like my father then. He used to pronounce my name just like that. Elen-i. It sounded wonderful, but then I suppose him being Greek has something to do with that" The old man just nodded and walked back to his taverna. It was the first time Eleni had noticed it.

She stood on the sand and looked firstly at the pretty house. Two large shuttered windows on the ground floor, each side of the lovely blue front door. Three shuttered windows upstairs; the one on the right she knew was hers. She imagined one of the others was the old man's and his wife's, so who stayed in the other one? She smiled as she spotted a large television ariel and a big black satellite dish clinging to the roof, they looked so out of place. Her eyes then went to a little kiosk attached to the side of the house. Here advertisements for ice cream, coca cola, water and chocolate stood in the sand. At the side of that were three steps up to a beautiful and so typically Greek taverna. She could see the roof was made of bamboo and raffia with a fabulous grape vine draped over, many of its fruit falling through into an eating area separated from the beach by a low bamboo fence.

Eleni walked slowly towards the steps taking in the scene before her. Ten little wooden tables, covered in check cloths, stood in the sand, comfortable whicker chairs surrounding them. Some of the tables were occupied with people eating, some with others just drinking. Some were watching an English football match on the TV perched over the bar, their chairs sinking deeper into the sand as they moved, animated by the scenes on the screen.

She smiled to herself. I wonder if they eventually get to be sitting on the sand, she thought. She noticed a tiny old lady taking fresh drinks over to a table, her bare feet hardly disturbing the sand floor as she walked.

"My wife Sofia and I am Tomas" The old man spoke, breaking into her thoughts. She took his outstretched hand and shook it and then held it in both hands.

"I am Eleni Russos, but then you know that from my passport. Thank you so much for bringing me here. It is like something out of a fairy tale, it is so wonderful" She shook his hand once more.

"Come, this is your table" He gestured towards a small table by the bar. "What can I get you? A drink perhaps, a salad. I make lovely Greek salads" he stood waiting for her to reply.

"I would love an ouzo and lemonade please. You will have to put it on my bill as I have no money with me at the moment."

"Little one you are my guest. Please do not concern yourself. I will fetch your drink" he turned and walked to the bar, returning moments later with her long cool drink.

"Wonderful" she said after taking the first sip. "Just as my father would have made" She smiled at him, not realizing those words had torn at his heart. "He used to make lovely Greek salads too. In fact he taught me how to cook many Greek dishes. We used to have a wonderful time in the kitchen. Perhaps you will let me show you one day when the taverna is quiet?"

"Perhaps you can little one, but for now you must rest. You have had a long journey and your body will soon tire. Tonight you must drink plenty of water, eat a little and then I will make you a night drink that will help you rest" With that he returned to his work in the kitchen.

Eleni sat watching as people from the beach gradually left their sun beds and filled the taverna's tables. Tomas and Sofia were kept busy with their orders for food and drinks, and even though her glass was now empty, she did not like to disturb them.

Tomas looked over "Help yourself. One more ouzo and then water for you" He laughed as he pointed to the little bar behind her.

Eleni rose and explored the many bottles behind the obviously old but very clean bar. Finding the ouzo she poured some of the liquid into her glass, then filling it almost to the top with lemonade she plopped in cubes of ice.

"Large beer when you're ready please love." A pale, very tall English man stood leaning on the bar. "And one of those drinks like that" he pointed to hers. "We will be on the swinging chair". With that he walked away, for a moment Eleni, thought he seemed familiar. Then she remembered he had been there when she had fainted. She felt slightly silly and thought how long ago it seemed.

She noticed the pretty chair at the end of the tables and saw him sit next to the woman who had also been looking down at her sprawled on the floor.

Feeling a little confused she looked over to Tomas who just nodded and laughed. Grabbing a white apron from the back of the bar door she quickly wrapped it around her costume, grinning at the thought of her friends seeing her dressed like this, and began to work.

Taking a large glass she carefully poured the beer then made the ouzo drink, placing them on a tray she took them over to the couple. Smiling and praying they did not remember her from earlier in the day she placed the glasses on the chair's side tables.

Back at the bar she rummaged around for some paper, and finding only an empty cigarette box ripped it open flat. Using a pen found in the kiosk she wrote down what the couple had had. Once again she was interrupted.

"Excuse me love can we have more over here" She looked up to see a man waving an empty glass.

Eleni walked quickly over to the old man.

"Tomas quick. I need a pad to write all of this down." Laughing he produced one from his back trouser pocket.

"The tables are numbered on the side, look." He pointed to an empty table. "Just write down what they have and then which table it is. I will work out their bills later. I am sorry about this Eleni but we are so busy this evening, it seems they are staying until the football match has ended, would you mind doing this for me? Just until we are straight. The holiday makers do not like to wait, they never seem to get used to the Greek way."

She patted his shoulder." Don't worry Tomas. I am enjoying it" With that she went over to the table where the man still sat with his glass held high.

"I'm sorry for the wait," She said smiling "What can I get for you"

Three hours later she was collecting the empty glasses and tidying the bar. It was as if she had been born to serve. The customers had loved her outfit. They loved the way she could speak English, German and French, all thanks to her top class education, but mostly they loved the way she smiled.

"Little one, thank you so much" Tomas was now raking the sand between the tables. "You looked as if you were having fun" he bent to pick up a mound of cigarette ends and spilt food. "That's better. So much easier than having to mop"

It was true. Within minutes the taverna looked spotless. Sofia had sorted the kitchen and wiped the tables, Tomas had raked the floor, and Eleni had cleaned the bar and glasses.

"Right" said Tomas "Now for our food"

Sofia came over to the little table by the bar where Eleni was now sitting.

"Thank you" She said softly "You were a big help" Her smile lit the whole of her pretty but wrinkled face.

Tomas returned before Eleni could reply. "Meze, crusty bread who's hungry?" He carefully placed empty plates down before filling the table with the meze dishes. Little portions of delicious food. There was a large bowl of Greek salad loaded with plump black olives, tzatziki, tiny pieces of octopus and squid, spiced chicken, and warm crusty bread. What a feast? It was wonderful. Eleni had forgotten just how hungry she was until now. They had large glasses of water, and smaller ones of delicious retzina.

Eleni sat back, full almost to bursting point, and watched as the sun slowly dipped behind a ridge of mountains on another island in the distance.

They were now the only people on the beach as the holidaymakers had at last gone back to their hotels and apartments. All she could hear was the sea gently lapping on the shore, her toes wriggled in the soft still warm sand. She felt so content.

"Here. Drink this. It will help you relax" Tomas held a steaming mug of delicious hot chocolate and hazelnut, topped with thick cream.

"This is a dieters nightmare," She laughed sipping cautiously at the hot drink. "And I don't think I need it to help me sleep" She said yawning widely.

"You may feel tired but you have had a very strange day. It may play on your mind and keep you awake, that will help. Trust me," Sofia said softly. Her voice was so gentle, she almost sang her words.

Eleni turned her chair to face the sea and slowly drank her chocolate. The sound of the sea and the lovely soothing drink soon had their effect and she fell asleep sinking deeper into the sand on her wicker chair.

## • CHAPTER •
## 3

Eleni woke to the sun streaming through the shutters, uncertain for a moment where she was.

Lazily she looked around and could see that the room was quite large, painted through out in a dazzling white. She spotted a small whicker table and matching chair by the window, a big round multi coloured carpet lay on the marble tiles between them and a long white wardrobe, its doors full-length mirrors.

By her bed, which she could sense was quite large, stood a little wooden table. On its top a very dainty lamp, its cream marble base the figure of a nymph, it was as if she were dancing, scattered by her feet lay some leaflets giving information about the island.

On the long wall between the bed and window she could see some photographs, she promised herself to examine them more closely later.

It was so simple, comfortable and clean; Eleni could tell that she would be happy here.

Stretching and yawning she pulled the sheet from across her body and was amazed to see that she was dressed in a long white cotton nightdress. The reality quickly dawned and she felt a blush creep over her face.

Oh my God, she thought. The last thing she could remember was sitting in the chair, sipping her drink and listening to the sea, so how had she got here? Who had undressed her?

Embarrassed she looked around the room to where she had thrown her clothes before her swim. They had gone. The room was tidy, her rucksack sitting on the floor at the side of the white wooden wardrobe. There was only one answer. Sofia.

After a long cool shower she rubbed her body with wonderfully soothing sun cream. Tomas was right, she had spent a long time in the sun yesterday and her skin felt tight. Dressed in shorts, t-shirt and sandals, her damp hair clinging to her back, she made her way downstairs and along the beach to the taverna.

"Kalimera Eleni" (Good morning) Tomas called as she approached. He was once again raking the sand by the tables "I hope you slept well"

"Kalimera Tomas, yes thank you I did. But I must apologise for causing you any trouble. I am sorry but I don't remember much after your nightcap. Please tell me what happened"

Eleni made her way up the steps and sat at the little bar side table.

"Coffee?" Sofia was at her side in a second "You look so much better this morning little one" Gently she stroked Eleni's hair "You were so tired last night Tomas carried you to your room and I put you in one of my nightdresses. I know it didn't fit too well, but I could not find one in your rucksack"

Eleni was again embarrassed. "That is because I do not own one" she giggled "Thank you so much Sofia, I have caused you so much work and yes I would love coffee. Thank you"

"It is no trouble Eleni. After all of your hard work yesterday it was the least I could do. But you should always wear something in bed; it helps to stop the mosquitoes biting. I have washed the clothes you traveled in, and your costume. Look" Eleni's eyes followed Sofia's pointing finger to a small washing line full of her clothes blowing in the gentle breeze, she felt chocked and lost for words. Standing up she kissed the cheek of this lovely little woman.

"Here we are little one. Coffee, one of my special pastries and a fresh peach. So fresh it is still warm" Tomas placed a tray with the breakfast on down on the table. The pastry looked delicious, as big as a saucer, covered in honey and sliced almonds.

"You are trying to get me fat Tomas" Eleni laughed

"It will do you good. It will put some sugar into your blood and give you energy." Tomas said walking past her table carrying his rake.

Eleni poured herself a cup of very strong smelling coffee and whilst waiting for it to cool a little took a bite from the pastry. It crumbled softly into her mouth, the honey running down her chin. Laughing she tried to catch the crumbs as they fell and licked her lips noisily. It was pure delight. As she sat eating she watched Tomas rake the sand around the beach umbrellas. Then he fetched the sun beds one by one from the pile at the back of the beach. Placing them one each side of the umbrellas, he angled them carefully to catch the maximum sunshine. Then dusted them down with a cloth. She sipped her coffee and watched as he carried small plastic tables and placed them in the sand between the beds. Next came clean ashtrays from the bar, and lastly white carrier bags were tied to the umbrellas. She smiled as she saw him stand back and admire his work. Work that he obviously enjoyed.

"You do that well Tomas," she said as he came back to the taverna. "But why the bags?"

"Well our visitors buy ice creams, water and cola. It is much easier for me if they put their rubbish in the bags and then when they are all gone I just collect them and put them in the bin. There is always a small amount of paper and things but it saves me so much time. Did you enjoy your pastry?"

"Yes thank you it was delicious. Just like my father used to make, you were right I can feel that it did me good" Her eyes shone as she spoke.

"You talk a lot about your father little one. You must tell me more when we have time" he saw the sad look in her eyes "That is if you want". He looked down at her, so beautiful, so young, and so much like his sister it hurt.

"Perhaps one day I will" She smiled but he could see her eyes were full of tears. He nodded towards her as he left and headed for the kitchen.

Sofia came to clear the table

"Do you want another pastry Eleni?" she enquired.

"Oh no Sofia. One is more than enough thank you. It will certainly see me through to lunchtime, and that peach was so juicy. Um!"

"What will you do today?" Sofia asked as she busied herself at the table.

"I would like to catch the bus Tomas told me about and go into the town. I can look around the shops and buy some essentials and then when I return have a lovely swim." Eleni rose to leave.

"If you walk over the hill and down onto the main road, the bus stop is on the left. Just ask the driver for stop number 1 and on your return it is stop number 25. They run very frequently so you will have no trouble coming home" Sofia's voice yet again sang as she spoke. "We will see you later then. Have a nice time"

"Thank you I will"

Eleni set off towards the hill behind a row of cypress and olive trees. As she walked she was surprised to see a clearing in the woods that Tomas had made for cars to use, his little Fiat and an old fashioned camper van its only occupants this early in the day. On the edge of the car parking space were small cabins containing showers, peeking inside one she was touched to see little sachets of shower jell and shampoo similar to the ones in her splash room. It seemed nothing was too much trouble for this lovely old couple.

Following Sofia's instructions she soon found the main road and spotted a bent rusty bus stop post. Looking at the sign she noticed that it did indeed have the numbers 25 in English and Greek, and that was it. No name, just numbers.

She watched as a bus passed on the other side of the road and turn round in an opening a little further on, before coming back towards her. Others had already formed a queue, so she waited her turn and asked for stop number 1 before handing over the fare. Luckily she found an empty seat by the window and watched fascinated as the countryside sped past.

They traveled high up the hillsides giving her a good view of the marvelous sandy coves below, she could see tiny boats bobbing lazily on the calm water. The road then dipped down into villages set right upon pretty beaches. Everywhere there were tavernas advertising their food, shops with everything you could want for a day by the sea set out on the pavements in front. Lots of lovely white cottages stood in fields, their red slate roofs reflecting the sun. She saw so many tubs bursting with bright red geraniums she was amazed.

At each of the remaining stops more and more people climbed on board, and the bus was full to overflowing by the time it reached Skiathos Town. Eleni found it amusing how the different had nationalities reacted to it. Being able to speak many languages she could understand everyone on board. She heard the English laugh, the Germans complain and the Greeks not notice, they just talked about the coming day.

She made a mental note as she got down from the bus. On the harbor side, opposite the red kiosk selling newspapers. That's where she would need to come to catch the bus back. She repeated it over in her mind and walked towards the shops, not realizing just how many red kiosks there were.

Eleni had a very successful morning. She bought a little travel iron, some washing powder, another costume, black of course, a long linen beach top, and a couple of pretty cotton tops to wear with her shorts. Lastly, a lovely red cotton sundress with a gold Greek key design around the neckline, it would look fabulous with her sandals back at the room, and a tan of course, she thought.

She gazed into quite a few of the many jewellers, promising to return and buy Sofia a present before she left, and of course something for herself.

As the sun grew hotter she stopped to look into an arty shop selling fabulous photographs of the island, at first because it was in the shade, but she was soon fascinated. She would definitely have some of those; they would look lovely with the ones her father had bought from an exhibition in New York. The photographs were all in black and white making their subjects seem so much more dramatic.

One was of a boy swimming with a dolphin; he was almost a shadow of the graceful animal as they rode the waves in unison, the sun glistening in the droplets of water on their backs. Eleni remembered this was similar to the one her father had now on the wall of his office.

Another of three beautiful sunflowers with bees collecting the nectar, their wings caught in frantic movement, their pouches already full of the precious powder.

A photograph of an old run down building, overgrown by long grasses and a grape vine, its lush fruit falling over the stone ruin. In the background the sun was setting over the sea. The photographer had captured the moment so well you could almost feel it. This was also similar to one on the wall at home.

Another caught her eye. A young girl standing on a cliff, one hand shading her eyes, her other arm raised as if waving. Her dress tight to her slim body as it flowed in the breeze and her long hair streaming behind her as she looked out to sea. Her face was partly hidden, but Eleni imagined she was beautiful; she looked like a little fairy. Peering closer she noticed how the sun refelcted the tears falling down her face. It was a masterpiece and took her breath away. She could almost feel the girls sorrow.

As she looked, now totally engrossed by the wonderful pictures she noticed a small one towards the back. It was of three young boys, all dressed in the old fashioned dark knee length shorts, and all were bare chested. Two were standing on a small rock in the sea, laughing as they pointed towards the third. Waves were breaking white as the water swirled around their feet. The other boy, who had obviously been running towards them, was caught the second he jumped on the rock. It looked as if he was flying. She looked closer, and squinting her eyes tried to make out their faces. Two seemed familiar. She peered closer, then BANG. Her head hit the glass of the window. For a second she was stunned by the suddenness of it.

A young man rushed from the shop and held her arm. "Are you alright?" He enquired in English "That was quite a knock you took. Please come and sit". Still holding her arm he led her into the shop. It was so cool her skin broke out in pimples immediately. "Please, please sit" He stood at her side until she was comfortable in a large cream leather chair. "Let me fetch you some water". He rushed off as if it was an emergency, giving Eleni just enough time to compose herself.

Taking the glass of ice-cold water from his outstretched hands she thanked him in his own language.

"You speak Greek?" he asked quite puzzled. Not many tourists had even the slightest idea of his native tongue.

"Of course. I am American but my father was Greek. What made you speak English?" she replied.

"I looked at your clothes, the fact you had tourist shopping bags, and because you were alone" She was amazed that he had noticed so much

"Greek girls love to shop in groups. They spend most of the time giggling in groups" He had a wonderful smile as he spoke.

"I feel such an idiot. I was trying to get a better look at the boys on the rock" She explained, "I just felt they were familiar. Did you take the photograph?

"No not me. It is one of my fathers, taken many years ago. He is the one flying through the air. His friend Tomas is standing on the rocks, and the other is their pal Marco." He waited for her to speak.

"I am renting a room from a Tomas, it is him in the photo, is that why I thought he looked familiar" She smiled up at him.

"Tomas. Which of his houses are you in?" he asked

"Which? How many has he got?"

"Tomas and my father own many houses on the island, and some on Alonysos just across the water. They rent them out during the holiday season. All of them have tavernas attached, so between them they make a good income."

Eleni laughed. "Good for Tomas. I am staying at Eleni Beach. It is wonderful. But why if they have a good income does he work so hard there?

"Tomas loves to be busy. He would hate to do nothing, Sofia is the same. They do it because they love it, and because they miss Vanni, their son. He lives in Athens with his aunt and only comes home for holidays. They only have one spare room, as you know, so it is not that hard really, and the taverna is only busy for short periods. Once the sun has gone down the people leave, and with it being not so easy to get to hardly any families go there. Only couples, his lovers as Tomas calls them. Please excuse me for a moment"

Eleni watched as he walked over to a couple looking at the photographs. He was right. She remembered Tomas as he admired his work on the beach that morning. She remembered the sachets of shampoo. Yes he did it for love.

The couple in the shop left after buying a lovely photograph of poppies, high on the cliff side, their tall stems bent against the wind. Once again it almost spoke it was so graphic.

"That was one of mine they bought. Mine are this side of the shop, the others are my fathers." His smile showed how pleased he was "Mostly the ones we sell are my fathers. He is a magician with his cameras, but just now and again mine too are bought. It pleases me very much"

She watched as he filled the wall space with an identical photograph to the one just sold. "We always keep the original and take copies." He said as he saw her looking.

"You are very good too from what I can see." Eleni stood and walked around, admiring the work of this pleasant young man. Her mind had already put him in the "George Michael" range with his looks and she felt a shiver each time he glanced in her direction.

Unfortunately her naivety and sense of loneliness was making her a simple target for the young man who thrived in the company of women. Sensing that she was about to leave he quickly introduced himself.

"I am Nicos Mandros." He held out his hand.

Eleni took it "Eleni Russos. Thank you so much for the water. I feel better now and I must leave. I have time for lunch and then I will get the bus back. It was so nice to meet you" Picking up her shopping, she began to walk to the door.

"Please let me take you for lunch. You are a guest of Tomas and he would severely tell me off if I did not look after you" Nicos was quickly after her. Pulling the blinds down to protect the photographs from the sun he slid the closed sign across the door and locked it, all within what seemed seconds.

"You must be hungry," she laughed.

No, he thought, I am in love. Again. He took her shopping in one hand, and held her arm with the other. No way was he going to let her go to lunch alone. He was a little scared by the feelings this beautiful girl had stirred in him. He smiled. His mother would be so pleased. How long now had she been on at him to find a girl? Now he had. He didn't dare ask how long she would be on the island. He just knew he wanted her forever, well for now anyway, perhaps he wouldn't say anything to his mother after all. No not yet.

Many of the shops were closing their shutters for the lunch break as the young couple walked towards the harbor, their owners greeting Nicos cheerfully, teasing him about the girl on his arm. Eleni smiled at them and nodded, acknowledging their happy banter with a wave. She was happy to be walking with Nicos; she too felt the magnetism that had hit him so hard.

He led her to a harbor side taverna and sat her down in the shade. Calling to one of the waiters he asked for her shopping to be placed behind the counter, then ordered ouzo for them both.

"I take mine with lemonade please Nicos" She said as he ordered. "My father used to tell me I should take it the Greek way, but I prefer it as a long drink" She smiled over towards him and he fell deeper as he looked into her huge dark eyes. Eyes so dark they were almost black. He studied her hair. Long, thick and black, just a hint of auburn shining like gold. Her skin, a lovely olive. She was so wonderful, so tiny and fragile; he could hardly tear his eyes away.

The drinks appeared quickly, and after letting her take a few sips he passed her a menu.

"What would you like?" His voice deep with emotion. "Please choose"

"Salad, tzatziki, and then fish souvlaki please" She saw a glint in his eyes as she closed the menu and passed it to him. Nicos nodded to the waiter and ordered the same. He could hardly think straight, let alone read a menu.

Eleni and Nicos sat in silence for a few moments, just gazing at people walking past. They watched as little boats came into the harbor, their bright colours reflecting in the water, and could just hear the tinkling of their bells.

They felt so comfortable together, so right. Eleni smiled over at him, pleased now to have bumped her head. Remembering the reason she had been looking in the window she began to speak.

"That photograph of the ruin, we have that in our home in New York. My father bought it from an exhibition a few months ago, and the one of the boy swimming with the dolphin. They are in his office. Was it your exhibition he went to see?"

"I am so pleased he likes them" Nicos replied whilst helping himself to salad. "We did have an exhibition that went to Athens, Paris, London and New York. Father sold many photographs, I did quite well too. It must have been ours that he went to, did you see it too?"

"Oh yes I went with him it was lovely. He was determined to have those photographs no matter what they cost. He said they reminded him of home."

"What a small world" Nicos was now fascinated. Just who was this girl? It sounded as if her father could be wealthy. But more than anything he wanted to know who she was with.

They ate their meal and chatted. He found out she was traveling alone. Her first stop had been his island, and then she was going to Kefalonia before returning to New York, but before home she wanted to see Athens, if there was time. The woman on the plane had wetted her appetite for the antiquities that she had only seen in books.

Lunch was over far too quickly for Nicos; he wanted it to last forever.

"Thank you so much" Eleni said as she rose "I must go now and catch my bus home. I will come to your shop again, and this time I will take you for lunch" She went as if to shake his hand.

"Eleni please. Let me take you back to the beach." He said her name just like her father and Tomas." I promise to drive carefully" His cheeky grin made her laugh.

"A Greek who drives carefully. That will be a first. OK come on. I don't really fancy a crowded bus after that lovely meal"

Nicos called for the bill and her shopping. He left a bundle of notes on the table and took her bags. "This way. My car is over here" he led her by the arm once again, this time into a tiny cobbled street, shaded by balconies brimming with tubs of bright geraniums.

She was a little shocked by his car. A bright red Audi coupe with cream leather interior, the top automatically opened when he pointed the control on his key ring. "I know" He laughed "A bit of a waste on the island, but I love it"

"It is beautiful, and just like mine at home. It was a birthday present from papa." A shadow came over her face. Nicos noticed that she spoke of her father often, and when she did this shadow formed. He would ask when the time was right.

They drove quite slowly down the island road, Nicos pointing out places of interest as they went. She laughed, as often he had to shout over the sound of the wind.

The journey was far too short for Nicos. He wanted to drive and drive with this girl beside him. She looked wonderful as her hair flew behind her, her eyes shone with laughter. But end it did, in the little clearing in the woods. Quickly he left the drivers seat and almost ran to open her door. Once again carrying her shopping he took her arm and led her along the sand towards the taverna.

"Nicos" came the shout from Tomas. "How lovely to see you. Please come you must take a drink" It was then he realized Nicos was holding Eleni's arm.

"Little one, are you OK?" He put down his tray and rushed over to her "Why are you with Nicos? Has something happened?"

Nicos told the story, and assured Tomas that not only was Eleni now OK but she had also been fed.

"It is good that you look after her Nicos. You would have had me to recon with if you had not" Eleni remembered what Nicos had said and she realised it was true. Nicos sat at the little table by the bar and accepted a drink from Tomas.

"Would you mind if I have a swim? I don't wish to seem rude, but I am so hot." Eleni looked towards Nicos. "Just a quick swim and I will be back" He smiled at her.

" Of course it is OK. You do as you wish Eleni. I will stay and talk to Tomas"

Nicos watched as she walked to the house and disappeared inside. Tomas frowned as he noticed the look on his face.

A short while later Eleni returned to the beach. Nicos almost choked on his drink, this time Tomas smiled.

They saw her walk gracefully across the sand, her black costume emphasizing her wonderful figure, and slowly glide into the water. Giving a little jump, she dived into an on coming wave. Nicos watched, his mouth open.

"Just like a dolphin eh Nicos" Tomas said softly.

"Yes Tomas, a beautiful dolphin."

"Be careful my friend" Tomas added, "She has been hurt very badly. Please be careful"

# • CHAPTER •
## 4

Whilst Nicos watched Eleni swim he told Tomas the events of the morning. He mentioned the photographs that had been of such interest to her, and the fact that her father had bought some of the exhibition ones.

"She said the boys seemed familiar, and even recognized you. I know papa was the one in flight, but who was Marco?" Nicos had not taken his eyes off Eleni as he spoke.

"It was her father." Tomas said softly "But promise me Nicos that you will say nothing. I must speak with her first. Promise me" Tomas noticed the shocked look on Nicos's face. "Promise me you will say nothing," he repeated sternly.

"You have my promise Tomas, but I ask that when you have spoken to her you will tell me also" Nicos looked worried.

"Of course I will, but only if Eleni agrees" Tomas and Nicos shook hands as if sealing a deal.

They both turned to look towards the sea as Eleni emerged from the water. She walked back to her belongings left on the sand and carefully dried herself on the previously disguarded towel. She put on her new beach top, which became transparent as she walked towards the taverna. Tomas again noticed the look on Nicos's face.

"Her heart has been broken, my friend, so do not play with her feelings. Give her time and give yourself time" Tomas placed his hand on Nicos's shoulder "Just give her time"

Nicos nodded, not really understanding, but agreeing anyway. He would give her all the time she needed.

Tomas was amused to see that after putting her towel behind the bar Eleni unhooked the apron from the door and began to serve the holidaymakers with drinks. Nicos watched as she poured the beers, and mixed the long drinks. He smiled as she went from table to table, speaking the different languages, and felt a little jealous when she laughed with the men. Eventually she came over to him. "Nicos have you forgotten the shop?"

"It will still be there tomorrow" He replied.

"Typical Greek" She teased and continued to pour drinks.

Suddenly a scream shattered the friendly banter. Tomas dropped his tray and ran into the kitchen, Eleni and Nicos not far behind.

"Sofia, Sofia are you alright." Tomas's voice reflected his pain at seeing his lovely wife on the floor. He knelt and cradled her head "Sofia what has happened."

Slowly she opened her eyes.

"Oh Tomas my arm. I think it is broken" They all looked towards her twisted arm, obviously broken. "I reached up for that large pan and slipped" They all looked up at the high shelf. "I fell towards the oven and in fear of getting burnt I put my arm out. Now look. What are we going to do? It will soon be time for the customers to eat." Her eyes shed tears as she spoke, and they could see the pain she felt.

"I will take you to the clinic in town. The customers can wait." Tomas gently helped her into a chair.

"No Tomas. I will take Sofia in my car it will be more comfortable for her, you follow in the van. Eleni can look after the bar and then I will return with papa. He will run the kitchen for you. I will wait on the tables and everything will be OK." Nicos took control immediately Eleni was very impressed.

The two men helped Sofia walk to the car, grateful for his offer, it was true it would be much more comfortable than Tomas's old van. Nicos thoughtfully put the top up and helped Sofia into the front seat.

Turning to Eleni he smiled, she felt her stomach twirl.

"I will be back soon. If it gets busy you must make them wait." She nodded and waved as the car and van left the clearing.

Eleni ran back to the house and quickly changed into shorts and t-shirt, she tied the apron around her waist and returned to the bar.

The time flew as Eleni served the customers. Luckily they realised that she was on her own, and many of them fetched their drinks from the bar to help. She wrote down on her pad their orders and hoped Nicos would be back in time to work out the bills.

She relaxed as she saw his car pull up. Nicos and a tall slim man walked towards her. They were so alike, you could tell immediately they were father and son.

"Eleni this if my father Alexi" They shook hands "He will cook and we will manage until Tomas is back"

Eleni could hardly believe it, the world-renowned photographer Alexi Mandros, cooking. Alexi too was shocked. Eleni Russos, who would have thought it. He hid his surprise by going straight into the kitchen.

Eleni followed and for the first time noticed how large the kitchen was. It was spotlessly clean. Baskets of fruit, salads, vegetables, and bread, covered one surface. There were large glass fronted fridges filled with fish and meats. Large silver saucepans filled shelves and hung from the ceiling, and on the floor a cupboard stocked with plates and bowls. Two large sinks dominated one wall and at the end of the room an old fashioned Greek oven, its fire already lit, a delicious aroma already floating from within.

"Well I think I can manage" Alexi smiled at Eleni. You are so much like your namesake it is incredible, he thought, as he watched her leave.

The meals he produced were wonderful, Tomas's had been delicious, but with Alexi each plate looked like a picture. He took such care with each dish, arranging the foods in a most artistic way.

As she worked Eleni suddenly remembered the photograph of the three boys. If one was Tomas and one Alexi, who was the third. Nicos had said he was called Marco, but thinking now, he too had seemed familiar. Was that her father they were with? But no it couldn't be. He came from Kefalonia not Skiathos. She dismissed the thought with a sigh and carried on pouring drinks.

Alexi was such fun to be with. He sang loudly as he cooked, clearly enjoying his chores. Occasionally Nicos would join in with the songs, entertaining the customers as he worked. During one song, that required a female voice, Eleni also sang.

After the meals had been finished Alexi appeared from the kitchen, wiping his hands dry on his apron.

"Come Nicos, Eleni, let us dance"

They stood in the gap between the bar and tables and linked arms. Alexi started to sing loudly again and the trio danced in the typical Greek way. The customers joined in the merriment by cheering and clapping.

By now they were serving themselves to drinks, and recording their orders on Eleni's pad.

Where else but Greece would you do that, she thought as she danced.

Tomas and Sofia were amazed at the sight that greeted them. The customers had now joined in and a long chain of dancers was on the beach. Nicos had made sure no one had come between him and Eleni, and he held her waist tightly as they moved. He felt so happy.

Alexi spotted Tomas and broke the chain.

"My friend how are you" he cupped Sofia's face in his hands and kissed her cheeks. "Let me look" She held her now plastered arm out for all to see. "Come you must sit down. I will fetch your supper." He pointed to the little table "Come Sofia"

Eleni and Nicos busied themselves with the bills and Alexi was once again in the kitchen. Tomas had put two tables together and was setting places for them all to eat.

"Come children, come" Alexi waved to Eleni and Nicos. He filled the table with all sorts of lovely foods. "Oh Tomas I have had a wonderful evening. I'm sorry it came about because of the accident, but please you must let me do this again"

"Of course you may" Tomas replied "But could you keep up the pace? I don't know dancing like that at your age"

They all laughed as they ate. Eleni looked across at Nicos, her eyes shone with happiness.

"The children did well." Alexi said as he helped himself to more chicken "And Eleni can dance very well. You know at times she reminds me of your sister Tomas, she too could dance. Marco taught you well little one"

The silence was broken only by the waves. Everyone stopped eating. Eleni looked frightened.

"You knew my father?" She asked, her voice shaking. Nicos reached across and held her hand to steady it. She glared at Tomas "You knew him yet you said nothing to me" The tears that flowed down her cheeks, tore at Nicos's heart. "You all knew and no one said anything" She was standing now, her body trembling. "The photograph. It is papa with you and Alexi."

"Oh little one, please come here" Tomas held out his arms and engulfed her in a long hug. She sobbed into his shoulder. "I was going to talk to you tonight, but with Sofia's accident. I'm afraid it got put off. Don't be angry with Nicos, he only knew when you were swimming and I made him swear not to tell you. I take it you told Alexi when you fetched him here?" He looked over to Nicos who just nodded.

Tomas held her face away from his shoulder and cupped it in both hands. "I did not know what to say little one. Please forgive me" He looked in such pain Eleni reached up and kissed his cheek.

"I will forgive you only if you tell me all about him" She whispered. "I want to know Tomas. Why was he coming here?"

"Let us clear this away, and then we can all talk" Alexi spoke as he began to collect the plates. "Nicos please make us a large pot of coffee and fetch the brandy. We will tell you all little one, but it will be a long night"

Eleni was in a daze as the others worked around her. Nicos placed the coffee pot and brandy in the middle of the table then fetched cups and glasses. He sat down beside her and took her hands.

"I will stay if you don't mind. I just want to be with you" He almost whispered the words not wishing to upset her but wanting to let her know he was there for her.

"Nicos, phone Athena and tell her we are with Tomas and will be late," Alexi ordered from the kitchen.

"Who is Athena?" Eleni enquired.

"Athena is my mama. I must let her know. When papa is with Tomas sometimes they stay up all night. They discuss business and then drink. Tonight will be similar I think. She will not be surprised if we don't return until morning." Nicos used his mobile phone and spoke quickly to his mother.

"Is she a photographer too?" Eleni asked

"No not mama. She does all the business paperwork and organizes the exhibitions. She is very good with figures and people. Papa only sees things through a lens. It is a good combination," Nicos explained." Our gallery in town is named after her although she doesn't spend much time there, she's usually off somewhere with an exhibition."

"Of course. The Athena Studios. I read the sign this morning" Eleni was beginning to relax "I remember now the exhibition in New York. That too was called The Athena Exhibition. I wonder could that have been your mother papa spoke to when he bought the photographs. A tall slim woman with black hair. Very well dressed I noticed"

"That sounds like her. She shops in Athens and Paris so she should look good" Nicos laughed "Papa pretends to be shocked when she returns. He says she spends a fortune, but really he loves it. He likes her to have nice things and he is so rich anyway. But still he teases her"

The others had returned to the table. Tomas poured the coffee, and Alexi the brandy.

"Eleni. Alexi and I have been talking and we think that if you tell us what you know about Marco first it will help us to tell our story. Do you think you can do that?" Tomas looked across at her.

Eleni nodded and felt Nicos's hand tighten on hers. It was comforting. She sat silently for few moments and sipped her coffee.

"Please remember much of the story is what he told me. I hope it will be all right". They all nodded.

"Just after the war" she began "Papa left Kefalonia to find his fortune in America."

Tomas frowned, he and Alexi looked at each other.

"His father had arranged for him to stay with a Greek family in New York until he was ready to live alone. He told me all about the long sea voyage and his wait at Ellis Island before meeting the family at the huge harbor. He couldn't get over how big everything was at first and how crowded. The family was very kind to him and helped him find a job.

At first he worked in the kitchens of a Greek restaurant. He said he didn't like it much as it was so different to the tavernas at home, but it did help him to learn to speak English working with others. Not long after he was offered a job as a gardener's assistant in Central Park. So during the day he worked there and then at night he worked in the restaurant. He hardly had time to spend his wages and so before long he had saved enough to move into his own apartment. The family were sad to see him leave, but helped him anyway.

One day in the park he came across a tramp sleeping under a thick bush. His orders had been to move tramps on but after he had woken the man they began to talk and shared papa's lunch. The tramp was an English man, who had been in a Japanese prisoner of war camp. When he returned to England he could not settle, and became rather eccentric, as he called it. His father had given him a large sum of money and he had sailed over to America. He came from a very high-class family, and his father did not want the embarrassment of having him around. Awful to think that a father could do that to a son, but that is life I suppose.

Not being used to fending for himself he was finding it more difficult than he had at first thought. His confidence had gone and he could not even find a place to live. Papa let him stay in the park, but that night whilst he lay in bed he began to think about the man.

Next day he invited him to stay at the apartment with him. The man accepted on the understanding that he did all the cleaning and cooking, also all the laundry. The one thing he could not do was shopping. He was so unsure of everything that he feared even going to the shops; he was a little older than papa but his insecurity made him almost childlike. Papa agreed and so began a friendship that was to last for years.

Richard Graves and papa worked well together. The flat was kept nice and clean, and gradually with help Richard began to regain some of his confidence. Being in the apartment all day he liked to study the newspapers that papa brought home. Evidently the stocks and shares section was his favourite. They began to buy and sell the shares that

Richard thought of as good, and shortly they were making a lot of money.

Soon they were able to buy a lovely big house in the city. It was quite run down, but between them they turned it into a palace. Richard designed the inside and papa the large gardens. It is so beautiful.

Papa gave up his jobs and they concentrated on making their fortunes. Much of their profits were put into gold and wonderful gemstones. Within 10 years they were millionaires. Richard was the brains behind the share dealing and papa looked after the gold side of things.

Soon they began to get noticed by people in high places. Everyone it seemed wanted to be their friends and they started to get many invitations to balls and dances. It is sad but, but even then Richard would not go out.

Papa loved to dance and it was at the Presidents New Year Ball that he met mama. He said she was so beautiful as she glided across the floor with another man that he could hardly wait for the dance to finish. She was only tiny and very slim. She had long deep red hair shot with gold; he said her skin was so white it was almost transparent. Her dress was of the palest green silk and she wore a simple gold necklace with a dolphin pendant, and thin gold bracelet.

Her name was Christina. She was just 19. Her father was the owner of a successful bank in the city, one that Richard and papa dealt with often.

Within weeks papa had asked her father for her hand. He did not approve at first as he thought my father was a little too old for Christina. He had no doubts of the ability of papa to support her, but as a father he only wanted the best for his daughter and would have preferred a younger man for a son in law. Her mother though could see how in love they were, and eventually persuaded him to let them wed.

The wedding took place at our home in order that Richard would be able to attend. We have a beautiful garden, filled with wonderful marble statues of Grecian dancing ladies, and large stone dolphins that are fountains. Papa filled tubs with red geraniums and planted sunflowers and poppies in time for them to bloom on the day. He had sweeping marble patios laid and had grape vines draped over pagodas, I just wish I could have been there to see it." She paused and looked towards the sea, deep in her thoughts.

"Papa spoiled mama with lovely jewellery and fabulous clothes; he loved to see her in nice things. They were so popular, the couple to have at parties, the ones first on invitation lists for banquets. They had marvelous parties at our home, inviting Presidents and Film Stars. They seemed to know everyone.

When she became pregnant with me he gave her a marvelous necklace of diamonds and when I was born, he gave her the matching earrings and bracelet. That set must be worth a fortune now.

One day when I was only five years old and she was walking with me in the park"

Eleni faltered and the tears once again fell down her cheeks. Nicos put his arm around her shoulders and she smiled weekly at him. She took a sip of brandy and began again.

"We were in the park when suddenly she could hear gun fire close by. Running with a child was not easy and we got caught in the crossfire. Mama was killed instantly, and I was also hit. Papa said he sat at my hospital bed for days willing me to live. I still have a large scar where the bullet went straight through" She rubbed her side with her hand "That is why I only wear costumes. It is still ugly even after all these years, and so red. But I am alive and that is all that counts. The men shooting had been arguing over a card game. It was such a waste of a life.

My grandmother never got over the shock and died shortly after. Grandfather unable to cope with the deaths of his daughter and his wife, became a recluse. He signed the Bank over to me and Richard found managers to run it for me. Grandpa lived for many years, but never left his home after grandmother's death. We would go to see him every weekend and try to cheer him up, but although he loved to play with me, he never really recovered.

After the shooting Papa decided that we would be safer out of the city and bought a lovely home on Long Island. Here he brought more statues and spent much of his time making the garden spectacular. I realise now that each of our homes is a tiny bit of Greece, he must have missed it so much that he wanted his own little piece. What I don't understand is why he did not come back before.

I love that home. I spent most of my time there as a child with Papa and Richard. I had a Scottish nanny, a lovely woman, but very strict.

Being English Richard insisted that we had a butler, and he personally chose the household staff. He was happier than I had ever seen him, but still he would go further than the grounds.

It was there that papa taught me to cook. Every Sunday our cook would have the day off, and we would take over. We had such fun, and made lots of mess, but our food always tasted so good. When we were alone together in the kitchen he always insisted that we speak Greek, and that is how I began to love languages.

I went to the best school Papa could find and when he realized I had a gift for languages he sent me to a school in Switzerland. I missed him so much at first, but soon began to love it. I made some very good friends and we had lots of fun." She smiled at the memories.

Papa and Richard were still making money, and the Bank was also doing well. I could have anything in the world, apart from my mama, the one thing I really wanted. I went to all the best places to eat, and dance. I spent holidays on papas yacht with my friends from school. I even went to Wimbledon one year. I love tennis and it was a birthday treat. Anyway the story is of papa not me.

He never married again. He spent his time looking after his business, his garden and me. He very rarely went out in fact. Only occasionally for meals with other business men, but mostly to museums and things, some times I would accompany him.

He loved art and we have a wonderful collection of paintings at home. He used to go to exhibitions in the city and it was at one of these that he bought the photographs. I remember him looking at them for such a long time. At the one of the ruin I thought he was going to cry. I remember him smiling at the one of the three boys and he just closed his eyes after seeing the young girl on the cliff. The lady at the exhibition would not sell that one, as it was the only one she had, no matter how much papa offered

I realise now that he must have recognized himself as one of the boys, he also purchased the one of the boy with the dolphin, and the photograph of the ruin, I don't know why other than he liked them. I caught him many times just standing staring at them.

It was about four months after the exhibition that he told me he was thinking of coming here. I wanted to come with him, but he said no, not this time, maybe next.

"It has done me good to tell papa's story. I have never told anyone before. I feel like a weight has been lifted, but I worry a little about what Tomas is going to say. I still don't understand why papa was coming here after all of these years." She gently lifted his hands and kissed them.

Looking into his eyes she pulled the sheet high and beckoned him to join her. Both of them were fully dressed but with the feel of her in his arms his body reacted as a man. She could feel the heat of his erection against her leg and stroked it with her hand. He groaned loudly and began to slowly undress her.

"Do you believe in love at first sight?" She asked coyly. Nicos nodded, at that precise moment he would have agreed with anything she said, his body needed her. "I am so pleased" She sighed, relaxing slightly as she looked deep into his eyes. No man had touched her in this way before, and although she felt nervous with Nicos it just seemed so right.

He stroked her body as it was revealed. So soft. So lovely. Removing his shorts he let her eyes wonder over his body before very gently he entered her. Their rhythm was soft and slow as they kissed and touched each other.

Lust took over and Nicos pushed harder and faster. He gave a loud groan as he climaxed, panting.

"Oh Eleni my love. You are so wonderful. I love you so much" He said kissing her roughly. "Now let me look at you properly". He pulled back the sheet and stared at her tiny body. The scar stood out immediately and she put her hand over it quickly to stop him seeing. Taking her hand he pulled her from the bed and stood her in front of the mirror.

He stood behind her and let his hands wonder over her skin.

"Eleni don't be afraid," he whispered hoarsely as her body trembled. "Be proud of your body, all of your body." He touched the scar gently. "Just look. Why do you hide it?"

"It reminds me of mama, but it is so ugly" Eleni's voice shook. "Each time I see it I think of her, it makes me so sad"

"And so you should think of her" He replied "You should never forget her but look. See the mark the bullet has made. It looks like the silhouette of a beautiful girl; the roundness of the scar is surrounded by her hair. See" He traced the red marks with his fingers. "You should remember your mama as she is with you here, it is nothing to be ashamed of, nothing you should hide."

# · CHAPTER · 5

Eleni slept through exhaustion but it was not a restful sleep. Many times she woke Nicos with her mumblings, and at one time cried out as if in pain. Now Nicos too was exhausted, but he was so pleased that he had stayed

As the dawn light began to creep through the shutters he rose and walked silently to the window. It was going to be a beautiful day he could tell, but what were his father and Tomas going to say. Was this precious girl going to learn something that would cause her pain? He hoped not.

"Nicos. You stayed" Her voice crept into his mind and he turned to see her smiling at him from the bed.

"Of course I did. I said I would" He walked back to the bed and sat down. Holding her hands he looked straight into her eyes "I want to look after you Eleni. I know this is probably not the right time, but I want to stay with you forever". Nervously he bent and kissed her lips. "How are you feeling?" he could see the crying had left dark circles under her eyes.

he coming to see? Tomas, Alexi, please help me? I feel so alone. I miss him so much" Her voice shook as she said the last few words.

It had taken all of her energy to tell the story and she broke down sobbing. Nicos held her tight to his chest, feeling her grief with her. Her body jerked as she cried, he felt so helpless.

"You have us little one" Sofia's spoke in her lovely way "Marco was a good friend of Alexi and Tomas. We will look after you, don't worry. But now it is bed for you. Tomorrow Tomas and Alexi will tell their story. Tonight it will be too much for you"

Nicos helped her stand and then swooped to pick her up. She was like a feather in his arms. He carried her over the sand to the house and up to her room. Gently he laid her on the bed. He knelt on the floor and stroked her hair and face.

"You must sleep Eleni. Sleep will do you good" he said softly.

"Please stay Nicos. I don't want to be alone tonight. Please stay" She looked so forlorn how could he refuse. His father and Tomas would think it improper, but she was the one that mattered.

"Yes I will stay." He wanted to say he would stay forever with her, but now was not the time. He covered her with a sheet and fetched himself a pillow and blanket from the wardrobe. Placing the pillow on the floor he sat down, he wrapped the blanket around his shoulders and leant his head on the bed. Holding her hand for comfort he spoke again.

"I will stay right here Eleni." But she did not hear. She was already fast asleep. Exhaustion and emotion had taken over.

As you will know he never made it." Eleni paused again.

"He flew to Athens and hired a light aircraft to bring him to the island. It crashed in the waters between the mainland and Skiathos, mechanical fault they said at the inquest. So now I not only have the Bank but also his business too. Richard is my guardian and he is running them for me, but I will have to make arrangements when I get back as he says he is going to give up. I have no interest in the running of business so I must find someone to do it for me.

For weeks after my father's death Richard slept in the garden, under a magnolia bush. It is his special place, don't worry he's not mad, he goes when there when he is troubled. It has affected him badly but he has promised that he will stay and work for now. He says he owes it to papa to look after me, and I know he will.

When he retires I might just sell the whole thing. I have more than enough money to last me for life. I could live here with no complications forever. I am alone in the world. Not only an orphan, but I have no one else at all. No grandparents, no uncles, no one. Richard is the only one to cares for me now." Her fingers unconsciously twisted a napkin as she spoke.

"The last few months have been a nightmare for me. Without Richard I could not have coped. We arranged father's funeral together, although he could not attend himself. We have sorted out much of his business, and we have sold the yacht. I could never imagine going on that again. He named her after me and it broke my heart just to step on board.

One day I realised I had had enough, I was worn out, and that is when I decided to come here. Ever since I was born I had lived in luxury. Had anything I wanted. My papa tried to teach me values, but it was so difficult. He was so rich, and now so am I.

Richard panicked. He said I was not to come alone, but I insisted. He is terrified I will be kidnapped. I have to phone him every day and I am surprised he hasn't arranged for someone to be watching over me here."

Tomas smiled to himself, she was so right.

"I'm sure this man Richard loves you little one. You must not blame him for worrying." He looked over at the couple on the swing, a different football shirt today he noticed.

" The reason for my journey is I want to know why? Why was papa coming here and not going to Kefalonia where he came from, or who was

"Oh Nicos that is beautiful. Only an artist's eye would see that. No one has ever seen me naked before, I have always felt so afraid" She turned and kissed him long and hard before looking back towards the mirror.

His hands continued down her flat stomach towards her thighs. He noticed a smudge of blood beginning to show between her legs. He was surprised how emotional it made him feel, and so masculine.

"I am your first?"

She nodded as a blush rose in her cheeks.

He picked her up and carried her back to the bed. This time he made sure she was satisfied before once again loosing himself in her wonderful body.

A short while later they were laughing like children as they showered together.

"If anyone comes now we are in big trouble" Eleni said, spitting out a mouthful of shampoo. "Tomas would skin you alive if he knew"

They dried each other with the large soft white towels and Nicos had trouble restraining himself.

"Eleni get dressed or we will never be ready for breakfast. And stop that" He was laughing but doing his best to sound stern as she gently but firmly scratched her nails down his chest. "Look what you are doing" His manhood rose once again." I wish we had more time you minx"

"Oh I think we have enough," She giggled as she launched herself back on to the bed.

Moments later Nicos lay back, lit a cigarette and sighed loudly.

"Three times before coffee. No man can stand that" Nicos was spent yet again. "Now leave me alone for a few minutes. Let me finish this before I dress." He blew a perfect circle of smoke. "And you had better move too" He playfully slapped her naked bottom.

Sofia could see from their faces as they walked along the sand towards the taverna, that they were in love. The way he looked down at her and smiled. The pink shine of her glowing face. It was lovely to see them so happy, especially after the night before.

" Kalimera children. Coffee?" she asked

" Kalimera Sofia. How is your arm? ." Eleni kissed Sofia's cheek.

"It is Ok. Now sit," She pointed towards the table.

They sat in silence at the little bar side table and watched the sea.

"This is such a marvelous place" Eleni sighed

"It is now" Nicos replied reaching for her hand.

Sofia brought coffee and an assortment of pastries. Some covered in honey and nuts, some with raisins in the dough, some with tiny pieces of peach. She fetched a bowl of fresh fruit and a jug of thick yogurt. It took her some time as she could only use one hand, but no amount of pleading from Eleni would stop her from serving them.

"Eat children. You need the sugar in your blood. It will do you good"

Eleni laughed, "That's just what Tomas said yesterday. Sugar in my blood is all well and good, but it will also make me fat. Where is he anyway?"

"He has taken Alexi back home to change. They have been here talking all night, hopefully they will be back shortly"

"I don't care if you are huge Eleni. I will love you anyway" Nicos sighed forgetting Sofia was still there. She just patted his shoulder and walked back to the kitchen.

After their breakfast they walked along the beach, their feet just in the shallows of the water. They were so comfortable with each other there was no need for words. The young couple just walked slowly along holding hands.

Eleni found a large flat rock by the waters edge and sat down, Nicos stood behind her and put his hands on her shoulders. They felt the warmth of the sun on their skin and the coolness of the water at their feet, a gentle breeze blew, it was a lovely moment.

The sound of Tomas's van and another vehicle made them turn to look. It was indeed Tomas and Alexi. Nicos could feel the tension rise in Eleni's shoulders.

"Do not be afraid Eleni. I am here with you. What ever they have to say remember I am with you." He kissed the back of her neck "Come on lets go and see"

As they walked slowly back, Eleni felt torn. She wanted to know about her father, but she was afraid. She held Nicos's hand tightly.

They were surprised to see Tomas and Alexi arranging some of the framed photographs on the taverna tables.

"They will help us to tell our story" Tomas said seeing their concern. "Come let us sit," He gestured to the tables still together from the night before.

Eleni and Nicos sat together with Tomas and Alexi opposite. Sofia sat at the end, facing the sea.

"I will start and Alexi will add his bit as we go along if that is OK little one." Tomas was hurting. How would she react? Would she hate him? He had no choice but to tell the truth.

"Many years ago I lived in the tiny village of Lassi on the beautiful island of Kefalonia. My family consisted of my father, mother, twin sister and myself.

My best friends were Alexi here, and your father Marco. We were all the same age, 13, and went to the same school in Argostoli, and so it is natural that we were very close.

The four of us did everything together. We played in the fields, swam in the sea; we helped with the olive harvest, and also with the grapes. We had a wonderful childhood, but the war was soon to change all of that.

The Germans came and took over the island. At first it was not too bad. They tried to be friendly, and as there was no fighting on the island mostly they treated it as a holiday. Some of the soldiers lived in barracks in Argostoli and others were sent to live in the villages with the locals. My father, under protest, was ordered to take in a young soldier, his name was Kurt Schumann, he was 19, just a few years older than us.

My mother tried to make him welcome, as Greek women are taught to do, but my father ignored him. At first we did too, but over the weeks we began to accept him into our little gang.

Kurt hated being in the army and was very homesick. Back in Germany he was on the verge of going to Art School, but the war had stopped all of that. He was very gifted and even though his Greek was limited he could describe flowers and birds like no one I have ever met. He could see the beauty in everything, his hands were never still as he emphasized the things he saw.

His job in the army was to take photographs of military things and it was an occupation he enjoyed very much. If only it had not been wartime he would have been so happy. When he was not doing army things, as he called his work, he would roam the hillsides with us, swim with us, he became one of us. His camera was always with him.

He took many lovely photographs of our island, developing them in a small-unused goat shed in one of father's fields. He said it was the best dark room he could ask for. Made of stone with a slate roof and only tiny slits for windows, it was perfect. He showed us how to develop films, and as his job was to take pictures for the army we were kept very busy. They provided everything he needed and soon the little goat shed was full. We put up wooden shelves for his chemicals, we made a little table for his trays, and we tied string across the room to dry the photographs on. It was our den.

Alexi here took a big interest and Kurt gave him one of his cameras as a present. That was the start of his love of the art." Tomas nodded to Alexi.

"Marco and I were more interested in the chemicals he had and we used to mix them for him. It was like magic when he placed black film into the trays and we would watch as the images appeared.

My sister would fetch our lunch, goat's cheese, bread, fruit and wine, and we would all sit in the sun eating, waiting for the pictures to dry.

Kurt told us stories about his home and family, and how after the war he wanted to go to America. It was the place, he said, where he would find his fortune, he believed anyone could find their fortune there. Marco loved these talking sessions and always had an unending stream of questions whenever Kurt mentioned America. Sometimes we would talk for hours.

I remember that even then Marco would sit with my sister as we chattered and ate, and many times I watched as they walked hand in hand across the fields after our meal. It always seemed so natural, we were all good friends, and unfortunately I was young and so innocent.

One of the first photographs Alexi arranged was that one" Tomas pointed to the one of the three boys.

"He set the scene and asked Eleni, my sister to take it, but as you can see she was too quick and he slipped not quite making the rock in time. We did not realise what had happened until it was developed and I remember Marco and I laughing, but Kurt and Alexi saw how marvelous it really was."

It was the first time Tomas had spoken his sister's name. Eleni was stunned for a moment. Tomas continued.

"Not long after came the boy and dolphin, yes that is Marco little one, your father." Now she understood why he had purchased the photograph.

"Unbeknown to us our fathers were organizing a resistance movement on the island, and soon traps were being laid for the soldiers. Some were killed and that is when everything changed.

We were told that we had to stay loyal to our country, to forget about Kurt, and do what we could to rid our island of the invaders. It was hard for us, we liked him, but we had to do as our fathers had ordered.

We began to help by digging holes in the roads; it made the trucks swerve and stop. We placed shards of marble under the wheels of cars and put honey in the petrol tanks. We threw stones through lorry windows as they passed on the road below, and put rope across the roads to make the motorcyclists crash. All sorts of tricks that would help the cause. It was a great adventure. But still we had Kurt staying with us. It was not easy.

The German Officers began to retaliate and shot some of the locals. Then it all turned very nasty. The soldiers began to rape women and young girls.

Father was afraid for Eleni; she was very beautiful, and very fragile. So he hid her away in the cellar under our home, letting her out into the air only at night. The big problem was Kurt. He knew she was there. He had lived with us and knew she was there." Tomas's voice cracked. It took several moments before he spoke again

"They killed him. They tried to make it look as if he had had an accident on his motorbike, but we knew better and the Germans knew better. They took a group of men, including my father and Alexi's father to Argostoli and shot them in front of a large crowd, then they threw the bodies over the cliff."

Tomas pointed to the photograph of the poppies on the cliff. Alexi spoke next.

"Nicos took that last year it looks so beautiful there now. No one would ever know of the horror those rocks saw.

Anyway we felt so awful about Kurt that we decided we needed to do something. We went to the place where his body had been found and planted three sunflower seeds." He pointed to the photograph. "We said a few prayers and said goodbye to our friend" Now Alexi was emotional.

Tomas had composed himself and continued.

"After this the resistance grew much stronger and Marco's father was in charge. He ordered Alexi to take photographs of the German bases around the island and he did. We would accompany him as if we were just three boys on a trip. We still used the goat shed to develop the films and with Alexi's skill the resistance made many raids. We did everything we could to help. They had murdered our fathers, we hated them.

A few years later the war ended and the soldiers went home. It was wonderful. I can remember the day they left so well. Everyone danced in the streets, everyone kissed, and it was truly wonderful. We had overcome them.

Mama allowed Eleni out of the cellar, and how she had changed. She was now a woman; her hair was deep red from lack of sun, her skin almost white. She had always been beautiful, but now she looked unreal. Like a fairy, a lovely fragile fairy"

Eleni interrupted "Tomas you could have just described my mother" her voice shook. Tomas nodded.

"You are so like her little one. You have Marco's hair and skin, but your face and body are so like her. You could easily be her daughter"

Eleni felt betrayed. Her lovely mama. Papa had only married her because she looked like this woman Eleni, she was even named after her, she felt a sudden hatred fill her heart. She felt so hurt.

Tomas could see the pain in her eyes, he spoke softly.

"I could see Marco was stunned. He had always been close to her, but I could see in his eyes, he loved her. He never left her side as we joined in the dances. He held her close when we stopped to drink. Then they disappeared.

Marco's father found them the next morning. Fast asleep and naked in the goat shed.

He was so ashamed of his son he ordered him to leave the island. My mother had protected Eleni for so many years only for her to be deflowered by him.

The day before he left he came to see us. I didn't know what to say, one of my best friends, and I didn't know what to say." Tomas shook his head.

"He pleaded with my mother to let him walk with Eleni one last time. She cried, and eventually they were allowed to go, but only if Alexi and I went with them. We were ordered not to let them be alone, not to go out of our sight even for a moment.

We made our way over the hillside to the goat shed where we sat talking awkwardly. He told us how he remembered what Kurt had said about America and that the next day his father was taking him to Athens in order to get the boat over.

He promised that when he had made his fortune he would return for her. Marco and Eleni held hands, she was crying. He begged us to let him take her inside the goat shed, just for a few moments. He said he wanted to say his goodbyes to her alone. We let them go.

Alexi and I talked much easier now they were gone, and the time flew past. Eventually I stood up and peered through a slit in the wall. Eleni and Marco were making love. I could not believe my eyes, and did not know what to do.

When they eventually returned to us I just flew at him. We fought on the ground, punching and kicking. I called him awful names and vowed that should he ever step on the island again or try to see Eleni again, I would kill him.

Mama was furious when we returned, she could see we had been fighting and asked the reason, looking from Marco to me and then to Eleni. I am ashamed to say that I told her. She slapped me so hard I fell into the dust.

"I asked you to look after her Tomas you have let me down" She turned to Marco "Don't ever come near her again" I could see the anger in her eyes. She dragged Eleni inside and Marco just walked away, his head down, crying. I never saw him again." Tomas stroked his face as if feeling his mother's hand once again.

"The next day Eleni went to the cliff and waved to every boat that left for the main land. She stood for hours. Alexi took that photograph and I made him promise never to let it go. As darkness fell she walked towards a clump of poppies in a nearby field. She pulled off a flower and split the pod, before scattering the seeds in the place where she had stood. When I asked her why? She replied that it was to mark the spot where she had died. I said she was being dramatic and left, my heart too was broken you see, Marco had been my friend and now he was leaving but I could not let her see my tears"

Tomas stopped talking and watched as Eleni walked over to the pictures. She picked up the one of the girl on the cliff and stroked the glass before doing the same with the photograph of the poppies.

"She must have loved papa so much." She said softly."How can I hate her?" Nicos went over and gently led her back to the table.

"For days she would not eat" Tomas said, "She was an empty shell. My mother decided that the best thing for us all was for her to go to our aunt in Athens. During the years she had spent in the cellar Eleni had read many books. She knew everything about our history, the wonderful buildings in the city and she wanted to see them for herself.

So a few days later I stood on the cliff and waved goodbye to my sister. She too had been ordered never to return. It broke my heat, my beautiful Eleni, gone forever.

How I hated Marco for doing this to her I could have killed him with my bare hands.

Mama could not settle, she had lost her husband and now her daughter, and so we moved to Skiathos. She wanted to forget, but I could never forget Eleni.

At first we rented a room in the harbor, it was over a busy taverna, and so small. I worked hard doing jobs in the kitchen, and helping the fishermen with their catch. I hardly had time for myself, but one thing I did do was write to Alexi. He was my only contact with home.

I began to do well in the taverna, learning from the owner how to cook and run the business. I also met his daughter, Sofia, and as our romance deepened, he looked upon me with great favour.

It was obvious that when we were to be married our little room would be too small, so I asked Sofia's father if he would help me buy some land in order that I could build us a home. In those days beach side land was very cheep and I was able to get all of this" He waved his arms wide. "Now everyone wants to buy land close to the sea, but I will never sell this. With the help of Sofia's brothers we built our home and after the wedding mama, Sofia and I moved in. I continued to work at the taverna and Sofia stayed here with mama.

Sofia noticed that more and more people were coming to the beach and she began to sell drinks and things from the house. She did so well that we built the kiosk on at the side and a little later added the kitchen and eating area.

A short while later Sofia gave me our son, Vanni. I gave up working in the town and came here to be with my family. I was so happy.

After the bad earthquake had wrecked Kefalonia in 1954, Alexi wrote and told me our village was gone. Every house had fallen. The goat shed now a ruin" They all looked towards the photograph.

"His mother, brother, and Marco's family, had all been killed and he was now homeless and alone, so we invited him to come and live here. He arrived with his only possessions, various cameras and the clothes he wore. He lived here and helped in the kitchen. During the summer he would take photographs of the tourists on the beach and sell them, it proved to be very popular and soon he was able to buy his own home in the town. He began to get a good reputation with his camera and converted the ground floor of his home into a little shop. It is the one you see today" Alexi was nodding. "One day a tourist offered to take some of the photographs and put them on display in his shop in Athens. Alexi was worried he would never see the man again, but took the risk anyway. They soon sold and the man sent Alexi the money, less his commission, it was a fortune.

The man returned some months later in order persuade Alexi to allow him to take the photographs of us, and Kefalonia, to put on display in his shop. He came with his beautiful daughter, Athena. Unwilling to allow the originals to go Alexi took copies of them and this time went with the man himself. The only photograph he would not copy is the one of Eleni on the cliff; he took this with him upon the understanding that it would not be sold.

They could have sold that particular one many times over, but Alexi remembered his promise to me, and no matter how much was offered it was not for sale.

Alexi stayed in Athens for quite some time. He took pictures of the antiquities and sold them in the mans shop.

He returned six months later, with his lovely wife Athena, plus a letter from Eleni. I could not believe it, after all of these years. Apparently she had been walking past the shop and recognized herself from the photograph. She went in hoping to find out why it was there; instead she met her old friend Alexi.

Her letter told me how she had used her knowledge of Greece to work in museums and as a guide in the city. Eventually with aunt Francesca's help she had started her own business, training guides for the tourists and now she was a wealthy woman.

She told me how she had never married and, even though I hated Marco she still loved him. She asked me to forgive him and explained that she was as much to blame for what had happened. She knew mama would never forgive her but she hoped I would.

I returned her letter and we arranged to meet on Alonysos so that mama would not know. Alexi and I had already bought several houses on the beachfront and so it was easy for her to come to stay.

I was so nervous the day I went over. I told mama I was going to look at another house that was for sale, but told Sofia the truth.

I spotted her as I looked from the ferry, and cried. She was still so beautiful. I could hardly wait to hold her once again. I ran from the boat and straight into her arms. We cried for a long time, it was wonderful.

It took me a while to realise that the young boy standing at her side was actually with her. I looked down and instantly realized that this was Marco's son. He was the mirror image of my friend.

Eleni explained that when she knew she was pregnant, mama with her old fashioned ways had banished her from our family. She had been forbidden to write or contact us ever again, but when she saw the photograph after all of those years she realised what a waste it had been. All those years apart, it was such a waste." Tomas shook his head in a bemused way.

"The little boy, Andros, was a delight. He looked so much like Marco, but many of his ways were Eleni's. She said that she could never forgive mama for sending her away, but if I accepted Andros, then she would forgive me. How could I refuse?

We talked for hours and ate in one of our tavernas. We played with Andros on the beach and had a truly wonderful day. They stayed at the house for over a month and I had many trips over to see them. Occasionally I took Vanni with me, I wanted him to know his cousin, but made him swear not to tell his grandma. Sometimes Alexi would come with Nicos, and he too would play with Andros. We loved to see the three of them together, it reminded us of ourselves when we were young.

The boys grew close, even though there was an age difference and they wrote to each other often. Eleni and Andros eventually returned to Athens but this time we kept in touch.

As the years passed they had many trips to the house on Alonysos, and I used to long for summer to come, as it would bring them close once again.

It was during that time that Alexi and I began to buy more houses, and tavernas. The islands were getting very popular with the tourists.

Vanni did well at school, he was a genius with figures, and Nicos followed Alexi in being an artist with a camera. When the time came for them to go on to better schools they went to Athens and stayed with Eleni and Andros.

Vanni and Andros began their own company, they were so alike in their aims, it seemed only natural. They now own a company that imports many goods from America, but they still live with Eleni. Neither has married, they are in fact married to their business, you know all about Nicos.

Athena proved to be a huge asset to Alexi, she loved to arrange the photographs in the shop, and serve the customers. Eventually she persuaded Alexi to have an exhibition in Athens. Not in her fathers shop, but in a proper gallery. It proved so popular that soon she was arranging more all over the world.

It was, as we know at one of these that your father saw the photographs. He bought the ones you have mentioned, but being unable to buy the one of Eleni, he asked Athena for the owners address. He said he would write and beg him to sell, he would offer what ever the price; he just wanted to own it.

He was amazed when she gave him the Gallery's address and he recognized Alexi's name, so he asked her more. She told the story, as she knew it, and during that week of the exhibition they met quite often.

Eventually Marco wrote a letter and asked Athena to deliver it. Alexi brought it here to the taverna, I felt so pleased to hear from our old friend once again.

Mama had died years before and I thought long and hard of how she would feel. Eventually I wrote, with Eleni's permission, and told him the full story. I said I forgave him. I told him he had a son.

Within days I received a telephone call. He was coming here and wanted me to arrange a meeting with Eleni and Andros. It was so nice to hear his voice again. We both laughed and cried, we talked for ages, it must have cost him a fortune.

He sent a letter with the date of his arrival, and some photographs of himself and some with you. That is how I knew who you were the day you arrived on the ferry.

I contacted Eleni, and she came over to Alonysos, wanting to see him alone, before he eventually met Andros. We all know what happened next.

I am sorry little one, if I had not written that letter, he would not have been coming to the island. It is my fault he is dead. Can you ever forgive me? I feel I can never forgive myself" Tomas broke down and sobbed. After a while Eleni spoke.

"It is not your fault Tomas. You were not to know what would happen. None of this was your fault I am not angry with you. I forgive you, but really there is nothing to forgive. It is my father I am angry with, I feel he used mama. He said he loved her, but really he married her because she was Eleni's double. I will find it hard to forgive him"

"But you must little one. Did he not make her happy? Did he not treat he with respect? You must forgive Marco, he did love Christina for herself of that I am sure" Alexi said with feeling.

Eleni nodded "You are right I know, but this has been quite a shock for me. I am sorry." She turned to Tomas "Tomas do you think I could meet Andros? He is my half brother, my only living relative. Please telephone and ask for me"

"I will I promise, but not today. I think we have had enough today" Tomas sounded exhausted.

"Tomas you must go and rest, Sofia go with him. Nicos and I will run the taverna for you. Have no fear, we will look after everything" Alexi was already walking to the kitchen. "And you Eleni can see to the bar"

Within minutes the taverna was busy with lunchtime customers. Eleni could hear Alexi singing as he worked in the kitchen. She watched as Nicos laughed with the customers and took their orders. She tied the apron around her waist and began to pour drinks. She just nodded to the couple in the swinging chair, she knew their order now, and took it over.

She had much to think about, but for now all of that could wait.

## • CHAPTER 6 •

It was an extremely hot afternoon and the customers stayed in the shade of the grapevine roof lingering over their drinks and food, but eventually they began to drift back to their sun beds.

Eleni collected discarded glasses and cleaned the bar ready for the early evening drinkers. Nicos cleared the tables and raked the sand. She could hear the clatter of pans as Alexi cleaned in the kitchen. It all seemed so comfortable. After the mornings tale from Tomas she had much to think about, but had welcomed the break and now felt much better.

"Nicos" she called "I have finished here and am going for a swim. See you later"

She returned to her room to find Sofia had already cleaned and tidied. She stared at the bed, where only a few hours ago she had given herself to a man for the first time. I am going to stay here, she thought. I don't want to live in New York any longer this is where I belong.

She put on her new costume and grabbing her towel ran down the stairs. Nicos watched as she ran across the sand and into the sea. He loved her so much, he wanted her to stay here on the island, but her knew her businesses would call her back, the homes she spoke of, and Richard, eventually they would pull her back.

After her swim, she slept for a while on an empty sun bed. She loved the feeling of the suns rays, seemingly soaking into her skin, skin that was now turning a wonderful deep brown. Tomas woke her.

"Eleni, little one" He shook her gently "I have spoken to my sister, and she has agreed that you should meet Andros. He is coming to Alonysos tomorrow and I will take you to see him if that is what you really wish?"

"Oh please Tomas, I would really like to meet him, but please can I go alone. I don't want to hurt you. You can take me to the boat, if that would make you feel better" She replied.

"I do understand you know. I will take you into town in the morning and fetch you back later, you can tell me all about it then" He smiled down at her, so glad that she had forgiven him. It was a huge weight off of his shoulders. As Tomas returned to the taverna Nicos walked down to her sun bed.

"I must go soon my love. My mother has coped on her own for too long. Papa is coming with me" He sat in the sand and stroked her back gently. "I will be back, never fear" he kissed her warm shoulders. "I will be back tomorrow"

"I won't be here tomorrow Nicos, I am going to meet Andros. Tomas is taking me to the ferry in the morning, and I am going to meet my brother" As she spoke she rolled over and Nicos could see her eyes shinning with excitement, or was it fear?

"Then I will come with you," He said

"No. I have asked Tomas if I can go alone. It will be much better" She saw on his face a look of disappointment "But I will call at the shop as soon as I return. I promise," She added quickly. She walked with him to his car, where they kissed passionately before he left. Eleni waved frantically as he drove off.

She returned to her room and began to sift through her meager wardrobe to find an outfit for the following day. Soon her bed was covered in shorts, tops, and her three dresses. Sandals lay scattered on the floor. It was going to be hard to know what to choose.

In the end she settled for her new red sundress and picked a pair of delicate bronze sandals from the floor. She put the items together. Perfect, she thought. Rummaging in her rucksack she found her little bag of jewellery. After a quick look inside she chose a tiny pair of earrings, matching bracelet and necklace. For a moment she held them in her hands and remembered way back to when Marco had given them to her. Her 15$^{th}$ birthday, so long ago it seemed, but as she thought of him, it could have been yesterday.

Brushing away her tears she stood and sighed. This is no good. I must pull myself together, she thought, the customers would soon be wanting more drinks. She picked up her little cloth beach bag deciding to take that with her the following day, not that it would be holding much, she just needed something to have in her hands. Right that's it, she thought, finished.

She put on her white shorts and a pretty red top, scooped up her hair and tied it back with her red band. Applied a little make up and she was ready.

As usual, the first customers were the couple on the swinging chair. She greeted them with a smile and poured their drinks. They talked for a while and Eleni made a note of their food order. She watched as they walked to the chair and she began to think. Every day they were there on the beach. Every afternoon they sat in that same chair and had the same drinks. They must be so much in love, but something about the way they sat, not quite close enough, and the fact they never seemed to hold hands or kiss, made her wonder.

She remembered seeing them in the town, looking in shop windows, but carrying no bags. She remembered they sat at a table in the harbor side taverna where she ate with Nicos; they seemed to be everywhere she went. As she thought she watched as Tomas went over and spoke to them. He looked round and caught her gazing over and the guilty look on his face told her everything. As he returned to the kitchen she called over to him

"How is Richard?" she laughed. He smiled back, knowing he had been rumbled.

"You must not be angry with him little one. He loves you so much, he just wants you to be safe." He said smiling

"Come on Tomas tell me all" She asked

"Well Richard was so worried when you were coming here alone he telephoned me. Your father had told him the full story and so he knew all about me. He asked me to make sure you stayed here, that was the easy part. We knew as soon as you saw my board with Eleni Beach on it you would want to come to" your" place. I already had some photographs of you so I knew exactly who I was looking for. As I say that was the easy bit.

Richard arranged for that couple, they are from an English security firm that he deals with, to come here also. They are staying in the camper van in the clearing." Eleni laughed, how many times had she walked past that van and not realised. "Mind you, you gave them a scare when you came home from town in Nicos's car. They panicked and had a taxi back, not daring to wait for the bus," Eleni laughed louder." Seriously little one. They are here for you and will be on the boat tomorrow. If you need anything, please don't be afraid to contact them. Richard would kill me if his little girl came to any harm."

"Thank you Tomas" She walked from behind the bar and kissed him "When do you talk to Richard?"

"Every day" came the reply. "He phones me everyday usually."

"Well next time tell him I'm OK and missing him too, and thank him for me please" Eleni looked right into his eyes "You know I phone him almost every day and he hasn't let on at all. You two are crafty!"

They had no further time to talk. The evening customers began to fill the taverna wanting drinks and food. Tomas switched on the television and another football match was being shown. It was going to be a busy night.

Sofia was in the kitchen, Tomas serving at the tables, and Eleni behind the bar. Wonderful, she thought happily as she poured yet another large beer.

They eventually sat to eat themselves about 10 o'clock. It was lovely at that time of night. The days heat had died down, the sky a marvelous black, was littered with tiny stars. The sea, empty of swimmers, calmly lapped at the shore. So peaceful.

Eleni looked across and laughed as she noticed the camper van lights were still on. "I hope they are comfortable Tomas" He smiled and laughed with her.

Eleni slept well that night. So much had happened during the day that as soon as her head touched the pillow she was in a deep sleep. She dreamt of Nicos, Marco crept in at times, and of course Richard.

Rising early she showered and dressed. Picking up her beach bag, she took one last look in the mirror and decided to wear her hair up. When she eventually went downstairs Tomas was in the hall, obviously speaking to Richard on the telephone.

"She is well and sends her love. And I must say she looks wonderful this morning" He was saying.

"Tomas let me speak to him please," She asked. Tomas passed the phone over "Richard. Hi." She listened for a second or two and began to giggle "Red" she said as her hand stroked her dress, then she was silent as he spoke again. "Yes I will behave, and yes I will phone you when I get back. Love you" She handed Tomas the phone and walked through the open door.

"Kalimera Eleni. You look beautiful this morning. Coffee?" Sofia was already laying the little table.

"Kalimera Sofia. Thank you. Yes I would love coffee" Eleni sat at the table. She could already feel the heat from the sun on her bare skin and moved into the shade, glad now that she had put on plenty of sun cream, not wanting to get burnt or too hot this early in the day.

The three of them sat and enjoyed their breakfast, watching the sea as they ate. It was so nice just to sit and look at nothing, Eleni thought. No one on the beach yet, just the three of them at the little table. Perfect.

When at last they had finished Tomas spoke.

"Come on little one. We must go now if you want to catch the early boat. I have phoned my sister and she says Andros will be at the jetty to meet you. She has spoken to him about you, so do not worry."

All of a sudden Eleni felt nervous, what if she didn't like this man? He must be 50ish by now so how would he react to suddenly having a younger sister?" her mind was spinning.

She said her goodbyes to Sofia and followed Tomas across the sand to the clearing. A smile broke over her face as she spotted the camper van, obviously already empty.

"They will be at the harbor," Tomas said as he opened the creaky van door for her. "Remember they are there for you if you need them"

The journey into town was very different to her ride in Nicos's car. The old van rattled as it bumped its way along the road. Being early they hardly met any other traffic, just a few goats grazing at the side of the road, and locals in similar vans to Tomas's, the drive was soon over.

The boat was waiting at the harbor side and Tomas took Eleni to a kiosk to buy her ticket. About 30 others queued as they waited to board. Eleni joined them and waved to Tomas as she climbed the well-used wooden steps on to the boat. She waved again as she found her seat on the top deck wanting to be there not only to catch the sunshine, now blazing down, but also so she could get a good view of Andros when the boat reached Alonysos. She saw Tomas drive off, and spotted Nicos standing by the kiosk waving, as the boat began to glide out into the open sea Eleni waved back.

The boat soon gathered speed and now she was very pleased to be on the top deck, as spray from the sea was catching those who sat lower. She watch as sea gulls dipped and floated not far from the boat, swooping occasionally to catch pieces of bread thrown to them by the crew.

Tiny green islands passed them by and she wondered if any one lived on them. They sailed passed a much larger island, where she could see tiny white houses around a beautiful sandy bay, and lovely little churches perched on the hillside. I must visit one day, she thought gazing at the pretty scene. Sitting there in the sunshine and watching as they passed the many islands the journey flew past. Suddenly she sensed a change in the boats engines and felt the slowing down of their speed.

Her heart began to race and she felt giddy as the pretty harbor of Alonysos came into view. She could see the houses and tavernas that were strung out along the shore. People were already on the beach, and children were playing in the shallow waters. She could see the village behind and scattered houses perched on the hillside, and soon she could hear the shouting of the crew as they docked.

Standing up she frantically looked down across a sea of faces below. She watched as the security couple disembarked, no time for smiling at them now.

Then she spotted him. It was as if her father was standing there. He stood quite tall, his body lean and muscular. His smooth jet-black hair only slightly ruffled by the breeze, and his tanned face turned up as he scanned the people as they left the boat. He wore a spotless white shirt; black shorts and sandals, on his wrist Eleni could see a slim black watch.

Everything about him said successful businessman and class in a rather understated way.

Slowly Eleni made her way down the tiny steps to the lower deck, grasping the cold metal handrail tightly as she went. One of the crew gently held her arm as she stepped on to the concrete harbor side. Slowly she walked towards him, still unnoticed, as he continued to look at the many faces.

"Hi there" It was the American lady from the plane. "How ya doin? Are you enjoying your holiday?" Her strong accent seemed so out of place. "Me and Harve" She nodded towards a much smaller man, bald and slightly dumpy, "have seen all the old things in Athens and decided to have a look around a few of the islands. It's so good to see you. What are you doing here? Who you with?" She stopped to draw breath.

Eleni was unsure what to say and looked around feeling confused. Andros walked towards her.

"I'm with my brother," she said quietly.

"Call yourself a brother!" The lady launched herself towards Andros "Call yourself a brother! Fancy letting this little girl travel alone. Just you look after her" With that she punched his arm. "And mind you do! Come on Harve, let's have a look at this cute place"

Eleni and Andros watched in stunned silence as the odd couple walked away. They turned to look into each other's eyes and suddenly burst out laughing. Holding her arms wide she fell into a wonderful warm embrace. Andros cupped her face and kissed her cheeks.

"My little sister" he breathed "I am so pleased to see you. Come on I had better start looking after you. Lets see if we can find a coffee in this cute place" he mimicked the lady.

Eleni laughed, "That sounds great"

They held hands as they walked towards the vast array of tavernas. "Some of these are Tomas's aren't they?" She enquired.

"No, not some. Tomas and Alexi own all of the water front ones. Come I will take you to my favourite. We have much to talk about" Andros gently guided her along.

They walked some way before he stopped at the end of the little village. The taverna he had chosen was right on the beach. It had coloured umbrellas over little wooden tables, the chairs surrounding them had cushions to match. It was bright and very pretty. Bouzouki music played softly in the background. Andros held out a chair for Eleni, and as he stood behind her she noticed how lovely he smelt. It was that fresh lemony aroma rich men have, but no one ever knows what it is called.

Andros ordered coffee and pastries. Eleni once again thought about her figure. If she kept eating like this she would be huge. He took her hand in his.

"Now little sister, we can talk"

They sat for a long time, drinking coffee, eating and chatting. She liked this man, her brother, she felt comfortable with him. He was so much like Marco in his looks, but in his ways he was so different. He wanted to know all about her life in New York, all about her life with Marco. He was hungry to know everything. Eleni felt a little sad that he would never have the chance to meet his father they would have got on so well.

She asked about his life, and was pleased to learn that his mother wanted to meet her; she had been scared that the older woman would hate her, and she was more than a little frightened of her own feelings. How would she react to meeting a woman who looked so much like her own mother? Eleni was confused, would the hatred she had felt yesterday return?

After yet more coffee they strolled hand in hand along the beach, continuing to talk as they went. Andros knew much of the story Tomas had told her, but after Eleni had been sent to Athens the story was bitty. He only knew little pieces. Pieces that his mother had learned from letters Alexi and Tomas had written. Eleni filled in where she could. When she reached the part where Marco had been coming to meet Andros he sensed a deep hurt in her voice.

"I miss him so much Andros. Richard does what he can, and he tries so hard, but I miss him so much" She wept into her brother's shoulder.

"You have me now Eleni. I know I can never take his place, but I promise I will look after you." He kissed the top of her head. "Right little sister you are going for a swim" He picked her up and waded into the sea. She screamed and laughed.

"Don't you dare?" She shouted, as he threatened to drop her into the water." Put me down" quickly followed by "No. Not in the water!"

"Look I have a long time of brotherly things to do to you so you had better get used to it" Once again he lowered her towards the water.

"No. You pig!" She cried laughing hard. He turned around, walked back to the sand and placed her gently down.

"That's just for starters" He kicked at the water splashing her with spray, and ran off down the beach laughing. She flew after him swinging her beach bag.

"Oh! Just you wait." she shouted after him. "I'll get you" By the time she had caught up with him they were both breathless from running and laughing.

"I think we are going to get on just fine" He mimicked the ladies strong Yankee accent again. Eleni cried with laughter when he tried to walk, well waddle, like her and fell into a heap on the beach.

"That serves you right for splashing me". She said as he tried to brush the sand from his now not so immaculate shorts.

"Children. Behave" A soft voice called. It was Eleni. She stood in the shade of an old olive tree on the edge of the beach. She was so tiny, her body wrapped in a wonderful pale green silk dress. Her hair, now white, pulled back from her lovely face by a green band. Large dark glasses shaded her eyes. In the scorching heat of the day she looked so cool, how could anyone look so cool?

Eleni stopped laughing and looked at this woman. At that moment she could understand Marco, this woman was stunning, tiny but with a marvelous aura surrounding her.

Andros took her hand and led her towards his mother. "Eleni I want you to meet my mother, also Eleni" He said laughing. The two women went as if to shake hands.

"Come here child" The older woman pulled Eleni into her arms in a warm embrace." Now isn't that better?" She looked at her son with a frown "Andros what a mess. Clean yourself up then you can take us ladies for some lunch"

They stopped in a different beach side taverna this time. The Olive Tree, as it was known, had been completely constructed from wood, it felt so cool in the heat of the day. The roof, the tables and chairs, even the floor, all made from the same lovely fragrant wood, fabulous. A gnarled and obviously ancient olive tree grew through a hole in the floor.

The food was excellent. They had salads; fresh fish and a mouth watering honey dessert. The talking hardly stopped, all of them had much to say and so many questions to ask.

Eleni had enjoyed herself so much she felt torn when it came time for her to get back to the boat.

"Come little sister. We will walk with you" Andros took her arm. "When can we meet again?" he asked.

"Why don't you both come over to Tomas's taverna? I should really be there to help Sofia until her arm is mended, but we will still have plenty of time to talk and Eleni can see her brother"

"That would be great. But I have to go back to Athens tomorrow. I should be back soon though and then we will come over"

Eleni acted upon impulse. Tomas and Sofia could manage surely, just for a couple of days. She hoped they would agree with what she was about to ask.

"Can I come with you Andros? You could show me your home and the city. Plus the fact I need to do some serious shopping" He laughed at the last bit.

"Typical woman eh, shopping. But seriously, yes that would be wonderful. I will pick you up tomorrow from Tomas's and we can fly over. My plane is at the airport on Skiathos so I have got to go over anyway."

"Hi ya" The voice echoed across the harbour. "Has he looked after you? Have you had a good day? Is this your ma?" The woman looked at the older Eleni.

"No. Its erm, my aunt" Eleni replied and shrugged her shoulders at Andros. "And yes we have had a marvelous day thank you" Andros couldn't look her in the eye; he was trying to stifle a laugh.

"That sounds lovely Eleni," The older woman said softly. "You can call me aunt. Two Eleni's in one place could become confusing, yes I would like that" She bent and kissed Eleni goodbye. She too smelt wonderful. This time Eleni recognized the aroma. Anais. It had been her mother's favourite.

She hugged Andros and kissed his cheek. "See you tomorrow big brother. About 9ish?"

"Yes about 9. Be careful" He replied.

Once again Eleni found a seat on the top deck, this time so that she could wave to her brother and aunt as the boat began to move.

They passed the islands on their way back but this time Eleni took no notice. She was deep in thought. Her brother, her only living relative, and how she already loved him. She felt a little in awe of his beautiful, fragile mother, but already knew that she would grow to love her too.

Eleni looked up towards the sky.

"You would be so proud of him papa. He is wonderful," She whispered. "So proud"

Nicos was waiting as the boat docked. She walked down the tiny stairs over the wooden steps and threw herself into his arms.

"I have had such a wonderful day. Andros is so nice, and Eleni so beautiful. A truly marvelous day" She kissed him again. "But now I must get back to the taverna and get ready. Tomorrow I am off the Athens. "She once again saw a look of disappointment on his face." But only for a couple of days." She changed the subject quickly. "I thought Tomas was coming to pick me up?"

" I phoned and said I would," He grunted as he led her to his car. He felt a pang of jealousy. He wanted her for himself. He didn't want to share her with anyone, and especially not with Andros.

# • CHAPTER •
## 7

Eleni hardly drew breath as she told Tomas and Sofia about her day. Nicos sat in silence feeling now almost angry. Andros this, Andros that, he was fed up with it ever since they had been children; all he could remember was Andros, Andros, Andros. Eventually she stopped and went to get her things ready for the following day.

"Sofia. May I go with her?" Nicos knew it was improper, but he wanted to be alone with her for a while. "I won't see her for days. Please may I go?" He was almost pleading. Sofia eventually agreed

"You can go but not for too long."

Once he had her alone Nicos was impatient to get her into bed. He swept her into his arms and kissed her hard. Pulling at her clothes he virtually threw her on the bed, before making love to her roughly, possessing her, letting his anger take control as he thrust into her. Afterwards a rush of guilt swept over him as he looked into her huge dark eyes.

"Oh my love." He kissed her gently this time "How can I wait until we are together. I need you so much. I think I want you to marry me.

Please say you will" That would shut Andros up, he thought. She stroked his sweating brow and kissed his lips. Having almost no knowledge of men, she didn't realise he had all but raped her his passion and anger had been so strong.

"Nicos I have loved you from the minute we met. I will marry you but you must do the right thing, had my father been alive you would have had to ask him, but now you must ask Andros for my hand. It is only right"

Nicos was ecstatic that she had agreed it was what he had wanted from the second they met. He knew they were so right for each other. But the thought of even speaking to Andros, let alone asking for her hand, left a bad taste in his mouth. It showed on his face and he gently shook his head. Ever since they had first met Andros had taken control he had been the oldest of the three boys and hadn't he just let them know. Wasn't he always the one to win any games, he was the one who could run faster and longer, swim quicker. He was the one, so clever at school, and now so rich. Nicos felt an almost hatred as he remembered their childhood.

Eleni propped herself up on her elbows and looked into his eyes.

"You know you must Nicos. Think about it when I am away. Now go, I must get ready. I will see you when I return and I hope you decide to ask him." She was angry "If you love me as much as you say, then you will ask. I will not marry you unless you do, just remember that" It hurt to say those last words but she meant them, at that moment she meant them.

Nicos dressed in silence and stooped to kiss her before he left.

"I am sorry for upsetting you Eleni, I didn't mean to."

She watched him leave and realised that he had not said whether he would ask Andros or not. Let him stew she thought still angry. If I'm worth marrying, then I'm worth asking for properly. With that she set about packing her rucksack with vigor.

Sofia watched as Nicos left the house, he looked sad and a little angry. Minutes later Eleni appeared, a similar look on her face.

"Is something wrong Eleni? Nicos left without so much as a wave. That is not like him. Have you two argued or something." Sofia was concerned. They looked so right together, so happy, what on earth could have happened.

"Oh Sofia. He has asked me to marry him, but he refuses to ask Andros. I know if papa was still here he would ask him, I don't see why he is so against going to see Andros." Eleni was almost in tears.

"I do think it is a little sudden Eleni, you have only known him for such a short time. Are you sure about this?" Eleni nodded "Nicos is a sweet boy but he is jealous little one. You have your brother now and he will have to share you. He will get over it I'm sure, I hope. When you get back you will see, he will be ready to ask" Sofia stroked Eleni's head softly. "Anyway are you ready for tomorrow? Have you packed all that you need?" she continued.

Deep down Sofia was worried. The young couple had known each other for such a short time, and hadn't Nicos already got a reputation for being a Casanova. If he ever hurt Eleni, Tomas would be very angry. She hoped things would work out well for the sake of them all.

"Yes thanks. I've got everything. I wish we were going tonight though. It would do me good to go now in fact." Eleni looked so down.

Sofia went to see Tomas. "Tomas please speak to Andros. Eleni and Nicos have fallen out and I think it would be better if they left for Athens tonight. What time is the last boat from Alonysos."?

Tomas looked at his battered old watch.

"It leaves in about an hour. I will call Eleni if you wish" Sofia nodded.

Moments later Tomas was greeting his sister on the phone. He told her about Eleni and Nicos and asked if it was possible for Andros to take her that night. He waited for her to speak to him and then smiled into the phone as she replied.

"Thank you Eleni. I will be over to see you tomorrow." He replaced the receiver and smiled at Sofia. "She says Andros would rather go tonight. He wants to show his sister Athens from the sky, and says nighttime is the best way to see it. I will go and tell her"

"No. Tomas let Andros come here and surprise her. Don't let her know we have interfered." Sofia stopped him from leaving the kitchen.

When Sofia returned, Eleni was already serving customer with their drinks. She greeted the couple on the swinging seat and asked about their day in Alonysos, not letting on that she knew who they were. It did her good to be doing something and now she was actually smiling as she went about her "self appointed" jobs.

The taverna was quite quiet, no football tonight, and nothing like as hectic as the night before, just nice and steady. Soon it seemed that they were clearing tables and raking the sand. An early night for them tonight.

"Right" said Tomas," Now for our food" He said the same words every night. Sofia and Eleni smiled at each other. As they chatted and ate Eleni looked up as she heard a car pull up in the clearing.

"Late customers Tomas" she said picking a large piece of feta from her salad. "We will have to start again".

"I don't think so little one. Look see who it is." Sofia waved into the darkness. "Welcome Andros. It is so long since you have been here. Its late though, what are you doing?" She pretended not to know the reason for his visit. Luckily he realised and quickly changed his greeting

"Hello Sofia, Tomas, sis. I hope you don't mind me calling this late but I wondered if Eleni would like to go to Athens tonight? The antiquities look spectacular at night from the air, I should have thought about it earlier. I have arranged a flight path and my plane is being refueled as we speak. So Eleni, would you like to go now, its only 10 o'clock?" Andros kissed Sofia and Tomas and hugged Eleni.

"That would be wonderful Andros. I don't know. We have not met until today and already I have seen you twice" Eleni's eyes lit up with excitement.

"Fetch your things then" He said "I have a taxi waiting" They all watched as she ran across the sand and into the house. "Now Sofia, tell me what is the problem?" Sofia told him about Nicos and Andros was angry.

"Of course he must ask me. If he won't then there will be no wedding. Eleni is my baby sister, and he should know that I would take my fathers place in this. It doesn't matter that we have only just met. He must do the proper thing. Tomas if you see him or Alexi tell them no wedding unless he asks. You did the right thing Tomas in calling mama. I will speak to Eleni when we are alone." Andros was quite animated, waving his arms in anger.

"Please Andros don't tell her we asked you to come tonight. Let her tell you in her own time." Sofia was worried about Eleni's reaction to her interference.

"Leave it with me Sofia. I will be tactful. Here she is and what on earth are you carrying. No sister of mine should have a rucksack. Eleni you look like a backpacker, not one of the richest girls in the world" He was laughing as she struggled with her bag "Louis Vitton first thing tomorrow my girl" He kissed her cheek "Come on then. See you in a few days Tomas, Sofia, and don't worry she is in good hands"

They walked past the camper van and Eleni smiled, this would give them a heart attack she thought. That is unless they are already on their way to Athens, knowing Tomas he would probably have told them whilst she had been fetching her things.

Andros led Eleni to the waiting taxi. He took the rucksack from her and pulled a face.

"This is disgusting and going as soon as you unpack. Ugh!"

They sat in the back seat and Andros began to tell her about the wonderful things she would see from the air. The Acropolis, Mars Hill and much much more.

"They are all lit up at night and look amazing" Eleni was speechless as she listened it sounded so wonderful. When she had first flown in her eyes had been tightly closed as they flew over the city, but listening to Andros, what she would have seen in daylight in no way compared to seeing them by night anyway.

The taxi sped down the road towards the main town, weaving its way through little villages, but never slowing down. Soon they were in Skiathos Town, and it was buzzing at this time of night. She noticed how lovely the harbour looked as lights reflected on the gentle sea, a flotilla of little boats bobbed on the waves. She saw the many tavernas full with diners, and heard their soft music floating into the sky.

She saw Alexi and Athena dining with Nicos, and for a moment it hurt. Andros saw the look of pain cross her face, but for now he would say nothing.

The airport was so tiny Eleni was shocked. She had not seen it before having arrived on the ferry and found it quite amusing. They passed through the checks almost unnoticed by the guards, who sat watching television and just waved them on. Andros took her straight through to the runway, which in the dark looked as if it went into the sea, where his little blue and white plane sat waiting.

He settled her in to a seat behind his and began the pre flight checks. She was amazed. He was the pilot, and although she had been quite nervous about the flight, suddenly she felt safe. Her brother, her big brother was flying her into the night.

The little plane rumbled and rattled as it sped down the runway before gliding off in to the darkness. The lights of the town looked beautiful as they gradually gained height. Eleni stayed silent as she took in the pretty sight below.

"Right then passenger. How are you feeling?" His voice sounded so funny coming through the intercom.

"I'm OK thanks Mr. Pilot. This is lovely." She replied before turning and squashing her nose against the window once more.

"It is only a short flight so I won't be able to talk much, but before we land I will try to point some things out for you. If air traffic will agree I will take you over the city" Andros turned and smiled at her. He so wanted her to enjoy being with him. How he had longed to know about his father, but to find he had a sister thrilled him to the core. He would look after her, and Nicos could go take a jump if need be, plenty of men would treat Eleni like the lady that she was. He thought about the rucksack and laughed to himself, no lady he knew would be seen dead with it, but that was his sister he supposed. He had learned a few things about her already and had soon realised she was a one off. Amazingly rich, yet very down to earth, very innocent. Their father had brought her up her well.

Soon all Eleni could see was dark. Occasionally the moon shone on the sea below and highlighted the waves, but other than that darkness. She thought of her father. This was where he had died. Here in this deep dark sea. She shuddered and felt slightly chilled.

The voice of Andros broke into her thoughts. He was talking to air traffic control and from what she could make out they were going to allow him to fly over the city. Evidently air traffic was light at this time of night and he could do one circle around. He thanked them and acknowledged the message, then checked on his speed and height. Eleni was transfixed as she watched him work.

Athens was all he had said and more. The harbour at Piraeus looked like a wonderland; with so many lights it could have been a Christmas tree. The Acropolis stood out against the ink black sky as if were floating above the city. There was so much to see she could have stayed up in the air circling all night.

"This is wonderful Andros. I have never seen anything like it in my life" She sounded like a child, her eyes were wide with wonder.

Churches were lit, amphitheatres looked unreal as lights showed them off against the dark. Huge statues looked so lifelike as the height of the little plane made their true size seem smaller. It was breathtaking and Eleni was disappointed when the plane began to descend.

"That was something I will never forget Andros, how can I ever thank you" She leant forward and kissed his neck, breathing in his lovely aroma as she did.

As the plane came to a halt a large black limousine pulled alongside. The chauffeur opened the doors as Andros and Eleni stepped out into the cool night air. Greeting the man Andros helped Eleni into the back seat after once again grimacing at her rucksack and throwing it into the boot.

"We are shopping first thing" he said quite seriously "I'm not having my sister going round like a tramp"

"I thought you said typical woman, when I mentioned shopping before. You've changed your tune," She said smiling at him.

"That was before I saw that monstrosity. It's a good job you have eaten as well, I'm not taking you out in that" he screwed him nose up at her shorts and t-shirt. "Roll on tomorrow. I wish mama was here, she would make a lady of you" Eleni punched his arm playfully and he retaliated with a bear hug.

They started their first brother sister mock fight, quite a difficult thing to do on the back seat of a moving car.

"What ever will he think?" Eleni said breathlessly nodding towards the driver.

"He won't even notice. They are paid to notice nothing yet see everything," Andros replied as only a very rich man could.

Eleni was fascinated as they drove through the lovely city, and it seemed all too soon that they pulled up at huge iron gates, which opened slowly revealing a long gravel drive.

The building before them gradually came into focus as they moved smoothly towards it. It looked superb, as did the grounds.

A huge fountain stood in the middle of the garden, and she could just make out statues, and pagodas draped with grape vines.

The house itself was of white stone, its bulk standing out against the dark sky. Large white marble columns and steps led the way towards a massive dark wood door. She had lost count of the windows as she concentrated upon the marvelous entrance lit in a similar way to the antiquities she had just seen.

"Is this your home?" She asked her mouth open in wonder

"Welcome Eleni. Yes this is my home." He raised her hand and kissed it tenderly "I never thought that one day I would bring my sister here. I never even knew I had you until today, and now I feel I have known you forever. This is your home too now" Eleni wanted to cry the air was full of emotion. Instead she pulled him into a hug.

"I love you big brother"

"And I love you little one"

The car stopped by the marble steps and Eleni noticed a young man walking towards them from the house. She assumed it was one of the staff until he launched himself towards her smiling. "Welcome Eleni. I am Vanni, Tomas and Sofia's son. Father rang to say you two were on your way. Where is your luggage?" Eleni shook hands and kissed his cheek having to stand on tiptoes to reach. She looked at Tomas's son. Tall and bronzed, his blonde hair designer ruffled, slight stubble on his chin. He dressed well and she noticed he smelled as good as Andros.

"Luggage. Call this luggage" Andros was holding the rucksack at arms length and pulling a face as if it smelt awful. Vanni and Eleni burst out laughing.

"Oh Andros you are such a snob. Come here let me carry it" Vanni took the offending bag from Andros in one hand and with the other guided Eleni into the house.

Together they led Eleni to her room, a graceful four-poster bed draped in white muslin greeted her as she entered. She hung her clothes in the wardrobe; so glad now she had brought her red dress with her, and threw the rucksack to the back. Andros is right, she thought, I do need to shop.

She found a wonderful assortment of oils and creams for her body, lovely rich shampoo, and beautiful gowns of silk to wear in the white bathroom that led from her room. Running herself a hot deep bath she carefully chose her oil from the fabulous range. Poppy.

The two men were amazed when at last she floated down the stairs wrapped in a dark green robe, her hair loose and shinning.

"Eleni you look wonderful and you smell divine. Come let us get you a drink" Andros led her into a huge room.

Three massive red velvet sofas dominated the floor, little wooden tables stood at their sides. A large wooden glass fronted bar, its doors now open, held a vast array of drinks and fine glasses. Swooping red velvet curtains fell to the shining marble floor gracefully.

"Slightly different to the taverna" She laughed. "Everything is so big. I can't get over it. I thought our house was big, but this is very impressive. And all those lovely things in my room, wonderful"

"That is mama. She says if we are to have guests then they should always have the best," Andros said proudly.

Vanni stood as she entered the room, his eyes lit up at the sight before him.

"Come in and sit down. You are so welcome. Right now tell us all about yourself" He said, his eyes taking in every detail of her. "Wine?"

"Yes please" She nodded and took the glass from him. Curling up on one of the sofas she took a sip and began her story, interrupted often by Andros who wanted to know as many details as he could. This time it hadn't hurt to tell her story, and she was pleased Andros was so interested.

The three of them sat for hours talking and laughing, until eventually Eleni excused herself, after all she reminded Andros, it was almost 3am. Vanni walked her to the bottom of the magnificent staircase and bid her good night. He stood and watched until she was at the top, then waved and blew her a kiss.

What a fabulous day it had been Eleni thought as she walked down the corridor towards her room.

She lay in the large four-poster bed and felt so happy. For the first time in months she felt happy, and safe. Did that mean that perhaps Nicos was not the one for her? How could she feel this happy when he was not there?

She drifted off to sleep before she could answer her own question.

# Chapter 8

Eleni slept well and woke to see the bedside clock showing 9.30. It was her longest sleep since arriving in Greece.

Back at the taverna she would now be helping Tomas with the sun beds and would probably have already eaten.

She rolled over in the huge bed stretched and yawned, before rising slowly.

Choosing a different fragrance this morning she treated herself to a lovely long hot shower, happily singing one of Marcos favourite songs as she soaped herself. As she returned to the bedroom, now wrapped in a fabulously thick soft white towel she heard a knock at the door.

Opening it slightly she peered through the crack.

"Its only me Eleni" Andros stood before her already immaculately dressed. "You sing a lovely song" he said "Anyway breakfast will be ready when you are then its off to the shops."

"Ok thanks. I won't be long. But where do I go?" So far Eleni had only seen the inside of her room and the one they had talked in last night.

"I will wait here and show you. I have a couple of phone calls to make so I will do them here" Andros had already fetched a tiny gold mobile from his shirt pocket. He began to talk so she closed the door and dressed quickly.

Thank goodness for her red dress and bronze sandals. She was already feeling a little scruffy being in the company of these two well-dressed men, and remembered longingly all of the wonderful clothes she had left at home. Once dressed she picked up her little handbag containing her purse and precious black AMEX card.

"You are in for a treat," she said kissing it with a smack before carefully placing it back inside the purse. "A real treat".

"Well that's a vast improvement" Andros said as she opened the door, ducking as she swung her bag in his direction. "Come on lets eat."

He gently took her arm and led her down the very ornate staircase, along a cool wide corridor and into an amazing conservatory.

Beautiful tall green plants in marvelous pots stood on a mosaic floor. A large white metal glass topped table with chairs took up the middle. It smelt fresh and cool, but it was the view that took Eleni's breath away. The city of Athens lay sprawled out below and she could see the harbour in the distance.

"Andros this is marvelous. It is just amazing. I didn't realise that we had traveled so high last night" She was stunned. "Our home on Long Island is beautiful but cannot compare to this. Only the gardens are similar. Papa loved his garden and I was surprised to see how alike the two are"

"Kalimera Eleni, Andros" Vanni strolled into the conservatory. "Sleep well?" He was so comfortable in his body she noticed as he walked over to another table laden with delicious food. His walk was almost a roll.

"Kalimera Vanni" they chorused, and then laughed.

"Yes thank you I slept mega well" Eleni answered now helping herself to the food.

As soon as they had filled their plates a maid appeared with a large pot of strong coffee. Eleni took a deep breath.

"Umm! There's nothing like the smell of fresh coffee. I will always love that smell"

They chatted over their meal and occasionally Andros's phone rang.

"He is always busy, always working" Vanni said picking up another pastry.

"That is good. Thank you Spiros" Andros said into the tiny phone before closing it. He turned to Eleni. "That was Spiros, head waiter of one of our smartest restaurants here in Athens, he has a table for us tonight. You must realize at such short notice he has worked a minor miracle."

"Thank you Andros that sounds lovely. So I take it I can't go in jeans?" She was teasing him.

"No definitely not. When we have finished its off to Gucci, Versacci, and Dior for you. We will come and make sure you get something nice" He tried to sound strict.

"Oh Andros. Anyone would think I had no idea of nice clothes and things. Papa always made sure I had the best, but usually I would have to do a chore for them" she smiled at the thought "I would sometimes have to clean his car, or rake the leaves in the garden, help chef in the kitchen, all sorts of things to earn my pocket money. I recall once when he bought me a lovely pair of shoes, I remember they were hand made by Pinnet of Paris. Anyway, when they arrived he saw me toss them in the back of my wardrobe. He was furious and made me work at the center every night for a week." She was laughing at the memory.

"The center?" Andros queried

"Yes. Papa and Richard, always remembered how they had started life in America, and set up a drop in center for the homeless by the beach. It started off as a soup kitchen and just grew. They have built on to it and now it has a proper kitchen, sleeping rooms, shower rooms, and even a little medical center. There is also a workshop where these people can make things to sell. Some of them are brilliant artists you know. So it was there I worked each night, serving food and handing out sleeping bags. He was like that, so very generous, but hated waste."

Vanni was laughing loudly.

"I can just see you dishing out soup"

"But now it is not just soup they get. Each year, on my birthday, we treat them to a Thanksgiving type meal. Papa said that as I was so privileged in life, on my birthday I should give something back. We used to have such fun. I dread my birthday this year, it will be the first time I have gone on my own. Oh and talking of my birthday it is next week so I must fly back in good time. Richard will go mad if I am not there" She looked at Andros.

"I will make sure you get back don't worry, but on the condition that you return as soon as you can. I need to spend much more time with you"

"Of course I will be back" she replied "Nicos has asked me to marry him. Mind you he refuses to ask you and I told him he must or no wedding" She sat upright as if in defiance.

"Nicos asked you!" Vanni spluttered.

"Yes he did. What's so funny about that?" Now she was angry.

"Nothing little one" Andros took her hand in his "The reason Vanni is laughing is that Nicos is always asking girls to marry him. He has quite a reputation. Please don't look like that it tears at my heart" Her face had crumpled as if she were in pain "He is an artist and very flamboyant. He loves to be dramatic and feels each time he is with a girl she is the one for him. He will swear he loves them, he treats them well, he will make them feel they are the only woman on the planet" Eleni was nodding" I am told he makes love like no other" Eleni blushed slightly "If he is serious he will ask, but please don't be too disappointed if he does not. You see he is jealous of me and Vanni" Eleni remembered Sofia's words" When we were children he was always last at everything. His head is full of beautiful pictures, but he claims he cannot run well, he cannot swim well and he always made excuses for not climbing trees or going into the caves. Vanni and Nicos spent many years growing together and then I came along and joined in. I think he dislikes me" He looked at her and she could see he was concerned. "He has a heart of gold though. He would help anyone in trouble, so he cannot be all bad."

"He is the first man I have really fallen for. I suppose papa protected me a little too much. I am almost 28 years old and have fallen for a gigolo. I feel so silly." They thought she was going to cry "But I suppose that's life. Live and learn eh" She looked at them both and sat up straight in a defiant manner. "Right then lets shop"

The three of them left the house and got into the waiting limousine. "Where do you want to go first?" Andros asked

"Gucci is one of my favourites so I will leave that until last, you can choose the first" She replied

"Woman's logic!" Vanni said laughing, he always seemed to be laughing she thought.

The three of them had a wonderful morning. Eleni was greeted at the shops as if she was royalty. She noticed that at each one Andros proudly introduced her to the madam as

"This is my sister Eleni Russos." And the women soon got to work. She watched as the models showed off their creations, sitting sipping ice-cold champagne as they walked up and down in front of her.

The morning flew past in a haze of marvelous clothes and shoes. Handbags so soft they felt unreal. Underwear sets of pure silk. She noticed Vanni was more interested in them than the dresses and nudged him in the ribs.

Eventually when Andros was satisfied that she was no longer a scruff he asked where she would like to eat lunch.

"As you have so kindly brought me all of this" She gestured to the pile of bags now safely stowed in the boot of the car "I will treat you" She whispered to the chauffeur and smiled as she noticed his eyebrows shoot up. "Come on, my treat, and it's a surprise."

The car seemed to float through the magnificent streets before coming to an abrupt halt.

"You cannot be serious" Andros was aghast "MacDonald's. Here in a city with such fine food you choose MacDonald's" Vanni was crumpled up laughing; in fact he was almost crying. Eleni too was giggling.

"You forget Andros I was brought up in America. As soon as I saw the sign I had a craving. I need a burger. Come on" The chauffeur held open the door for her, he did not even look round as she led the way in.

"OK let me order." Vanni went with her.

"Just coffee for me" Andros said "No make that water" he had spotted the paper cups and was aghast.

Eleni and Vanni returned to their table with a tray full of burgers and fries, coffee and cola plus a bottle of luke warm water for Andros.

"Don't you ever tell anyone I have been in here?" He sounded like he was telling children off for being naughty. "Never breath a word"

Eleni licked her fingers as the various sauces ran from between the bun, Vanni followed suit. They picked at the fries with their fingers and eventually when the tray was left with only rubbish on Eleni sat back.

"Oh I needed that. Delicious Umm."

"Delicious! How could that have been delicious?" Andros asked rolling his eyes in disgust.

"It was really," Vanni added.

"You are as bad as she is Vanni. Uncouth that's what it is uncouth" Once again the others burst out laughing.

"Come on. What's next?" Eleni cleared the table and picked up her bag.

"Home for a rest, or swim if you like first, and then tonight I am taking you for a proper meal" Andros led the way to the car taking long strides as if trying to get away as quickly as he could.

The driver took them around the city and between them Andros and Vanni gave her a running commentary. They knew so much about the city it was like having a guide in the car. She sat mostly in silence listening and gazing out of the window. What a beautiful city it was.

The maid took Eleni's parcels and bags to her room and between them they unpacked carefully. Vanni knocked at the door just as they were finishing

"Fancy a swim?"

"Oh yes please. Just let me get my things" She pulled her costume from a drawer and grabbed a towel.

"No need for that" Vanni took it from her "There's everything down there already" They walked down the stairs and through the conservatory and into a large low shed like building standing to one side. Only it was built of white marble not wood. A lovely pool house, one end wall was glass from floor to ceiling.

There were nice bright rooms to change in, super soft towels to dry with, creams, oils and everything a swimmer could possibly need. Vanni showed her where to go and went off to change. She hung up her dress and noticed the stale smell of burgers, perhaps Andros was right, it smelt disgusting, but it had tasted so nice she thought.

"Andros is working in his office. If he gets chance he will join us, but if not you will have to put up with me" Vanni called from the water.

"How come you are not working?" She asked as she slid into the pool" I thought you two worked together"

"We do but I do mine at night mostly. We are now an international firm and what with time differences and things one of us has to work at night. After our meal tonight I will go to the office." He replied.

"But when do you sleep then" She asked

"I am lucky that I only need a couple of hours at a time so I will sleep after our swim, and then again in the morning before breakfast."

She watched as he moved smoothly and quickly through the water noticing his powerful shoulders as they rose with each stroke. She felt a shiver. Nicos has certain awoke the woman in me, she thought, even if he is a love rat he has done one good thing. She swam off to join Vanni.

They stayed in the pool swimming, talking and playing ball for almost an hour.

"Right time for a rest. Fancy a drink?" Vanni pulled himself up on the edge of the pool and out of the water, he pointed to a lovely patio area just outside.

"That sounds great." Eleni used the steps; she was trying to be ladylike. After drying herself and putting on plenty of cream she joined Vanni outside where sun beds were arranged on a marble floor. The view was as spectacular from here as it had been in the conservatory.

"Athens, what a wonderful sight" Eleni was again overwhelmed by the view before her.

"Ouzo?" Vanni asked as he poured himself a drink from behind a small stone bar. Eleni noticed a brick bar-b-que and pretty wooden seats standing on the lawn nearby.

"Yes please, with lemonade and ice. Someone has thought of every thing here," She pointed to the eating area. "I take it Eleni has done all of this".

"No actually. Andros and I did this part. Eleni comes here to swim but she prefers to eat in the conservatory with her friends. This is where we bring our pals, we can make lots of noise, have loud music and it doesn't disturb anyone in the house. Good eh?" He placed her drink at the side of her bed.

"Thanks. Um delicious" Eleni lay back and let the suns rays sink into her skin. The warmth making her relax and feel good.

"Tell me more about Nicos. I can't believe I have fallen for a rat" She looked over to where Vanni lay, the cream on his body glistening in the sunshine. Not an ounce of fat on his long lean limbs. She felt a stirring and sensed her nipples rising; she smiled to herself as she willed them to go down. This morning she had been upset by what they had said about Nicos, and here she was hours later admiring another mans body. You are turning into a tart, she said to herself.

Vanni told her many stories about their childhood and how Nicos had been as a boy. She noticed that he often glanced at her breasts, her nipples now aching they were so large. He gave a lop sided knowing sort of grin and continued. He said how he admired Nicos's work and liked him, but sometimes he made him mad. When Andros had joined them, Nicos had at first tried to dominate the new boy, but then sensing that he was getting nowhere decided to dislike him instead. Vanni shrugged his shoulders.

"He is as Andros said, very flamboyant and likes to shine out from the crowd. I mean have you seen that car of his. It cost a fortune to ship over to the island, an island with one road. That says it all to me" Vanni snorted.

"His car is wonderful. In fact it is exactly the same as mine back home. Papa gave it to me so don't you knock his car. Anyway I have decided to wait until I get back and see how he is with me. I can't and won't believe it was all lies" Eleni replied. She finished her drink and decided to go to her room. "I think I will have a sleep in the cool before getting ready. Andros has said to be ready for cocktails at 9. I think I had better make a real effort tonight" She said a little mockingly.

"He loves you already Eleni. He is so pleased that you have come into his life; you are the link to his father. Don't tease him. He only wants the best for you, he wants to be there for you." He looked up at Eleni "You know Andros is a brilliant business man. You could do no better than to have him look after your affairs you know. He would love to be connected to his fathers business." Vanni was serious for once.

Eleni sat down again. "Vanni do you think Andros would come to New York next week with me? I would love him to meet Richard, and I am sure Richard would feel the same."

"He would be over the moon little one if you asked him, but if he goes then I do to" He was smiling again "I want to see where you live and we can help at the center on your birthday."

"OK you're on." She replied "I will ask him tonight at the restaurant." Eleni ran off over the marble tiles and on to the soft warm grass. She skipped up the steps and into the house. It could be the answer to my problems, she thought, Andros running my business, not that I want the business anyway, but still.

Up in her room she rang Richard. He was delighted to hear from her and glad she was enjoying Athens. He agreed that it could be a good idea about the business, but wanted to meet Andros first.

"I will make a few enquiries before I decide" he said, and she knew he would delve deep into anything he could find out about her brother. She said her goodbyes, promising to be in New York for her birthday, and then rang Tomas. She told them what a marvelous time she was having with the others and hoped Sofia's arm was holding up to the extra work. She asked if Nicos had been to see them and was disappointed to learn he had not.

"I expect he is busy at the shop, or out and about taking more photographs" Tomas growled down the line. "Why don't you phone him yourself?" He suggested before handing the phone to Sofia. The two women had a long chat and eventually Eleni said her goodbyes.

She tried Nicos's mobile number and found it was switched off. She then tried the shop, Athena answered.

"He is out at the moment" She said "I will get him to phone you when he returns. Oh and Eleni, do not always believe all he says. I love my son, I would die for him, but sometimes he makes me very angry. I fear he falls in love far too easily yet it is always the women who seem to get hurt. I don't wish to upset you little one, but he can be very jealous of Andros and Vanni." Eleni was quite shocked. Even Nicos's mother was now warning her. Perhaps she should start to take notice of them all.

Just before 9 she checked herself one last time in the mirror. Tonight she had chosen a beautiful black Gucci cocktail dress and soft leather high-heeled sandals. The maid had put up her hair in a chignon, with curly tendrils falling around her neck. For once she had applied full make-up and doused herself in Kenzo Flowers perfume, her favourite, and her new silk underwear made her body feel wonderful. She had only brought along her simple gold jewellery, but it looked good with her outfit. Grabbing the bag that matched her shoes she was ready.

Both Andros and Vanni stopped talking as she entered the room

"My goodness" Andros exclaimed "You see I said we would make a lady of you. Come here let me have a good look." She glided over to where they stood "You look marvelous Eleni. I shall be so proud tonight" Andros bent and gently kissed her cheek.

After a delicious cocktail made with peach schnapps and champagne they strolled out into the night air and the waiting car.

The men sat either side of her as the limousine sped through the outskirts of Athens and up high into a nearby hill. They turned into a long gravel drive and towards a beautifully lit building. It was obviously an ancient mansion. She would see the now familiar marble columns leading towards the entrance and noticed a long deep red carpet over the steps. This is one special place, she thought. As the driver held open the door she could hear faint music from within and smelt a combination of mouth-watering aromas.

Andros took her arm and proudly walked towards the entrance, Vanni followed a couple of steps behind. They were greeted by a bowing Spiros, who Andros had spoken of earlier and led to a table overlooking the city.

"You have made me a very proud man Eleni. Did you see how other dinners looked as we walked through? I wanted to shout out loud that this beautiful lady was my sister, but no doubt the gossips have been working overtime and they know already" His glowing face said everything. Eleni took his hand and gave it a gentle squeeze. She could not reply she was too emotional at that moment.

Their meal was superb and the conversation interesting, but light. Quite often the three of them would burst out laughing as they listened to one of Vanni's stories. It was truly wonderful.

Eleni was surprised when after the meal they were escorted by Spiros into a huge ballroom, where dance music was playing gently. Other dinners sat around tables, or stood at the windows, some were enjoying a leisurely dance around the shinning floor.

They sat at the table Sprios had indicated to and Andros ordered champagne.

"You are spoiling me brother" Eleni said smiling widely "Thank you this is a lovely night. I'm sorry about lunch time, I hope I didn't offend you" She remembered his face at the sight of MacDonald's. It seemed an age ago now.

"I am pleased you are enjoying yourself Eleni. And no, I was not over upset about today, but please don't take me again" Andros was smiling too. "Why don't you young ones dance?"

Vanni held out his hand and Eleni felt the electricity as she took it. His skin felt so soft and once in his arms the closeness of his body played havoc with her senses. His lemony smell weakened her knees and for a moment she had trouble in keeping in step. They danced and chatted until suddenly Vanni led her back to the table.

"I think a little rest before you have the last dance with Andros." He smiled at her and she wanted to melt.

"Andros I have returned this wonderful lady to you. You are lucky I didn't run away with her" He teased "I have told her to rest a little before the last dance with you.

"Thank you Vanni. More champagne Eleni?" She nodded and sipped at the cooling drink. Needing to calm herself she visited the powder room and ran cooling water over her wrists before touching up her make-up. Surely I'm not falling for Vanni, she asked herself as she stared at her own face in the mirror, but she already knew the answer. Yes she was.

The last dance was announced; Andros stood and bowed to Eleni.

"My I?" He asked holding out his hand. She nodded and let him lead her to the floor.

"Thank you for a magical night Andros. It has been really wonderful" She lost her step as she stretched to kiss his cheek.

"I am so pleased you have enjoyed it little one. I hope we have many more nights like this" His smile said everything. They floated around the room, Andros nodding occasionally to other couples as they moved. Eleni could tell he was a proud man and pleased to be showing her off. All to soon the dance finished and he led her back to the table.

Her mind was made up. She would ask him to run her business; after all, he would have inherited them if Marco had married his mother. She began to think deeper.

"Is everything alright Eleni? You look so serious." He asked looking into her face.

"No everything is fine. I was just thinking about home that's all and wondered if you would like to come and meet Richard"

"And me" Vanni interrupted.

"That would be marvelous thank you. I promised to get you back for your birthday and I shall. Tomorrow we will book tickets for all of us. Would you mind if mama came with us. I know she likes to shop in big cities and she would really love to see where Marco lived. She has taken his death hard you know. She had so hoped to meet him once again; I think she never stopped loving him, never even looked at another man. Such a waste as you have seen she is a beautiful woman, and so kind."

"Of course she must come. I would love to shop with her and you are right she is a beautiful woman." Eleni replied. It was the first time she had realised that other people had felt Marco's death the way she had. "Will you fetch her?"

"Yes. I will phone tomorrow before we sort the arrangements and then I can book the hotel," Andros said happily.

"You will not Andros" Eleni said quite sharply. "You will all stay at my home. I want you to stay with me. I will phone Richard first thing"

The waiter brought coffee and delicate chocolates to complete the evening, and what a wonderful evening it had been she thought, just wonderful.

The car was waiting as they stepped into the night air. The black sky littered with millions of tiny stars was the perfect backdrop to the wonderfully sights of the city.

"You know I will never tire of seeing Athens at night" Eleni said as they sped off. The men agreed with her.

Back in her room she undressed and slid between the crisp cool sheets of the huge bed.

Within minutes she was fast asleep, a smile staying on her face as she slept.

It felt as if she had only just closed her eyes when she woke to someone knocking at her door.

"Eleni are you awake yet?" It was Vanni. She glanced at the bedside clock. 10.am. She flew out of bed and grabbed her silk gown. Tying it tightly round her waist she opened the door. "You little monkey. You were still asleep" said Vanni laughing as usual "Do you want breakfast here?"

"No its OK thanks. Coffee will do this morning anyway after that lovely meal last night. Is everything OK?" She looked into his eyes.

"Yes. I woke to tell you Andros has flown over to Skiathos this morning to fetch Eleni and he has asked me to look after you until he returns. Evidently he has some business to sort out on the island, which will take a few days, and then he will be back. He has booked the tickets to New York for the weekend and has instructed me to make sure you have some decent luggage. I don't think he likes your rucksack much" Eleni was laughing with him now. They looked into each other's eyes and Eleni began to melt. She felt her heartbeat quicken and her skin begin to prickle. He took her hand and kissed it gently, making her shiver. His lips met hers so suddenly as he pulled her into his arms.

"Oh Eleni you are so beautiful. I'm sorry I should not have done that. Please forgive me."

"Vanni. There is nothing to forgive. It's just I'm a bit embarrassed, the fact that I have just woken and must taste awful" She was cursing herself for not being showered or having cleaned her teeth.

"You taste wonderful to me." He had that lop sided smile on his face again. His hands slowly untied her gown and he began to stroke her breasts. She groaned from deep within and felt her nipples harden under his touch. She held his arm and led him over to her still warm bed. He undressed quickly and once again began to kiss her naked body. This time he kissed her all over; lay her down, let his tongue run down her stomach and even further. She came to a mind blowing climax within seconds and winced as he entered her. His muscular body pounded at her as she met his rhythm, their pace quickening as he too reached satisfaction.

They lay entwined breathing deeply for a few minutes. His body pushing her into the soft mattress as he lay on top of her. Slowly he rose up on his elbows and began to stroke her face.

"I should be working you know" He was laughing yet again "You will have Andros angry with me if I do not get it all done" he bent and kissed her.

"Let him be angry then" She kissed him back and began to stoke his chest. "You have a wonderful body Vanni. A girl could get to quite like it you know" She continued to let her hands wonder and she could feel him rising again whilst still inside her. It was the most fantastically sexy feeling she had ever known. Not that she had had that many. Only Nicos and Vanni, but she was learning fast.

The second time was much slower and she had to slap him, as this time when he brought her to satisfaction he refused to stop the rhythmical movement until she somehow found the strength to push him away. He moved her onto her knees and entered her again. This time he collapsed on her back, flattening her hot face against the pillow. He held her arms wide apart; it was delicious to feel his power.

They lay still, only the sound of their breathing breaking the silence. As she lay thinking about the past moments she realised that neither of them had taken precautions, but who cares she thought, certainly not me, not at this minute.

Slowly Vanni rose, kissing her shoulders as he moved.

"I must shower and return to the office for a short while, but I will be back soon and then we can go for your luggage." Eleni watched as he strode across the room and into her bathroom, following when she heard the water begin. She ran herself a hot bath adding lots of aromatic oil as the steam rose. Laying herself down in the soft bubbles she began to sing.

"You have a lovely voice" Vanni shouted from the shower unit "It is the sort of voice that makes me want to make love to its owner" Now he was laughing.

"Not again you monster. Go and get your work done." She flicked some of her bubbles in his direction as he emerged from behind the glass doors. "And in any case I'm starving now, I need some breakfast."

"Give me a few minutes and I will join you" Vanni planted a kiss on her nose and went to dress. "See you in the conservatory in half an hour" He shouted as he left the room.

Eleni relaxed in the bath and let her mind wonder. She thought of Nicos, and how only a few days ago she had felt so in love. Now she had been with Vanni, her passion had been transferred. I am so fickle, she thought to herself.

As she dressed her mobile phone sprang to life. It was Nicos. She felt her face blush with guilt as he spoke.

"I'm sorry I missed your call. Mama told me you had phoned." He sounded all tinny. "I rang to tell you I have not changed my mind. I cannot and never will be able to ask Andros. I'm sorry Eleni but I must break off our engagement"

"Nicos. What engagement. You asked me to marry you but would not ask my brother. That is not an engagement in my books." She was angry with him now. Fancy ringing to tell her it was all off, why hadn't he waited until they were face to face. She had forgotten that only minutes ago she had been making love with Vanni. It was Nicos now who dominated her mind. She remembered what the others had said and realised they were right, but she could not dislike him. He had taught her so much in the little time they had been together. He had been so kind to her. She still felt something towards him.

"Nicos, listen. I am sorry that you feel like that, but I do hope we can still be friends. I would like it very much if we can still have a drink together now and again. Still laugh together. Can we. Am I asking too much?" Now she was crying. The first man ever to ask her to marry him, and he had broken it off. She felt old, at her age crying over her first love. Nicos heard her sniffle and felt a little sorry for her.

"Eleni I will always have a space in my heart for you. Of course we can be friends." She noticed he sounded slightly relieved. "As soon as you return we will drink together. I promise." They said their goodbyes and Eleni sat on the bed and cried. Vanni heard her sobbing and stormed into the room.

"Little one. What on earth is the matter?" he stroked her damp hair. "Tell me please" he held her close.

"Nicos had just dumped me" she said between sobs "I know I should be pleased after what has happened this morning, but I still feel sad. He was the first man to ask me to marry him. Oh Vanni I feel so ugly and old" He laughed and held her closer.

"My poor little girl. You are experiencing your first break up. You should have done that in your teens you know. You are not old, and you are certainly not ugly. I think you are wonderful, and so innocent I could eat you" Growling he pretended to take a bite of her arm "Please stop crying. We told you about Nicos, and in any case you have me now. I am all yours Eleni. That is if you will have me?" He peered into her tear-streaked face. "I know Nicos said he loved you, but now I am telling you I love you. Come on get dressed. I need some coffee" he pulled her to her feet and pushed her towards the wardrobe. "And try to look like a lady" He mimicked Andros and soon had her laughing.

They sat in the conservatory enjoying their coffee and pastries in the mid morning sun.

"Why have neither you or Andros married?" Eleni asked him. "Two very eligible bachelors, rich and handsome men."

"Well Andros is married to his work, but he does have a lovely lady who I am sure you will meet shortly. Paris her name is and she is perfect for him. I keep on at him to marry her and Eleni approves so I don't see his problem. Perhaps he will one day if he can find time. As for me, well I have been waiting to meet the right woman. I have had many friends, but none that is quite right. In any case I too have the business at heart. I am the same age as you don't forget so I'm not in any hurry yet."

Eleni felt a stab of jealousy when he spoke. Many friends he said, I bet they were all beautiful women too, she thought.

They finished their breakfast and went to the ever-waiting car. Athens looked its magical best as they drove through the outskirts. It was as if the city was on another planet from the rest of the world. It had that aura that set it apart and Eleni felt it deep down.

They stopped outside the Louis Vitton emporium and the driver held open the car door.

"Come on scruff lets see what we can do with you today" Vanni led the way. As Andros had introduced her yesterday, today it was Vanni who spoke.

Eleni chose a deep gold leather case and matching flight bag, also a beautiful black and gold handbag. She bought a lovely soft dark green leather briefcase for Richard and waited until his initials had been set in gold on the front.

"He is a very lucky man," Vanni said as they inspected the finished article. "It is a beautiful present"

Eleni was pleased with her purchases so far but decided that she needed another look in the Gucci shop. Vanni pretended to be bored with shopping but took her anyway.

The madam greeted her as if she had shopped there many times, and soon produced some wonderful garments for Eleni to look at. She chose a couple of cocktail dresses and some comfortable trousers for traveling, some pretty silk blouses, and two pairs of sandals. More underwear and she was done.

"Right that's it I think. Time for lunch." She gathered her bags together and headed for the door "Where shall we go today?"

"I will show you a lovely place" Vanni said his voice quite deep "You will love it"

They put her bags in the boot of the car and sat comfortably in the back holding hands.

"I am glad Nicos phoned this morning Eleni. I am sorry that you were upset, but I am glad you see because it leaves you free for me now." He looked into her eyes. "I said before that I have never met the right woman, but I have now. I know we have only met a few days ago, but I feel you are the one for me" He leant over and kissed her gently. "I will give you time if you need it, but as for me I am certain."

"I think you are wonderful Vanni, and I can honestly say I don't need any time. Nicos was there for me when I needed him. He was kind and nice. He taught me such a lot, I asked if we could be friends and he has agreed. I think I confused his kindness for love. I am so very naive you see and as you said innocent, but I am pleased to have met him." Eleni replied. It was true, what she had felt for Nicos was nothing compared to the strength of her feeling to Vanni.

"That is good then" Vanni patted her hand "Let us go and get to know each other"

Eleni was surprised when the car stopped outside of Andros's house. "I thought we were going somewhere for lunch?" She quizzed him

"We are little one. The best lunch in Athens" Vanni replied. "Go and unpack then come down to the pool, I've got a surprise for you"

She took her bags to her room and collected her costume. No need for a towel she remembered.

As she walked across the lawn towards the pools house she sensed the smell of delicious cooking food wafting in the air. Her stomach gave a low rumbling growl.

Eleni made her way into the changing rooms; she hung up her clothes and put on her costume. Instead of going in to the water she went straight outside to find Vanni cooking on the bar b que. She poured herself a long drink and lay on the sun bed watching as he prepared the salad and turned the meats over the coals. She laughed when she read the logo on his apron. "Beware man cooking" it read, and was suddenly shocked when she realised that was all he had on.

"Come on. There is only you and me. If we are going to get to know each other properly let's make a start" He was his usual jolly self. "Get that costume off!"

Eleni was amazed. Lunch in the nude, but what the heck. Nicos had shown her how to accept her scar, and she knew the rest of her was not that bad, so off it came. For a couple of minutes she was slightly uncomfortable but she soon relaxed as her drink and the sun began to work their magic.

"Right then. Lunch is ready." Vanni announced, "Come and get it" Eleni stood slowly. She felt self-conscious. Now he would see the mess on her side, but she realised that he must have seen it this morning and not even mentioned it. She took a deep breath and walked over to the picnic table where lunch was ready

"My little zebra. Come and eat"

"What did you call me? A zebra?" She asked sharply.

"Well you are. Look where your costume has been. You have stripes in your tan, and a little white belly" Now he was laughing hard. "You must come here every day until we go to New York and sunbathe naked." He saw the look on her face "Don't worry. I told you this is mine and Andros's playground. No one comes here; no one will disturb you I promise. If that umbrella is open like that "He pointed to a brightly coloured beach umbrella "That is the sign to say we are here. Do not disturb. OK"

Eleni examined her body. Vanni was right. She had quite deep marks where her costume had been.

"Ok if you are sure. I hadn't noticed before, I didn't even think about it. I suppose I should get a bikini instead." She could not believe she was talking of buying a bikini. After all of these years trying to hide her scar she suddenly realised it didn't matter any more. Thank you Nicos she said to herself.

"Zebra indeed" she swiped at Vanni with her napkin.

They ate a delicious meal of salad, taramasalata, and char grilled garlic chicken; they drank smooth rose wine, and talked. It seemed so natural for them to be sitting there talking and eating. They went together so well.

After the meal they lay on the sun beds and talked some more before Vanni dozed off. She studied him whilst he slept, his superb body glistening in the sun, and she remembered how his skin had felt against hers. She smiled as he snored very softly and soon she too was asleep as she listened to his rhythmic breathing.

She woke to the touch of his hand gently stroking her stomach, and kept her eyes closed as his fingers wondered over her skin, she smiled as his hand slid between her thighs. He entered her slowly, teasingly. Oh so annoyingly.

"No" He said as she started to open her eyes "Keep them shut" It was so erotic. There she lay in the open air, eyes tightly closed, being made love to. He stroked every part of her body; he licked her breasts, and kissed her lips. Moments later they called out together.

"I love you" He said as he collapsed on top of her, kissing her again "I love you so much. My little zebra." She kissed him back and smiled.

"You were right Vanni. This is the best place for lunch. I shall remember this for ever"

The next few days were taken up with them making love and laying in the sun. They didn't even bother to go out at night to eat, choosing to stay at the house.

Eleni went with him into the office and watched him work. She slept when he did, ate when he did, and thoroughly enjoyed every minute of their time alone. Just the two of them. It was wonderful just like a honeymoon.

She noticed her suntan stripes had now faded, and how her body had shaped up from swimming each day.

She felt so happy when after making love and she told Vanni that she loved him. His smile lit the room as he twirled her round.

"I knew you would in the end. I mean who could resist me!" he laughed.

The following morning at breakfast he produced a wonderful display of red roses and a beautiful set of gold and diamond earrings. She was so moved she almost cried.

"You can have the rest of the set the day we marry" He announced "I have already got them in my room. I have got to ask Andros first I know and then we can set a date."

"Vanni. You have forgotten one thing" She said

"What my love?"

"You haven't asked me yet"

"Right. Tonight put your best dress on. We are going out. I will show you"

For the rest of the day she hardly saw him. She sunbathed, swam and slept on her own. As evening came she bathed and asked the maid to help her with her hair. She wore a beautiful gold silk underwear set and chose a dark gold Gucci cocktail dress. Finally some wonderful Pinnet sandals with a tiny bag to match. She put on her new earrings and her little gold necklace. She looked and felt fabulous.

Vanni took her to the restaurant in the hills that they had been to with Andros. Spiros met them and led them to a table in the center of the room. Eleni was a little disappointed not to be able to see Athens from it and would have preferred a window table, but still it was nice just to be here. She noticed throughout their meal Vanni said little. He kept looking at her and smiling. When the time came for them to go through to the dance room he suddenly stood up and banged on the table with a spoon.

"Ladies and gentlemen. If I can have your attention for one moment. As you can see I am here tonight with the wonderful Eleni Russos" Eleni wanted to crawl under the table as she felt all the eyes turn to her. "Eleni is the most wonderful woman in the world and" He knelt at her feet "I would like to ask you to marry me" A huge cheer went up as he waited for her reply.

Now she felt like a million dollars. She should have seen this coming after their discussion this morning. Trust Vanni to make an exhibition like this. She stood up and replied.

"Yes I will"

Vanni took her hand and placed a fabulous solitaire diamond ring on her finger

"I will love you forever" He said as he kissed her. "And I have already asked Andros. He is as pleased as I am. Next I must tell papa." Vanni beamed as a constant stream of diners came and shook their hands. A grinning Spiros was asked to take champagne to every table in order to toast the couple.

"If this is the proposal, what will the wedding be like?" She asked laughing. "Thank you so much for this" She turned the ring on her finger "It is beautiful. Thank you"

"Our wedding is going to be like a fairy tale. I promise you a day to remember"

They opened the dancing as if it were their wedding. The other diners clapped as the young couple floated around the room as if in dream, smiles lighting up everyone's faces as they passed by.

As they left the floor Eleni was amazed to see Andros and his mother striding into the room. They greeted each other with a kiss

"Sorry we are late. Air traffic control kept me in Skiathos. But I can see you have already done the deed" he raised Eleni's hand before kissing her. "I am so happy for you little one come let me dance with you"

Eleni smiled as Andros proudly took her around the room. He asked if she was sure about Vanni. Was she happy? All sorts of questions.

"You sound like my papa" She said laughing at yet another question.

"Eleni. Your papa is not here and so it is up to me to take his place. It is a roll I am proud to hold. You know I am here for you." She felt her eyes fill.

"I love you Andros you make me feel so safe"

"Tonight we celebrate little one. Tomorrow I will talk to both of you. There is a lot to discuss. Come let us rejoin the others." The dance finished and Andros led her back to their table.

What a marvelous night she thought happily, she gazed down at her ring and smiled across at Vanni

Marvelous!

# • CHAPTER •
## 9

She woke to Vanni kissing her shoulders.

"I must go Eleni. I don't think Andros would be too pleased to find me here do you?"

She snuggled around him and whimpered

"Please stay. It's so comfortable with you here"

"I can't little one. Now they are back we must be careful. I will see you at breakfast" he kissed her before getting out of the warm bed and dressing. She stifled a giggle as he tiptoed across the room and opened the door quietly. Looking furtively through the tiny gap he had made he quickly blew her a kiss before disappearing into the hallway.

Eleni pulled the covers around her body and lay back with a contented sigh. She felt happy enough to burst. Vanni was such a wonderful man, what he had done the previous night was amazing. To be proposed to like that must be every girls dream, yet it had actually happened to her. She went through in her mind over and over how he had got down on one knee, the things he had said, the way they had danced, she looked again at her ring. Vanni I love you, she thought. You make me feel special, safe, loved. I am such a lucky girl.

Andros was missing from breakfast this morning puzzling Vanni slightly.

"He is working early so that he has plenty of time to talk to you two," aunt Eleni explained. "He asked me to tell you he will be free at 10. If you would kindly go to his office then" It was more of an order than a request Eleni thought.

The meal was a quiet affair. Aunt Eleni talked only if necessary and the other two just gazed at each other and ate very little.

"Come on. Lets go and see what he has to say" Vanni pushed away his still full plate. "I am as nervous as a teenager" He tried to lighten the mood but it fell flat.

He took Eleni's hand and together they walked slowly down to Andros's office.

"I wonder what is so important Vanni." She said quietly, her heart fluttering. She felt nervous, as Vanni had said he did, but she didn't know why.

For some reason Vanni knocked before opening the office door. Never before had he done that, after all it was his office too, but he felt as if this meeting was somehow special.

"Come on in" A smiling Andros waved to them from behind his large oak desk, it faced the one Vanni usually used. "I have finished for now so let's get talking. Coffee?"

"No I'm OK thanks" Eleni said shakily. She sat where Andros indicated and Vanni had the chair next to hers.

"Right then I will get down to it" Andros was leaning on his elbows and looking very official. "Yesterday afternoon I received a phone call from Vanni asking for your hand Eleni. Nothing would give me greater pleasure in seeing my sister marrying.

I take it you realised Vanni is my cousin, and that makes him your half cousin. That thankfully will not prohibit you, but I hope you can see there are many things to think about." He paused. "Tell me Eleni, why did you come to Greece?"

"I came to find out why papa was going to Skiathos when he was killed." She replied shakily.

"And have you found that out?" He asked

"Yes. Tomas and Alexi told me all about it, and I repeated the story to you and Vanni the other night. Of course once I knew I had a brother I wanted to meet you to" She smiled at him nervously.

"Well let me continue." Andros sounded very serious as he spoke. "You followed Marco's trail and found out about his life. Whilst doing this you meet Nicos, whom you immediately fall in love with and agree to become his wife" Eleni nodded, now she was looking at her feet. "He refuses to ask me for your hand and you leave Skiathos with me to stay here in Athens" She nodded again "It is here that you meet Vanni and once again you fall in love." Now the tears had started to flow. The way Andros was talking made her feel silly, dirty, and so childish. "Last night was a beautiful night. I am pleased that Vanni treated you the way you should be treated and am sorry we did not get back in time to see him on one knee. Spiros told me all about it though" She looked up to see him smiling "You see little one. I want to make sure you are happy. I want my best friend, my cousin, to be happy. It just seems so sudden. I want you to wait before you actually get married. I want you to wait one year. Get to know each other properly. Court her properly Vanni." It was Vanni's turn to nod "I have given my approval of your engagement and have spoken to Richard" Eleni gasped "Yes Eleni you forgot to phone him. He was a little hurt but we spoke for some considerable time, and now I am looking forward to meeting him"

"But a year. It is such a long time Andros." She pleaded

"Eleni it will fly past I can assure you. You have not thought about your business and also of Vanni's. People like us cannot just get married. We have to think about the consequences to our finances. It can be quite complicated. The months will fly past believe me. We have to think about a safe place for you to marry, somewhere security can be tight. We also have to think about where you will live after"

"But I have a home in Long Island" she interrupted

"Who's home Eleni? Marco and Richard bought those houses in America. On your fathers death they automatically went to Richard. They are both his. You see I have learned a lot from him. Now to the businesses. The bank is yours and run by managers, that is good as it gives you an income without the worry. The gold and gem side of things is split between you and Richard, and the shares are spilt equally as well.

Have you any idea of how rich that makes you little one." She shook her head.

"Well it can be no ordinary wedding I can assure you. You my love are a multi millionairess. Athena Onassis you are not but I can tell you that you are not far behind. Marco must have been a wizard with his requisitions and Richard brilliant with his. Someone has to take control of all of this well before you can think of marrying. I know it sounds awful to talk of finances when you are in love, but you can see it makes sense surely?"

Eleni looked at Vanni and this time they both nodded.

"You talk of security Andros, but there is none here. Back at Eleni Beach I know there are a couple that keep their eyes on me. But since then no one, so why worry?" Eleni quizzed him

"You are so wrong Eleni. Ever since you left American soil you have had people with you." Andros replied. "Yes the couple at the beach, but what about on the plane?"

"I didn't notice anyone then" She said biting her bottom lip nervously. "Was there someone on the plane too?"

"Of curse there was. Richard has done a very good job. You have people everywhere as I said."

"Tell me Andros. It feels a bit creepy not to know who they are"

"Well your driver in America is one, then you got on the plane and there were two more"

"Not that loud lady and her husband surely" She laughed "The one that thumped you on the arm in Alonysos" Andros nodded.

"That was her sign to say she was handing you over to me. She is one of the best money can buy. Who on earth would think she was security? The two at the beach, they work for her. Here your maid is not just a maid, and the chauffeur not just a driver. We have cameras in the grounds and alarms on the house and gates. You see it is not just for you. Why do you think Vanni and I work from home? It is because we too are targets; we are all targets of kidnappers and terrorists. We only visit our offices when necessary as can run everything from here. Mama has her own guard on Alonysos and we have ours. At home you have had people watching you around the clock since you were born, even your car has a tracking device fitted, but I realize now that you had no idea."

Eleni was shocked. It made her skin crawl to think that she was watched all the time.

"When we get to New York Richard and I have agreed to go through some paper work and make a start. You see no one is against you marrying if that is what you want. If you are truly in love one year is nothing, and anyway Eleni it will take you that long to sort out the arrangements and of course a dress" Andros's voice was much lighter now. "Vanni too must see to his finances. Our company here is split like the ones in America, we have to make arrangements to secure ourselves."

"But when I marry Eleni it will be for life Andros. There is no need to worry" Vanni spoke quickly.

"Yes I know that Vanni, but what if one of you dies, what happens then? Don't say it can't happen as we all know it can. What if children come along? What if I die, where will that leave you then? It is a good thing this marriage, it has made me think of many what ifs. Our solicitor will meet us when we return from America, he also agrees it is about time we sorted things properly." He looked at the young couple "Please don't look so serious. All of this is quite normal for people of our standing. Right then go and enjoy the rest of the day. Tomorrow we are off to America and I am so looking forward to seeing where papa lived. Promise you will give me a tour Eleni. I want to know everything."

"Of course I will Andros. And thank you for looking after everything. We know you are right. I realize now I made a mistake with Nicos, but I just needed someone to be there and he was. He was so kind; I suppose I was a sucker, as we say in America. I just leaned on him and thought it was love. This time I know for sure" Eleni took hold of Vanni's hand "Very sure"

Once outside the office Vanni took her in his arms.

"His is right Eleni. I am so glad he has pointed all of those things out to us. A year will pass, quickly I promise" he kissed her tenderly "Now I too must work. Phone Richard and then why don't you go and see Eleni, I'm sure she would love to talk to you about the wedding. I think we should let her help, she has such good taste and knows all of the right people, and of course being a woman she would love to be involved" Vanni kissed her again and went back into the office he shared with Andros.

Eleni took her phone down to the patio outside of the pool house. She sat herself down on a sun bed and spoke at length to Richard. It was wonderful to hear his lovely English voice, he was so pleased for her and it made her realise that the wedding would have to be in the Long Island house in order that he could be there. She would have to talk to Vanni.

She said her goodbyes and lay silent for a while, just looking at the wonderful view before her and thinking. Andros was so good to her he had really taken his roll to heart. She knew whatever decisions he made would be in her best interest, she hoped he would agree to run her businesses. She had completely forgotten to ask him before, but would make a point of doing it once they reached America, and she had spoken to Richard. She hoped he would agree it would be for the best.

She felt a little sad that the place she thought of as home was nothing to do with her now. It was a place she loved, and now it belonged to Richard. I suppose really that's only right; after all it was him and papa who bought it in the first place. They had achieved so much together it was good that Richard should do well out of the partnership. She thought.

She phoned Tomas, who had hardly answered before Sofia took the receiver from him. She was so pleased about the engagement Eleni could tell she was crying. She wanted to know everything about Vanni's proposal and said she wished they had been there to see it. Her enthusiasm was catching and soon Eleni began to feel excited once more. They talked for a long time discussing the arrangements and Eleni realized that Sofia was talking of a Skiathos wedding. It was going to be difficult to please everyone, she thought, and smiled to herself. Andros was right again; it was going to take some time to sort out.

She left the sun bed and went to look for aunt Eleni, hopefully if Vanni was right she could help her sort things out. Eleni found her still in the conservatory, reading the morning newspaper.

"Have you seen this?" She pointed to an article on the front page. Eleni shook her head. "Well let me read it to you, here sit down. It is about the English Honors List. You know what they are I assume?" Eleni nodded. "Well it states here that Richard Graves, presently living in America, has been awarded a Knighthood for his outstanding charity works. Evidently the Queen is doing a tour of America in September and will Knight him in New York" Eleni almost snatched the paper away in her haste to read it for herself.

"You know I have only just been speaking to him and he never said a word." Eleni panicked as her eyes quickly scanned the words. "But it says she will Knight him at the President's Office in City Hall. He doesn't go out of the grounds. He couldn't even go to papa's funeral. I must get home. I need to see him, I must call him again"

"Calm down dear. We will be leaving here tomorrow so don't phone him now; let it wait until you see him face to face. If he is so certain he will not leave his home, then we will have to persuade him otherwise." Aunt Eleni spoke soothingly. "Now tell me what you had in mind about this wedding. A year is hardly long enough for the arrangements. It will be the wedding of the year here in Athens"

Eleni groaned inwardly. She had Richard in New York to consider, Tomas and Sofia in Skiathos and now aunt Eleni in Athens. How on earth was she going to please everyone? It was supposed to be hers and Vanni's day yet it was already beginning to become a pain. If only I hadn't sold the yacht, she thought, we could have sailed to each place and had three wedding days, then everyone would be happy.

That's it, she thought. The answer to Andros's security problems, no one would miss out, and she and Vanni could have their honeymoon at the same time. Wonderful. She must find Vanni and tell him. It just meant that she would have to buy another yacht. If Andros was right and she had millions then she could buy just what she wanted. Oh if only tomorrow would come soon. Suddenly she needed to be home.

It seemed an age before Andros and Vanni finally emerged from their office.

"Right then who's ready for a nice lunch?" Andros asked rubbing his stomach. "Shall we go out or would you two like to eat here?"

"Can I talk with Vanni first?" Eleni asked her eyes were shinning with excitement "And then I would like to stay here. I need to pack this afternoon, so lunch here would be lovely. That is if it's OK with everyone else?"

"Of course it is fine with me," Aunt Eleni said. "I feel it has been quite a morning for you men, and you to Eleni, so I will tell cook we are all here for lunch." She gave Andros the newspaper and pointed out the article about Richard before going off towards the kitchen.

"This is wonderful Eleni. I bet he is over the moon" Andros said

"He didn't mention it to me when we spoke on the phone, but I imagine he is very nervous. I can't wait to see him. We must get him to the ceremony and I don't know how we are going to do it. It says The

Queen will Knight him at City Hall, but how are we going to get him there?" Eleni had forgotten about the yacht as her concern for Richard grew.

"Drink anyone?" Vanni asked "And don't worry Eleni. We will sort things out once we are in New York" He handed her a long glass of ouzo and passed a traditional one to Andros. "Let us toast the new Knight, and a toast to my lovely bride to be" he raised his glass and Andros followed suit.

"To my beautiful sister" he added

## CHAPTER 10

Eleni had a troubled night. Vanni had been busy in the office making sure everything was OK whilst he and Andros were away so it meant she was alone. All she could think about was getting home. As dawn broke she was still awake and feeling troubled and worried about Richard. I might as well get up and go for a swim, she thought, anything is better than lying here.

She dressed quickly in jeans and t-shirt and made her way through the house and down towards the pool house.

It was a beautiful morning. The sun was just rising over Athens, the sight rivaling that of nighttime. She could see the port was busy already, lorries and cars were vying for space, and large boats stood ready to take them to wherever.

High in the cloudless sky she could see the vapor trail of an aeroplane as it silently cut through the bright blue stillness.

The grass on her bare feet was slightly damp and yet nicely cool, birds were singing. It was a good day to be alive, she thought. The sleepless night now far behind in her mind as she opened the door of the pool house.

Still thinking of the wonderful sights outside she went into the dressing room and changed in to her costume. It was only as she made her way to the pool that she could hear someone was already in the water. It was aunt Eleni.

"Kalimera aunt" she said as Eleni stopped at the end of the pool, ready to turn and swim back.

"Kalimera. You are early little one. Is something troubling you?" She asked.

Eleni noticed that although the older woman was wet, she had no make-up on and her hair was plastered to her head, she still looked fabulous.

"No I didn't sleep well that's all." she replied, sliding into the water "I am so worried about Richard. I know Andros and Vanni think I am over reacting, but I know him. He worries so much and when he does his confidence goes. Then he sleeps in the garden, hardly eats or anything. He is such a lovely man and is so kind, I just want to help."

They swam together for a while before aunt Eleni spoke again.

"After our swim, come with me for coffee and you can tell me all you know about him. I will help you to help him if you will let me."

"Oh please. That would be great." They swam for a while in silence.

"Right that's my 50 lengths done." Aunt Eleni had stopped at the shallow end "I will shower and change, meet you for coffee in the conservatory in a while. We have until 11 before we have to leave for the airport so we can have a good chat. The boys have a lot of work to do this morning so they are having their breakfast in the office, which means we will be alone. See you shortly"

Eleni watched as her aunt left the pool, and then swam a little more before following her still wet footsteps.

After a lovely long hot shower she felt so good compared to how she had been in her room. The swim and shower, plus the wonderful morning had lightened her mood considerably. She trotted across the grass and entered the conservatory from the garden. The smell of strong coffee hit her nostrils and made her mouth water.

"Come Eleni. Sit down and let us talk. Coffee?" Aunt Eleni had already started her breakfast.

Eleni helped herself from the delicious array of pastries and fruit and took them to the table where a steaming pot of coffee awaited her. She poured herself a large cup and sipped at the hot liquid. No milk, cream, or sugar, just very strong and very black. She felt it energise her immediately.

"Now tell me about Richard Eleni, the more I know the more I will be able to help. Once we get to New York we have got 3 weeks before the ceremony, but we are only staying for 2 so we need to get cracking."

"No if he is willing to go, I will stay and go with him. I cannot leave him to face it alone. If all goes well I will return to Athens after, and then hopefully I can go to Kefalonia, the last leg of my original journey" Eleni drank more coffee and nibbled at her pastry. She thought for a moment.

"Really I know very little of Richard. Papa met him when he was working in Central Park." Once again she began the story of her father and his business partner. "Papa found it strange though that Richard could never cook or eat red meat, or pork, and he would only drink white wine, never red. Papa didn't question it and still to this day I have never seen him eat or drink anything red." She said softly. "They bought a lovely home near to Central Park and between them turned it in to a magnificent house. Papa told me once that it took hours of coaxing to get Richard to leave their old apartment and get him to the new house. He went eventually in the back of a taxi with his head covered in a blanket, and papa said he cried all the way. When my parents married they even had the ceremony in the garden so that Richard could be there." She stopped and stared at the other woman "You see it is hopeless, he couldn't even go to papa's of their funeral, I don't see how we can help"

"Carry on Eleni."

"Well after mama was murdered we moved to our home on Long Island, papa thought it would be safer there. I remember Richard would only go if we put him in one of the removal trunks and closed the lid. He traveled in the back of the lorry with the furniture, whilst we went in a posh car. Papa had already built him a place in the garden and he slept there for over a week, before eventually coming inside. He smelt awful and looked painfully thin, but with chefs help we soon got him fattened up and well again. That's it really. He still lives there, still won't go out. But its funny really, when he is well he has to have brand new underclothes and shirts everyday. He has them sent especially from London, Saville Row I think it is called. It must cost him a fortune, but he says he can't bare anything old next to his skin. I mean he even has brand new socks everyday too. His old stuff goes to charity shops in the city." She paused for a moment to get her breath. "He bathes twice daily, you could set your clock by him, always in fabulous oils, and he loves nice aftershaves.

He does do a lot for charity. He and papa set up a center for the homeless on Long Island, but he also funds places in England and a nurses training center in Singapore for some reason. That's all I know. He seems quite happy with his newspapers and computers, his new clothes and his white wine, but something must have made him like this. He will never talk to anyone about it.

Oh one more thing I don't know if it means anything but all of the staff at home are English, he chose them himself. We have cook, two maids, a housekeeper and two gardeners, two drivers, and of course Michael, our butler. He is so starchy and very English. He even irons Richards newspapers would you believe" Eleni was smiling as she remembered how The Times was flattened each day before being placed on a silver platter and presented to Richard as if it were The Crown Jewels.

"Thank you Eleni. I found that very interesting and it has given me a lot to think about. It was so nice to hear you talk about Marco. I feel he turned out to be a good man." She looked sad for a moment. "I wish I could have just met him that one last time"

"Oh Eleni I had forgotten. I am so sorry. You loved him very much didn't you?" Eleni was on her knees by her aunt's chair. "I will show you everything, and tell you everything I know about him when we get home. I promise." Aunt Eleni looked at her watch

"Goodness its almost 10 o'clock. We must move little one, or we will be late"

The two women made their way back to their rooms to get ready. Vanni was already sitting on the bed when Eleni entered; he made her jump as she spotted him.

"Not that ugly am I?" he asked laughing "You almost left the floor then"

"No you're gorgeous. Its just I was deep in thought. I have been talking to Eleni, she wants to help Richard. By the way, I will be staying in New York a week or so longer than we planned. I hope you don't mind. I have so much to do"

"As long as it's not too long. I can't live without you for too long." He put on a dramatic voice and held his hands over his heart.

"Don't be daft" she replied "And then when I come back it's off to Kefalonia, will you be able to come with me then?"

"You bet I will." He now sounded eager "Just me and you. Lovely. I think Andros is right though. It looks as if the year is going to fly past. We are going to be very busy I can see. Right are you ready?"

"I got everything packed last night, so go and get your stuff whilst I change then we can go and meet the others" Eleni was already picking her traveling clothes from the wardrobe. A nice pair of dark cream linen trousers and a silk blouse, a slightly lighter colour. She looked stunning. Her skin was now almost mahogany, and her jet-black hair fell loosely over her shoulders. It was all Vanni could do to keep his hands off her; instead he kissed her cheek and patted her bottom.

"See you in a few minutes." He said as he left the room.

Soon all four of them were downstairs, once again in the conservatory, their cases and bags pilled by the door. Andros took all four passports put them with the tickets then passed them to his chauffeur, who, he told Eleni, would check them all in whilst they went straight to the VIP lounge. "So much nicer" he said.

"Richard is going to love you Andros, you can be so English at times"

One car took the luggage and documents and another, the large limousine, took the group down the hillside towards the airport.

As they walked through the noisy, people filled checking in area Eleni noticed the loud American woman and went to wave. Andros stopped her quickly.

"Careful Eleni remember they are security"

"Sorry Andros. I didn't think. Are they on our flight?" She was still looking, and even if she couldn't wave, she could give a little smile.

"Yes. They will be in the seats behind. You can talk a little then if you wish, but only as if you are travelers. OK"

"OK brother. I get the message." Eleni smiled up at him.

Up in the VIP lounge they sipped champagne and ate tasty nibbles. Andros was right again, this was lovely, Eleni thought. She looked out across the runway and spotted a huge Boeing with the American Flag painted on its tail. All of a sudden she felt homesick. It seemed ages since she had left New York, ages since she had spoken English for longer than a phone call, and even her last Big Mac seemed so long ago. She smiled as she remembered Andros's face when she had taken him for lunch, but she also remembered the taste. Her mouth watered for home.

As before she sat and watched the films shown as they flew. She drank plenty of water, and at times snuggled up to Vanni and slept. It was so different to her journey before. Then she was alone, worried of what she would find out about her father. Puzzled as to why he had been coming to Greece and so sad that he never returned. Now she was no longer alone, no longer afraid. Now she had a brother, an aunt, but most excitingly a fiancé.

Feeling restless she remembered Andros's order and began to talk to the loud American woman, but only about the lovely things they had seen in Athens and the fabulous shops the city boasted. Eleni told her of her forthcoming wedding and showed off her ring. It helped to pass quite some time on the long dreary flight back to her homeland.

Eventually the captain announced their descent into JFK airport and Eleni squashed her face up to the window. She could see all the familiar landmarks of the city. The Statue of Liberty standing proud in the sunlight. It was then she cried. Home again at last. Vanni held her whilst she wept and stroked her hair.

"I hope you are not going to do this every time we return?" He said softly

"No it's OK. It's just that it has been one hell of a journey for me. Such a lot has happened. Sorry"

"Nothing to be sorry for little one. It's good to let these things out" He kissed her brow "Come on the door is open." Eleni hadn't even noticed they had landed let alone stopped at the terminal.

"Vanni. Can is ask you something really stupid" She looked to see him nod "What day is it, and what time is it. I have completely lost track." He burst out laughing,

"It is Monday 15th August and the time is 12.30 pm. Is that OK madam?"

"Yes thank you. And don't tease" She dug her elbow into his ribs, and then altered her watch.

Once again they were whisked through, this time to the VIP exit. The security was much tighter here and all of their bags were opened. Their passports were scanned and fingerprints taken, even photographs of their eyes, but eventually they were allowed on to American soil.

"Well I have never been through anything like that in my life." Andros exclaimed, "I feel dirty somehow, slightly abused." The others laughed at the horrified look on his face.

"It is since 9.11 Andros. Security here is very tight. It has to be, I thought you would know that" Eleni was teasing him.

"Come on you two stop bickering" Aunt Eleni said, "Let us go now. I'm rather tired after that flight and need to refresh myself. Which way is it?"

Vanni pointed to a blue sign. Exit. They all followed the arrows and after quite a long walk found themselves by the entrance.

Suddenly Eleni waved and ran over to one of the waiting cars. It certainly stood out from the rest, a beautiful silver gray Rolls Royce. Vanni thought she was going to kiss the driver.

"This is ours come on." She waved enthusiastically at the others.

As soon as they were all seated in the marvelous car, and the luggage safely stored in the boot, they were off.

This time it was the others who sat watching as the strange sights of New York sped past. Eleni asked the driver to do a little de-tour as she pointed out places of interest and showed them where Marco and Richard had first met as they drove past the park and down towards the river.

The high metal gates of her home opened slowly as they pulled into the gravel drive. She could see the sight of the house impressed the others; it was truly beautiful today with the afternoon sun glistening on its many windows. It was a large colonial home, typical of the area, but somehow Marco had managed to add a little taste of Greece to the building. At that moment Eleni felt it was the best thing she had seen for ages.

Michael opened the doors for them and greeted her with.

"Good afternoon Miss Eleni. Welcome home." Vanni wanted to laugh at his greeting.

"Good afternoon Michael. This is my aunt Eleni Yannisos, Mr. Andros Yannisos my brother, and my fiancé Mr. Vanni Yannisos. Mr. Richard has told you we are all staying here I take it."

"Of course Miss. If you would all like to follow me I will show you your rooms. Your luggage will be with you shortly" He didn't show anything on his face but the introductions must have registered in his brain, instead he walked towards the house and beckoned them to follow.

"Michael. Where is Richard?"

"Sir Richard is in the garden Miss. He has been there for a few days now. I am sure he would be pleased to see you though. He has been a little worried I do hope you can help. He so deserves this honor"

Eleni hardly heard the last bit; she was already running towards the bottom of the garden. Vanni followed quickly.

She slowed down as she reached a huge magnolia bush. "Richard" she called softly "It's me Eleni. Can I come in?" She made it sound as if she wanted to enter a room.

The bush moved slightly and she could just see him lying below the branches.

"Eleni it is so good to see you. Sorry about this but I will soon be better. I hope anyway. Please explain to your guests that I will be with them in a day or so." With that he disappeared back into the bush.

Vanni looked puzzled. Eleni spoke quietly.

"Come on. Lets leave him be. He will come out when he is good and ready and not before" She took Vanni's arm and led him back to the house, and up to his room.

After long showers and changes of clothes they all felt refreshed, but it had been a long flight and they all felt a little weary. One by one they appeared outside where Michael served much needed pre dinner drinks on the patio as the sun set over the city.

The outside space was similar to the one at the pool house, but without the wonderful sights of Athens below. This time all they could see were skyscrapers dominating the horizon as Eleni pointed out landmarks to the tired group.

A little later they enjoyed a leisurely meal served in the dinning room and all decided on an early night. It had been a long day, a very long day, everyone felt worn out.

Back in her own bed Eleni soon fell into a deep sleep, Vanni was in the adjoining room, but he was also shattered. Tonight they slept alone, after that who knew what would happen.

The time difference, jet lag, whatever it is called, saw Eleni wake very early. Just like in Athens she woke as dawn broke over the island. For a moment she could hardly believe she was back in her own room, her own bed, and then she remembered Vanni next door.

She cleaned her teeth and brushed her hair before going through the middle door and sliding in to the bed. Automatically he rolled over and swung his arm around her waist.

"Good morning Miss Eleni" he said softly trying to mimic Michael. "And what can I do for you?"

"Let me think" she answered her hands already wondering down towards his boxer shorts. He didn't ask again. Moments later they cried out together.

"Shh.!" She giggled. "We don't want to wake everyone" She lay down on his chest listening to his thudding heart, gently he pulled the covers over her. They cuddled together and slept for a while. She woke him nibbling on his ear.

"Now I am starving. Come on lets go for breakfast". "

"Shower first and then I'll meet you downstairs" he kissed her nose and helped her to stand.

As Eleni walked back into her own room she thought she heard a noise outside, peering through a crack in the curtains she was surprised to see aunt Eleni walking in the garden. She was heading towards the magnolia bush.

Eleni watched as the old lady made her way towards one of the many marble seats dotted around the garden. She looked around at the lovely statues and plants as she walked, and Eleni could see her gazing at the dolphin fountains. I wonder if she is thinking about papa, she thought to herself. I wonder how she feels to be in his house?

Eleni quickly showered dressed and went to join her aunt.

"Kalimera aunt" she called as she neared the older woman who was now deep in thought.

"Kalimera Eleni. Please come and sit with me" she patted the seat beside her. "I was just looking around, I can feel Marco's presence. It is very strange for me to be in his home. I hope you understand" She looked at Eleni, her eyes filled with tears.

"Of course I understand. Shall we go for breakfast now and I will show you the house afterwards?" She asked.

"No Eleni. I would like to be alone. You go and join the others; I would like to stay here. It doesn't matter about breakfast I will get something later"

Eleni was worried, any minute now Michael would be serving Richard his breakfast here in the garden. She knew that if aunt Eleni were still to be here he would not come out to eat.

"Please aunt, come with me, some breakfast will do you good. Please come"

A wonderful English voice boomed from under the magnolia bush.

"If the lady wishes to stay in the garden Eleni then please be good enough to let her."

Eleni was a little shocked.

"But I don't want either of you missing breakfast Richard."

"Do not concern yourself about me Eleni. I will eat when Michael brings the tray, I will eat with your aunt. We have not been introduced yet, and although I do not look my best at present, I am sure we can manage. Now go and see to your other guests, and tell Michael I also have a guest for breakfast if you please." Richard sounded a little agitated.

Eleni left the odd couple and walked back to the house. She met Andros making his way towards Richard and Marco's office but had no time to speak as Michael also appeared.

"Ah Michael. Richard and my aunt wish to have breakfast served in the garden. Apparently they will eat together"

"Of course Miss Eleni" he answered as if was the most obvious thing in the world. "Please tell me does your aunt prefer tea or coffee in the mornings?"

"Coffee please Michael, and she likes it strong thank you" She called racing after Andros who was now opening her father's office door. He turned to greet her; a huge grin lit his face.

"Eleni. Richard has sent the key for me. He has asked if I would like to make a start on sorting your affairs." He waved a piece of paper. "He has even given me instructions as to where everything is, and the telephone number of your solicitor. Very organized I must say"

"He is like that." Eleni replied.

Together they walked into the room. The lovely smell of leather came wafting into their nostrils the minute they set foot inside; it came from a huge Chesterfield Sofa standing to one side. The two side-by-side desks were of dark mahogany, as were the cupboards and coffee table. The desks were covered in large leather bottomed blotting pads, silver penholders, old-fashioned telephones, and up to the minute computers. Large mahogany chairs stood proudly behind.

A wonderful cream Adams fireplace dominated one wall and above it were the photographs of Marco with the dolphin, and the ruined goat shed. The room was a strange mixture of old England, modern times with a little bit of Greece thrown in.

Andros stopped in his tracks and gazed around. He went over and stroked the sofa, before looking closely at the photographs. He touched the cupboards and let his hand wonder over the desks.

"It's like walking into the past" he said very quietly "To think my father spent many hours in here, and now I too am here. Which was Marco's desk?" Eleni pointed to the one on the left. "Eleni please leave me. I would like to work alone."

"If you need anything Andros, pull on that rope" she pointed to a thick cream silk rope hanging at the side of the fireplace "and Michael will come."

Andros was already in a world of his own and didn't reply. He was shaken by the strong feelings that had come over him. He had never met his father, but here in this room it was as if he were with him. He sat behind the desk Eleni had pointed to and cried.

Eleni left him and went to find Vanni.

"It's only two of us for breakfast Michael. I think we will eat on the patio thank you," she said as he passed on his way with Richard's tray.

"Yes Miss Eleni. If you would like to take a seat I will be with you in a moment" He disappeared into the garden.

Eleni knocked on Vanni's door

"Are you ready yet?" she called as she let herself in "It's just me and you this morning. Come on I'm starving"

Vanni emerged from the bathroom already dressed.

"So am I?" he said "I wonder what has caused that?" he said laughing. Eleni had completely forgotten about their love making even though it was only a short time ago.

They walked hand in hand to the patio and sat. Michael soon appeared at her side and breakfast was underway.

"What shall we do today?" Eleni asked. "Do you fancy a tour of the city, a lazy day here or what?"

"I think a tour would be nice. You can show me all of your old haunts" He replied with a grin.

Eleni asked Michael to inform the chauffeur they would like to go after breakfast and see the sights. He nodded and once again disappeared into the house.

"What about the others?" Vanni said "Won't they want to come too?"

Eleni explained that Andros was making a start on her paperwork, and Eleni content to stay here.

"Perhaps the traveling has tired her, she can go another day." She added and looked down towards where her aunt sat. She looked so fragile, so tiny sitting amongst the large flowers and bushes, so lonely, Eleni thought, and suddenly so old.

They finished their meal and went off to see what New York City had to offer.

"I feel like a tourist," Vanni said, as the fabulous car seemed to float silently along the drive "Doing the sights."

"You are a tourist." She replied, "Now where shall we go first? I know the center. I must go and make sure everything is ready for my birthday do on Thursday"

The car disappeared from view as the gates slowly closed behind it.

# • CHAPTER •
## 11

Aunt Eleni watched as Michael slowly made his way across the lawn. She thanked him as he placed the tray at her side.

"If you require anything else madam, just call?" He said primly. "Sir Richard I will bring your newspaper in a moment" Eleni found it quite amusing to see the butler speak to a bush but kept her face straight. She watched as he walked back to the house and returned with the newspaper on another silver tray. Bending down he placed it on the grass and then left.

Aunt Eleni poured herself a coffee and began to inspect the food that had been brought. She heard the bush move but didn't turn around.

"Madam. May I present myself? Richard Graves at your service" She looked at the tramp like figure bowing before her and smiled.

"Eleni Yannisos." She put out her arm. "I am very pleased to meet you" He raised her hand part way to his lips and blew a kiss.

"Please excuse me madam, I am a little grubby, as Eleni would say, but rest assured I will smarten myself up as soon as possible." She saw a lovely grin sweep over his face and a sparkle in his eyes.

"Please call me Eleni," she said patting the empty seat at her side. "I take it the tea is for you?" He just nodded so she filled a delicate china cup. They sat silently for some time enjoying their drinks, neither touched the food laid out on the tray.

"All of a sudden I feel rather silly" Richard said breaking the silence. "Here I am in the company of a lovely woman and just look at the state I am in. I take it Eleni has told you I sometimes retreat to the garden. It keeps me sane, if you understand"

"I understand completely" She replied "And I envy you. There are many times I would like to forget the rest of the world, but I unfortunately, have nowhere I can go."

"Please tell me more I am intrigued, obviously I have heard of you. Marco spoke many times about his friends back in Greece, but tell my only if you wish and only what you wish."

She could see the look on his grimy face he was concerned.

"You know who I am" She began, Richard nodded. "The mother of Marco's son. I had hoped for many years to meet him again, he promised to come back for me, and now he is dead. I feel my life has been wasted. Meeting Eleni and coming here I can see that I was a fool to wait, he had got on with his life. I just waited" Richard wiped his hand on a napkin and gently covered hers in a comforting way. He nodded urging her to go on.

Eleni felt the need to speak, it was strange she had never felt like this before. She looked into his eyes and immediately knew he would understand what she was about to say.

"When I grew up I spent many happy hours with my brother Tomas, friends Alexi and Marco. We were always together, but even from an early age it was Marco who took my eye. He was always the best at everything, the strongest of our little gang, the one who did things we others would not or could not do.

When the war came my parents were ordered to take in a young German soldier, Kurt. He was only a little older than us and soon he became part of our group. He taught Alexi the art of photography and showed us all how to appreciate beauty.

He taught me much more though. I had never seen such blue eyes in my life before, they shone like ice, his hair was almost white it was so blonde, and in his uniform, he looked wonderful.

He awoke the woman in me.

My father was a very quiet man but suddenly one day he said I was to go into the cellar and live for a while. I tried so hard but no amount of pleading from me would make him change his mind.

I could not believe it; they had put my bed in there, and all of my things. There was a fire glowing in a chimanea and a bowl for washing. A mirror had been put on the wall just above an old wooden commode.

It looked like the prison it was going to be, and I knew immediately I was being locked away for a long time. I was only a child and didn't understand, why me, what had I done, was I so ugly? I felt so frightened.

Mother said it was for my own good, to protect my innocence but still I didn't understand. I wanted to be free. Run through the fields with the boys, swim with them, but no.

Father used to bring my meals first thing in the morning and then again late at night. He would only allow me to walk in the air after I had eaten supper. I saw the moon and stars, but no sunshine for many many months.

Often I could hear the planes flying over, but never got to see them. Many times I heard my brother talking, but never got to speak to him. Many times I heard Marco laugh, but never laid eyes on him.

I was trapped by my father in this awful cellar. I was locked away for three years or so Tomas told me. I completely lost track of time.

My mother used to send me books to read, books about our history and the ancient Grecians. I read until my eyes were sore. I took in all the knowledge these books had to offer, for me it was the only way to stay sane.

They locked me away to save my innocence but gave me books full of love and lust. The Greek Gods were magnificent in their lovemaking. I learned so much from them and gradually believed that I was one of them. When I looked in the mirror and could see this thin white face staring back, hair so long and so dark from lack of light, I convinced myself I was a Goddess.

I explored my body whilst growing into a woman and dreamt of Apollo, Zeus and Achilles; my mind was full of carnal thoughts. I learned the art of seduction; my father would have been disgusted. I know he thought he was protecting me, but some days I just longed to be with a man, any man. I thought of Marco.

You see I am ashamed of myself."

Richard squeezed her hand.

"When father stopped coming to the cellar mother told me he had been killed along with Alexi's father and some other men. Evidently the Germans had blamed papa for Kurt's death. They had put him in papa's care and he should have looked after him. My mother told me the truth, papa had killed him in order to save me, but I hated him for it. Kurt was such a lovely boy and wouldn't have hurt anyone; he hated the war, as much as we did, he was so gentle.

I begged mama to let me free, but she said it was far more dangerous now than before and she would obey father's wishes to keep me safe.

How I loathed him, he had taken my freedom, and the life of Kurt. I vowed to get my revenge, and went back to my books. I lived a make believe life with the God's on Mount Olympus.

When eventually the occupation was over and I was once again set free, the first thing I saw was Marco. He didn't stand a chance. I knew how to capture him, and I did.

How he had grown in those past years. He stood strong and proud, he looked marvelous. That night the inevitable happened and we became lovers. Marco's father found us and ordered him to leave the island, he said he had disgraced his family and abused my father's name. He disowned him, banned him from seeing me again, it was awful to hear some of the things he said.

But just before he left we did meet again and Andros was formed, if you understand?" Again Richard nodded.

"My brother saw us in the goat shed and there was a terrible fight. Tomas vowed that if ever Marco stepped foot on the island again he would kill him. They had been friends for life and I had come between them suddenly I felt so awful.

But, I had paid my father back for imprisoning me and killing Kurt. I remember looking to the skies and shouting to him what I had done. Then I wept.

I realised that now I loved Marco, the years of dreaming had become a reality and I knew in my heart I loved him more than anything in the world.

I had thought about him so often and imagined how we would be together, yet my actions were driving us apart. I wanted to die, wanted to go back into the cellar and start again. Wipe out that night completely.

On the day he left I stood on the cliff and waved to every boat that went across the water. I had no idea which one he was on, or even if he saw me, but I did not leave the cliff until after dark.

He had said he would return and I promised to wait, even if it took forever.

That night I was distraught, Alexi comforted me and I allowed him to treat me as a woman." Eleni looked towards the sky and sighed.

"If only people had not been so hasty, I hadn't been so hasty, our lives could have been so different

Shortly after I found out I was pregnant; my mother was horrified, but not as much as me. I had no idea whose child it was, Marco's or Alexi's, but I was determined to keep my baby.

Mother said I had disgraced my father's memory, and she banished me to the mainland to live with my aunt Francesca, papa's sister. She had left Kefalonia many years before and I had never actually met her until the day I arrived at Piraeus.

My mothers parting words stung by heart, she said I was a whore and no daughter of hers.

I left my island heartbroken knowing she was right, I was a whore.

Once in Athens I could not believe my luck, I was suddenly free. I was so close to the God's that I had read about, their homes, their statues, it was wonderful. Instead of being a punishment it was the best thing in my life. The city made me a very happy girl. Aunt Francesca was wonderful, so out going, so modern and she loved the thought of having a baby in the house. Oh so different to those I had left behind.

I started to use the knowledge I had learned in the cellar, about the cities antiquities, and with the help of my aunt, began to conduct tours. I loved these buildings, every stone, every column, and I spoke with feeling.

After the war many people were traveling and they wanted to see the places they had read about in newspapers, or seen on the films. They all loved they way I spoke.

My tours proved so popular that soon I was training others to take groups around. I had had my beautiful baby boy and this suited me much more. I enjoyed the teaching and it was then that I also learned to speak English.

The English love Athens and all of my pupils were taught the language. My little company grew and when aunt Francesca died leaving me her house and possessions I was wealthy enough to buy the wonderful home I live in now.

It didn't seem to matter that I was alone, that I had lost touch with my family. I had my son and beautiful home, my days were filled with teaching and I was very happy."

Tears trickled down her cheeks.

"It wasn't until I saw the photograph of me waving goodbye to Marco that I realised I had wasted so many years. Years when I could have spent time with my brother, my friends, perhaps even married. I wondered if Marco had ever come back to try and find me.

I stood looking at the photograph and eventually entered the shop. I was amazed to find one of my old friends inside. Alexi was there, the one who had actually taken the picture. We embraced and cried. We talked and he told me that Tomas and my mother now lived on Skiathos and had done for many years.

Neither of us mentioned that night on the cliffs, nor ever have done since.

I realized then that even if Marco had returned to Kefalonia he would not have found me. Not only had my mother and brother moved, but also the big earthquake had wiped out any remaining friends and relatives. It would have been hopeless for him.

I was able to get in touch with my brother though, and we had a wonderful meeting on the island of Alonysos. He told me my mother had barred him from ever speaking to me, but he had decided just this once to go against her wishes. We had already spent too many years apart, he said, and promised to forgive me even though my mother could not.

Tomas was married and had a son, that is Vanni, now Eleni's fiancé, and Alexi had a son Nicos, and so with Andros we had made a new gang of friends. As the years passed we would often meet on Alonysos where Tomas and Alexi had brought many houses.

Eventually Vanni came to live with us whilst he was at university, and then when he and Andros began their company he remained, and still does to this day. So you see, now I had two boys to look after. My days were full.

We had all done so well in our lives, but still I pined for Marco. I still believed he loved me. I still waited. I was determined to prove my mother wrong I was no whore; I had just been a very lonely and confused young girl.

When Tomas told me Marco had been in touch I couldn't believe it. He too had seen the photograph of me, at an exhibition here in New York. He met Athena, Alexi's wife who ran the exhibition and had written via her.

I was so excited when Tomas told me Marco was coming to see us. I was like a young girl again, so happy.

The news that his plane had crashed was that painful I wanted to die. I wanted to hide, go back in my cellar and start again. I cannot begin to describe the searing pain I felt. I cried for days. My last chance had gone. I felt I had wasted my life waiting for him and now this.

Meeting young Eleni was very strange, she was like a breath of fresh air, but also the daughter of the man I had loved for so long. I could see that she was Marco's daughter the minute I laid eyes on her, but I could also see she was very much like me. Tomas explained that Marco had married a girl called Christina and that Eleni's description of her could have been of me. It was strange to think that his wife had been so similar, I felt pleased in one way, but hurt that he had not stayed faithful to me.

Coming here has made me see that it was her he loved. The photographs of them on their wedding day, the ones that are on display in the dining room, you can see in his eyes how much in love he was. The pictures of her with the baby, and later as a toddler, ones of them all together, they prove that he had forgotten me.

I can see a likeness between us, but Christina was so much younger and so beautiful.

I can understand now that until he saw that picture of me he had forgotten, and I can see why. Christina was very special.

I realised then that I had been living a dream. Suddenly I feel so old, so worn out. I would give anything to be able to begin again.

I came here to try to find a piece of Marco, try to make sense of my life but I fear it is a huge mistake."

Richard patted her hand.

"Please don't think like that Eleni. You have not wasted your life. Look at your son; he is a good and clever man. It is all down to you. Look at your home and that is down to you. You have worked hard for the life you have. Please do not think you have wasted anything." He paused "To me you look beautiful. Your mother was so wrong, I am sorry she hurt you" He was slightly embarrassed never having said that to a woman before. There had been times, many years ago, when he had thought of certain women as beautiful, but until now had never actually said it, but now he meant it. She was stunning in his eyes, and yet so relaxing to be with, he felt so comfortable and safe.

"Thank you Richard. I am afraid I have talked for so long our drinks are cold. Once I began my tale I could not stop you must forgive me."

"Well I'll get Michael to bring some more, and whilst he does I will go and change." He pointed to a little white stone building hidden by the bushes "Marco made sure I had everything here. All the facilities I need are in there if you understand my meaning? I will try not to be too long."

With that he strode out towards the building then stopped by the door and turned towards her.

"It has been so enlightening Eleni. Your story is similar to mine in some ways and has given me much to think about. Thank you for sharing it with me." He disappeared inside.

Within minutes Michael appeared with a tray of hot drinks and chocolates.

"Sir Richard has requested morning coffee. I hope it is suitable madam? Can I take it he is showering?"

"I think so Michael. He has gone in there," Eleni pointed to the building.

"Good. Good" Michael repeated. "He is back with us. Thank you madam, you have done him good. Perhaps now you can persuade him to go to the ceremony at the City Hall. It will take a miracle I know, but if I may ask you to try?"

"I can see you are very fond of him aren't you" Michael gave a nod "I will certainly try for you then"

"Thank you madam. He works so hard for others, but something always stops him when it comes to himself. Please do not let him know I have spoken to you like this. It is not really the proper thing, but I can see you think kindly of him" Michael was embarrassed to have spoken so emotionally and yet he was pleased. This gentle woman had worked wonders already.

They both turned as the bush behind rustled. A hand came from underneath and took the newspaper from the silver tray.

"I am sorry Eleni. I am not quite ready. May I ask that you come back after lunch as I would like to talk some more."

"Of course Richard. I will take a walk after my coffee and return a little later." Eleni was trying to treat Richard's behavior as normal "Would you like Michael to bring you lunch? If you would like I can have lunch with you here?"

Michael looked towards the bush waiting for a reply.

"Yes please. I would like you to join me."

Michael smiled

"Yes Sir Richard. The usual?"

"Yes Michael. The usual, but for two, thank you"

Eleni finished her drink and took a couple of chocolates to nibble on as she walked around the garden.

She studied the statues closely and smiled at the dolphin fountains. Marco had never forgotten his homeland, even if he had forgotten her.

As she walked she could feel Richard's eyes on her and smiled, she felt so much better for telling him her story she hoped he would tell her his. There must be something in his past that had resulted in his behavior, hopefully she would find out after lunch.

A small fairy like marble figure caught her eye and she moved closer. It was partly hidden by beautiful orange geraniums but she could see it stood on a stone base. Her heart almost stopped as she read the inscription. "My wonderful Christina. You were my life, my little fairy. I will love you forever. Marco"

The words stabbed at Eleni. He had loved this woman whilst she had waited. All those years she had waited. She wanted to cry, she wanted to die, but instead she fainted.

Richard rushed from beneath his bush and knelt at her side.

"Eleni" he stroked her face and cursed himself for being dirty. "Michael come quickly!" he shouted. He looked towards the fairy and realised she had been reading the inscription. This lovely woman did not deserve this. He wanted to hold her; comfort her; he wanted to take the hurt away.

Never far away Michael was already running towards them.

"She has just fainted Sir Richard. Do not alarm yourself." Now he was worried about both of them. "Help me to sit her up." Between them they raised Eleni who slowly opened her eyes.

"What a silly thing to do." She said still a little shakily and deathly pale "Please may I have some water?"

Michael left Richard propping her up and went quickly towards the house. He returned shortly with his silver tray bearing water and glasses.

"I have telephoned for the doctor and informed Mr. Andros, Sir Richard." He bent down and helped Eleni to drink.

"Thank you Michael. Here comes Andros, he will help you to your room Eleni." Richard was glad to see the younger man run across the lawn.

"Mama. What has happened? Are you ill?" he said as he neared the trio on the grass.

"No Andros. I have just fainted. It is all the traveling I expect. It has taken its toll." Eleni had now regained some of her colour. "There is no need for the doctor Michael, I think I will rest in the shade now. I'm sure I will feel much better after some lunch"

"Madam you will let the doctor see you, and then, only if he agrees you may come and have lunch in the garden. I insist you speak to him first." Richard spoke forcefully.

The men helped her to her feet and Andros held her arm as he walked slowly her to her room.

"I will be back for lunch Richard" she called.

Richard watched as the group disappeared into the house and then returned to his bush. He removed the newspaper from the ground and folded it neatly before placing it on the garden seat. He walked purposefully towards the little building, this time he entered, determined that when Eleni returned he would be presentable.

## CHAPTER 12

The doctor examined Eleni and pronounced her tired but fit. He agreed that the travelling had taken its toll and ordered her to rest, or at least stay at the house for a couple of days. No sight seeing for her, not that she was really interested. She had seen what she had come for, Marco's home. She had wanted to see where he lived, his garden, learn a little about his life, and now she had the answers to all of her questions. Deep down she had known for years that he would not return for her, but something had made her keep waiting. Now she felt empty.

She lay on her bed for a while after the doctor had left. She thought about her life and realised it had not been wasted, she had a wonderful home, she had her business and she had Andros. Yes. She could have married, her life could have been different, but it was too late now.

She glanced at her watch and decided to return to the garden. She had to admit that Marco had made it a beautiful peaceful haven; it was no wonder Richard liked to stay there.

After their journey from the airport she had no wish to see the city. It was so ugly compared to Athens, so crowded and busy, the huge skyscrapers overpowering, no she would stay here until they returned home.

She freshened herself up and went back into the garden. As she neared the magnolia bush she was touched to see a little table had been laid. Two pretty chairs stood either side and silver candlesticks had been placed on it's top.

"Madam. Richard Graves at your service" Richard appeared from behind the bush. This time he was dressed in a well-cut dark suit, white shirt and striking green silk tie. He took her hand to his lips and kissed it gently. "Your servant madam." He bowed slightly. "I hope you are feeling better?"

"Richard you look wonderful. Yes thank you I feel much better and I can see you are too." Eleni's smile lit up her face. "This is so nice thank you" She nodded towards the table.

Richard held out a chair and helped her to be comfortable. He poured her a small glass of white wine and one for himself.

"To a beautiful lady." He raised his glass and drank. "Thank you so much for joining me."

Michael soon appeared with a lovely assortment of light foods, tiny salmon and cucumber sandwiches, various cheeses with biscuits, large prawns with salad and a lovely bowl of fruits. It was a perfect for a hot afternoon.

They talked as they ate, enjoying each other's company. Richard was so attentive and polite Eleni began to feel like a young girl again, flattered by this lovely man.

After eating they sat back and as if by magic Michael came to clear the plates away. Shortly after he returned with an assortment of tiny cakes, and a large pot of coffee.

"That was perfect thank you." Eleni felt so relaxed. "I haven't enjoyed lunch so much for a long long time."

"I am very pleased to hear you say that my dear" Richard replied, "Do you mind?" He fished out a packet of Dunhill cigarettes and a gold lighter. She shook her head.

"Of course not."

They chatted whilst he smoked

"I only have them now and again I feel it finishes a meal." he said drawing deeply. "It helps me to relax.

"As long as it helps then enjoy them." Eleni studied his face. He was handsome in a rugged sort of way, his hair, now thinning was so white, and he had striking green eyes. She had already seen that he was tall and even though he must be almost 70, was still slim.

"Would you like to tell me your story? Sometimes it helps talking to a stranger, it has certainly helped me." She asked cautiously, not wanting to send him back under the bush.

He stared at the table and she could see that he was thinking. They sat silently whilst he considered her offer.

"Yes. I think I would" He said eventually "I must warn you though it is not a pretty story, quite gruesome in fact. Are you sure? The only people I have told were my parents, and then with drastic consequences. Not even Marco knew the full truth, but somehow I feel I can talk to you"

"Just tell me what you want. If you feel upset then stop." She said gently and reached across the table to touch his hand. He took it in his and stroked her fingers. "I don't want you to feel uncomfortable, and we have plenty of time"

He looked into her eyes and began.

"When the war started my father, a high ranking officer in the RAF was called upon immediately, The Prime Minister needed him, no less.

My brothers and I were all expected to join up and we did, it was a duty, which we were happy to do. To Fight for King and Country. It was an exciting time, we all wanted to do our bit.

Marcus and Julian, my brothers, joined the RAF, as was expected of us all, but I enrolled for the army. Straight away I was in bad books, my parents were livid, but I wanted to break away, do what I wanted for the first time in my life. I suppose I was just being a bit of a rebel.

I had had a very privileged upbringing being the son of an officer and my mother coming from a very wealthy family. We lived in a huge mansion, had servants, went to the best boarding schools, and had our lives mapped out almost. I can imagine now how they must have felt, but I was determined to do what I wanted. This was my chance to be me.

I quickly climbed the ladder and became an officer myself. It was only then that my father started to accept my decision, and when I was seconded into a specialist unit, he almost crowed with delight.

Our unit was sent to the Far East where we were employed in many undercover operations. I can remember it well. We lived dangerously, sometimes too dangerously, but we still managed to have fun. We had to; death and destruction were our work we needed fun to help us forget.

Unfortunately during one raid Japanese soldiers captured some of our unit, and some were killed. I was one of those unlucky enough to end up in one of the hell camps." Richard stopped and stared into the sky. "It is an awful thing to say but there were times when death would have been the better option. We were subjected to terrible torture by our captures, but I will not go in to details, I could not for my sake as much as yours." His fingers tightened around Eleni's.

"Those of us that survived were made to work in the jungle. Clearing places for them to hoard equipment and fuel. We spent our days hacking down trees in searing heat. Mosquitoes and bugs biting our already weak flesh, very often we would disturb snakes or huge ants nests. The work was grueling but our food was awful. Rice in thin soup day after day. Soon we looked like walking skeletons, many fell ill, and many died.

A cut or a bite could soon become infected and many lost limbs to gangrene. The medical facilities were pathetic, and although we were lucky enough to have a doctor amongst us he could do nothing for many of the prisoners.

Some tried to escape, only to be captured and murdered. The usual punishment for trying to escape was to be tied to a wooden frame and then laid across young bamboo shoots. Bamboo grows very quickly, I will leave you to imagine but it was an awful way for men to die, but still we tried. To give up trying, was to give in to these awful men. Every night we would plan and plot but I had to stay, being the highest-ranking officer in camp, I had to stay put, but I did my best to help.

I was in the camp for two years, but at the time it seemed much longer.

I saw many men come and go. We buried so many I lost count. We always tried to give them a decent burial, but being so weak ourselves it was difficult to even dig the graves. We sang hymns, and said prayers, all the time each of us wondering who would be next.

We had no idea how the Allies were progressing, or what was happening in Europe and each time a new prisoner came he was grilled for news of home. We needed to know, needed something to hold on to, any news was better than nothing.

A lorry brought in three new prisoners one morning. They were from D Force, Royal Engineers, and had been captured during a scouting mission. It gave us all hope. If these men were not far away, that meant others were not far behind. These were the men that cleared the way. Experts in explosives, brilliant in making traps, and such like.

Our hopes were heightened when the camp commander ordered some of us to destroy paperwork and records from his office; we knew then that the British were close. We tried every trick to delay our captors, hoping daily that this would be the end to our suffering. We knew someone would come and find us it was just a matter of when.

One morning we heard explosions and gunfire in the distance, all of us cheered and then knelt and prayed. The noise came from far away but it gave us all hope.

That afternoon a few of the Japanese soldiers came over to our dormitory and picked four of us out, they marched us to a clearing at the back of the camp and ordered us to dig. They stood over as we moved the hard earth, their guns waving if we stopped to rest. It took the four of us hours in that awful heat to dig a trench deep enough for their needs.

We had no idea what it was to be used for until they marched every prisoner towards us. They lined everyone up and began to fire." Eleni saw the horror in Richard's eyes. It was as if he was living it over again. "They just kept on firing straight at us. Wounded men fell screaming into the trench, others silent, already dead. I stood with my friend and we held hands, trying to comfort each other. When he was hit he fell and so did I but I could feel no pain, and it took a moment for me to realise that he had dragged me down with him. We were still holding hands, but he was dead, I was alive.

Bodies continued to fall on top of me, blood and bits of flesh covering every part of me, it was horrendous. I could hear the wounded crying out, until eventually they too succumbed to the eternal sleep.

The shooting stopped and so did the cries of the wounded. It was so quiet. No sound from the soldiers, no sound at all. Still I dare not move. I just lay still not knowing what to do. Blood flowed all around, and soon I was totally soaked.

A big black cloud of flies descended buzzing loudly as they fed, rats come from nowhere, and birds picked at the bodies." He shivered at the recollection

"I waited until darkness and slowly inched my way to the top of the trench. I peered over the edge and could see lights on in the camp commanders office. It seemed as if all of the soldiers were in there. They must have assumed that they had killed all of the prisoners and had not bothered to leave any guards.

Slowly I pulled myself up and out of the trench and as I did the office door opened. I rolled quickly under a bush and pulled the branches together. From a small opening I could see the whole camp, and prayed that they could not see me.

I stayed there for two days and nights. Watching and waiting, sleeping occasionally, but so weak from dehydration, and so hungry. The bush protected me from the heat of the day, but it could not protect me from the sights in the trench. It was a terrible. These men had been my friends. The stench was awful as the bodies soon decayed in the humidity and heat.

I must have dozed off when suddenly I heard shouting from the commander's office. Soldiers were running around screaming at each other. Some came over to the trench carrying shovels and began to cover the bodies with soil, but the sights and stench beat even them, so they dropped their tools and ran away.

I could hear gunshots, much closer now, and cried with joy when I saw a soldier fall. The British had arrived. I was safe.

The Japanese put up a good fight and it took hours before they were overcome. As the British entered the camp I saw the commander slice himself open rather than be taken prisoner. Only a hand full of soldiers remained alive and they were soon placed under guard in our empty dormitory.

The sound of English voices was a joy to hear and I wanted to greet them, but still I dare not move, I could not move. I felt safe under the bush; it had protected me for days.

Eventually when each of the dormitories had been searched and found to be empty a corporal walked towards the trench. I saw him put his hand to his mouth and nose in an attempt to stop the smell. He looked over the edge and retched at the gruesome sight, and as he turned to go I called out. He knelt down and peered into the bush.

"Sergeant. We've got a live one," He shouted, and then he spoke softly. "Come on matey, out you come" He put his hand into the bush to help me out. His eyes widened at the sight of me as I slowly slid my way from beneath the leaves. What a mess I must have been, covered in baked on blood, so thin my bones showed through my skin, no wonder his eyes almost popped.

I was so traumatized I could not speak and I felt so disgusting as a young girl ran to his side. She stood for a moment looking at me, staring straight into my eyes, and then she took my hand and slowly led me towards the nearby stream.

She stripped off my clothes and walked with me into the water, then she washed me all over, using rolls of grass to scrub my skin clean of blood. She pulled me gently under the surface and washed my hair, rubbing my scalp hard with her tiny fingers. Once she was satisfied she had removed all of the blood she led me from the water and lay me down on the ground where covered me with large flat leaves from a nearby tree. Slowly she took each leaf and broke it in her hands, squeezing its juices on to my body before laying them back down over me. The fresh smell of those leaves was wonderful; and I could feel their sap sinking into my skin.

She said she would have to leave me for a few moments but promised to return, and said I was not to move. Although she spoke English, it was with the strangest accent I had ever heard, a mixture of all sorts.

She came running back with a clean set of clothes, where she had got them from I have no idea, but when she dressed me they felt marvelous.

Over the next few days, whilst the British soldiers rested in the camp, this little girl nursed me. She made wonderful broths, and tea the like I have never tasted before or since, lovely rice pancakes filled with berries and fruit. Every day she would boil water for me to drink, and every day she made me drink plenty I can tell you. She took me each morning and again at night to wash in the stream, scrubbing my skin with rolls of grass.

She made a paste out of crushed flower heads and smoothed it all over me every night. The dried on blood had stained my skin, but slowly with her treatment it began to return to something like normal.

She picked flowers and stuffed a pillow in order that when I slept their perfume filled my senses. She said she wanted to cleanse me. She understood how I felt.

She told me her name was Nabia, she was only 12 years old, and the soldier who found me was Corporal Luke Gould. She had been traveling with this group of Royal Engineers for years, ever since they had saved her from a rapist and certain death. All of her family had been murdered and so she had attached herself to this unit.

I understood then why her speech was so comical. She had lived with Scots, Welsh, Cornish and men from the Midlands, but she was actually born in Kuala Lumpur.

I was still very weak spending most of the time in bed; and I used to watch as she busied herself around the dormitory each day. She swept and cleaned, sewed and cooked, and as she did she sang. Her voice was like crystal, so clear and pretty, and occasionally she would do a little dance.

At night she slept on the floor by the Corporals bed as if protecting him. She told me how ill he had been with malaria and how she had nursed him, just like she was nursing me. Corporal Luke, she called him, and you could see from her eyes when she spoke, she loved him deeply.

We eventually moved out and made our way down to Singapore. Nabia and I did the journey in the back of a captured lorry and during that time we talked some more. I could not believe that this little girl had been through so much, seen so much, in her short life, and yet she still managed to smile.

When we reached Singapore I was taken on board a ship and joined many other released prisoners. All of us had horrendous tales to tell, many had bad injuries, many just sat and stared, but all of us were free.

The ship was bound for England and the unit of Royal Engineers was also traveling with us. I met up with Corporal Luke again and asked about Nabia. I could see he was upset so when he told me they had found a safe place for her I didn't ask further. I wish I had now, but it's too late.

It took us three weeks to sail home, and in that time I grew much stronger. I was still painfully thin and shaky, but gradually things got better. My skin now took on a glow from being in the sun, but my hair had turned white. I looked like an old man, I was barely out of my teens yet I looked so old, but I kept telling myself at least I was alive and free.

Many times at night I would wake after dreaming of that awful trench. I was the only one to survive and the pangs of guilt wreaked havoc with my mind. I wanted to hide; I wanted to be under the bush. I know it sounds silly, but I had felt so safe under there. Hidden from everything. Hidden so well that if I had not called out to Corporal Luke no one would have ever found me."

Eleni could see that talking was taking its toll on Richard. He was reliving the nightmare and she was concerned for him.

"Please Richard say if you want to stop. We can continue tomorrow if you want.

"Dear lady. I would really like to carry on, but if I am boring you please say" His voice had regained its strength

"How could anyone be bored with such a story? Please continue"

He smiled across the table at her and began to speak again.

"When the ship docked at Southampton we ex prisoners were the first off, I never saw Corporal Luke again, not even to thank him. We were taken to hospitals all across the south of England and after check ups and de briefings, those of us who were deemed fit were sent home.

How I had looked forward to being home. For days I had been thinking of going through the gates of our drive, seeing my home, hugging my mother, and now it was about to happen.

The army arranged for a car and I shared the journey with two other ex prisoners. We had no possessions and so there was plenty of room. We sat silently watching the wonderful green English countryside pass by. I cannot tell you how marvelous that was, England in spring, what a contrast to that we had been used to.

The other two were dropped off before me and I watched as wives, mothers, children and fathers greeted their men. The streets had been decorated with flags; neighbours stood clapping, everyone seemed so happy to have these men home. It was very emotional.

My homecoming however was so different. My father greeted me with a handshake and mother gave me a quick peck on the cheek. Oh so English; and so unwanted. I could see they were uncomfortable, pleased to have me home, yet so uncomfortable.

I needed a hug, a long comfortable hug, not just a peck. I wanted to talk to my father, but all he could do was tell me about my brothers. I was as if they were trying to ignore what I had gone through. I felt like crying, I had looked forward to this moment for so long and it had been such a disappointment.

Over the next few days I noticed mother looking at me slightly strangely. It was as if I was dirty. I could see disgust in her eyes. It was a very painful time. Father rarely spoke at all. I felt as if I was going mad. I so wanted to tell them what had happened and in the end I did.

We were having our Sunday lunch and I just froze at the sight of the roast beef, blood oozing from it as my father carved, I watched as he placed the slices on my plate and I began to shake. The butler was pouring red wine and it all became too much. I remember thumping the table and telling them what had happened. I can remember shouting, crying and I couldn't stop, once I had started I just couldn't stop.

Mother left the room, too upset to speak, and father just got angry. He was angry that I had upset my mother, and angry that in his words, I was not man enough to forget. He slapped my face and told me to pull myself together, stiff upper lip and all that rot. I will never forget the look in his eyes, he looked at me as if I was a monster, he hated me, and he felt I was weak. To be the only survivor was to him worse than me dying, by surviving I had somehow let him down.

Afterwards I went into the garden, initially just to walk in the clear air, but I stayed. I found a bush and stayed right there. I felt safe again, hidden from life, hidden from everyone. It was a wonderful feeling.

The gardener found me next day and told my father. He couldn't understand me, could not come to terms with my "eccentric behavior," he didn't even try. If only he had spent some time with me, talked about it, if only he had held me, but no. Instead he came into the garden and threw an envelope stuffed with money to the ground.

"Get yourself sorted you are an embarrassment to this family, a man in command should never leave his troops." That was all he said, then he walked away. I knew what his words meant; I should have died with the others.

I took his money; it was all he had to give me, no love, and no compassion, just money. I collected some of my belongings from my room and then made my way to Liverpool, where I bought a ticket on the first ship that was sailing. Luckily for me it was a speedier trip than that on board the troop ship, as I could not bring myself to go outside of the cabin. I had food and drinks brought to me, but the long days without company or fresh air took their toll. I was once again a wreck.

When we arrived our first stop was Ellis Island to be passed for entry. The offices were full of people from all parts of the world. It was noisy and cramped, smelly and the air stale. Children were crying and men shouting. I could not get out fast enough.

Once I had been passed I got on the boat to come over to New York, but I was so confused I just jumped into the first taxi I saw and asked for the city center. The driver must have thought I said central, and dropped me off at the park.

I had only been there for one night when Marco found me. He talked about his work, shared his food, and told me how lonely he was. I remember him coming back next day and coaxing me from under the bush, gently talking, not rushing and not loosing patience, he was marvelous. It took us a long time to reach his apartment, but not once did he try to rush me. He was just what I needed.

Life with him was so different. He never once questioned my opposition to going out; I think he was just pleased to have someone looking after his home.

We used to talk about Greece and sometimes of you, Tomas and Alexi and the things you did as children. He taught me how to cook his favorite dishes and a little of your language. He always had time for me, but never asked anything in return.

Before the war I had been training at a London Stockbrokers and when he began to bring newspapers home, I found I once again loved to read the financial news. To start with I studied companies and bought shares in my mind. I soon realised that now the war was over patterns were forming and certain companies were doing very well so I asked him to buy some shares properly.

When I asked him to sell them soon afterwards we could not believe the amount of profit I had made. It was then that we decided to go into a partnership. From then on things just went up and up, the profits we were making were terrific and so Marco began to buy gold.

I imagine you know the rest, but that basically is how I ended up here. Marco was my family now and then along came Christina and later

Eleni, they were some of the happiest days of my life. No one expecting anything of me, everyone just accepting me for what I am.

I'm sorry to tell you Marco did really love Christina, it would be a lie not to. She was such a lovely girl, a child really; well compared to us she was a child. So pretty and delicate, but you must remember this. He could never have forgotten you as he gave his daughter your name and that in itself is a great honor.

When Christina was murdered it was only Eleni that got him through. He protected her as best he could, a little too well at times I think. She is not very worldly wise and as you know very impulsive, but still she is the daughter I never had and I love her so much. Anyway back to my story.

After Christina's shooting we still worked together, but not nearly as hard as before. Luckily everything we did was from home, computers are such marvelous things. We had no need to employ anyone else, so we only had ourselves to please. Work if we wanted to, if not then we didn't. We had made our fortunes and had lost some of our appetite to make more.

As the years passed my work changed and unfortunately for reasons of high security I cannot tell you about this. Other than to say I rank amongst my closest friends The American President and British Prime Minister. Perhaps one day I will tell all, but for now that will have to do." He smiled across at Eleni; pleased to see she was still interested by the look on her face.

"Then one day not so long ago, Marco took Eleni to the Athena Exhibition. You know what happened then" Richard sat back and looked straight at Eleni, he could see the sadness in her eyes.

"You still have not told me why you will not go out Richard." She said softly "I can understand that you need to come in to the garden, but I cannot understand why you are a recluse"

"That look in my fathers eyes, even my mother looked at me as if I were a disgrace, they made me feel hideous. I could see disgust, I could see loathing, and that is how I think others see me too. It is as if when people look at me they see a monster. There are times when I wished I had died along with my friends." Tears trickled down his cheek." Between them they finished what the Japanese had started, they broke me as a man"

"Oh Richard. You are a lovely human being not a monster you must not believe that. I cannot understand how your parents could be so cruel; I would stand by my son no matter what. I would die for him if need be. Please believe me you are not a monster, all I see is a frightened young man who needed the comfort of his family, needed support and needed to talk. Your mind has stayed closed for so long, it has stayed under that bush, the one that saved your life, gave you comfort, but now you are out in the open. I hope you stay there" She paused for a moment." Has it never occurred to you that your friend pulled you down with him on purpose in order that you would survive? Haven't you ever thought that he was protecting you?" She looked across at him. "Tell me this. If it had been the other way around, would you have not tried to save a friend?" They sat silent for a moment or two.

"That is a wonderful thing to say. Perhaps he did know what he was doing and like you say acted to save me." Richard was smiling and his eyes seemingly searching the grass for answers. "He held my hand so tightly I thought he was afraid, but looking back perhaps you are right. In fact when we stood in front of the trench he did make me stand slightly behind." He sighed deeply. "If I am to believe that Eleni then you are not the only one to have wasted their life. I too have wasted so much time. Why oh why did we not meet before. Things could have been so different. I feel like a weight has been lifted, how I wish I had spoken before but it was never the right time, the right person listening, madam you are a tonic to me. I must say I am surprised that we could both talk so freely I don't really understand do you?"

Richard looked puzzled, what was it about this woman that had made him speak, why did he suddenly feel the need to talk after all of these years. Perhaps she was the Goddess she had once dreamt of being.

"I'm not sure myself. I think I needed someone who I knew would understand, an age thing maybe, sorry I am as unsure as you. One thing I do know though is our parents have much to answer for." She smiled at him timidly.

"Just one more question Richard if you don't mind. Why the new clothes each day, they are sent from London are they not?" she asked. "Eleni told me about them, I hope you don't mind"

"When Nabia had striped and washed me that first time I told you that from somewhere she produced clean clothes." Eleni nodded "Well I cannot tell you how wonderful they felt. They may have been army issue but it was such a feeling I find it hard to explain. These clean things that were fresh replaced the awful smell and feel of the old ones. I think you will understand." Eleni nodded again" My father always had his clothes from Saville Row and I suppose in my mind I am showing him I am as good as him. That feeling each day when I put on a brand new shirt reminds me that I am alive, I will never tire of that feeling.

It is so strange though, when I am here under the bush I sometimes go days without washing or changing. It is just as if I was back in the camp. I don't understand it myself really. I think it is just a need I have, like you say go back and start again. You want to go back to your cellar; I want to go back to the bush. I wonder what Freud would make of all of that." He sat back laughing.

They both turned towards the house as Andros came running across the lawn.

"Mama I have just had a call from Paris. She is coming here to interview the President and to do an article on the Queen's visit."

"Paris is Andros's lady friend Richard." Eleni explained, "She is a freelance journalist, one of the best. I am glad she is coming. I wonder where she is staying?" The two men shook hands as Eleni introduced her son.

"She can stay here with all of us my dear. We have plenty of room." He addressed Andros "When does your young lady arrive Andros?"

"She will be here in the morning. I will get a taxi and meet her. I will be lovely to have someone to see the city with. It seems ages since we have been together." Andros had the flush of a young boy about him as he spoke.

"You will do no such thing, please take the Rolls." Richard said "And please inform her she may stay here with us. I will let Michael know we are expecting another guest." He picked up a little brass bell and gave it a shake. Michael as usual appeared within seconds.

"We are to have another guest Michael, and please make sure the Rolls is ready for Andros first thing in the morning."

Michael nodded

"Yes Sir Richard. Will you require anything else?"

"Yes please. I think we will have some champagne and fresh peaches. Eleni is that all right with you. Andros?" They both agreed and thanked him.

"Now Andros tell me how you are getting on with all of that paperwork?"

"Very well thank you. You are very organized I have found it remarkably easy I must say. Eleni will have to go far to find someone to take your place." Andros replied, "I think that two more days should see me through. Tomorrow I will spend with Paris, the next day is Eleni's birthday and then I will get back to it."

"Oh I had forgotten Eleni's birthday" aunt Eleni said with a gasp. "I must go shopping tomorrow. I wonder where is best. I don't want to go far, to be honest I don't like the look of New York much. Is there somewhere close by I can shop Richard?" She put her hand to her mouth and gave an embarrassed giggle. "Sorry I forgot. How would you know?"

"Well its high time I found out," Richard said reaching for her hand "I will come with you and together we will find something nice."

"Don't run before you can walk Richard. Please take things slowly. If you still feel the same in the morning then by all means come with me, but if not don't worry"

Andros watched in amazement as they looked at each other. Surely not. He could see a spark that flashed between them and wondered if they could see it themselves.

Richard poured them all a glass of champagne and stood. He raised his glass.

"If you are with me I can conquer anything. To tomorrow my dear lady"

Andros was now certain and smiled to himself. It was about time his mother had someone else to occupy her mind; she had spent enough of her life pining over Marco.

Eleni looked at Andros

"Please don't say anything to the others about Richard shopping. Not yet anyway. I don't want Eleni becoming too excited, you know how she gets over everything."

"She always has been excitable." Richard added "Ever since she was a child. She could wait for nothing, but Marco always made her work for her things. It was quite hard on him at times, as whilst he wanted her to have everything, he could see how easily she could become a spoilt brat, as the Americans say. There were times though when I felt he should have let her find her own feet. He kept her very close, a little too close I think, and now she is having to learn very fast. And talking of my little girl here she is."

They all turned to see Eleni racing across the lawn towards them, a large bag bouncing at her side. Vanni followed not quite so energetically.

"Richard you look fabulous." Eleni flung herself into his outstretched arms. "Here I have a present for you from Athens." She handed over the lovely briefcase.

"Thank you my darling it's wonderful. I can keep all my papers together. Thank you." Richard smiled before kissing her cheek and then gestured towards her aunt. "Your aunt is the reason I look so much better. I think she may be a miracle worker in disguise."

"I think you are exaggerating slightly Richard." Aunt Eleni was blushing like a young girl. "More champagne anyone?

# • Chapter •
## 13

That evening they ate in the wonderful dinning room. Andros, sitting near the middle of the long dark mahogany table, watched as his mother and Richard often gazed towards each other. They were at each end, and whilst young Eleni talked about her day, they might as well have been on their own.

Eleni had shown Vanni as much as she could cram into one day, it was no wonder he sat silently Andros thought, he must have been worn out. She told them of the sights they had seen, the shops they had been in and where they had eaten lunch. She had taken him back to the restaurant Marco had been employed in when he had first arrived in New York. It was a large busy place now, but the food was still as good.

"Not as good as Tomas's though" she added "You know I really do miss that little taverna. I just felt so at home. I think we should go and see your parents Vanni, after this trip, and anyway I have still kept my room on and must owe him lots by now." They all laughed.

"I agree Eleni." Vanni said "I haven't been home for such a long time. I must go back to Athens first though and after that we can visit the beach"

"I think it is lovely that Tomas named his beach after you aunt Eleni. So romantic." The young girl addressed her aunt.

"Oh no. It was called that many many years before Tomas brought the land, but I do think the name had something to do with it. He is my twin, you know, and he did miss me greatly" Aunt Eleni once again glanced at Richard. "I have never been there myself yet. We have always met on Alonysos, perhaps I will go one day." Andros realized it was her way of asking Richard to go with her.

After their meal Richard ushered them into a spacious lounge where Michael served coffee and liqueurs. Andros noticed how comfortable his mother looked sitting next to Richard on the beautiful leather sofa. Gazing around the room he saw how, like all of the other rooms, it was so English. The large house itself was more like a Grecian home on the outside, but inside it was lovely old-fashioned English.

"I love the way you have furnished your home Richard," He said still looking around. "How on earth did you manage to get all of these lovely things." He wanted to add, without going out, but stopped himself just in time.

"At first I used to shop through catalogues sent from England, but these days I do it all over the Internet. I may be getting on a bit, but I have still managed to learn about that." He laughed. "That's how I get my clothes, do my share dealings, and everything really. My father would turn in his grave if he knew I was ordering my clothes from London, via a computer. Not the done thing old boy." He put on a different voice and then laughed again.

Eleni felt quite emotional, Richard was actually poking fun at his father, the man he was so afraid of, but whom he so wanted to be like. She watched as he sat back smiling and lit his Dunhill.

Andros finished his coffee and stood.

"Right I'm off for a walk around the garden and then it's bed. Paris is arriving early tomorrow Vanni, and Richard has kindly let be have the Rolls to go and meet her."

"Oh but I wanted it tomorrow Richard." Eleni wailed "I was going to take Vanni to the center we didn't get chance today. I want to make sure it is ready for Thursday."

"Eleni you sound like a little child. I want, I want. You can go in your own car" Richard said sternly.

"Well now you sound like papa." Eleni added, her lips pouting.

"I promised him that if any thing happened to him I would look after you young lady, and that includes stopping you getting your own way every time. I have said Andros can have the car and that is an end to it."

Vanni was beginning to realize just what he had taken on with this lovely but slightly wild young girl.

Andros just smiled as he left after kissing his mother goodnight. Vanni and Eleni followed soon after.

"Just us again dear lady." Richard said gently. "More coffee?"

"No thank you Richard. I think I too will go to my room. It has been a long day." She stood ready to leave. Richard took her hand and kissed it gently.

"It has been a long rewarding day Eleni. Goodnight sleep well my dear." She looked into his eyes and smiled.

Eleni undressed and slid into the large comfortable bed where she lay thinking of Richard and his story. Little did she know he too was lying awake, and he was thinking of her? Slowly they both drifted off into dream filled sleeps.

Andros had already left for the airport when the others came down for breakfast.

"Mr. Andros left about an hour ago madam." Michael informed Eleni as he helped her to her seat. "They should be back shortly."

Once again Richard sat at her side. She was pleased to see him look so well. He was dressed in casual, but smart trousers and tweed jacket, and his cologne was delicate and light. They ate quietly, listening to young Eleni as she mapped out her day. Firstly she was taking Vanni to the center to prepare for tomorrow, and then she was going to phone her friends to make sure they were coming to her party at night.

"Is everything ordered Richard?" She asked taking a bite from her toast.

"Ready and waiting. I have contacted the caterers and everything is in order. You just speak to your friends and don't worry about the rest." He replied.

"Come on Vanni." she said hurriedly "Lots to do today so lets get on with it."

Richard watched as the youngsters left in the red sports car.

"I hope he realises just what he has got there. I think he will have to keep a tight reign on her."

"I think you are right Richard, but it will do him good. He has had it too easy in life so far. It will do him good." Aunt Eleni was laughing, remembering Vanni's face as he had been hurried through his breakfast.

The beautiful Rolls Royce silently floated into the drive just as they were finishing their coffee. The chauffeur held the door open as Paris emerged. She was stunning. Tall and slim, she had short cropped red hair, and her features could have been sculptured from marble. She wore a well fitting, very expensive looking navy suit, and multi coloured Hermes silk scarf hung loosely around her shoulders. No one would believe she had just been on a transatlantic flight she looked immaculate.

Walking like a model, her long body sashaying as she made her way towards the breakfast patio. Andros followed slightly behind a huge smile on his face. She was obviously much younger than him but at that moment he looked like an excited child.

"Paris I am so pleased to see you again." Eleni stood and kissed her cheek "You look well. May I introduce our host. Richard Graves."

"I am well thank you. Pleased to meet you sir." She put out her hand. "Thank you for inviting me to stay." Her English accent surprised Richard. He shook the offered hand and was pleased to receive a good strong response. This is no ordinary woman, he thought to himself as he looked into her huge amber eyes, eyes that shone with an almost fire like quality, no ordinary woman at all.

"You are welcome. Please sit. Coffee?" Paris accepted and sat down. "Eleni tells me you are to interview John, sorry the President"

"Yes I have an appointment with him tomorrow, but now I know who I'm staying with I would love to interview you too." Paris had no time to waste. "Obviously I have heard all about your charity work and the fact you are to be knighted next month, but I would love to know more and I take it you know The President well?"

"Paris please not now." Eleni was concerned. Paris might unnerve Richard in her haste.

"Its alright Eleni. I would be flattered Paris, but not today. You must rest and get ready for tomorrow. The President is a much bigger fish than me anyway."

"Don't worry about Paris Richard." Andros joined in the conversation. "She has her own time clock and never suffers from jet lag. She travels so much it comes naturally to her to adjust. Just like that." He clicked his fingers.

"Well I have things to do today and tomorrow is Eleni's birthday, so how about Friday?" Richard asked but Eleni was worried he was moving too fast for his own good. "Time to go dear lady. Are you ready?" He put out his hand to help Eleni stand and smiled at her as he did. "We will not be too long, but just ask Michael if there is anything you need."

He led Eleni towards the Rolls.

"A bit of style I think. Do you know I have had this car almost thirty years and never been farther than the drive in her? Such a shame I think, don't you?"

As Eleni let Richard guide her into the back seat, she was still concerned. If this man had not been further than the drive in such a long time, what a monumental step it was going to be. He slid in beside her and asked the chauffeur to take them to Tiffany's. It was the only shop he knew the name of, he told Eleni with a smile.

As the car swept down towards the gates, Eleni held Richards hand, she could feel the tension in him, as they swung open.

"You don't have to do this you know" She said quite tearfully" I will understand."

"My dear lady. This is something I so want to do. I have wanted to for so long but until you came along I have not had anyone who would understand. You have opened up the world for me; I don't know how I will manage when you have gone back to Athens though, so I must make the most of the days we have left." He looked quite sad. "I already know I will miss you terribly." She tightened her grip on his hand.

It was quite a long drive into the city and Eleni watched as Richard looked out of the window. He could not believe how busy the streets were. The buildings, so many and so tall, the smell of stale air even invading the car, and people everywhere.

"I don't think I like this very much" He said quietly.

"Shall we go back then?" Eleni asked.

"Oh no. Its just I don't think I knew quite what to expect. It all looks so dirty and crowded. I like clean air and space I am afraid, not this." He felt disappointed in what he saw.

The car stopped outside the huge Tiffany's building and the chauffer once again held open the door. Richard hesitated for a moment and took a deep breath.

"Right then tally ho!" He stood on the pavement and held his hand out to Eleni. She was amazed by the inner strength this man must have, it was no wonder he survived that Japanese hell camp.

She held on to his arm tightly, guiding him through the huge glass doors and into the shop. They stopped occasionally to look at the goods on show and chatted happily. Eleni could sense his discomfort but decided to stay quiet. She knew he would let her know when he was ready to leave.

She chose a pretty pink cashmere jumper and a beautiful multi coloured silk scarf for Eleni's present. Richard decided to buy a slim gold bracelet set with tiny rubies.

"It goes nicely with those." He said smiling, but Eleni could hear a tremor in his voice.

"She is a very lucky girl. Are you ready now? Shall we go?" She didn't want to overdo this first outing.

"Not until I have chosen something for you." He replied "Now go and look at something over there whilst I make my choice. Go on off you trot." He pointed to another display. "And don't go peeking or sneaking back until I wave."

This was an even bigger step for him Eleni thought as she walked slowly away. To stand in this huge shop, surrounded by all of these people, was like climbing a mountain for him, but she did as he asked.

She soon became engrossed in the wonderful clothes on show and began to calm down. Every so often she glanced in his direction and could see that he was talking to an assistant. They were discussing something in depth, she could tell, as their heads were quite close together. The poor chauffeur was doing his best to keep watch on both of them, a sight that Eleni found quiet amusing as his head swiveled from one to the other and back. She began to feel excited wondering what Richard was buying and by the time he turned and waved, she felt like a teenager. She walked quickly to his side.

"Right dear lady. Time to go I think." He took her arm and led her though the crowd towards the door.

Once safely back in the car Richard let out a huge sigh of relief.

"You did really well Richard. I am so proud of you." Eleni leaned over and kissed his cheek. "I can't believe you made me go away though."

"It is all down to you Eleni. I could feel you watching me even though I said not to. I felt safe knowing you were there. Thank you." He patted her hand. "I would like to keep this to ourselves if you don't mind." She nodded

"Andros won't say anything, and I won't" She told him "Do I have to wait?" She pointed towards the little gift bag Richard was holding.

"Yes madam you do. Tomorrow is Eleni's birthday and you can have it then." She watched as he smiled to himself. "A bit naughty of me I know, but I have decided tomorrow it is. Shall we go somewhere for lunch?"

"I think I would like to go home if that is Ok with you. I don't feel comfortable in the city. It feels so cramped and crowded compared to Athens. The air is not the same."

"I know what you mean. I had not realised until today. I have spent so long at home, in my office or in the garden, I had forgotten how ugly cities could be. Is Athens so beautiful then?" He replied. Eleni nodded and told him all about the marvelous buildings, statues and shops. The wide streets, filled with people and cars, yet feeling open. He watched as she spoke and could see the love of the place in her eyes. He asked about her home and she described the wonderful views from the conservatory and garden. It was obvious to him she loved her home as well.

The journey sped past as she talked and soon they were back at the house gates. The car slowly came to a stop and they could see Andros walking towards them.

"Richard, how are you feeling. I was a little worried you have been gone for some considerable time." Andros was genuinely concerned. Not only for Richard, but also his mother, how would she have coped if anything had gone wrong?

"Andros kind of you to ask but we had a lovely time thank you, but now we are both hungry and a little tired. Would you and Paris like to join us for lunch, I take it the others are not back yet?" Richard helped Eleni from the car.

"No. Poor Vanni" Andros laughed "She will wear him out at this rate." He kissed his mothers cheek. "Are you alright mama?"

"Yes thank you Andros, but as Richard has said a little tired and hungry"

Richard informed Michael that the four of them would like lunch in the garden and Andros went to fetch Paris.

Eleni sat at the table, still by the bush after yesterday's meal there, and sighed. It had been quite some morning at had taken its toll. Not as young as I think sometimes, she thought to herself, one shop and I'm tired.

The four of them sat in the shade of the trees and bushes enjoying a superb light lunch. It was similar to the previous days, tiny sandwiches and cheeses, white wine and cakes served with coffee. As before Eleni thought it was perfect.

Paris was unable to pass on the opportunity of eating with Richard and led most of the conversation. She asked easy questions at first but slowly began to delve deeper. When Richard sat back and lit his cigarette Eleni took this as a sign.

"I think I will go for a lie down now if you will excuse me. Richard I think a rest might do you good too."

Together they walked back to the house.

"Thank you Eleni. I am tired now. You do look after me"

He was too polite to say he had had enough of Paris's questions but Eleni read his thoughts.

"Paris is a lovely woman, but she can be a little overpowering at times." She said "Don't think you have to do this interview, just remember from now on you do what you want." He smiled down at her in acknowledgement of her wisdom.

The little red car rattled the gravel as it came to an abrupt halt. Eleni and Vanni jumped out.

"Hi everyone. Have we missed lunch?" She called excitedly.

"Andros and Paris are still in the garden. Richard and I are going for a lie down. Why don't you go and tell them all about your morning. You can tell Paris all about the center." The older woman smiled to herself. Now that was a good paring. One who asked questions for a living and the other who could talk non stop.

Vanni still looked a little shell-shocked as he followed her across the lawn.

The two older ones smiled at each other and went inside.

# CHAPTER 14

That evening Paris took the other younger ones out to a good restaurant that she knew.

"Paris knows all the best places to eat in just about every city in the modern world" Andros said proudly "Will you two be alright here?" He looked towards his mother and Richard. He knew the answer but asked anyway.

"Yes thank you. We will have a nice dinner and then it's an early night for me." Aunt Eleni answered, Richard standing at her side, just nodded.

They waved as the Rolls swept down the drive.

"That poor chauffeur. He has been on the go all day" aunt Eleni said with a light sigh." And I expect that lot will want to be out late too"

"That is his job my dear. In any case not every day is quite so hectic for him. Come on let us dine in peace"

They enjoyed a lovely meal, chatting occasionally, just comfortable to be together. Richard could see that Eleni was tired and after their coffee and brandy led her to her room.

"I hope you sleep well Eleni." He bent to kiss her hand "Until tomorrow dear lady" As he once again stood straight Eleni stretched up and kissed his cheek. His hands held her for a moment and then he pulled her close.

"I feel so hopeless" He said after a while "I have never in my life kissed a woman properly, held a woman close, or anything." He suddenly looked so young and confused.

"Then let us find out together" Eleni led him into her room. "Remember I too have missed out on many of the nice things in life."

He held her tightly but kissed her gently.

"We must be fast learners" He joked "That was wonderful"

Together the helped each other undress, it was a new experience for them both.

"I can't believe this Eleni. Here I am over 70 and this is my first time"

"Lets pretend we are 21 again Richard. What would you have done then?"

Once naked their inhibitions left them and they made love slowly and meaningfully. Exploring each other's bodies as they learned. Eleni gently stroked the scars on his skin, left from his time in the camp.

"Nabia did a good job on those," she said before kissing the largest mark.

"You are the most wonderful woman in the world," he said kissing her nose "Not that I know many, but still" He laughed. She elbowed him gently in the side. "Can you imagine Michael's eyebrows if he could see me now?" This time they both laughed.

"I know one thing Richard. He would be very pleased for you, and for me" She said." Will you stay all night? It would be so nice to wake up with you"

"Madam I am going nowhere" He said sternly "You are stuck with me I'm afraid to say"

Michael was walking down the corridor as next morning they emerged from Eleni's room, and his eyebrows did certainly rise, but only very slightly, he smiled as he saw how happy Richard was. He had served him for the last 30 years and would give his life up for this man. His own wife Molly was housekeeper and living here had meant they had had a wonderful life. This was their home as well as Richards. It was the only home they had had since marrying and emigrating to America. That was all due to Marco and Richard. Mostly Richard.

"Good morning Michael" Richard said with a huge grin "Is the birthday girl's breakfast ready yet?"

"Good morning Sir Richard, madam, I will make sure it is." He replied as solidly as ever, even though he was still a little shocked.

The couple sat at the breakfast table and chatted as they ate. The younger ones gradually appeared looking a little worse for wear. Andros kissed his mothers cheek before sitting down.

"Happy birthday Eleni" They all chorused when she eventually appeared. Michael popped a champagne cork and poured her the first glass.

She clapped her hands in excitement as she spotted the pile of presents on the table and quickly began to unwrap them. She loved the pink jumper and scarf vowing to wear them for her party tonight. Andros gave her a pretty marble statuette of a dolphin and Paris's gift was a lovely leather handbag.

Vanni made her wait for his, teasing her that she was like a child, and not a 28-year-old woman. Eventually he gave in and produced a fabulous black and white photograph of the taverna at Eleni Beach. It had been taken from the sea and showed the pretty house, kiosk, with Tomas and Sofia sitting at the bar side table. A thin black frame helped to show it to perfection. Eleni was almost moved to tears.

"Oh Vanni thank you. It is beautiful" She showed Paris and explained who the people were. "Looking at this makes me want to go back even more," She said stroking the glass. "We must not leave it too long Vanni"

"There is one more present Eleni." Richard said sliding a box across the table "I went shopping yesterday and picked it myself" The words hit Eleni like a sledgehammer and tears flowed down her cheeks.

"You went shopping" She looked at Richard who was now holding aunt Eleni's hand tightly "You wonderful woman" She shot up out of her seat and hugged them both.

"Well aren't you going to open it?" he asked slightly embarrassed by the attention.

Her fingers shook as she pulled at the paper and she gasped as she opened the box lid and saw the pretty bracelet.

"Oh Richard it is beautiful. I shall treasure it forever. It goes so well with my scarf and jumper" Then she laughed "But I suppose it would" She looked across at the obviously happy couple. "I love you both."

They settled down again to finish breakfast chatting amicably and enjoying each other's company.

"Paris what time is your interview?" young Eleni asked

"I have to be at City Hall by 12 o'clock so I had better go and get ready" she replied "But the interview is at 1. I have to be searched etc first, and then they go through my questions. But don't worry I will be back in time for your party." She rose from the table and gracefully walked into the house.

"So its us three for the center. Come on lets go, they will be expecting their turkey and trimmings for lunch." Vanni, Andros and Eleni left together squashed in her fabulous but smallish red sports car.

"Its just the two of us again my dear. What would you like to do today?"

"I think a drive around the city. I would hate to come all this way and see nothing, even thought I'm not really that keen. Then after lunch we can learn a little more about each other." She smiled cheekily over at him "Don't you agree?"

"I think that sounds wonderful but first I would like to give you this" Richard passed her a tiny velvet box

She held the box and stroked the top

"You know this little thing means so much to me. I have no idea what is inside, but the box is so important. It somehow represents your first day of freedom."

Slowly she opened it and gasped. Inside was a lovely gold necklace with a large single diamond at its center. "Richard I am almost speechless.

It is absolutely beautiful" She leaned over and kissed him "Thank you so much"

"No thank you dear lady. I can't thank you enough. Let us go and have a look at the city then."

Eleni brought her car to an abrupt stop on the tarmac outside of the center.

"Who taught you to drive?" Andros asked "I think you should ask for your money back"

"Cheeky" she replied. "I'll tell you it was papa and he said I was very good."

"Well that says it all" Vanni joined in "You drive like a Greek" Eleni punched them both.

"Right then lets get going. Who wants to peel the potatoes?" She laughed as she led the way into the center.

Andros was amazed how clean and bright it was, and very spacious. A long table had already been placed down the center of the room and he could hear the clatter of people already working in the kitchen.

Once again Eleni had a pile of presents to open, only this time it was obvious that they were hand made. Little wooden carved figures, pots with pretty plants in, and a badly knitted scarf. He was proud of how she accepted them not showing once any sign of dislike, and thanking the givers profusely.

They had a busy morning, as Eleni had said they would, peeling mountains of potatoes, carrots and chopping cabbage. The other cooks had already put the turkeys in the oven and their smell made them all feel hungry. Dishes of cranberry sauce were placed on the table, and piles of knives and forks.

"Don't you think there might be too much Eleni?" Vanni asked "There's hardly any one here to eat all of this"

"They will be here soon Vanni. Lots of them you wait and see." Eleni was now stirring a huge saucepan of gravy.

She was right, no sooner had she spoken than people began to arrive. Tramps and homeless, their clothes in tatters, their faces dirty. He was surprised when they all went to her and wished her happy birthday before disappearing into the shower block at the side of the center. He was so touched as he watched her speak to each and every one who came through the door. This crazy woman was something else, he thought.

Soon lunches were being served at a frightening rate. Vanni remembered his question about having too much, but now feared they would run out. One thing though, they didn't have time to eat themselves.

"How long have you been doing this?" Andros enquired as he helped to wash some plates.

"Papa and Richard set up the center years ago and as long as I can remember we have done this on my birthday. I told you before, Papa said I should always give something on my birthday as I had so much during the year. I sometimes come here at night as well. Then they only get soup, bread and sandwiches though, but it all helps when you are hungry. There is plenty of space for them to sleep, and as you have seen they can wash too. You know I was dreading today Andros. It is the first time I have done this without papa, but having you here has made things so much better" She held her arms out and they fell into a long hug.

"Happy birthday my little sister." He kissed the top of her head

They all worked hard until almost 3 o'clock.

"Right that's it I think" Eleni looked around the once again spotless kitchen "Time to get ready for my party" She gathered her presents and once again thanked those who remained. "These people who work here are wonderful you know. They are here day after day getting food ready." She said as they walked back to her car. She threw Andros the keys "Show me how you drive then. "

Andros felt slightly nervous and when he stalled the car the others burst out laughing. He couldn't remember the last time he had driven. Taxis and limousines were his usual mode of transport, or give him an aeroplane any time. It soon came back to him though and they arrived back at the house safe and sound. Eleni was still laughing

"I drive like a Greek eh." She teased before gasping with delight "Oh! Just look at that," She pointed to a huge pink and white marquee erected in the garden. Waiters and waitresses were carrying trays of glasses, setting tables and putting up balloons. They looked like ants as they trailed across they lawn. Eleni stood and clapped.

"Do you always do that?" Vanni enquired "It seems to me every time you get excited you stand and clap"

"I know I can't help it" she said "I will probably do it on our wedding day too" She turned as the gates opened to allow a lorry through "Oh! This must be the group. Richard has certainly gone to town this year. What time is it? Oh goodness I had better go and change. Guests will be here about 7" She was that excited she was almost going in circles.

"Calm down" Andros said putting his hand on her shoulder "Go and have a lie down, then a nice bath, then get ready. You will be worn out if you carry on like this. In fact I think we should all have a rest. It looks as if Richard and mama are already in their rooms. I expect Paris will want to chill, as she says, when she gets back, so come on lets go" He ushered the others into the house. "Right off you go, and rest" he knew they would spend some time together first, and hoped that Paris would be back in time for them to have some time for love as well.

Little did he know that was exactly what his mother was doing right this minute.

Eleni and Richard had spent an interesting morning driving around the city and then after a nice lunch had retired to her room where once again they began to learn about each other.

"I like this type of lesson the God's taught you well" Richard said as he held her silky naked body in his arms "Can we have lessons every day please miss?"

"I hope so darling. But what is going to happen when I return to Athens. I am going to miss you so much." Eleni sounded sad.

"Will you stay a little longer?" He kissed her nose "I would like you to stay if you can"

"I will try, but you know I have to go back at some stage, I have things to do and sort out, but I don't really like New York I'm afraid. It's a little overpowering. How I wish we could be together in Athens or preferably on Alonysos" She said softly.

Andros had been right; Vanni and Eleni fell into each other's arms as soon as she had closed her bedroom door, and within seconds were in her bed naked. Discarded clothes littered the floor.

"So much for resting" Vanni said grinning "It's a good job your big brother can't see you now"

A film of sweat shone on her spent body. Eleni just giggled.

Back in his room Andros was thinking of his own love life and was pleased to see Paris arrive a short while later. Her eyes were sparkling fire with the excitement of the interview and she threw herself into his arms. Her energy and euphoria of the past few hours was released as she attacked Andros's body. He did not complain, he just enjoyed her enthusiasm. It had been far too long since they had been together and after their first lust had passed they rested before making love much more slowly and sensually.

"I do miss you Paris, but if you behave like this whenever we meet I think I can put up with it" he said teasingly. She had been quite some tiger.

She answered without words, using a kiss to his lips and then moving slowly down to his chest, to say how she felt. Smiling she saw his eyes close and heard him groan. Taking her time she treated him to all the things she knew he liked.

"Who said the English are reserved?" He laughed "That is the sort of thing that will give me a heart attack, you naughty girl," He added once his breathing had returned to normal. "Come here" he pulled her down upon his chest and held her tight. "You know I love you don't you. You are the only woman for me even if I can't tie you down. Not wife material are you really, not yet anyway" He felt her head move with a nod.

"And I love you too. Perhaps one day when I have had enough of traveling and writing I will let you have me, that's if you can fit me in your busy schedule." She said softly looking up at him.

"That day cannot come quickly enough, just don't leave it too late my darling, you realise I am not that far short of 60" He kissed her nose "Now let me sleep. We had a late night last night and I have been working all day at the center, now we have the party, so sleep."

"Don't talk rubbish; you are only 58, miles away from 60" she said softly. "And a pretty fit 58 if I may say. He pulled a sheet over and they settled down, their arms and legs entwined.

A couple of hours later Richard and Eleni, Andros and Paris stood on the patio and watched as the birthday girl greeted her guests. They saw her accept gifts and introduce Vanni, who looked slightly uncomfortable at meeting so many new faces.

"She's invited 200" Richard said as the marquee began to fill. Music and laughter drifted up into the air and some of the younger ones started to dance. "I had been slightly worried about today" he added "It is her first birthday without Marco, but I think it has helped her having all of you here. Please let me thank you on her behalf. She is so precious to me, thank you."

Andros looked across at Richard and then to his mother. He noticed how her fingers stroked the necklace around her neck almost unconsciously. As her hand dropped to her side he was able to see it better. It was new, if he was not mistaken. Eleni had never been one for jewellery, just the owner of a few simple necklaces and pairs of earrings. This one he could tell was something else, the central diamond sparkled as it caught the lights from the marquee. Richard he thought, you old devil.

It was a lovely night. The food and drinks were excellent and Eleni was in her element. With Vanni at her side she positively glowed as she made her way around her guests talking and laughing with people on every table.

Just before midnight Richard interrupted the dancing, gave a little speech then informed her that the older ones were retiring. She wrapped her arms around his neck and hugged him

"Thank you for a fabulous night Richard, and for my present." She kissed his cheek before hugging aunt Eleni, Andros and Paris. They waved goodnight to the other party guests and the four of them walked together across the lawn.

"What time will you want to see me tomorrow Paris?" Richard asked "Not too early I hope?"

"I thought about 11 if that would be OK with you. It would give me time to write up my notes from today and get myself ready." She replied

"That would be fine with me. In my office at 11 then, oh and don't' worry Andros you can still work in there. We can have the sofa my dear"

They said their goodnights as they reached Andros's room and Richard led Eleni to hers. Michael appeared from nowhere as they walked along the corridor.

"Michael. From now on I will take my early morning tea in here please. Tea for two. Thank you" Eleni stifled a giggle at the look on Michael's face; it was one of shock, surprise and elation all in one split second, and resulted in a strange smile. She knew how fond of Richard the butler was and was pleased to see how he smiled at this request.

Richard closed the door behind them and took her hand

"You don't mind do you?" he asked rather shyly. "I should have asked you first, but seeing Michael there it just came out"

"Of course I don't mind Richard. I think it would be wonderful to wake up with you and share your tea. I can think of nothing nicer." She kissed his lips tenderly. "Now I am very tired so lets get into that lovely bed and cuddle. I want to feel you close"

"Say not one word more madam. Your wish is my command." He stood to attention.

It was so comforting to feel him next to her she wanted to cry. Richard sensed a change in her mood and asked what was bothering her.

"Oh its just me being silly I suppose. It just feels so nice being in here with you. So comfortable and natural and so cosy. I was thinking of how I will manage once I get back to Athens. I only have a few days left, I could stretch it for another week, but what is another week." Richard pulled her closer.

"Don't worry my darling it will all be fine you wait and see."

They kissed goodnight and drifted off to sleep, his arm over her waist as if they had lain like this for years.

Andros and Paris were also wrapped together. No more love making tonight, just a nice comfortable kiss and cuddle.

"Just like an old married couple," he said before turning off the bedside light.

"There you go again. You realize you have dropped a million hints, but never once asked me outright?" She said nuzzling his ear. "Think about it. Goodnight"

Andros lay for some moments. Think about it? Did she mean he should ask her? Did she mean all of his hints had fallen on deaf ears? Women! Why couldn't they just say what they meant for a change? He would never understand them, he thought miserably. Well perhaps he should do something. Better to have asked and received a no, than never to have asked at all, he smiled at this witticism. Right then he would. Not quite like Vanni did in Athens, no something much more subtle.

He fell into a light sleep dreaming of going down on one knee at the top of Mars Hill, The Acropolis in the background. He felt restless. Knowing Paris she would prefer it if he chased her down the Olympic Track in the center of the city, shouting out his request.

For some reason the photograph of his mother waving goodbye to Marco came into his dream. He woke suddenly. That was it. He would take Paris to Kefalonia and propose right there on the cliff top overlooking the sea. He went back to sleep, this time with a smile on his face.

In Eleni's bedroom she and Vanni were also drifting off to sleep. They had enjoyed an exhausting love making session and were still wrapped around each other. The sheets twisted and partly lying on the floor.

"Vanni when can we go back to the beach?" Her fingers made circles in the soft hair on his chest. "I have really enjoyed coming back to New York, enjoyed my party and everything, but deep down I want to be back there. The city seems so stifling and busy. So hot and muggy I want to get out and go back do you think we could build our house there. Just by the car park, in that little clearing, you know where I mean" He nodded "You could do your work on your computer, and I could help Tomas and Sofia. It would be marvelous."

He turned to face her fully.

"What about your business? Have you decided if Andros will take over for you? I don't think Richard wants to be much longer at the helm." He said softly before adding. "I too would love to have our home on the beach and I'm sure papa would let us have that land, I will ask him when I phone tomorrow if that is what you really want. We have almost a year to build something special. It is a superb idea. I could easily work from there and visit Athens when necessary. Clever girl. I love you." He kissed her nose.

## • CHAPTER • 15

Aunt Eleni sat in bed sipping her tea lazily. The sunshine beaming through the window was warming and comforting. How wonderful it had been to wake up with Richard again. How safe she had felt. Now he was showering in her bathroom and she could hear him singing softly to himself.

After bringing in the tea tray, Michael had produced a selection of silk ties, a brand new shirt, underwear, and his dark suit as if it were an everyday occurrence.

It all seemed so natural to the three of them, but she wondered how Andros would react if he knew what was going on.

"You look lovely sitting there with the sun in your hair. Very beautiful"

"I think you are exaggerating slightly, but thank you for the compliment. You don't look so bad yourself. Why the suit?" she asked as he held up the ties for her to choose one. She nodded towards a lovely navy and green one. "It will go with your eyes," she said.

"I always dress for the office, always have done, habit I suppose. Today is work first and then the interview I shan't see much of you I'm afraid until later" He sat on the side of the bed and took her hand in his. "I will miss you dear lady"

"Promise you won't let Paris bully you this morning. She can be a little forceful at times, that's why she is so good at her job, but please if you have had enough, say so." Eleni was concerned that Paris might just upset Richard again. "Richard can I ask you something?" He nodded, frowning slightly "Have you accepted this award" He nodded again

"Yes I have. John phoned me and insisted, you know who I mean, and Michael was absolutely over the moon when the letter came. It was almost as if he had received a Knighthood and I felt that I couldn't let him down so I replied accepting. That's when I got all worked up and had to go into the garden. I was so scared, how could I accept if I couldn't go to receive it." He looked bewildered "But now I have you. Please Eleni you must stay for the ceremony. I cannot go without you." Eleni heard the fear in his voice.

"Of course I will be there." She replied softly stroking his cheek "At your side if that's what you want. Now go and get your work done. Paris will be on the dot you know. She can't wait to talk to you" They kissed gently and he held her face in his hands.

"If you are with me I can do anything" It was a wonderful thing for him to say, but also worrying. What on earth would happen to this lovely man when she returned to Greece? How would he cope? How would she cope? But she knew she could not stay here. New York was not a city for her no matter who was there.

Richard left her with a smile, a little wave and strode off towards the office.

He was amazed to see Andros already at Marco's desk and Vanni at his.

"Sorry Richard" Vanni said quickly "We have just been catching up on a few things. Hope you don't mind?

"No. Take your time. I only have a few share prices to check, and perhaps sell a few. I have slowly been winding down since Marco died, so I only have a few to work on these days. Hopefully it won't be too long before I have sold them all but the gold will take much longer I feel. Can't make too much in one year or the tax man will be after me." Richard sat on the sofa and watched as the two men worked on the computers. They were so much faster than him. He could hear the keys rattling as they stared at the screens. He walked over to the fireplace and pulled the rope at the side. Michael appeared quickly.

"I'll have my paper as soon as it arrives please and coffee for us all." Michael acknowledged the request and left the room silently.

Paris joined them soon after, holding the door as Michael returned with a trolley. He handed Richard The Times, ironed flat as usual, and set the coffee tray on the table.

"Thank you." Richard said, "We will ring if we need anything else" Michael bowed and left.

"I was hoping to do a bit of this first" Paris gestured towards her notes "Hope you don't mind?"

"No. You go ahead. I will have a read of this I'm not going anywhere" Richard poured himself a coffee and sat reading the newspaper.

Paris opened her laptop and began to type furiously. Occasionally Richard looked over and was surprised at the speed of her fingers as she worked. It convinced him there and then not only to give up doing Eleni's work but also his own. These three younger people worked so fast it made him feel old and snail like. He would leave his work for now, they would only laugh at him he was so slow. One thing he would have to do though was to contact his tailor on London.

"Right. That's it." Paris shut her laptop with a loud click. "I think a coffee then the scoop of my lifetime" She smiled at Richard who looked surprised. "Don't look at me like that Richard. You are the biggest scoop I have ever had. Who else has interviewed you, tell me that? When the announcement of your award was in the papers it was just a written piece. No photograph or anything. No one has seen you for years. I am so lucky. I might even retire after this. I mean it doesn't get any better then sitting here with you" She smiled at him over the rim of her cup.

"I think you are exaggerating a little Paris." Richard said more than a bit embarrassed.

Andros was staring at them from the other side of the room. Had he heard that correctly? Paris might retire after this?

Now he was sure. Once they had finished here he would take her to Kefalonia. His stomach churned slightly. What if she said no. He hoped it wouldn't spoil things between them if she did. But she might just say yes, and then he would also panic. Women! Who would have them? He went back to his work smiling, confused, but more than a little excited.

He could hear Paris buttering Richard up with compliments, and asking questions at the same time. She was brilliant at asking about one thing and getting long detailed replies for answers. Andros began to feel slightly worried if Richard would cope once she really got her claws into him.

"The reason I asked to interview you was to simply find out about your charity work which is the reason you have been given this award, so we will begin if that's OK" Richard agreed "Then tell me all about your centers."

Richard began to explain how when he arrived in America he was homeless and living in the park, and how with Marco's help he ended up as he was today. He told her he wanted to give something back. To help those who were in a similar position, even if it was only a roof over their heads and a bowl of soup. She asked about the nursing school in Singapore.

"You have done your homework," He laughed, now a little nervous. How could he tell her about that without telling the whole story? "Can we come back to that later?" Paris agreed and asked him about his yacht.

Andros looked over again His yacht; he didn't know he had one.

"Well, for many years Marco used to take Eleni for holidays on his yacht, and when he died she decided to sell it. She said she couldn't go on it ever again. It seemed such a shame, she really is a beautiful vessel, and so I bought it from her. Not that she knew it was me" He giggled slightly "She is going to be a little angry I think when she finds out. Anyway, I bought the yacht and now it is used by charities in the city, mostly for children to have fun." Richard continued to tell Paris about some of the underprivileged children and where they had been. Many sent him photographs and many wrote letters, others drew pictures. He went to one of the cabinets and pulled out a bulging file. He handed it to Paris. "Here. You might find some of this interesting" Paris flicked through and asked if she could look at it later. Richard agreed.

They went on to discuss other projects that Richard funded, like the drop in center for ex servicemen in London. He explained that when he had read about the many homeless and injured servicemen returning to

England he decided that he should do something. It was only a small center, but quite popular he believed.

"The old boys go to talk about the war I think." He added, "Many of them love to relive their experiences, and to talk to people who went through similar times"

Paris continued to question, and Richard answer.

Eventually they returned to the subject of the nursing school. Richard stared at the coffee table and thought. His silence made Andros and Vanni both stop working and watch. It was obviously a subject that worried him. Eventually Andros spoke

"If this is too much Richard I'm sure Paris can stop for today"

"It is hard you are right. The thing is if I tell you about that I will need to tell the whole story or it will not make sense. I cannot lie and make something up, so here goes. It seems strange that I went so many years without telling anyone, and now within the space of a few days I will have told my story twice".

Andros and Vanni were mesmerized as Richard began his tale. Paris had no need for questions and she let him speak, she switched on her tape machine and sat back. Up until then she had been making notes, but now she wanted to watch his face as he spoke, it changed so often as he talked, she could see he was reliving the time. It was fascinating. All three of them were enthralled by his remarkable story.

"So you see the reason for the school now. I owe my life to that little girl, she was my nurse and I really hope she survived." He sat back shattered and emotional "It's thanks to your wonderful mother I have been able to speak like this you know" He stared right into Andros's eyes and it was then he realised how much Richard already loved her.

Paris was ecstatic

"Richard, thank you so much. This is definitely the piece of the decade. It will keep me busy for days. Do you want to read it before I e-mail it to the UK?" She asked excitedly.

"No my dear. I will trust your judgment." He smiled "But promise me one thing." She nodded willing to agree to anything at that moment. Her editor would be on cloud nine when he received this article. "Please do not send it until after the ceremony. I would like you to wait until then" She agreed a little reluctantly, but she did agree to wait.

"May I have a photograph to send with it?" Paris asked. Andros thought she was pushing it a little now. Richard was such a shy person deep down.

"Only if you wait until I have my award". Richard had just made his mind up about a very important thing. "Shall we go for a little lunch now" He glanced at the grandfather clock in the corner as it struck 2. They all began to sort their work ready for the break. "Andros may I have a word?"

"Of course Richard." He stayed behind the desk as the other two left. "Is something wrong?" He could see the frown on Richards face." Has all of that bothered you?" He knew his mother would be furious if Richard was in anyway upset.

"No dear man, nothing like that"

When they joined the others on the patio both were smiling broadly. Richard kissed Eleni on the cheek and sat down beside her.

"Sorry to have left you on your own for so long. We have had a very interesting morning"

"Oh I haven't been alone. Eleni and I have been walking in the garden and talking about her party. It was a lovely night don't you agree" Richard nodded blushing slightly. Andros smiled to himself realising the meaning of his mother's words.

"Well after lunch I shall reclaim my computer" He looked across at Vanni, "I need to do a little work and then I am all yours. How would you all like to go out tonight? Paris, I leave it in your capable hands to find us somewhere for a nice meal. My treat" Richards eyes shone as he spoke "It will be the first time ever for me, so make it somewhere special please. If you make it for about 9 it will give me time for a short rest."

They continued their lunch chatting about Eleni's party and her mountain of presents. She told them about her and Vanni's plans to build a home on the beach and made him promise to phone Tomas after lunch.

"You don't like to wait for anything do you?" He said laughing "Little miss I want now" She punched him in the ribs returning his laughter.

"Well I will have to this time. Big brother says I must" She looked at Andros, who just nodded. "But at least it will give us time to plan a lovely house and get it built. You know how fast they work in Greece.

It might take even longer than a year" They all laughed and nodded in agreement at that comment.

"Right" said Richard. "Time for a little stroll and then to work" He took Eleni's arm and led her towards the garden "I'm sorry, you have been around here this morning, but I want you to myself for a few moments" They strolled and chatted. Examined the wonderful flowers, at this time of year still in full bloom.

"Some of these remind me of home," She said gently stroking a bright red poppy.

"Eleni" Richard said taking both her hands in his. "Would you like to go and choose an outfit for the ceremony? I am going to order my morning suit this afternoon and would like it if you would be my special guest. I have been given two seats and have promised Michael one, the other is yours. I have asked Andros to speak to Paris. She will go with you. I do not want to see it until the day, I would like it to be a surprise." He stared at her "The only problem is the colour. I have had a letter giving me the instructions for the day, and the Queen will be wearing light blue. Not one of your colours I imagine anyway, but I thought I would just let you know" Eleni put her fingers over his lips to silence him.

"Richard you are babbling now. But yes I will go and find something appropriate, I will speak with Paris later." They continued their stroll and inspection of the garden before returning to the patio.

"Paris would you do me a huge favour?" Aunt Eleni asked, "Come with me to find a suitable outfit for the ceremony"

"I would love to Eleni. Tomorrow?" She enquired; "This afternoon I have a meal to sort out" she teased Richard. "No peace for the wicked"

Vanni and Eleni left the table and went off to phone Tomas, Andros and Paris stayed talking, and Richard took Eleni to his office. She watched as he began to type his e-mail, looking up now and then deep in thought. Suddenly with a flourish he hit a key and raised his arm.

"That's it. Two morning suits ordered."

"Two?" she queried

"Of course my dear. One for me, and one for Michael. I hope he will be pleased."

"You are such a kind and generous man. I'm sure he will be more than pleased, but how do you know his size?"

"I order all of mine and his from London. Can't have a shabby butler eh" He smiled warmly at her. "They keep our measurements and I just pick the materials etc. Easier than trawling through the shops for him, and of course me up until now. Mind you I can't imagine I will ever do anything else but order from London. Now just a little bit of work on my shares and then for a lie down. Would you care to join me madam?" His face lit with a boyish grin.

"Of course Sir Richard." She replied blushing very slightly.

She sat on the sofa and watched as he worked. She noticed how he frowned one second and then smiled, his fingers slowly tapping at the keys.

Andros and Paris entered the room after knocking at the door.

"I'll just finish off if that's OK?" he asked Richard, who gestured for him to sit at the other desk. It shook Eleni to see her son behind his father's desk as if it were his own. The resemblance was striking she had always known that, but here in this room, it brought Marco back to life.

"Be my guest. How is it all going?" Richard replied picking up his pen and scribbling down a few notes.

"Just a little more really. I don't think I will need to work tomorrow, not on Eleni's things anyway. Just a little of my own and then I can have a few days off before we return to Athens"

Richard put down his pen and looked across to the other desk.

"Andros I want you to take over my business, in fact I have decided I'm going to give it all to you."

Andros was shocked

"But you can't"

" Yes I can. In return I will ask for a handsome allowance, so don't worry about me being penniless. Marco and I built this up together and as you are his son it is only right that you should have a share. I would like you to manage Eleni's inheritance, and the rest is yours. But as I say I will expect an allowance"

"But Richard" Eleni interrupted

"No Eleni. I have made my mind up and it is like a weight has been lifted. I will be free to do what I want. I already have more than enough to see me through, and I have two wonderful houses. One of which I am going to sell perhaps even both. And now it is time for me to see some of the world. I have the yacht and intend to use it for myself. I want to see Athens for myself" He smiled at her.

Andros was speechless, as he noticed was Paris.

"So tomorrow Andros, whilst these lovely ladies are shopping, we will get things moving" He nodded as if that was the end of things.

"Time for my rest. Eleni?" He stood and held out his hand. "A rest for you too I think. We will see you both later." With that they left the still astonished pair.

Paris could see Andros was emotional. It was a wonderful gift Richard had just given him, not just in the monetary context, but the fact that it was connected to his father. She walked over and stood behind him gently massaging his shoulders. There was no need to say anything as slowly her fingers worked their magic.

"I think I need a rest after that" he said eventually "I feel stunned"

"Come on then. Let me show you how to relax properly"

Paris was brilliant in the art of full massage and he smiled knowing what it would lead to.

"Now you are one of the riches men in the world I think I had better make it a very special afternoon" She leant over and switched off his computer before leading him from the room.

"My room I think. Can't have Michael thinking I'm spending all of the time in yours"

Andros let himself be led like a child. He was still in shock, Richard had just given him part of his father, and for that he would be eternally grateful.

# • CHAPTER 16 •

Paris sat Andros by the window whilst she ran a warm, deep bath. She poured wonderfully smelling oils into the cascading water before testing it with her hand, and then she lit aromatic candles placing them around the bathroom. She stood back and surveyed her work before fetching the still shocked man.

He let her slowly take off his clothes and held her hand as he stepped into the water. Once he had lain down and was beginning to relax she returned to the bedroom and rang Michael. She asked for wine and fruit to be brought to her room.

"You cheeky thing" Andros said laughing

"Well Richard did say if there was anything that we required" she replied. Whilst she waited she flicked through her diary and looked for a restaurant. She picked one she knew and phoned. It had fabulous views of the city, close to the river, and from what she could remember the seafood was exquisite. Richard had left it a little late, but once the manager realised whom the table was for there was no problem. He was pleased to give them the best table in the house.

A knock at the door announced the arrival of the fruit and wine.

"He's not daft that Michael is he?" She said filling the glasses. "I never said it was for two, but he must have known," She giggled at the thought of the slightly stuffy butler knowing they were both in her room. "Right now to sort you out" She took the drinks and handed Andros his. He watched as she slowly took off her clothes "Move over let me in"

They were the last ones to appear on the patio later that evening, but Eleni could see her son looked much more like his old self. He had been shocked by Richards gift and it had showed on his face. Now though he positively glowed. Well done Paris, she said to herself.

Richard was impressed by the choice of restaurant, and could not get over the way the waiters fussed over them as they ate.

"It's because you are who you are" Paris said "Having you here is a big feather in their cap, and they will let everyone know believe me." Their meals were superb, and as Paris had promised the fish exquisite.

Vanni and young Eleni talked throughout of their plans for the new home. Having spoken to Tomas that afternoon, who was more than pleased to give them the land by the beach, it was all systems go. They talked about bedrooms, bathrooms and furniture, and Andros could see just how excited they were. He would keep his news for another day and was pleased to notice Richard said nothing either.

Champagne was ordered to accompany their dessert and Richard stood to make a toast.

"Thank you all" he said quite emotionally "To tomorrow and beyond" He raised his glass and gazed at Eleni. Andros noticed the spark that lit his mother's eyes, and he smiled to himself. That was one exceptional man she was looking at. They echoed the toast and once again Andros watched his mother, but he noticed this time she looked away sadly.

The journey home was a noisy affair. The wine and champagne had loosened their tongues, all except Richard and his mother Andros noticed. They sat side by side in silence. Perhaps young Eleni's enthusiasm for the new house was a little overwhelming for them.

"I think I will take a little stroll in the garden before retiring" Aunt Eleni said as the car pulled to a halt outside the magnificent house. "It will help settle that lovely meal" She smiled at Richard. "Thank you for a fabulous night"

"That is a good idea mama. Would you mind if I came with you?" Andros wanted to speak to his mother alone. Paris felt a little snubbed. She had further plans for his body, but they would now have to wait.

Richard watched as Andros and his mother walked across the lawn towards the flowerbeds. He too was concerned. He had noticed Eleni's silence and wondered if he had done something to upset her. He asked for coffee on the patio and sat down to wait for their return.

Andros took his mothers arm.

"Mama what is wrong. I noticed in the restaurant you looked a little sad. Please tell me"

They sat at the little table by the bush.

"It is difficult Andros. You see I came here to feel close to Marco, and have ended up falling in love with his friend. At my ripe old age I have found love, but I am afraid. I cannot live here, I don't feel comfortable, and New York stifles me. Tonight in the restaurant all I could see were those tall buildings and masses of lights across the river. I want to look out of a window and see the Acropolis, or the Aegean, not piles of concrete." She paused for a moment "My problem is I don't know what to say to Richard. I have mentioned to him that I am not comfortable here, but I don't think he realizes just what that means. If I go back to Athens I will loose him, if I stay I will be unhappy. Please tell me what to do. Today he gave you his business and said he wants to travel on his yacht. I could cope with that, nice places to see and fresh air, but he didn't ask me. I am so confused" Her voice trembled.

"Oh mama. You have no need to worry. This afternoon, just before lunch, Richard asked me if I thought you would marry him. He said he was going to ask you, but wanted to talk to me first. He wants to be with you whether it is in Athens, or on his yacht. He is worried that you will turn him down." He gave a laugh "I think the two of you are as confused as each other." He hugged her close "Just like a pair of teenagers. Come on lets go and join him I can see he is waiting, but promise me this you will not let him know I have told you. He doesn't want anyone knowing just yet." He kissed her brow and helped her to stand.

By the time they reached Richard she was smiling.

"Eleni was something wrong?" his face was showing his deep concern.

"No Richard. Nothing was wrong. I just needed that little walk. I think I have eaten too much. May I join you for coffee, and then I think bed" She sat at his side and watched as he filled another cup.

"Andros?"

"No thank you. I have a busy day tomorrow so its bed for me now" Andros knew Paris would be waiting, although after this afternoon's session he didn't feel much like making love. Sometimes she forgot just how much younger than him she was.

The older couple sat in the warm night air, this time in a more comfortable silence. Richard was first to speak.

"Andros is right, tomorrow will be a busy day. I must start to transfer things over to him and I want him to help me sell the other house. He has spoken with young Eleni and she is very happy for him to run her side of things so it should not be too long before everything is sorted." He reached over and held her hand. "I was so frightened for a while then. You looked so unhappy and I felt so useless. Please tell me." His voice was pleading.

She rubbed his hand and told him of her fears. She spoke of her conversation with Andros, but did not mention what he had told her.

"It sounds so silly to say I am in love at my age, but Richard I am"

"Eleni I love you too" He kissed her cheek. "Take me to Athens"

"Pardon?"

"Take me to Athens. If we are behaving like teenagers as Andros said, lets us do it properly. Come on why wait? At our age why wait for anything?" He giggled happily as he spoke.

Leading her into the office Richard switched on his computer. The screen sprang to life and he started to tap on the keyboard.

"There you see. Tomorrow morning 9 am a direct flight to Athens." He tapped away again and as before finished with a flourish. "That's it then. Booked."

"You have got to be kidding me. We can't just go like that."

"Yes we can my dear, and more to the point we are." He went to the bell pull and summoned Michael. He explained the situation to an ever more surprised butler and asked for the car to be ready, he also asked him to inform Andros as soon as he was able.

"What about your passport? You will need a passport" Eleni was trembling with shock.

"I have it here" Richard pulled it from the desk draw "Never given up the old British passport, well European, even though I had no intention of going any where. Doesn't have that nice ring does it European passport. I am English and proud of it." he laughed. "Come on let's pack" he took the stunned woman by the hand and led her to her room. "You won't need much my dear and you can take me shopping when we get there if I forget anything." He opened her door "Right I will go and get my things. Can I put them is your case? I have just remembered, I might have a passport, but do not have a case. Silly me" Richard sounded like an excited child as he left her standing open mouthed.

She stayed motionless for a few moments and then began to laugh. This man was incredible; all of her earlier fears had now disappeared. Before she had time to decide on what to take Richard was back, his arms full of clothes.

"How long are we going for and month?" she laughed, "I thought we were shopping once we got there?"

"To be honest Eleni I haven't got a clue. The last time I traveled was to here and all I had was on my back. Help" She sorted through his things and gave a lot back. She remembered to pack brand new shirts and underwear, but decided on only one suit, and one pair of trousers. A couple of jackets and she was done.

Her things took up very little space, and it was a good job. She had all she would need at home so why bother, she thought. Remembering home she picked up the phone and rang to warn them. She could tell they were as shocked as Michael.

Richard sat mesmerized as she spoke in her native tongue. It was the first time he had heard her, and loved her singsong voice.

"Michael is going to wake us early, so come on lets get into that lovely bed" he said when she had finished her conversation "You can speak Greek to me. It made me shiver all over when I heard you"

"You are one crazy man." she laughed.

Andros first down for breakfast, found it highly amusing when Michael broke the news.

"Sir Richard has asked me to tell you, you will find all you need to begin the transfers in his desk." He added after telling him about his mother's trip "And he also asked if would you be good enough to inform the others"

"I certainly will" Andros replied wondering how young Eleni would take the news. He waited until all four of them were round the table and dropped his bombshell.

"If we had known we could have gone with them," Eleni wailed. "We could have gone to see Tomas."

Paris too was a little put out.

"I wanted to ask a few more questions. I could have gone with them as well" She whined.

"Eleni, Paris, has it not occurred to you that they want to be alone" Vanni said quietly. "And in any case we go back in a couple of days. Don't be so impatient" It was true Eleni had forgotten that their stay was coming to an end. So much had happened in the last week or so, it had slipped her mind completely.

Much later on in the day when Andros was at Marco's desk, and Vanni working at Richard's the telephone rang. It was his mother. They had arrived safely, and she wanted to apologise to him. She told him how Richard had treated it all as a big adventure and was now completely in love with flying.

If he needed any advice on the paperwork he was to phone, but not be surprised if they were out. Richard wanted to see everything she said.

She sounded so happy it made Andros smile. He said his goodbyes and told her to behave, a comment that made her giggle.

Paris came into the office just as he replaced the receiver

"Why don't I come with you when you go back?" she asked him. "I would love to talk to Richard a little more, and you can show me where Vanni is going to live."

Andros was pleased. This would be his chance. Take her to Skiathos and then on to Kefalonia. Plus it would give them more time to be together.

"I think I can arrange that. Why don't you look on the Internet and book it now?" He said. "This is our flight number" He passed her a note. "All you will have to do is change mama's ticket"

Within minutes Paris had done just that.

"What did we ever do without computers" she sighed "Right to work" she set about Richards story with vigor.

Eleni felt at a loose end and more than a little unsettled. The other three all had their work to do so she decided to visit the center. A trip to the doctors might not be a bad idea either, she was thinking of all the unprotected sex she was enjoying, but the center needs me and it may be the last chance I get, but at least I know it will survive. The center won.

Marco had left a generous provision in his Will, which meant it would be able to continue. She was pleased about that; it had always been a favorite project of his, and now hers too.

Andros would be angry that she had gone without telling anyone, but tough, today she felt a bit rebellious.

She brought her car to a skidding halt, as usual, and went to join the other workers. They were delighted to see her; another pair of hands was always welcome. She started in the kitchen. Sacks of vegetables needed washing and chopping before going in the huge metal saucepans already on the cookers.

She stood at a sink by the window and stared out over the beach and river as she worked. She smiled to herself, as she thought of Richard and Eleni flying off like that, so romantic. It was hard for her to believe that he had actually gone. All those years of staying in the house grounds and now it seemed there was no stopping him. She wondered what aunt Eleni had said that had made such a difference, but what ever it was it had worked.

Suddenly she put her knife down and stared towards the river. A beautiful white yacht was gliding into the marina a little further up the beach. It was her father's.

"Here they come" the head cook announced, "Richards children are back" Eleni was stunned and asked what she meant.

"Its one of the trips he organizes. Children from deprived homes, and disabled kids. They have holidays on the yacht. They meet their parents here when they return so come on let's look lively. Get that coffee on and those muffins" She clapped her hands emphasizing her words.

The others workers sprang to life while Eleni took in the news. Her yacht used for children's holidays, it must have been Richard who bought it from her then.

She was soon brought out of her trance like state as the room erupted in noise. Children of all ages and ethnic origins were descending upon them. They quickly found seats at the long central table, or made room for those in wheelchairs. Paper, pencils and crayons were produced and they all set about drawing and writing about their adventures. The staff served cola and muffins, and then coffee as the parents began to arrive.

"This sort of holiday means the world to these kids" A voice said at her side "That Mr. Graves is such a generous man" Eleni looked at the woman beside her. Her clothes were worn, and her hair lank. She watched as she approached a little girl in a wheelchair and bent to hug her. The little girl's face lit up as the woman kissed her. She waved to the others as her mother pushed her towards the pile of cases now by the door, handing Eleni a crude picture of a dolphin as she passed.

"Please give this to Mr. Richard and tell him Sally said thank you. It was amazing. Best thing ever in my life" Eleni looked at the crayon drawing and began to cry.

"It gets us all like that at first" The head cook said "Look I have a handful" she waved a pile of paper. "Come on lets have a drink" She led Eleni to the serving hatch and handed her a steaming mug. "Deep breath now, come on, don't let them see you upset. They have just had the holiday of a lifetime and they don't want to see tears" Eleni did as she was told and began to feel a little better.

Richard, what a lovely man you are, papa would be so pleased that his yacht was being used for something as wonderful as this, she said to herself.

The staff from the yacht had arrived and the afternoon flew as they all helped parents to be reunited with their children and luggage. She noticed a few of the children only had little rucksacks for their belongings and it reminded her of the one she had left in Athens. It seemed so long ago now since she had set off with it on her back. Her journey had turned up so much in such a short time it was hard to take it all in at times.

She was soon jolted from her thoughts as more parents arrived, or carers in the case of some.

Every child had only good things to say as they left and they had all either written a little letter or drawn a picture for Richard. As she bent to listen to another tale of their holiday Eleni realised how important it had been to them. They chattered non-stop about their adventures and she found herself laughing along with them as they told their stories.

Eleni learned that it had lasted three days and during that time they had sailed down the coast, had a bar b que on a beach, swam in the warm sea, and even had some school lessons on board. Richard had provided nursing staff for those with problems, and she learned how the disabled children had enjoyed having their treatment up on deck. Better than being in hospital, she heard one boy say, I hope I can come again, he continued and then handed her a letter he had written. She hoped Richard had made provisions for this to continue and she decided to speak to him and ask if she could contribute.

Once they had all gone Eleni and the other center staff sat down to recover. They were all exhausted.

"It's like this every time." The head cook said sipping at her coffee "Right make the most of this it will soon be time to get ready for the evening rush. How's that soup doing?" She got a mumbled reply from the kitchen. "OK, then lets talk"

Eleni spent some time telling them about her plans to live in Greece and how she hoped that she would be able to come over a couple of times a year, promising to keep up her birthday treat.

She collected the children's pictures and letters flicking through them as she walked to her car. Some were good, some a little strange, but she noticed every one had a name and kisses on.

What a lovely rewarding afternoon it had been.

# • Chapter •
## 17

The beaming faces of Richard and his mother were the first thing Andros saw as he walked through the arrivals gate.

Almost immediately he could smell that wonderful aroma of Greece. It had been a long and at times bumpy flight from New York but now walking towards the smiling couple he felt invigorated. Home again. Eleni greeted them all with a hug and kisses, Richard gave firm handshakes.

"How has it gone?" He asked as Andros wheeled his case towards the waiting limousine.

"Nearly all done thanks. Just a few papers for you to sign and that's it. Oh, the house in the city is for sale. I contacted that estate agent like you said and he is sorting that. Its all in here" he patted his briefcase. "More to the point how are things here?"

"It is the best thing I have ever done. Your mother was right. Athens is a wonderful city, so full of marvelous things. I don't think I have seen half of them yet." Richard looked at him beaming, and then added quietly "You know I did the most surprising thing. I proposed to her at the Acropolis." Andros stopped walking "I got down on one knee right there at the top, can you believe it. Me in all of that dust." He went silent remembering the day

"Well come on Richard tell me?"

"She said yes. I am so lucky. Its still hush hush though. She is a little worried young Eleni might get a bit over excited, so mum's the word for now. I want to tell the world, but she is the boss" He put his finger to his smiling mouth. Andros patted his back

"Congratulations, and don't worry I won't say a thing. Promise"

They all piled into the huge limousine, chattering loudly as it sped towards Eleni's home.

"You know I don't think I will ever get tired of these sights," Richard said quietly to Eleni "Thank you so much for bringing me here"

"What do you mean? Me bringing you here, you kidnapped me." She replied laughing "But you are right. I don't think there is a person on earth who would tire of such lovely things to see. Everywhere has it's own beauty even New York, but I feel that city is for the young, this is more for the likes of you and me."

The car pulled up at the front of the house where waiting staff were soon taking suitcases to their rooms.

"I fancy a swim," young Eleni said stretching "I feel like a prune after that flight"

"Good idea. Mind if I join you" Paris also felt in need of a little exercise.

"See you down there in a mo" Eleni was impatient. "Vanni what about you?"

"No. You two go ahead. Andros and I have things to do." He replied.

"You two are always working" Eleni shouted as she ran up the stairs to fetch her costume.

Minutes later she was in the water. The two women swam in silence to begin with. It was so nice to feel the water on their skin, feel their limbs stretch after being in the plane for so long. They decided to have a lay in the sun to complete their relaxation treatment.

"I don't know "Paris said, "We spend all of that time sitting down, but I feel like I have run a marathon. I must be getting old, flights never used to bother me, but this last couple have. Fancy a drink?" She walked over to the little bar

"Ouzo and lemonade please. It's seems ages since I had one, oh and lots of ice thanks."

Paris passed the drink over before lying on the remaining sun bed.

They let the sun's rays sink into their skin and Paris began to talk. She spoke about Richard without giving too much of his story away. She realised Eleni would find it distressing to know the whole truth so she began to talk about Marco. She asked a couple of questions and the replies soon had her brain working overtime. What a story Eleni had.

She told her about her trip to find out why he had been going to Skiathos, the photographs and how they related to her father, and how they also told aunt Eleni's story. Paris was intrigued. She began to probe, cursing that she had not got her tape machine with her. It was such a fantastic story.

"We must go to Skiathos and you can show me the photographs. I know you want to go anyway, but would you and Vanni mind if I tagged along?"

"Of course not." Eleni replied, "Why are you going to do an article on my father?"

"I think a book is more appropriate." Paris was deep in thought" I could combine Richards story with that of Marco and aunt Eleni." Now she was excited, her weariness gone in a flash, her eyes once again sparkling." You know I have been coming to this house for years and never once suspected that there would be such a story here. Right under my nose at that, I never even queried it when Andros told me about you. He just said he had been reunited with his younger sister. I am definitely getting old if I missed that remark."

"When would you like to go over to the island?" Eleni asked not aware of the other woman's excitement. "If it were up to me I would go tomorrow. I can't wait to get back to the beach. I have really missed it, even though I had only been there a short while I felt like it was home. Do you understand?" Paris nodded her mind already buzzing.

She would do a short article on Richard when he received his award, that would be the taster, and then she would do a book of all three stories. She could make this her parting assignment. She knew she would never get anything better than this, and her mind was made up. Andros would be pleased she knew, perhaps she should surprise him and turn the tables. Ask him to marry her, but that could wait for now. No rush, after all they will have been together for 10 years soon. No point in rushing now.

It was obvious to her that evening that Andros, Vanni and Richard had much to do over the next few days, so she suggested to Eleni that they go over to the island on their own.

"You can all join us later" she said, "Can you phone Tomas and ask if we can have one of his houses for a while please Andros."

"Why don't you stay with me at the beach Paris. I'm sure Tomas and Sofia would love to have you" Eleni asked her. "Vanni do you think Tomas would let Paris have your room for a while?"

"I will ask him for you. When will you be going"? He replied

"Tomorrow" the both chorused.

"I'm afraid I won't be able to fly you over" Andros said "I have too much to do here, but I will get the driver to take you to the ferry."

"You can fly?" Richard was amazed "You never told me he could fly Eleni."

"Don't get too excited Richard. I only have a license for small aircraft, mine is only a four seater. It comes in handy when mama is in Alonysos. I can just go over to Skiathos and then across on the boat taxi. It makes life much easier. But like I say it's only a small plane"

"I don't care. Will you take me up for a spin one day." Richard was like a little boy "Sorry I should have said please." They all laughed at the look of horror on his face in forgetting his manners.

"I certainly will. When do you plan to go mama?" Andros asked.

"When you have some spare time Andros. I will leave it in your hands. If Paris and Eleni are going tomorrow, we four can go whenever you can have the time" Eleni looked over to Richard "But I think it had better be sooner than later, before Richard bursts"

"Right then. Lets say you two go alone tomorrow and we will come over in a couple of days."

"Great" said Richard "I for one can't wait. Will you be able to show me a few of the islands as we fly over?"

"Richard just remember we have got to be back in New York soon." Eleni reminded him "It will have to be a short visit this time. We can always go again"

The girls packed their things that night and both made sure their men were happy.

Paris gave Andros another of her superb bathtub massages before slowly seducing him on the bed. Sensuously she rubbed aromatic oils into his warm skin. She began at his toes and then gradually made her way towards his stomach, flexing her fingers and teasing him as she went. Having reached his neck she began to go back towards his feet. Stopping to lick and tease once again. When she was satisfied that he could not wait any longer she straddled him and began to rock. His hands held on to her slim hips, trying to move her quicker, pushing her body down to take every part of him that she could. They collapsed together, breathing heavily.

Andros held her still momentarily, allowing himself time to recover.

"That has got to be top of my list for how I wish to die," he said eventually." Paris. I love you" He held her to his chest and kissed her tenderly. "You know that don't you. I really love you woman"

"Yes I do. And I love you" She kissed him back. "I think I will get one of Tomas's houses, you know. It will give us time to be alone rather than with everyone at the beach and you can rest. You work far too hard you know. Work Work Work, it will do you no good."

"That sounds a good idea, I'll leave it up to you" He purred. Slowly he rolled her to the vacant part of the bed and pulled the sheet over them. "Now to sleep. You have an early start" They curled around each other and began to relax.

In young Eleni's room it was a similar picture, but they still being in the early days of their relationship, had made love without finesse. It was still a case of fire with these two. Not waiting until they were naked before Vanni taken his woman. They had ripped at each other's clothes the second the door was closed. Vanni pushed her up against the door and pulled open her blouse roughly, while she undid his shirt and scratched at his chest. Undoing the buttons on her skirt he let it fall to the floor.

"I think you needed that," she said breathlessly a short while later.

"I'm sorry my love. Let me treat you like a lady now" He carried her to the bed and began to stroke her soft skin. Their youth and energy allowing them to be able to make love once again so quickly after their first encounter.

Richard was just content to hold aunt Eleni in his arms and kiss her tenderly. As they lay entwined he talked about Andros's plane. He was so excited he could hardly wait. Eleni realised that so many things were new to him after his years as a virtual hermit, she just hoped they would be given time to experience many more. She knew age was against them, but promised in her mind to show him as much as she could. They slowly drifted off to sleep, finding a warm comfort just being together.

The girls had already left when breakfast was served and the others sat in the conservatory watching the boats leave from Piraeus.

"I wonder if they are on one of those?" Richard said innocently peering through the glass wall. "Perhaps I should go and wave to them all" He realised just what he had said and was mortified "Oh Eleni I am so sorry. I let my tongue get carried away."

"Don't worry Richard. It was many years ago." But the remark had stung her slightly.

From the ferry the girls were looking the other way, the house was far in the distance but they could see the sun glinting on the conservatory windows.

"I bet they are all in there having a nice breakfast," Paris said as she strained her eyes. "Better than the ferry food anyway."

"Oh I quite enjoyed my pastry. Not as good as Tomas's, but OK for now" Eleni replied. "Come on let's go to the front and see if we can spot some dolphins"

They made they way cautiously along the deck. The ferry was rolling slightly as it sailed out of the harbor. They were lucky; this early ferry was not over full so they managed to get seats right at the front.

The wind blew Eleni's hair back and she turned her face up towards the sun. She remembered her first journey and how she had thrown the flowers. She told Paris and when the time came pointed to where she thought they had gone. All the time Paris was making notes in her mind, and could hardly wait to add the things she had learned to her computer files.

It was quite a long voyage, much further than from Thessalonica and Eleni got a little bored. It was to Paris's advantage though, she fetched them some coffee and began to probe further. Eleni pleased to have something to think about told her as much as she knew.

"I think once I have talked to Tomas and Alexi a trip to Kefalonia is on the cards." Paris said her thoughts out loud. "I need to get the feel of their village and see for myself the places the photographs were taken"

"Can I come with you? I would love to see where my father lived as a boy. It was on my list of places to go the first time I came, but things and people got in the way."

"I think we should all go. I bet aunt Eleni would like to go back too." Paris said with enthusiasm "And I'm sure Richard would"

"I'm not so sure Paris. It might upset her, you will have to tread carefully"

They watched as the ferry was steered carefully into Skiathos harbor and listened as the crew shouted to each other. Although the ferry had not been full, it still seemed crowded as everyone made their way towards the stairs together. People pushed and shoved, and the girls became parted.

"See you in a minute" Paris shouted as Eleni got swept away with a crowd. "Wait for me over there" She pointed to one of the red kiosks.

"OK" was all Eleni could reply as once again her tiny frame was moved involuntarily. She almost fell down the wooden bridge and onto the harbor, pleased to be on dry land again. She walked over to the kiosk to wait and looked around. I bet it hasn't changed in centuries, she thought as she gazed at the tavernas and bars. She caught the lovely smell of garlic and herbs and closed her eyes. Wonderful, she took another deep breath, this time it was of car fumes.

"Ugh!" she said out loud and turned to see Nicos drive down the harbor road in his car. The sight made her jump slightly. She had forgotten all about him, but how could she forget the man that had made her a woman? She promised herself that one day soon she would go to see him and explain, even thank him, well no perhaps not thank him exactly.

Paris ran over to her side.

"Are you OK? What a scramble that was"

"Yes I'm fine. Come on lets get a taxi" They linked arms and made their way over to the line of waiting cars. "Eleni beach please" she asked.

The driver constantly turned to talk as they sped along the road. He was pleased to have two such good looking women in his car and wanted to make a good impression. In fact he was doing the opposite. His lack of concentration was terrifying them and they could not wait for the journey to end. Both breathed a sigh of relief as the car skidded to a halt in the clearing. Eleni paid as Paris admired the view.

"This is wonderful. I have never seen anything so beautiful" her reaction was the same as Eleni's had been that first day.

"Come on this way" Eleni led her towards the taverna. Tomas spotted them and quickly came over. He hugged and kissed them both even though it was the first time he had met Paris.

"Welcome to Eleni beach Paris. Come, come. Let me show you your room."

Paris was dumbstruck, so this was aunt Eleni's twin brother. She could see a resemblance in his eyes and mouth, but that was it. This lovely old man was wrinkled by the sun and hard work. She followed the other two over to the house and stared at its front before entering. She tried to remember every detail as her journalists mind once again took over.

Tomas opened the door to the middle room and beckoned her in.

"This will be yours." He said with a smile. Paris nodded and thanked him. He showed her the adjoining bathroom and opened the spare wardrobe with a flourish.

He was so pleased and excited to have them both there, he almost fell over his own feet as he rushed around the room.

His nephew's lady, and how glamorous she was, plus Eleni, his son's wife to be. Sofia will have so much to ask them, he thought as he continued to buzz about. Eventually he left them in peace.

Paris unpacked her things and plugged in her computer. She began to tap away as soon as it sprung to life.

"Come on you. That can wait" Eleni stood in the door way already in her swimming costume. "Let's go and see Sofia and then have a swim"

"You go. I will come in a bit. I must just get some of this down and then I will join you. I will send Andros an e-mail whilst I'm about it. Let him know we are here." Paris didn't even look up she was so engrossed in her writing.

Eleni left Paris tapping away and went to see Sofia. She hardly had time to ask about her arm before the old lady engulfed her in a hug.

"Oh its on the mend" she said holding up a now rather grubby plastered arm. "The sooner this is off the better"

They hugged and kissed, Sofia cried, she was so happy.

"How is my little boy?" She eventually asked, "I am so pleased he is coming home. It is all thanks to you Eleni." She hugged her again. "Now where is Paris?"

Eleni explained that she was typing on her computer and would be down shortly. She sat down at the table by the bar and began to sip a long cool glass of fresh orange juice with just a hint of ouzo. Delicious.

Paris slowly walked along the sand, her feet kicking up the soft warm powder as she moved. This is heaven, she thought to herself. She looked across at the sea, rippling slowly on to the shore. Some people were swimming and others just lying in the sun. It was a different world to what she was used to, so calm and relaxing.

"Welcome Paris" Sofia greeted her with a hug and kisses "Please sit. Let me get you a drink" Paris joined her friend at the little table by the bar.

Eleni waved to the couple on the swinging chair. They must have the best job in the world, she thought, staying in such a wonderful spot as this with only her to look after. She had noticed them in a taverna when the ferry had docked, obviously they were expecting her. She wondered what they had done while she had been away, but looking at them she could see they were much closer than before and occasionally she saw them hold hands. Perhaps Greece had spun her magic on her minders at last?

"I can see why you want to live here," Paris said sipping at her cooling drink "It is wonderful" Eleni nodded in agreement.

They finished their drinks and went for a nice long swim. No need for a towel here, they just lay on sun beds let ting the heat of the sun and the gentle breeze dry their bodies.

"No more work for today" Paris said stretching almost cat like "I'm going to enjoy the rest of today and then start tomorrow" She yawned and rolled over. "Heaven"

Paris forgot her words that evening as she sat at the little table making notes. Eleni had happily resumed her job behind the bar and being alone gave her time to reflect. Her pen rushed across the pad, as she wrote quickly not wanting to miss or forget anything.

This was definitely going to be her parting piece and she wanted to make it perfect.

# · CHAPTER · 18

Paris was in her element. She had e-mailed her interview with the President before leaving Athens, and had received rave reviews plus a very large credit to her bank account. She may well be the woman of a very, very rich man but that did not stop her enjoying her independence money wise.

Her small piece on Richard had also been sent, and hopefully that too would be received well. No one had ever interviewed him before and for it to be printed on the day of his award, she knew it would make an impact, although it would be nothing compared to when the full interview was published.

Hopefully she would be able to follow it up with a photograph of the day and a further interview with his reaction. She knew he was a patriot and for him to meet the Queen and be knighted would be the highlight of his life. He had promised not to speak to any other journalists, but she realised there would be many there waiting to pounce. He would be expected to say a few words and she hoped he would keep them to a minimum. If his photograph appeared with just a small paragraph in the newspapers, leaving her article to take center stage, she would be one happy lady.

Now she was able to take her time, well a couple of days, to start her next project. She already had a mountain of notes to piece together; it seemed as every time she spoke to someone they had another piece of the story to tell.

She watched Eleni as she served customers their drinks. It was lovely to see how happy she was, and slightly incredible knowing how much she was worth. This girl need never work for her living, she was immensely rich, and yet here she was carrying trays of drinks and chatting to the customers as if she were just the same as them. Perhaps her next book would be based upon her?

Paris went back to her notes. I'm getting carried away; she thought to herself, I haven't started this book yet.

Tomorrow she would try to talk to Tomas and then she wanted to speak to Alexi. She realised that this short break would not be long enough for her needs; it was a pity really that she had to go back to New York, but that was her life. Jetting here and there, sometimes only staying in a country for a few hours before flying on again. She had always reveled in the excitement of meeting famous people knowing that the man in the street would read every word, but now something had changed. Perhaps because she had interviewed just about every Head of State, every President, even the Prime Minister, in fact very few people now interested her and she was loosing her appetite a little.

Richard's was going to be the crowning piece in her career, so where was there to go now?

Andros, that was where.

The following morning as she and Eleni sat at the little table eating the most delicious pastries she had ever tasted, she watched as Tomas went about his morning ritual. Sweeping the sand and laying out the sun beds, she began to make more notes.

"Don't you ever stop?" Eleni asked, "Every time you sit down you start to scribble away."

"Every time I sit down I see something else, or hear something else that will be used in my book" Paris replied smiling. "I don't think I will be very good company for these next few days. I have so much I want to ask everyone. Sorry"

"That's OK" Eleni replied, "I'm just happy to be here". She watched Tomas for a while "I think I will go into the town this morning if you are going to be busy. Do you want me to see Alexi for you? I could ask him to come here if you like."

"Yes please. That would be great, if you think he won't mind"

"No he will love it. Alexi and his son Nicos are ladies men and I'm sure he would be honored and flattered to come. I will ask this morning." Eleni left Paris to her notes and went to change.

She chose the pretty red sundress, tied her hair back, and made an effort with her make-up. She needed to feel nice to give her confidence. If she looked good, then she felt good.

The bus came within seconds of her getting to the stop. Timed that well, she thought to herself climbing on board.

"Stop no 1 please" she said and handed over her money. No spare seats this morning so she walked down the aisle and reached for one of the leather straps, that hung from the roof. It was quite a stretch for her and she had difficulty at times in staying upright as the bus sped down the road. She was glad to have put plenty of body spray on as her arm was stretched high quite close to an old ladies face. But it could have been far more unpleasant for the woman, she thought looking at some of the men on the bus.

By the time the bus reached Skiathos Town the bus was full to the brim. So many people crushed together it seemed quite unsafe.

Eleni was pleased when eventually she was able to step into the fresh air. She promised herself a taxi back. It might be a case keeping her eyes shut on the way, but she would at least have some room.

She had a stroll through the shops and treated herself to a nice pair of leather sandals; they were flat, strappy and amazingly comfortable. She found a lovely perfume shop and had a free spray of Flowers, cursing herself that she had left her own bottle in her room. The fabulous aroma freshened her up instantly.

Finally she reached the Athena Gallery and taking a deep breath entered. Nicos was talking to some customers and pointing out different photographs on the wall. He stammered slightly when he saw her, but continued until the sale had been completed. Eleni watched him for a while and then looked around herself. She stared at the photographs that had given her the answer to so many questions, and hoped Paris would see them when she spoke to Alexi.

"Kalimera Eleni. You look beautiful" Nicos came over and kissed her cheek. She felt his soft lips on her skin and his hands on her hips, he smelt wonderful. It was hardly surprising that she had fallen for him he just oozed sex appeal.

"Kalimera Nicos. It is good to see you. No hard feelings?" Her voice shook a little.

"No little one. I could not be angry with you for long. Do you forgive me also?" He thought about the young Swedish holidaymaker who had taken up his spare time since Eleni had left. She had returned home, and now Eleni was back, what a life!

She smiled and nodded, totally innocent of what he was thinking.

"Of course." She stretched up and kissed his cheek "And I have come to take you to lunch like I promised. When can you have your break"?

"This minute" He said. "Let me just tell mama and then I will be with you." He was already picking up the phone. He spoke quickly to Athena explaining that Eleni had called to take him to lunch and he would be out for a couple of hours. "Right then, I will shut up the shop and off we go" He rushed round pulling down the window shades and turning the door sign to closed.

It was a rerun of before Eleni thought as he ushered her out of the door closing it with quite a bang. He carried her parcels and held her arm, leading her carefully past the tourists now filling the narrow streets.

"Same place OK?" she asked a little breathlessly, wondering if this had been such a good idea. The spark that she had felt that first time he had touched her had returned instantly.

"I eat there every day, so that's OK by me" He replied. As they walked he waved and talked to other shopkeepers, happily showing Eleni off to them once again.

They sat at the same table and Nicos asked for her shopping to be placed behind the counter. He ordered her drink with out asking, he had remembered. The waiter brought menus with their drinks and Eleni was pleased to have something else to think about. Nicos was certainly all man and it frightened her that he had aroused these feelings once again.

She chose a different meal, chicken souvlaki, but still with salad and tzatziki. Nicos ordered the same.

"Well little one, now we know we can be friends, tell me what has happened since you left me" He made it sound as if she had run away. She supposed she had in a way, but she had been angry at the time with his refusal to speak to Andros. How different things could have been if he had not been so pig headed.

They talked as they shared their salads, and occasionally sat looking out over the harbor. He was pleased she was happy with Vanni, but made it plain she was settling for second best. He made her laugh when he tried to look hurt, only managing to pull a strange face instead.

Eleni told him what had happened to her, and tried to convince him Vanni was not inferior to him in any way. They chatted through their main course and after she had refused a sweet, through their coffee.

They sat back full and content. Both happy that they could still enjoy some time together without the usual bickering of a broken relationship.

"Eleni Hi" It was Paris "That bus was a nightmare, so full it was frightening" she stared at Nicos "Sorry I didn't realise you were with company"

Nicos stood and introduced himself, taking her hand and kissing it gently. Eleni felt a stab of jealousy as she noticed Paris flinch at the electricity of this man.

"I was hoping to speak to your father at sometime. Did you manage to ask him Eleni?" She said after sitting down. Nicos ordered her a drink.

"No sorry Paris. I was going to after lunch, but you can pass a message on with Nicos now you are here" Eleni replied.

"No need for that" Nicos said eyeing Paris's long slim legs "I will take you when we have finished here. Papa is in his studio at home. Let me phone him" He pulled out his mobile and rang Alexi.

"There that is fixed. Papa will see you in about an hour. He is flattered that such a famous journalist wants to speak to him"

Eleni noticed Paris blush slightly as he stared into her eyes. He is working his charm yet again she thought.

Whilst they sat and drank Eleni felt as though she was invisible. Nicos was talking happily to Paris and had transferred his interest to her. She called for the bill and her shopping and made an excuse to leave.

"I need to get a few more things," She said after paying. "See you back at the beach Paris"

Nicos stood and kissed her goodbye. He thanked her for lunch and promised to come to the beach soon. He had been a gentleman, so why did she feel disappointed.

She walked off feeling their eyes on her back and prayed that she would not stumble. The last thing she wanted to do was trip but the more she concentrated the harder it seemed.

She did walk around the shops, but bought nothing, and eventually when the heat began to take its toll she returned to the harbor and looked for a taxi.

As she stood waiting Nicos and Paris sped past in his red car. They were talking and didn't even notice her. She stamped her foot like a child, angry with herself as much as anything for feeling this strange jealous cloud that had settled on her.

The journey back was the usual terrifying ordeal, although she did manage to peer out of the window a few times to see beautiful white beaches as they sped past.

She looked down at her lovely diamond ring, sorry Vanni, she thought. I have behaved like an idiot. She smiled to herself at the thought of seeing Vanni again. He certainly was the man for her, so why did she feel like this?

She took her shopping to her room and went for her usual swim before putting on the old apron and serving the customers. Tomas could tell she was down and asked if everything was all right.

"Yes thank you Tomas. It's just me being silly. I had lunch with Nicos" she thought it better to tell him than let it come from a gossip. "I owed him a lunch and it gave us time to talk. Everything is sorted now. I think the shopping; heat and a full stomach are a little too much. Don't worry I will work it off"

She went to serve a group of men watching the seemingly never-ending football. They were English and it was pints all round. They drank at a quite a fast rate, keeping her busy for the rest of the afternoon.

She forgot all about Paris and Nicos as she joked and laughed with the now tipsy group.

Alexi had welcomed Paris in much the same way Nicos had. He was warm and friendly and answered all of her questions. She had not brought her prepared list and notes with her but managed to remember most of the points she wanted to cover.

The three of them sat on the terrace of Alexi's hilltop home. From here she could see most of the island below, the beaches outlining one side and a mass of cypress trees the other. It was wonderful, so relaxing, yet so exhilarating to be with two such charismatic men.

She had noticed on entering the house that it at first looked typically Grecian, but as she looked around she could tell that artists lived here. Its contents were superb, surprisingly very few ornaments, but the ones she could see were amazing. Bold colours looked even stronger against the white walls and marble floor tiles, but now as she sat sipping delicious wine, it was the tremendous view that took her eye.

Alexi managed to fill in a few missing points as they spoke. He told the story from a different angle to the others, although as yet she had not sat and probed them properly. He was more interested in telling her about Kurt, and how he had taught him to use a camera. He laughed as he remembered how crude and big his first one was, nothing like the digital ones of today, he said.

"It was huge! But still I managed to take some lovely pictures with it." Paris remembered the ones in Richards office and would not have described them as lovely, more like incredible.

Not long after she had arrived Athena came home, and insisted Paris stay for their evening meal. She asked about Andros and was amazed to hear of Richard and Eleni. Athena wanted to talk girls talk, and so Paris's interview with Alexi finished rather abruptly.

"May I speak to you again?" she asked him "When I return from New York"

"Of course you may. I have enjoyed it immensely, such a nice change for me" He replied "Just call into the shop when you get back and we can arrange something then." His eyes sparkled mischievously; she felt them strip her body of clothes with that one look.

Her own body began to react automatically and she felt slightly shocked, she needed Andros to be waiting in her room, she needed a man.

Athena once again took over the conversation and more wine was opened. Paris began to feel a little woozy having missed out on lunch, and she looked forward to the coming meal.

Paris and Nicos remained outside while Alexi and Athena went to see to the food.

"You two stay and relax we won't be long" Athena called as they disappeared into the dimness of the huge lounge which led from the terrace.

Paris did just that. The wine was definitely taking effect.

"Just look at that sunset," she said, "It is a wonderful sight from up here. The sea has turned red over there" She pointed.

"That is Koukounaries beach. I will take you one day to watch the sunset from the sand if you would like?" He didn't tell her it was the beach next to Tomas's bay.

"Please. That would be lovely." Paris tried hard not to slur her words.

When eventually the food arrived she concentrated on eating things to soak up the wine. Lots of fresh bread, some feta cheese and then a plate of pasta. Eventually her brain stopped whirring round and she began to feel a little better, but she still knew she had been drinking. Was it the wine or the company, she thought to herself? Or perhaps a little of both.

"Thank you for a lovely afternoon and meal" She said. "Would you take me back to the Tomas's please. I must get working on my notes" She had no intention of doing any work. She just wanted to get away before she showed herself up. The pasta was not mixing well with the wine.

"Of course. Would you like to go now?" Nicos was already on his feet. He held her hand to steady her and led her to his car. "In you get" He opened the door and helped her in.

She was so pleased the roof was up; she needed all the fresh air she could get.

Nicos could see her colour drain as he negotiated the winding, very steep hillside road.

"Would you like to take a walk?" He shouted over the noise of the wind and car.

"Yes please. Sorry is it that obvious?" She replied with difficulty. He smiled and nodded.

He continued to drive for a while and eventually stopped at the edge of a striking golden sandy beach.

"Koukounaries" he said helping her from the car. "We can walk for a while if you wish"

He held her hand gently as he led her along the shore "This is the beach where the sun turns the sand red. The one we were looking at from up there" He turned and pointed to the top of the hill. She could just make out the lights from Alexi's house.

The walk and sea air were working miracles. Her stomach settled and her brain once again seemed to stop moving.

"Sorry about that. Too much wine and no food is not the best idea" She laughed, "This has done me good thank you"

"Let us walk to the rocks up there and then we can go back" Nicos said before kissing her hand "I'm glad you are feeling better, but let's just make sure" He led her towards a rocky mound and helped her over to the other side. "It's a little dark over here but the moon will light our way" His voice was now smoky. She could smell sex oozing from him and the pit of her stomach fluttered. She knew she should turn round, but her legs disobeyed her.

The beach the other side was beautiful. The moon was giving the sand a fabulous silvery glow and the sea looked like a mirror. Paris stopped and held her breath. She thought Eleni beach had been stunning but this was something else.

Very gently Nicos turned her head towards him and kissed her. At first she resisted, but the setting and his obvious manly appeal connected with the wine, she let herself be seduced.

Slowly he undressed her kissing each part of her body, as it was unveiled, lingering over her breasts. Once she was naked he knelt in the sand and licked her skin, she gasped as ripples of electricity shot through her now aching body.

He could see she was ready and began to remove his own clothes. Being a well-practiced seducer it took only seconds. He spread his shirt on the warm sand and entered her slowly, so slowly she squirmed and pulled at his hips, begging him to push himself harder. Instead he tormented and teased her until she could take no more.

As her breathing began to calm he carried her into the shallows of the water and laid her in the warm sea. It was the most erotic thing she had ever done, so sensual, so beautiful, she felt incredibly alive.

They lay naked in the shallows for some time, watching as the moon inched slowly over the velvet sky. It felt as if they were the only people in the world.

Eventually they returned to the pile of clothes on the beach letting the warm breeze dry their skin as they walked.

Paris was silent.

She was mortified, what had she done? In all the years she had been with Andros she had never been unfaithful. To make matters worse it had been with the one man who Andros did not really like. How many times had he told her about when they were young?

She felt disgusted with herself, but she had to admit it had been fantastic, if only Andros would find time to do this sort of thing her life would be perfect.

# • CHAPTER •
## 19

They were both silent as Nicos drove Paris back to Eleni beach. Luckily it was only a short distance, but that made Paris feel even worse. To think she had acted that way so close to where the others had been made her stomach churn. She could so easily have been seen.

Nicos on the other hand was feeling smug. Not only had he taken Eleni's virginity but now he had made love to Paris as well. How lovely revenge was, he thought, first his sister, then his woman. Andros would have to find out and soon. Nicos would make sure he did.

All that pain when he had felt so inferior to Andros and Vanni had vanished, now he had reaped his reward.

He stopped the car in the clearing by the beach and opened the door for her. She just smiled at him and walked away. He could see her mind was in turmoil, and it pleased him. She was a stunning woman and should she split from Andros, well he might just make a play for her. He could do a lot worse and it was about time he settled down. He gazed at her long legs and remembered how they had gripped him; yes he could do a lot worse.

Paris was relieved to see the taverna was deserted; she didn't want to speak to anyone tonight. She wanted to think. How stupid had she been?

She ran up to her room and straight into the bathroom. The contents of her stomach, which had threatened to show earlier, made a rapid exit. After she sat on the floor and cried.

Eleni woke to hear sobbing from the room next door and went to investigate. She found Paris in a crumpled heap on the bathroom floor and knew instinctively what had happened. She knelt down and held the sobbing woman.

"Shh Paris. Don't cry. We have all made mistakes where Nicos is concerned, but don't worry I won't say anything and nor will he. It's our secret. Don't worry." She rocked the distraught woman in her arms trying to comfort her.

Eventually Paris calmed down and Eleni was able to help her shower. The easiest way was to strip herself and go in with her. It was a little cramped but she managed. Paris just stood as Eleni washed her hair and body, knowing that she wanted to rid her skin of his touch.

After drying Paris and then herself, Eleni led her to the bed and tucked her in; it was as if she were a child.

"You must put this to the back of your mind Paris. Andros will be here tomorrow and he will worry if you are still upset. Don't let Nicos spoil what you two have. Anyone can see that you are so together, don't let him spoil that." She gently stroked her head and kissed her cheek. "I will see you in the morning"

As she left Paris managed to murmur.

"Thanks Eleni. I owe you one. A big one."

Both women lay sleepless for the remainder of the night.

Tomas was concerned when he saw them walk towards the taverna next morning. Paris had dark circles under her eyes, and her face was blotchy. Eleni just kept yawning.

"Kalimera Eleni, Paris. I can see you did not sleep well. I am sorry." He said as they sat at the little table. "You must rest today, both of you. Take a nice swim and rest. I will make sure you have the best sun beds on the beach" His kind words made Paris want to cry and Eleni sensed it. She held her hand under the table and gave a squeeze. As Paris looked up she saw Eleni smile and was suddenly determined to put the whole episode behind her.

The girls had their pastries and lashings of hot strong coffee. They talked and soon both began to feel better.

Tomas's suggestion of a swim certainly helped as they splashed about in the warm gentle waves.

"Come on let's have a sunbathe" Eleni called after being in the water for some time "Look my fingers are all wrinkly, a sure sign we have been in long enough"

Paris looked at her hands and noticed they too were now showing signs of wrinkling. My body feels like one big ugly wrinkle, she thought.

They helped each other spread cream on their skin and lay down to rest. The sun soon began to work it's magic as its ray's sank deep into their bodies.

"That is wonderful" Paris sighed. "Thanks for last night Eleni. How did you guess?"

"I know Nicos" she replied. "He is a serial womanizer so every one says, and I fell for his charms too don't forget. Just put it behind you and concentrate on the others arriving this afternoon. We must look our best, or at least try"

They dozed in the sun for quite some time. Only the lovely smell of garlic and herbs bringing them back to earth.

"Lunch time" Eleni said taking in a deep breath. "Umm I'm starving. Come on lets go get changed. It won't be long before I have to serve the drinks. I hope there's no football on today it drives me made."

"I imagine Tomas loves it. He must sell lots of beer when there is a match on "Paris replied, and both girls laughed.

"Come on let's go" Eleni was pleased Paris looked so much better, and the fact that she could laugh meant so much.

Eleni's wish did not come true. Yet another match on the TV brought the group of men into the bar, a busy afternoon was in store.

Paris went to her room and began to pack her things. She had decided to go to New York a little earlier than planned. There was no way she could face Andros until she had sorted her head out. Nicos had been wonderful last night; it was a night she would never forget. She felt confused. Why didn't Andros do things like that? It was always her that made the first move, and suggested other positions. Andros would not dream of making love on a beach at midnight, or anywhere unusual.

Nicos had done more than seduce her, he had made her feel so good, so sexy, a real woman in a real man's arms, and he had awoken doubts about Andros. She loved him, but after last night she felt slightly unsure. She desperately needed space to clear her head.

After the Queen's ceremony she would return to complete her book and face him. Face them both.

Her hands shook as she folded her clothes; luckily she had not brought too much only expecting to stay a few days this time, and once she had finished she went to speak with Eleni.

"I'm leaving for Thessalonica shortly." She had deliberately chosen the longest route in order to avoid any chance of meeting Andros in Athens. "My agent has just phoned and wants me in New York to do some more interviews. If I leave now I can get the 1 o'clock ferry. I will ring Andros from the boat and explain. Hopefully they will be over themselves soon anyway" Eleni hugged her knowing it was a lie. "You will all be over in a few days so I will see you then. Take care." Paris said as they hugged.

Eleni watched as Paris walked across the sand and up the hill. Andros would be so disappointed, but Eleni knew her friend could not face him at the moment. It would be much better if she managed to get her head together before coming face to face with him.

She went back to serving the group of men and prayed that Paris could work her way out of her despair.

Paris reached the old rusty bus stop in minutes. She boarded and asked for stop number 1. Her heart felt like lead, but perhaps a little work would help. She would phone and arrange to speak to the Queen's trip organizer and get the low down on the American tour. It was a start, not a huge step but a start.

Once on the ferry she sat and stared at her mobile. She would have to phone him sometime, so better now than later. She pushed the hotkey number and waited. The ringing sound went on for sometime and she feared she would have to leave a message if he didn't answer soon.

"Paris darling sorry for that. I was just in the process of turning." She looked to the sky and saw a little plane in the distance. She could hear from the background noise that Andros was not alone. "Are you alright there on the beach. Won't be long now before I see you." She let him speak for a while before interrupting and telling her lies once again. "I will miss you so much but never mind we can make up for it when we get to New York. You can give me one of your special massages." His words brought tears to her eyes "I love you. Please be careful. Richard says to tell you to stay at the house. He will let Michael know you are coming." Andros paused "Hey I can see the ferry. Stand up and give me a wave." Paris waved frantically at the little plane. "I can see you darling. Don't forget I love you. Bye for now" With that he made the wings tip towards her and then back. She waved harder, the tears streaming were down her face.

Richard thought it was so exciting. He too could see Paris on the ferry below; well someone waving anyway, he could not quite make out her face. When the plane tipped he whooped with joy.

"Do that again Andros. It was fabulous"

"You behave Richard" Aunt Eleni said not wanting to feel that sensation again; it had made her feel quite queasy. "Let Andros concentrate. We will be coming in to land soon. Here, look at the island," She pointed to the window hoping the sights below would satisfy Richard for now. "I feel so excited and a little nervous" she added "Surprisingly I have never been to Eleni beach before, and to think you will meet Tomas and Sofia today." She was smiling broadly. "It seems so long since we have been together"

"I can't wait. I've spoken to him many times on the telephone and now we will meet in the flesh" Richard said "I hope he likes me?"

"Of course he will silly. If I like you then he will"

The little plane bumped slightly as it landed on the short runway at Skiathos airport. Andros steered it towards the terminal building and brought it to a stop. He did his checks, and then opened the door, the steps were lowered and the three of them left.

Andros went into the little office to pay his landing fees and order a taxi.

"Right. Come on this way" he led them over the tarmac and out on to the road. A car pulled up and he spoke to the driver. "This is it. In you get"

The three of them sat still as they sped along the road. The driver went a little too fast for Richard to be able to see all of the bays and beaches, but he still spent the journey with his nose pressed up against the window.

"Eleni will be so disappointed Vanni is not with us. I bet she is all excited. I hope he has phoned" Andros managed to relay to them in the back seat. The driver had opened the front windows and the noise was making it difficult to be heard. Eleni just nodded, she hated shouting, so unladylike.

They pulled up in the clearing and Eleni mirrored Richards's comments.

"It is so beautiful. I can't believe it"

Tomas ran to greet her.

"Welcome to Eleni Beach." He hugged and kissed her "Come let me show you my home" He held her arm tightly, ignoring the others. They followed behind as Tomas led his sister across the sand. "Sofia, quick Eleni is here" he called to his wife who rushed from the kitchen. The two women embraced and cried.

Young Eleni waved to her aunt and Richard from the end of the taverna. She was speaking on her mobile, obviously talking to Vanni. She clicked it shut and came over to the chattering group.

"He is staying to work" she said sadly "Work. That's all he does"

"Now Eleni don't be a child" Richard said sternly "He enjoys his work and you will see him soon. Stop being a baby."

Tomas sat his sister at the little table by the bar and fetched drinks. Sofia produced a selection of nibbles and the talking began in earnest. Eleni introduced Richard properly and told them of her trip to New York.

It made life easier for Sofia that Paris and Vanni were not there. The two Eleni's could share one room, while Richard and Andros the other. It was only for one night anyway. This was just a short visit before they all returned to America.

She was sad that her son was not there, but he had promised to come soon. In any case he would be living here before long. She gazed over to the clearing trying to imagine what his house would be like. It would be so wonderful when Eleni and Vanni married, and who know's, she thought, little ones could be on the way soon as well. After all Eleni was quite old, she smiled to herself; at that age she already had a rapidly growing Vanni to care for.

The rest of the afternoon was utter chaos. Young Eleni, Tomas and Sofia served the customers, returning as often as possible to the little table to talk. Everyone was pleased when at last the football finished and the group of men returned to the beach. The trio soon cleared the tables and prepared for the evening trade.

Tomas took his sister on a tour of his home wanting to show her as much as he could. It was a landmark day for both of them. They had wasted so many years apart, now every minute was precious.

Eleni loved the way he showed off his home. She could see how much he loved each brick, but then having built it himself it was hardly surprising.

She decided to have a short rest as the heat and excitement were beginning to talk their toll. Tomas showed her into young Eleni's room and hoped the bed would be big enough for them both.

"But we are two little ladies Tomas, I'm sure there will be plenty of room." She stressed. "Please tell Richard I am resting. He cannot get enough of new people and new places so I'm sure he won't miss me too much." She lay down as Tomas closed the shutters.

"Rest well Eleni. I will see you later." He closed the door gently behind him and returned to the taverna.

He passed the message on to Richard who just nodded and kept on talking to Sofia. She was telling him all about beach life and he was lapping up every detail.

Aunt Eleni dozed for a short while, but the excitement stopped her from sleeping. She sat up and gazed around the room spotting the little photographs on the wall. She opened the shutters to allow the light to shine on them and walked over to look.

She gasped, as she looked straight into the happy faces of her parents, herself and her brother. It was a picture taken many years ago, the last picture of them as a family.

The one at its side showed the grinning trio, Marco, Alexi and Tomas as they emerged from the old goat shed. She could almost hear them laughing it was so graphic. Kurt must have taken them.

She could not decide if they made her happy or sad. Her reaction was firstly to smile, then to feel the tears in her eyes. Stupid old woman, she said to herself.

She swilled her face and reapplied her make up. Tomas had brought her overnight bag to the room and she changed her clothes ready for their evening meal. She took one last look at the pictures and went to rejoin the others.

The evening was superb, the afternoon heat had subsided, and now the temperature was perfect for eating. Many of the customers on hearing that Tomas had his sister staying came over to meet her. They were all surprised to see this elegant woman stand next to the wrinkled old man and be proudly told that they were twins.

When Alexi, Athena and Nicos arrived the party began in earnest. As usual Alexi was the first to sing, and the first to dance. He pulled aunt Eleni from her seat and Richard watched in amazement as she tripped over the sand floor. Tomas joined them on her vacant side, and Nicos took photographs as they danced.

It was such a happy night, but the three old friends all felt a little sad that Marco could not be with them. So much had happened since the four of them had danced together on that fateful night many years ago, but suddenly it was as if time had stood still. If only he had been with them this night would have been perfect.

Young Eleni was more than pleased to be busy serving drinks, she found it hard to even look at Nicos let alone speak to him. It made her angry to see him talk to Andros as if nothing had happened. She could tell Andros was just being polite in answering his questions by the way he kept his replies short. She noticed how he turned away frequently to watch his mother dance, it spoke volumes. Eleni was worried, if he ever found out, could he forgive Paris? She doubted it very much.

The dancing, eating and drinking eventually finished and they all retired to bed.

It was the first time Tomas had left the taverna in a mess, Eleni promised herself to be up early in the morning to help him clean up.

The two Eleni's lay side-by-side, a little uncomfortable a first, so they talked for a while. The main topic of conversation was the photographs on the wall, and as they talked they slowly began to relax. The evening's merriment had tired them both, and soon they were fast asleep.

Richard and Andros had gone through a similar ritual in Vanni's room. Only to find it would not work, this time the large comfy bed was tossed for. Andros lost and spent the night curled up on the sofa.

Young Eleni woke as dawn broke, the suns rays lighting the room with a lovely glow. She tiptoed to the bathroom where she could still hear the soft snore of her aunt as she slept.

As quietly as possible she dressed and went to help Tomas.

He had not arrived at the taverna yet so she began by collecting the empty glasses and putting them in soak. Then she cleared the tables of plates and left over food. She was just about to begin raking the sand when he appeared.

"Oh little one thank you. My head is throbbing this morning, what a night eh?" he took the rake from her and started on the sand. Eleni returned to the glasses and before long the taverna looked spotless.

"Now for the beach. Come on Tomas I will help you" She led the way and began to carry the sun beds down towards the waters edge.

Eleni watched as the others came from the house. She could hear them laughing as they walked and noticed all three were in bathing costumes.

"Richard has never swum in the sea" Andros called to Tomas. "So we are going in with him. Won't be long."

She stood and watched as slowly Richard inched his way into the water. Aunt Eleni and Andros were by his side encouraging him all the way. It was strange to think he was experiencing so many new things so late in his life. Aunt Eleni had certainly worked some kind of magic over him, she thought. She heard him yelp as a wave showered cool water over his chest. Aunt Eleni and Andros were laughing loudly.

"Come on Richard, nearly there" Andros encouraged. "Right dip now" All three of them bobbed beneath the surface.

Richard laughed like a child as he swam, letting the waves lift and then drop him down again gently. It was lovely to see. Eventually the wet trio came towards the shore.

"That was amazing!" Richard said puffing "I would love to do that every day for the rest of my life!"

"If we live on Alonysos you could" aunt Eleni whispered in his ear. "And I would come with you" She kissed his cheek.

"Would you do that for me? Would you really live on the island forever with me? What about Athens?"

"You know I would. I just want you to be happy my love, and Athens is only a hop and skip away so we could visit quite easily." She smiled at this lovely man who had made her happy at last." I would do anything for you" They stood in the shallows of the water and kissed passionately.

"Just look at the love birds," Andros said. "I hope I am like that at their age. I can just see me and Paris being like them."

"I really hope you are." Young Eleni said softly, praying once again that Paris's secret remained in tact.

Sofia served breakfast when the trio had dried and changed.

"Kalimera Eleni, Richard, Andros" She called as they walked towards the little table "I hope you enjoyed your swim."

Richard talked non-stop about the fish he had spotted in the clear water, and how he felt as if he were floating when the waves had come. It was almost as if he thought no one had ever swum before. He managed to make an awful mess with his pastry getting crumbs all over his shorts. Aunt Eleni brushed them away gently

"Concentrate on your food Richard, just look at yourself" she said laughing and smiling, his enthusiasm for new things warmed her heart.

Everything was so different for him now. No longer did he seem afraid of meeting people, although at times she could see his shoulders tense.

No longer was he paranoid about dirt. Had he not proposed to her kneeling in the dust, something that just a short time ago would have seemed impossible. He still liked clean things, but no longer did he insist on everything being brand new, as long as they were clean he was happy.

Here he was drinking strong coffee and eating pastries for breakfast, his English routine well and truly broken. There had been times when she noticed him fumbling about, obviously missing the organization of Michael, but other than that he was fine.

The little table struggled to accommodate the breakfast guests, but they squeezed around not bothering that they were knocking into each other. Young Eleni had joined them and what with Tomas, Sofia,

Andros, aunt Eleni and Richard it was full. Full of happy people talking and eating.

Tomas looked towards the clearing when he heard a car stop.

"It is Nicos" he said happily" I hope he doesn't want breakfast I don't think we can squeeze another one in."

"Kalimera everyone. Just a flying visit I'm afraid but thank you anyway" He said refusing Sofia's offer of breakfast. "I've brought these." He handed Andros an envelope. "It is the photographs of last night. Oh. And could you give this one to Paris for me?" He passed over another envelope. It had her name in bold letters on the outside.

Andros took them and joined in as they all thanked him. He was puzzled, how did Nicos know Paris? Young Eleni read his thoughts.

"We met him in the harbor the other lunchtime" she said hurriedly. "Paris asked to interview Alexi and Nicos took her to meet him."

She had answered his question without him actually asking, a little too quickly, he thought. "Perhaps he took some photos then. You know how stunning Paris is." Eleni decided it was time to stop talking, she realised she had already said enough by the look on her brothers face.

Luckily aunt Eleni had taken the other envelope and opened it. They were all now laughing at the pictures before them. No matter when Alexi or Nicos took photographs they were always works of art, and even though they were now laughing at the images they could see that an expert had taken them.

Andros tried to join in the merriment but his mind was elsewhere. Eleni could see her brother was nervously tapping his fingers on the other envelope and in his eyes she could see pain. How could Nicos inflict this on someone and so easily? She thought. The contents might well be innocent, but just by giving it to Andros he had put ideas into his mind.

They all kissed Tomas and Sofia goodbye and promised to be back after the ceremony.

"Paris wants to interview me next" Tomas said puffing out his chest." And I am going to tell her what a horrible sister you were" He teased. Aunt Eleni elbowed him softly in the stomach.

"And I will tell her what a bully you were" They hugged once more. "See you soon brother"

They squashed into the taxi and set off for the airport. This time the driver was much slower and Andros was able to point out places of interest to Richard, who once again lapped up the information.

He was so eager to get back into the sky he left the car first and walked across the tarmac.

"What about your case" Aunt Eleni called.

"Sorry I forgot. I expected Michael to bring it" He replied quietly. She noticed a sad look on his face.

"You miss him don't you?" She asked tenderly

"Yes. He has stood by me for years. Michael and Molly have always been there for me no matter what. He used to iron my newspaper and then put it in a plastic bag if it was raining when I was poorly" She knew Richard was referring to his times under the bush "You know he never asked why I went there, just carried on as usual. I wonder what will happen to him when we live here?" He marched away carrying his case, his back ramrod straight, but she could tell he was upset.

The little plane was soon high in the sky, Andros impressing Richard greatly. He loved to sit and listen as he conversed with air traffic control, he found it exciting. He watched as Andros fiddled with switches and knobs, tapped glass-fronted dials with his finger, and swept the aircraft around the sky. It was then he wished for a second that he had followed his father into the RAF. To do this every day would be wonderful. He smiled to himself, that was one more thing he wanted to do daily, any more and he would run out of time.

This morning they were routed over the city and Eleni was able to show him the sights of Athens. He was stunned it looked so beautiful in the sunshine. He spotted the Acropolis and gently took her hand and kissed it.

"My favourite place" He whispered. Eleni smiled and blushed slightly, that was another thing he loved about her.

Andros brought them to a stop and once again did his checks. A group of mechanics came towards them ready to give the plane a thorough going over.

"Is something wrong?" Richard said a little panicky.

"No. I always have them go over it when I return. It's a safety thing." Andros replied and young Eleni wondered if the pilot of her father's plane had been as careful.

The limousine was waiting on the tarmac, but not to drive them home this time, to deliver their luggage for New York and of course Vanni. Eleni fell into his arms before telling him off for not coming to the beach to see her. They spent a few minutes swapping kisses and then walked to the terminal.

"Talk about jet setters" Andros said. "It's no wonder Paris gets a little edgy at times" Each time he mentioned her Eleni felt goose pimples shoot up her arms. She said another prayer.

The long flight was uneventful. They watched a film, and ate the tasteless food. Richard refused to eat with the plastic cutlery and settled for his bread rolls instead.

"Not the done thing. Plastic, disgusting" he said in his sharp English voice.

Before long they were all dozing in the stuffy air that surrounded them.

Andros stretched as they left the plane.

"That's better," he said holding his hands above his head.

"Right lets get the cases then its off home" said Richard excited now at being back in America.

The Rolls Royce stood out against the yellow cabs and large American cars. Richard spotted it and raised his hand toward the chauffeur.

"Here he comes," he said smiling. "In we get" He ushered aunt Eleni into the back and made sure she was comfortable. The others were left to fend for themselves.

No one spoke as they drove through the busy city streets. What a day it had been. Waking up on that wonderful beach, off to Athens and now in America. They were all stunned and not one of them had any idea what day it was.

The house gates slowly swung open and Richard spotted Michael waiting by the large central door. Eleni watched as he sat upright and smiled.

"Sir Richard, madam" He nodded to Andros and young Eleni" Welcome home. I trust you had a pleasant trip?" His voice was like glass.

"Yes thank you Michael." Richard replied. "Its good to see you, are you well? I have brought you something. Let me see." Michael was taken back a little by Richards's lack of protocol as he rummaged in his flight bag. "Here we are" he handed the still slightly shocked butler a large bottle of Jamieson Whiskey. "Your favourite, and this is for your wife" he passed a little pink parcel tied with silver ribbon. Aunt Eleni and the others could not help laughing at Michaels surprised look.

"Thank you Sir Richard. Very kind of you."

"Not at all dear chap. It's taken me long enough to go on holiday so I had to mark the occasion somehow." Richard looked down to the mess on the drive. The contents of his bag now scattered in the gravel. "Oh dear."

"Leave it with me sir, you go and settle in" Michael began to collect Richard's belongings. What a turn up for the books this was. He thought, thankful for the bottle, it certainly was his favourite.

"Is Paris at home?" Andros asked him rather quietly.

"No not yet Mr. Andros. She is working at the Queen's temporary office in City Hall this afternoon. She did say to tell you she would be back about 5"

"Thank you Michael"

Young Eleni picked up her case and went to her room. Vanni followed wondering what the matter was. She had been quiet since they took off from Athens. Just answering if he spoke, not starting a conversation herself. Something was bothering her.

They all freshened up and met for tea on the patio.

"Wonderful" Richard said as he took the first sip. "English tea. Sorry Eleni I didn't mean Greek was bad, its just this is the best. It's the way Michael brews it"

Aunt Eleni could smell the city again, its clammy heat and fumy air. The sooner the ceremony was over the better. They could get back to Athens and make plans to live on Alonysos. She could not wait, but promised herself not to let it spoil Richard's time here. After all it could be his last visit.

211

They heard the gates open and saw Paris arrive in a taxi. Aunt Eleni noticed how Andros stiffened at the sight of her and how Paris's eyes crinkled as if looking for something.

Andros rose and went to meet her. He held her at arms length for a second before kissing her cheek.

"How was the interview?" he asked almost choking, it was the last thing he wanted to talk about.

"Fine thanks. I will say hello to everyone and then go and write my notes up" She was as nervous as him. She could tell from the way he walked towards her something was wrong, if that Eleni had spilled the beans she would never speak to her again, but perhaps Nicos had, what then. She had to get inside, get away from everyone, she couldn't think straight and wanted to break down. Pulling on all of her inner resources she walked to the patio and welcomed the others. She chatted for a short while before excusing herself.

Moments after reaching her room Andros knocked and entered.

"Good to see you Paris" he tried to sound welcoming "Nicos sent you this" He held the envelope out to her and noticed she looked scared. "He took some photographs the other night at Tomas's and asked me to give you this" He waved it once again. She took it from him and threw it on the bed. "Don't you want to open it" She shook her head.

"Not now Andros. I need to get my thoughts and notes down"

"Well I want you to open it" he said forcefully "I want you to open it this minute"

Paris was frightened. Had Nicos had his camera with him that night? Had she been so drunk? Slowly she tore the envelope open and pulled out the photograph. A huge sigh of relief left her as she realised she was not the subject. But she began to frown it was a beach scene. The reality hit her. He had taken a picture of their beach in the moonlight. Andros snatched it from her hands and held it up. He studied its contents and flipped it over.

"How could you?" he asked, tears now running down his cheeks. "Just look at the back" He held it towards he "Go on look at the back" She sat down on the bed, her world crashing around her ears. I will remember forever. Nic XX, it read.

"Andros I" she began but the words would not come out "I will leave now" She got up and went towards the wardrobe.

"No you will not" he said angrily "You will pretend nothing is wrong for their sakes" He gestured with his head. "You will not spoil these next few days for mama and Richard. Then you can go" His words cut into her heart.

"Andros I love you. I am so sorry. Please" She held her arms towards him.

"Don't touch me ever again" He stormed out of the room and almost knocked his mother over.

Aunt Eleni tapped at the door and was shocked to see Paris sobbing on the bed.

"Come on now it can't be that bad" She cradled the crying woman. "What ever has caused this" Paris cried harder. Eleni took her face in both hands "Look at me Paris. Tell me everything."

She was a shocked by Paris's story but not surprised. Nicos shared an amazing aura with his father, it was animal, sexual, irresistible, and she knew only too well the effect they could have.

So no, she was far from surprised, just very disappointed. Not just in Paris, but also Nicos, his silly quest to get back at Andros had gone too far this time.

Nicos was the one to blame, couldn't Andros see that, he would have to be told.

Well no, Eleni thought, it was Andros himself; he had started this stupid thing with Nicos. He was partly to blame and she would tell him so.

Just when everything was going so well this had to happen she thought.

• CHAPTER •
20

The next few days were very tense for everyone. Richard was a bundle of nerves as he tried on his new morning suit. Paris and Andros had made an effort to be civil, but they were not fooling his mother for one second. Vanni and young Eleni had their heads together planning their new home every minute they had. Aunt Eleni just watched and waited.

The night before the ceremony she and Richard paced the lawn. She feared he would crack more than once, but with her help he managed to sleep in the chair by his bush, and not under the leaves. She stayed with him. It did nothing for her completion to have such an awful night, but as long as he was well, that was all that mattered.

She led him slowly to the house as dawn broke, to find Michael just about to bring them tea.

"We will have that on the patio thank you Michael" she said softly "Thank you" She could see he was as concerned as her and she had noticed more than once in the night his curtains had moved as he looked out over them. "Please fetch your wife and join us"

"But madam?" he was stunned

"I wish to speak to you both. Please fetch her, and some more cups, before the others come down."

Michael went into the house and immerged moments late with his chubby little wife. She was typical of an old English mansion house cook that Eleni had read about in lovely storybooks.

"Please sit. Tea?" she asked the silent pair.

Michael looked uncomfortable to be sitting at the same table as his master, but nodded his approval of her offer.

"Right. I want to ask you something very important. I realise today is a very special day for all of us, especially Richard, you Michael, and me of course." She took a sip of tea. "The thing is after today we will be returning to Greece and I had hoped that you would agree to come and work for us at our home in Athens. You will have the use of quite a large staff house; the people that work for me at the moment live in the city. We will also need you when we stay on Alonysos. It seems to me Richard cannot do without you Michael. Do you think you could consider it and let me know" Richard sat upright, his eyes shining.

"You wonderful woman. Of course they will," He answered for them

"Now Richard. It is Michael and Molly's decision not yours. Let them think about it please." She turned back to the smiling faces of the couple and knew their answer but continued to speak "Please give it your consideration as I said and let me know before we leave. And don't let him bully you." They laughed at her last remark.

"Madam. We do not have to think. Of course we would be honored to serve you both. We would love to accept." Michael said instantly.

"There I told you" Richard said raising his teacup in a toast. "Here's to Greece"

For once Michael let him self go and echoed Richard's words. His wife followed, she had tears in her eyes.

"Oh madam. Thank you so much. Michael has been at a loose end without Sir Richard. I thought he would wear the carpet out he has paced that much." They all laughed again. "Plus we will be so much closer my sister and her children. They live in Switzerland now and I haven't seen them for years." Molly realised this was an opportunity not to be missed.

"Good. Then I will sort out our tickets and see about work permits." Eleni was pleased with herself. The uncomfortable night now a distant memory in her mind. "Is everything ready for later Molly?"

"Of course madam. It will be wonderful. Trust me." Molly's face lit up with a lovely smile.

"Good then I think I had better get ready to meet The Queen and you too Richard. Come on. The hairdresser will be arriving soon and the make-up lady. The fitter from Dior should not be far behind" Eleni spoke as they walked into the house. "First a long soak in the bath and then" Richard let her ramble on, he was so pleased and surprised by what had just happened, she might as well have been speaking to the wall. He missed the last bit completely.

The morning passed in a whirl for them all. People came and went. Flowers were delivered with cards congratulating the new knight to be, everyone and everywhere had a busy, excited feel.

Aunt Eleni received a wonderful bouquet of pink roses from Richard, just as her hair was full of hot rollers. She read the card. To my beautiful girl, on this special day. Thank you. XXX. She wanted to hug him but he had been banished to his own room for this morning and they would not meet until it was time to leave.

The make-up lady did a marvelous job on Eleni's face. She had superb bone structure and lovely features, but the night spent outside had taken its toll. When Eleni was finally allowed to look in the mirror, all traces of tiredness had vanished; instead she stared at a younger version of herself. The lady left with a hefty tip, to go and see to Paris and young Eleni. The hairdresser was already with them. Eleni wondered how Paris would be feeling.

Finally her outfit was revealed. It was a very pale peach dress and jacket, which fitted like a dream. She had a matching tiny handbag and glamorous strappy high-heeled sandals of the softest leather. Dior had done her proud. Her hat was of the finest little feathers. They were attached to a small invisible band that stretched from ear to ear; it allowed some of the feathers to fall towards her face. She looked marvelous and felt it. She put on her lovely gold necklace, a small gold bracelet and smiled. What a day this was going to be.

Finally she was ready. Collecting her little handbag she walked slowly to the door and by habit turned to look around the room. She felt so happy, but things could have been better she thought, oh well never mind.

The others were waiting on the patio as she made her entrance and she could see the champagne was already flowing. Molly passed her a glass as she floated past.

Richard and Michael in their morning suits and looking very handsome stood talking to one side. Andros and Vanni both wore dark navy suits and each of them had chosen navy ties with a splash of colour to match their ladies outfits. Good, they had remembered, she thought.

Paris wore and amazing red suit that fitted her long frame like a glove, although she had red hair, it looked marvelous. She wore the tiniest of pillbox hats and short veil. A top model could not have looked more stunning.

Young Eleni had also chosen Dior, but her suit was of an antique pink. Her jet-black hair was decorated with a hat similar to Paris's, and with her dark olive skin she too could have graced the cover of any glossy magazine.

Richard turned as aunt Eleni walked outside.

"My darling you look like a dream" He kissed her gently "Will we all do for you madam?" He swept his arm wide.

"You all look fabulous what a handsome family we are. Thank you" She felt a little tearful, realising they had no idea what was coming.

They all turned as the gates swung open and a strange car entered the drive. It was a huge old-fashioned black Rolls Royce, a little flag of The Queens colours flapping on the front.

Young Eleni stood and clapped her hands wildly.

"Just look at that"

"Oh God" Richard mumbled and held his stomach.

"Just remember what you said to me once Richard. For King and Country" Eleni smiled into his eyes and held his arm tightly. "Come on and don't forget your top hat. Michael picked up both toppers and walked towards the car. Standing to one side he opened the huge door for them

"Sir Richard, madam"

"Michael today you are my friend, not my butler. Please call me Richard" Michael was even more uncomfortable. All of this was quite unheard of, but if that is what Sir Richard wanted, then that's how it would be.

"Come on Paris" Aunt Eleni called.

"How come?" Andros asked as Paris picked up her red handbag.

"I am an official reporter today. Covering everything Richard does." She went to leave but he held her back by her arm.

"Yes?" she queried.

Looking straight into her eyes he could see the pain in them and it tore at his heart. He kissed her cheek, purely to keep up appearances he told himself. He smelt her womanly odor and felt her soft skin against his lips. Oh Hell. She looked so stunning he wanted to take her back to the room this minute, but the thought of her with Nicos made him push the love he held to the back of his mind.

"We will see you later then at the reception." Was all he could say stiffly. She nodded and joined the others in the magnificent car.

"Why do they have to go so early?" Vanni asked

"They have to be searched and checks done. I think. Don't they have to have a rehearsal too?" Andros said still remembering the look Paris had given him as she left.

"But surely that will leave plenty of time?" Vanni was still puzzled.

"Oh I don't know why" Andros almost shouted. "You will have to ask them afterwards"

"Don't blame Paris" was all young Eleni could say. She was so angry with her brother for being such a pig to his woman she wanted to say much more, but today was not the right time.

Andros stared at her and drank another glass of champagne.

By the time it was their turn to leave Andros had downed even more champagne. Eleni noticed a slight stagger as he walked to the silver Rolls. The car had been polished to perfection and a tiny Union Jack flew on its front. She felt so proud. Proud of Richard. How she wished Marco had been here to see this.

The car swept down the drive and was soon cruising along the busy roads. She could see people stopping to stare as they drove past and felt a tingle. It was a fairly long way to City Hall but they all sat in an uncomfortable silence.

The car gradually slowed then stopped at the orders of an armed policeman. Their driver handed over an official pass and a uniformed officer checked the passengers before they were allowed any further. They were then directed to the foot of some beautiful white marble steps that led to a very impressive building.

Young Eleni could see more armed policemen at every turn, and barriers to keep the crowds at a distance. How The Queen lived like this she could not imagine, everywhere she went it must be like this, she thought.

Andros, Vanni and Eleni were accompanied up the steps by two of the Queen's footmen, resplendent in their marvelous traditional gold uniforms, and shown into a huge reception room.

All of those being honored today had been allowed two special passes into the main chamber room and then six other passes into the reception afterwards.

The President has obviously had an unlimited supply judging by the heads of State that were present, Eleni thought as she looked around the room.

She accepted a glass of champagne from a waitress and watched as Andros finished his in seconds. She hoped he would not show himself up and nudged Vanni. She quietly asked him to keep an eye on Andros and was pleased when he replied with a whisper that he already was.

"Well make sure he eats plenty of that." She nodded towards the buffet table laid out at the side of the room.

As they mingled with the other guests Eleni proudly introduced her fiancé and brother to some of the many people that she knew. Vanni was very impressed by the importance of those who stopped to talk, and by the way Eleni spoke to them, not changing one little bit. She was obviously used to being in such company, he thought.

Suddenly the huge wooden doors opened and a line of trumpeters heralded the arrival of the main party. They watched as a large man dressed all in black stood in the doorway and unrolled a scroll of paper.

"Isn't it all exciting?" She said and Vanni hoped she would not start to clap, well not just yet anyway. He watched as she stared in amazement at the goings on. Still really a child in many ways.

The trumpeters stopped and the man began to speak, his voice loud and as clear as glass.

"My Lords Ladies and Gentlemen" he began "May I present Sir Michael Cook" He was America's Head of Armed Forces, "and Lady Cook" The grinning couple walked into the room to polite applause. "Sir Anthony Barrett and Lady Barrett" he was America's Head of Security. They had both received honorary knighthoods for their work.

"Oh God" Eleni spluttered when she spotted Richard.

"Sir Richard Graves and Lady Graves"

"What?" Andros said fiercely.

"Lady Graves? They must have got married" Vanni said quite innocently

"But when? Why didn't mother tell me?" He was angry now and his mood was made no better when he turned and spotted Paris. She was talking to another man and obviously enjoying his company judging by the smile on her face.

She looked up and saw him, her face clouded over instantly.

The rest of the procession went by in a blur, until Eleni heard the man in black speak again.

The courtier announced The Queen and President. Vanni quickly held on to her hands, which looked very much like they would erupt into wild clapping any second. Her smile said thank you.

Eventually after managing to catch Richards eye young Eleni was soon admiring his award.

Andros took his mother to one side.

"Is it right?" He asked breathing alcohol fumes into her face "Are you married?"

"Yes we are. Isn't it wonderful? We had a civil ceremony this morning after the rehearsal. Just us two, Michael and Paris." She waved her hand showing off a wonderful gold band encrusted with diamonds.

"Why didn't you tell me, and why was she invited and not me?" He was so angry his face was now a fiery red.

"Why? You ask me why? After the way you have been for these last few days, you have been sullen, bad tempered and downright nasty. I have seen the way you have treated Paris, and anyway she had no idea until we got here. Only Michael and Molly were in on it. It has been planned for some time now but hopefully with you all present." She paused "How could I not want my only son at my wedding, but you made it so difficult. In the end we decided that none of you would come, but with Paris tailing Richard for the piece she is doing, we could not get out of having her with us." She stared straight in to his eyes and could see his hurt, but it was his own fault. "For the first time in my life I have had to make a decision between you and someone else. Richard won today, but believe me it was very hard. Don't you dare do anything to spoil today for him or for me do you hear. We have arranged for a wedding meal back at the house, and you are all welcome, but do anything to mar the occasion and I will send you to your room." She spoke to him as if he were a child, which at that moment he certainly looked. He stumbled with the shock of it all and Vanni was at his side in a flash.

"Come on its time for home" He grasped his arm and bundled him out through the door. He quickly kissed Eleni as they passed "I think we had better make an exit. See you all later."

Michael stepped in to help, glad of something to do.

" I will come with you Mr. Vanni." He said not waiting for a reply as he took Andros's other arm. He wanted to hit him for the way he was behaving. Did he not realise he was in the presence of Her Majesty? Michael was disgusted.

The two Eleni's embraced.

"Oh I am so happy for you and Richard" young Eleni said emotionally "What a wonderful day for us all" She stretched high and kissed Richard's cheek." Now tell me all about it."

The tale of the wedding was repeated, the ring looked at over and over again, but this time it was greeted with smiles and more kisses.

Paris had rejoined them and added her bit, telling of how surprised she was and how marvelous her article would be with that to include. Aunt Eleni took her to one side and told her of how Andros had reacted.

"Try not to worry Paris I will speak to him. Its about time he grew up." She gently stroked the young woman's arm trying to comfort her.

The day that had started with so much promise was rapidly beginning to fall apart.

They smiled, as Richard repeatedly told of his short conversation with The Queen and how she held that wonderful sword.

"Just here it was," he pointed to his shoulder "It was huge and so heavy for her" He turned to tell it again.

"John. How good to see you" He shook hands with The President. "What a marvelous day. Please may I introduce my wife Eleni, or should I say Lady Eleni"

"Richard congratulations" The President returned his strong handshake "Lady Eleni, I am at your service" The President bowed slightly "Paris how nice to see you again, and so soon. Thank you for your article, you were very kind to me."

Paris was astonished. It had taken weeks of arranging before she could speak to The President for the interview, and yet here he was on first name terms with Richard. Then she remembered Richard's words from before. John, he had said and then changed it quickly to The President. She would have to investigate further, but not now, she had other things on her mind.

"Eleni. You look lovely" He kissed young Eleni's cheek. "How are things?" This was even more amazing, he knew Eleni. She would definitely have to probe a little more.

"Fine thank you John. Are the girls here today?" She asked before kissing The First Lady.

The President explained that his daughters were away at present and gutted to be missing this as they would loved to have seen Richard get his award.

Paris's professional head began to read more into this. It was obvious Richard and Eleni knew The President and his family well, so was his award for charitable works or something else?

Young Eleni answered one of her unasked questions.

"I was at finishing school with his daughters. We had a whale of a time I can tell you, they are crazy." She giggled.

They watched in awe as The Queen retired, her courtiers following closely behind, the trumpeters sounding a fanfare.

Suddenly it felt as if a light had gone out, everyone stayed silent for a moment.

"That was so fabulous" young Eleni whispered to no one in particular "All so exciting"

The group walked slowly from the magnificent room, thinking of what they had just seen, not wanting their time in there to end.

"Oh Richard that was fantastic" Young Eleni stood on the steps and clapped her hands. "I have been waiting to do that all afternoon," The others laughed. "Come on here's our car"

They made their way carefully down the steps to where their own Rolls Royce stood proudly waiting. Richard ushered them in and looked round for Michael.

"He went some time ago Richard. Andros was feeling a little unwell so he and Vanni took him back to the house." Aunt Eleni was trying to hide the fact that Andros was drunk.

The car glided along the road and towards home, they all sat quietly, reflecting upon the fabulous events of the day so far.

The gates swung open as they neared and young Eleni gasped with delight.

"Oh just look at that" The garden and patio had been turned into a fairy light grotto. Hundreds of tiny lights twinkled brightly against the slowly darkening sky. The table usually used for breakfast was laid out beautifully.

"Well we couldn't let our wedding day go without a little celebration" Richard said patting his wife's knee.

Michael now back to his usual self and feeling much more comfortable, opened the car door.

"Sir Richard, Lady Eleni welcome home and many congratulations" he nodded slightly.

Molly had certainly done them proud. The meal was superb and the wines delicious. How Vanni and Michael had sobered Andros up his mother never knew, but he was and it made her feel much happier. He still spoke to Paris in a clipped voice but at least he was speaking, but she noticed for most of the evening he was silent, and he drank very little.

They rounded off the meal with champagne and a beautifully decorated cake. Molly had worked so hard, aunt Eleni thought; she must remember to get her a nice thank you gift.

The events of the day, coupled with the awful previous night, began to take their toll and Eleni asked Richard if they could retire. He agreed readily, his wedding night, he could hardly believe it.

After they had gone Paris began to probe young Eleni about Richard's award and was it really for charity work? How come he knew The President so well?

"Well I know he does a lot of work for The President, and we have had the British Prime Minister here a few times, but we were told it was for charity. Who knows if it was for something else? Who cares anyway?" She said innocently. I do thought Paris. "Time for bed I think" young Eleni yawned. She was tired but full of happy memories.

Vanni took Eleni's arm and led her into the house. He hoped she would stop talking about the day soon; he had visions of her chattering away in her sleep.

Paris rose to leave. "I will be gone tomorrow," she said as she walked away. "Goodbye Andros." He just smiled awkwardly. God she looked so fantastic. It had been murder for him to sit by her at the table and smell her perfume, feel the slight touch of her leg against his as she reached for different things. How he wanted her.

He followed her to her room and pushed the door open just as she tried to close it.

"You think that's it. Goodbye Andros, it that what you think?" Roughly he shook her by the shoulders. "Is that enough for you?" She nodded her face full of fear. "Well it's not for me"

He ripped open her jacket and pulled at her bra, it gave way instantly. "Whore" he said with a husky voice "Whore."

The fine material of her skirt gave way just as easily as he tore it from her body. She stood with her hands crossed over her breasts, in a pathetic attempt to protect herself from him. He gazed at her long slim body, now only clothed in high heels, stockings and a flimsy red thong.

He groaned loudly and pounced.

Paris stood no chance but she fought nonetheless, her self-pride not allowing her to give in until the very last moment.

The fire in her eyes told Andros what a huge mistake he had made. He felt ashamed, angry and physically sick.

What had he done?

## CHAPTER 21

Richard's rhythmic breathing did little to relax aunt Eleni. So much was spinning around her mind she doubted very much if anything would help. She had lain awake most of the night going through the events of the day, but mostly thinking of the tale Paris had told.

Her mouth was dry and her head beginning to throb. She decided to go and make herself a hot comforting drink. Perhaps that will help a little, she thought gazing down at her sleeping husband.

Slipping carefully from the bed she put her dressing gown on and tied it tightly around her waist. Tip toeing slowly she left the room closing the door softly, and headed for the kitchen.

Michael would be angry for not waking him she knew, but it did not seem right. She was perfectly capable of making her own drink, and in any case she did not want to speak to any one at the moment.

She stood in the doorway leading out on to the patio sipping a comforting mug of steaming tea. At last her mind began to calm down. She took deep breaths of the fresh cool air and she could feel herself starting to relax.

The sky was brightening as the sun rose behind the skyscrapers of the city; silently she stood and watched the morning arrive. She smiled as little birds flew amongst the bushes and pecked at the lawn for food. A squirrel ran up the trunk of a huge cypress tree at the bottom of the garden. It was a beautiful morning.

Turning as she heard footsteps behind her she was surprised to see Paris walking towards the door. Suitcase in one hand, laptop in the other.

"Good morning Paris you are up early" Eleni said quietly "I thought it was Michael" she stopped and stared. "What has he done to you?" She could see dark rings around Paris's eyes, her beautiful face was swollen and blotchy, her whole body gave the aura of defeat.

Paris shrugged her shoulders.

"Nothing I did not deserve." She looked a broken woman. Her clothes were fabulous as usual but the body in them looked tired. "I am returning to Skiathos today. I have spoken to Tomas and he has agreed to let me have one of his houses in the town. I am going to stay there until I have completed my book, and then who knows where I will go. Back to London I expect. Thank Richard for me please. I have finished my article on him and will wire it from the airport. I just hope I have done him justice."

"I am sure you have." The older woman replied sadly. "We will be on Alonysos next week, so please come and see us. I know you want to talk to me. If you feel able we can go together to Kefalonia, I can show you the places everyone has told you about. Just you and me if you like." Her heart was breaking for this lovely woman she had known for many years, and come to look upon as the daughter she had never had. "Take care" The two women embraced.

Eleni watched as Paris got into a waiting taxi and waved as she left. Her son was going to get the talking to of his life she thought sipping her now cold tea. She took her mug back to the kitchen and made her way up the stairs.

Passing the door of Andros's room she paused before entering. He was asleep.

She walked quietly over and looked down at her son, she could see scratch marks on his arms and face, and it made her smile. At least Paris had put up a fight, good.

She saw how old he was beginning to look and frowned. If her son looked like this, what on earth did she look like? She wondered if Marco had looked like this in his sleep. She tapped his bare shoulder.

"Andros wake up" She shook him gently "Wake up I want to talk to you." Slowly he opened his eyes and Eleni saw how bloodshot they were. He grunted and sat up.

"Is something wrong mama?" He managed to say through dry lips.

"You could say that" She replied, "How could you?" she sat on the bed "I have just seen Paris, she has left. Do you realise what you have done, how stupid you have been?"

"But you don't know the whole story" He said pleadingly

"Oh but I do. She told me herself, I know all about it and I still say you are stupid."

"But to go with Nicos. How could she? First my sister, then Paris, I bet he planned it to get back at me for something." Andros felt awful. He didn't need a lecture from his mother, not now.

"Tell me Andros since you met Paris have you slept with any other women?"

"Yes but its" she interrupted his words

"Don't you dare say it's different for men." Eleni was angry now "Have you not realised it is partly your fault." Andros tried to interrupt

"Listen for a change Andros. When you were younger, you Vanni and Nicos were friends. I used to watch you run, I used to watch you swim. I could see how Nicos always looked up to you, but what did you do? Ridicule him that's what. Every time he came last in a race, whether you were running or swimming you would tease him, poke fun at him. Did you never stop to think why he was always last?" Andros shook his head, it throbbed even more.

"Then I'll tell you. When he was running through fields, speed was not important, but the flowers and birds, butterflies collecting their nectar, the clouds in the sky above. Of course he came last, he was looking with his artists eye at all around him.

When you were swimming, he had no interest in ploughing through the water at speed, but stopping to look at the tiny fish at his feet. The way the waves rippled and caught the sunlight.

No matter how hard he tried, he could not catch you up. He so wanted to be like you, but his mind wanted to see the things you passed by.

Did you ever take time to look at his photographs, the pictures he drew? Did you ever listen to him describe a beautiful moment. No not once.

When you and Vanni set up your business, did you ever think of asking him to join you? No. Can you imagine how hurt he must have felt?

You had come into his and Vanni's lives and ended up taking his best friend away. You took his friend from the island where they had been born and lived, can you imagine the hurt he must have felt.

You made him your enemy. No one else.

It is no wonder he dislikes you, or so he thinks. Deep down he still wants to be like you. I saw you together at Tomas's that night. He tried so hard to talk, but all you did was turn away."

"But why did he have to pick on Paris?"

"She was easy pray Andros. She is a very beautiful young woman and as such catches the eye of many men, or had you not noticed.

Ever since you met her have you once flown to be at her side. No. OK you went to the island but then that was to take me and Richard, not solely to see her. Every time you two have been together it is because she had taken time to come to you. She has flown from the other side of the world just to spend a night with you, and what do you do? Work."

"But she travels all over the world, it is part of her job." Now he was beginning to feel queasy on top of everything else.

"Yes it is and why do you think she does it? Because she knows she can only keep your interest for a short while that's why. She knows deep down that you love her but you treat her so casually.

Tell me. When did you last buy her something, a trinket, some flowers, anything?"

"I can't remember, but she buys what she wants anyway." He replied insensitively "She has her own money, I can't remember."

"Not once I bet, that's why you can't remember. She is a woman Andros; she needs to be treated like a woman. Nicos could see that and I bet he made her feel like the only woman in the world."

"But he plied her with drink and seduced her" He wined.

"Look at it from her point of view. She wanted to meet Alexi and when young Eleni went into the town she decided to follow and see if she could arrange a meeting to speak to him. Eleni had said she would do it, but Paris needed to be sure, so she went herself. She met Eleni and Nicos as they finished their lunch, so she joined them for a drink.

Nicos oozes charm; he has so much it is only natural that she liked him. When he offered to take her to meet Alexi there and then she could not refuse, she was thinking only of her work.

She sat on the terrace and drank wine with them, two men who simply have the knack of making a woman feel special, and they talked. It is hardly surprising that she relaxed in their company they are very attractive men.

When Athena came home she insisted that Paris stay and eat with them. Hence more wine. This poor girl had eaten nothing since breakfast and so it is hardly surprising she began to feel a little tipsy. Nicos noticed and offered to drive her home. She felt so ill on the way they decided to stop and go for a walk to clear her head. They walked along the moonlit beach and if Nicos is anything like his father, he would have taken his time to describe what he was seeing. Describe the moon, the stars, and the gentle waves on the sea. They talk pictures as well as take them you should listen to him one day."

"No chance of that. Not after this." Andros said angrily "Any way how do you know so much about Alexi and Nicos, and what kind of men they are?"

She looked at her son and sighed.

"The day Marco left the island I stood on the cliff and waved to every boat that sailed. My heart was breaking. Why was he going, why did he not stand up to his father and my mother. We could have married, we were old enough. I could not see why he had to go. Tomas and Alexi were with me but Tomas left after a short while. He and Marco had fought earlier and he felt I was just being a dramatic female.

Alexi stayed, he took some more photographs and we talked. We talked about Marco and the way he used to listen to Kurt when he spoke of America. Alexi said he knew Marco would go one day and this was his chance.

He was so kind and understanding. He offered to marry me. Here he was, so young and handsome offering to take on a woman who loved someone else just to save her reputation, I could not believe it.

We sat on the grass and he talked about the lovely things he could see and he told me he had always wanted to be with me, but Marco had been the only one I had ever really looked at.

As I turned to speak he kissed me. We made love on the cliff top. He was so gentle, so loving; it was nothing like it had been with Marco, with him it was frantic. Alexi made me feel wonderful, he made me feel beautiful. That is how I know. He won me over with his charm; his soft voice and I fell for it just as Paris did.

Even though it was hard, I could not accept Alexi's offer of marriage. I knew I loved Marco so much, and I had believed him when he said he would return. I had to wait for him, I just had to.

Afterwards as we lay in the grass and stared at the sky I felt so ashamed, I had made such a big mistake. Just like Paris. I had let Marco down, even though he had just sailed out of my life, I felt I had let him down so badly, I had wanted it to be Marco lying with me; just as I imagine Paris really wanted it to be you.

My mother sent me away and until you were actually born I had no idea whose child I was carrying, but I could see instantly that Marco was your father. My relief was immense." Eleni was crying her son looked so hurt.

"I am sorry Andros, but please learn from me. Even though I had been with Alexi it was Marco that I loved. I realise now that I wasted my life waiting for him to return, but still I am glad I did not settle for the easy option." She paused for a moment.

"Paris loves you; she did not want to hurt you. She did not set out to do what she did. She is distraught at what happened, and wishes she could put the clock back. She loves you so much, but she needs to be treated like a woman.

She stood no chance as they walked along the beach. Any woman on this planet would have fallen the way she did. A romantic stroll, wine in her veins, a man who lavishes attention, you tell me who could resist that. If his touch were as gentle as his fathers, then she would have not been able to refuse.

Please don't let her one mistake spoil what the two of you have got. I know you love her so don't let her get away. Come with us next week to Alonysos. Go and see her, tell her you forgive her, make her feel wanted, loved, spoil her."

"I don't know if I can mama. I feel betrayed. But you are right I do love her so much." Andros was emotional as he spoke "I was going to ask her to marry me you know. Look" He pulled open the bedside cabinet drawer. "Look." He opened a little velvet ring box. Inside sat a beautiful ruby and diamond ring. "It is the colour of her hair, you see I have bought her something." Tears streaked his tired face.

"Andros don't let those feelings go to waste. Come with us and give her your ring. Ask her forgiveness for the way you have treated her, be a man and accept her apologies.

Remember I saw her bruises this morning; I think you need to beg her forgiveness you must have treated her very badly, I feel quite ashamed of you.

Please don't waste your life wishing you had acted. You are no longer a young man my son; make the most of what time is left. Take time to enjoy yourself. Stop taking her for granted, and stop working so hard. Take some time to be with her, look at her work, help her, and be interested in her as a person.

Make your peace with Nicos once and for all I beg you. Please don't waste the friendship you once shared."

Andros lay back on the bed, his mother was right; he had treated Paris like dirt. Her lovely suit in tatters, her skin scratched and bruised. He did not deserve to be forgiven.

As for Nicos, well that was a different matter.

He smiled weakly at his mother

"I will try" came his meek reply.

# CHAPTER 22

Richard stared in wonder as the little plane began its descent into Skiathos airport. His nose had been permanently pressed against the window as they flew across the sea from Athens.

He could see the little houses of the town grow as they neared, the blackness of the once distant island suddenly become green. He watched as tiny boats made their way across the waters towards the harbor, bringing in freshly caught fish, or returning tourists from their day trips. He spotted the splash as a dolphin jumped in the waves below.

How his life had changed in the past few weeks. It was hard to think that he had missed out on so much, but now he was determined to make up for lost time.

He unconsciously held Eleni's hand a little tighter. This wonderful woman, now his wife, had done so much for him.

The horrors of his time in the camp had been trapped in his mind until she came along. She had listened to him, unafraid to ask questions.

It was all he had needed, to be listened to and understood. She too knew how it felt to want to reverse time and start again. She knew how it felt to be an outcast. She understood his every move. His wife, he could hardly believe it.

He turned for a moment and smiled at her, she was so lovely, he thought to himself.

He went back to the wonderful sights just a thin pane of glass away and waited for the rush of excitement as Andros brought the plane into land. This was his favourite part, the earth rushing towards him, would they make it? It always made his heart beat faster, he loved it, and he felt alive.

He was a little disappointed as the plane gently touched down on the tarmac, how he would love to have a bumpy exciting landing. Oh well perhaps one day.

The first time he had flown made him realize how his father and brothers must have felt. He could only imagine their excitement as they whizzed around the skies shooting down enemy planes. Dodging bullets and ack ack from the ground. How alive they must have felt being in such danger.

"Come on time to leave." Aunt Eleni almost had to drag him from his seat. "The water taxi leaves shortly and I don't want to miss this one or we will have a long wait."

Richard didn't mind if they did. He loved just sitting in a taverna and watching the people pass by. No one looking at him in a bad way, in fact no one even noticing him as they walked slowly along. His father had been so wrong, he was no monster, he was just like everyone else, no longer did he have to hide. It had taken this lovely woman to make him to realise that.

They arrived at the harbor with only a few minutes to spare.

Now for the boat, he loved that too. The feeling of the wind on his face, the spray from the sea, the smell of the salty air. He enjoyed the noise as the boat rode the waves splashing a fine spray as it went back down with a loud thump. Everything was so exciting, but as with the flight, to him the journey was not nearly long enough.

The little boat slowed as it reached Alonysos harbor and he could see people on the beach and in the sea.

"I promised you would be able to swim every day. That is my house there." Eleni pointed to a little white cottage that stood a few yards from the beach. "No excuses, you must swim everyday." She laughed.

"You try and stop me" He replied, his gaze taking in the tavernas and shops. He could hear the faint hum of bouzouki music in the air." What a fabulous little place?" he continued, "It looks like paradise."

"Welcome to your new home Richard" She said, "I hope you will be very happy here" They kissed like young lovers. "I hope Andros will be happy too" she sighed.

Andros had taken them to the water taxi and then strolled around the harbor. He had hoped to catch sight of Paris; she would not be hard to spot in a place like this. With her tall figure and red spikey hair she certainly stood out from the crowd. He wanted to see her from a distance. He wanted to feel his reaction. He wanted to see if he could forgive her.

"Andros good to see you." It was Nicos, not what he had wanted at all.

"Nicos Kalimera." The two men shook hands. Andros felt like punching him but remembered his mother's words. "You are looking well my friend" It was so hard to be pleasant, but he was trying. "And your parents, are they well?" The thought of his mother with Alexi came into his mind and he stiffened slightly.

"Yes fine thanks. Come and have some wine," Nicos pointed to the Gallery "It is cool in there."

"Not today" Andros felt he had had enough of being nice for one day "Perhaps tomorrow. I must get to the beach now, but I had hoped to see Paris first. Do you have any idea where she is staying?" It hurt for him to ask, but he needed to know if Nicos was seeing her.

"I think she has a room in the harbor. I have seen her walking about, she is always making notes." Nicos laughed, "Tomas will know for certain. Ask him."

"I will. Thanks. Bye." Andros walked away relieved to be leaving, the palms of his hands were damp from the strain of being civil.

If Nicos had known exactly which house Paris was in Andros had no idea how he would have reacted, more than likely he would have given in to his feelings and really laid in to him.

As he walked he began to relax, and he realized the meeting with Nicos was not as awful as he had at first thought. He had been dreading his temper flaring, but no. He had been quite civilized and was pleased with himself. He must tell his mother, she would be proud of him he was sure.

Vanni and young Eleni had taken a taxi to the beach when they had arrived, but Andros decided to go on the bus. It had been such a long time since he had ridden on it he had quite forgotten how crowded and smelly it could become. People jostled for the few empty seats, and being a gentleman he stood and held the leather strap.

As the bus bumped along the road he stared from the window, this was such a pretty island. He decided to take some time to see much more. They had always stayed on Alonysos when he was young, the other boys coming over to see him, now it was his turn to see their island.

As they passed through a tiny village he spotted Paris sitting in a taverna. Her head was down and she was writing. She looked amazing, her skin had turned a delicious golden brown and her hair shone in the sunlight. He shouted quickly for the driver to stop and grabbed his case. He almost knocked people over in his haste to leave but he didn't care. He needed to be with her, he would have walked over broken glass, hot coals, anything just to hold her again.

He stood at the side of her table and watched as she scribbled away. She looked up vacantly and tapped her teeth with her pen, obviously deep in thought. She spotted his shadow and turned.

"Hello Paris." he said gently and saw her flinch.

"Andros. What brings you here?"

"You do." He replied. How he wanted to hug her, but he knew he needed to be gentle. "I have come to beg forgiveness. I am so sorry. Please do you think you can ever forgive me?" He looked at a vacant chair and raised his eyebrows. She nodded so he sat down. "Would you like another drink?" Again she nodded. Andros waved to the waiter.

"Ouzo for me and Paris what would you like?" He knew she always drank campari and tonic, and he usually just ordered without asking, but he had certainly listened to his mother's words, "do not take her for granted."

Paris was a little touched. Firstly by his being there, and secondly because he had asked what she wanted. He had asked to be forgiven, yet not mentioned her mistake. Things were looking up. She loved him so deeply, but after that awful night, she was wary.

"How is your book coming on?" he asked as the waiter set the glasses down "May I read some of it?" Now he was taking an interest in her work.

"Fine thanks. But no one can read it until it is finished." She replied "Not even the Eleni's or Richard."

"OK. Then I will wait. I read your piece in the paper on Richard. It was lovely. The thought of him going through so much, it is no wonder he had no confidence. I heard him telling you that day, but to see it in black and white was something else. But what I could not understand is why he had so much contact with The President and British Prime Minister?"

"That is another story that is waiting to be told" she smiled at him. "There is much more to Richard than any of us know. I have started to probe into his life a little more deeply and you would be astonished what I have found. But as I say that is another story. I think my next book in fact."

She found it relaxing talking about her work, and was slightly surprised that Andros was interested.

They sat in silence for a while, Paris returned to her writing. Eventually she put her pen down and sat back.

"That's it finished for today" she smiled at him "That was Tomas's part. I spoke to him yesterday; it is a lovely, but sad story. Very interesting, but then you know all about it from your mother don't you." She gathered her things together. "Here's the bus I must go. Thank you for the drink"

"Please don't go Paris. There is so much I want to say."

"Not now Andros. I think we have done well for today, lets not push it too far."

"Then meet me tomorrow. I will come to the harbor and we can eat together. Please Paris." He pleaded She looked at him and thought.

"OK then. The taverna at the end of the harbor, the one with the huge fish tank outside, 8 o'clock. See you then." She disappeared in to the crowd already on the bus.

Damn. Thought Andros, I will have to wait for the next one; he was going in the opposite direction to the town. He sat back and ordered another drink; at least he now had time to plan tomorrow night. He would make a real effort. His mother was right as usual; he would do all he could to win her back.

By the time the bus appeared Andros was feeling very sleepy. The heat of the afternoon and the drinks, combined with the effort he had made, had left him tired. So tired in fact he could have sat at the table for the rest of the day.

Sluggishly he stood and picked up his case, he was sure it felt heavier than earlier and looked down at it frowning. I must be getting old, he thought.

The bus was crowded as usual so he stood as near to an open window as he could. The combination of bodily odor and sun oil mingling to give a sickly aroma, but luckily he did not have far to travel this time.

His case got heavier by the minute as he walked up the hill and towards the beach. He could already smell the sea and took some deep breaths. Quite invigorating.

Walking through the clearing he stopped and looked at the wonderful sight before him. Golden sand and a turquoise sea. He needed a swim desperately.

Vanni spotted him through the trees, he was with young Eleni and they had begun to mark out the site of their house.

"Andros. Welcome" he called skipping over the bracken towards him. "Here let me take your case. Surely you haven't come on the bus?" He laughed. "That's not like you."

"Never again Vanni." Andros replied "It's OK thanks I will take this to the room. I assume we are sharing?" Andros knew Sofia would not allow Eleni and Vanni to sleep together, well not until they were married. Vanni might just creep into her room later on, but as long as his mother was unaware, it would be OK.

"Of course" Vanni winked "See you later."

Andros left him and waved to his sister as he walked away.

He unpacked the few things he had brought and undressed, it was so nice to feel the air on his hot skin that he stood by the window for a few moments enjoying the sensation. He stared out over the sea and thought about his meetings with Nicos and Paris. He had wanted to kill him, strangle him with his hands, but no he had spoken politely. With Paris he had wanted to hold her, tell her he was so sorry, love her, instead he had talked about her work.

He felt the need to lash out angry with himself for being weak, but yet he was pleased with his handling of both and decided the next step.

He would go into town tomorrow, by taxi not bus, he smiled at the thought, and find her a little present, but what? It had to be something special, yet not over the top. Something she would appreciate, but nothing to daunt her. How he wished his mother were here, she would know. Perhaps he would phone her later.

He waved to Tomas as he walked across the hot sand and straight into the water. It was wonderful. Any tension he had felt soon melted away as he swam as far out to sea as he dared.

As he turned to go back to shore he could see the little taverna and house, looking up the hill he could see the sun glinting on the windows of Alexi's villa, high up amongst the trees. He wondered what the view was like from so high up and hoped one day to find out. It must be at the highest point of the island, he thought.

Treading water he took time to gaze along the coast. He could see the next bay and knew instantly it was the beach Nicos had taken Paris to. He had to admit it was beautiful. He would go there too he promised himself.

He struggled slightly as he swam back to shore. He had come out much further than he had realised, and was not as fit as he had hoped.

Puffing slightly he fell on to any empty sun bed and let the suns rays work their magic. He was asleep in seconds.

"Andros you will burn." It was young Eleni. She looked so funny standing at the side of him he burst out laughing.

"What on earth have you got on?"

"My overalls, well Vanni's spare pair. He insisted that I wear them when we go into the woods, I'm glad really; there are so many brambles and things. Good fit eh." She danced a twirl in the sand showing off her outfit, which was much too big. "So chic."

He noticed how the legs and sleeves had been rolled up into huge lumps of spare material. The waist could have fitted her twice.

"Oh very fetching." He replied with a smirk.

"Come on then get up, you don't want to burn. What would Paris say if she saw you all red?"

Of course, thought Andros, she doesn't know, or does she? He remembered her words "Don't blame Paris."

"Eleni sit down for a moment will you" He patted the sun bed. "You know about Paris and Nicos don't you?" She nodded "Why didn't you tell me then?"

Eleni sat down and explained what had happened. She told him how utterly distraught Paris had been, and how she knew she had lost him.

"She loves you Andros, but now she is frightened of you. Yes, I know about the other night too aunt Eleni told me, she was very shocked. How could you hurt Paris like that?" She stared at her brother with sad eyes. "I was shocked as well. I always thought you were kind and gentle. A lovely man, but now I feel different somehow" She sighed. "But I will forgive you if you show Paris you know what a pig you have been and beg her to forgive you. Please don't let her get away Andros, it would be such a waste." She was pleading for her friend. Andros stared at his sister.

"I love her and I know I have been so stupid, a pig, as you say. She has made one mistake, a huge mistake, but all I could think of was Nicos. I could not see past his grinning face. Mama has told me off good and proper." He laughed nervously. "And she has said it is all my fault. I have driven her into his arms almost. I don't know if that is true, all I know is I want her to love me, I need her."

"Well tell her then, show her." Eleni banged on the sun bed sharply in frustration.

"I intend to never fear. Everyone is allowed one mistake I suppose. It just the thought of Nicos that sticks in my throat. Mama says he is a woman's man. Is that true?"

"You could say that." Eleni was watching her feet as they drew circles in the sand "He has a way of talking that mesmerizes you. He talks pictures if you understand, he sees so much in one glance. It is fascinating to hear."

"So I have heard." Andros was beginning to get tired of people singing Nicos's praises.

"Come on. Out of this sun." She pulled at his arm.

239

He stood up quickly and chased her along the sand. The long legs on her overalls made it difficult for her to run, he caught her easily and wrapped his arms around her waist. He plucked her from the sand and walked towards the water.

"Don't you dare?" She cried as he dangled her over the waves. "Vanni help" She was crying with laughter "Help."

Vanni ran towards them. He launched himself against the struggling pair and all three ended up in the sea. They splashed the water high into the air as they attempted to cover each other with spray.

The noisy laughing trio brought gazes from snoozing holidaymakers on the beach. Some sat up to watch them, joining in the laughter, others ignored the noisy group.

Eventually an exhausted Eleni struggled from the waves, her wet and now very heavy overalls making it even harder to walk. Vanni nodded at Andros and they ran towards her picking her up in their arms. She screamed again, thinking they would return her to the water, but instead they carried her to the house. It was a strange sight as they dangled her, an arm and a leg each, her body dangerously close to the sand.

"What a sight?" Tomas said smiling.

"But a lovely one. See how they laugh together, so happy. Vanni and Eleni were made for each other." Sofia replied as she watched them through misty eyes.

That night they all stayed at Tomas's. Eleni was busy serving drinks while Vanni and Andros sat talking at the little table. Vanni told of their plans for their new home and thanked Andros for making them wait a year.

"It will give us time to do it properly," He said smiling "We can build a lovely home in less than a year. Anyway how come you have stayed here, I thought you would be on Alonysos?"

"I wanted to see Paris" Andros replied."Has Eleni said anything to you?" Vanni nodded.

"She told me everything." He looked towards the sea "I was worried about you my friend. I have never seen you behave so badly. You came very close to disgracing yourself, and spoiling your mothers special day." Andros had forgotten all about that.

"Was I that bad?" he asked not really wanting to know the answer.

"You were horrible. When Michael and I got you home, firstly you threw up all over the patio, and then you became a little violent. You wanted to take on the world, lash out. Luckily Molly knew a special remedy and made you drink it. God knows what was in it." He laughed "But it calmed you down and we were able to clean you up. By the time the others returned it was as if nothing was wrong. I knew different." He paused "Eleni told me what you did to Paris as a way of explaining a few things. I am ashamed of you Andros. You raped her."

Andros could see the look of disgust in Vanni's eyes; it was similar to that of his sister earlier. Vanni spoke further.

"You forget my Eleni has also been with Nicos, yet you do not see me acting like that. I have accepted that she made love with him. I have accepted that he knows her body like I do. But so what? I love her and will put it out of my mind.

This afternoon reminded me of when we were children. The three of us splashing around only then it was you, Nicos and I. Do you remember what fun we had. Don't let one mistake cloud your memories, and don't let what Nicos did ruin your love for Paris."

Andros could only nod in agreement. He could not believe how awful he had been. Not only did he have to apologise to Paris, but to his mother and Richard too, and he supposed Michael, but first he would begin with Vanni.

"Thank you my friend. I am truly sorry." He held out his hand, which after a moments hesitation Vanni shook "Forgive me?" Vanni nodded.

## CHAPTER 23

Andros was pleased when Vanni left to be with Eleni in her room later that night. He wanted to be alone, wanted to think. He had upset so many people, where did he start?

He tossed and turned on the uncomfortable sofa until eventually exhaustion sent him to sleep as dawn broke.

Vanni crept back into the room and slid between the sheets on the bed.

"Andros are you awake?" He called softly. "You should have had the bed. It's too late now but tonight you can sleep in here."

"Thanks." He whispered back, but tonight I wanted to be with Paris, he thought.

A long hot shower worked wonders on his tired body and he looked and felt almost human at breakfast. He listened as Eleni talked about her plans for the day, more work on the house. Vanni agreed, the sooner they cleared the space, the sooner they could turn their plans into bricks.

Andros enjoyed their lively chat; even though he was in no mood to talk himself.

He called for a taxi on his mobile wanting to get to the town in plenty of time. He needed to have a proper look around the shops. His present to Paris had to be just right.

He stared from the car window as it sped along the road, quiet at this time of the morning. A few locals with their donkeys and little fiat trucks were the only ones they came across.

The fishermen were still unloading their catch when he reached the town. He was in for a long wait until the shops opened. Finding an empty table at the taverna Paris had chosen for tonight he sat down and ordered coffee.

Slowly people began to emerge from their beds and the usual parade along the harbor began. Andros sat and watched them stroll. He could feel the heat from the sun begin to warm his skin and knew they were in for yet another scorching day.

"Andros. You are an early bird." It was Nicos "What brings you to town at this hour?" Nicos sat at the table and waved his arm in the air. "More coffee?" Andros nodded.

"I have come to buy a present for Paris." He began "I know what happened between you two and I also have behaved stupidly." He couldn't believe he was going to tell Nicos his thoughts but he was. This was the beginning he needed. "I want to get her something special, something that will show how much I care."

Nicos looked at the man he had admired for so many years. This man who had always been so strong, who could run so fast, swim so fast, whose woman he had taken, and felt a little pity.

"I too am sorry for my behavior Andros. I should not have done it. And as for sending the photograph, well that was cruel of me; if I could turn back the clock, believe me I would. Paris is a wonderful woman, so graceful and beautiful, but now she looks so sad. It is my fault. I am sorry too I expect you want to fight me but here." He held his hand out just like Andros had done to Vanni. Andros took it.

"Thank you my friend." Nicos said, "Let us start again. Now tell me what have you in mind for her?"

"I haven't a clue. Perhaps a pen?" Andros replied with a shrug of his shoulders "What do you think. Will you help me?" If Nicos was so good with women let him think of something Andros thought.

"No. No. No. A pen. She would like it I am sure, and it would remind her of you, but it is a gift to her work, not herself. Now lets think of something very personal. I will help you." Nicos sipped his coffee.

"What about some perfume?" Andros tried again

"Yes that is a good idea. What does she wear?"

"I don't know." Andros replied sadly. Nicos waved his arms in despair.

"What? How long have you known her Andros and you don't know what perfume she wears? This is going to be hard. Now tell me what do you know about her. Describe her to me, what do you see."

Nicos was surprised; it was always one of the first things he asked his women, which is your favourite perfume? He could tell from their reply what sort of woman they were. Fiery ones liked spicy smells. Shy ones liked light flowery smells. He knew them all.

"She is tall and slim. She has bright red hair. She is a journalist." Andros began.

"Stop Andros. You are describing what every one sees. Let me tell you what I see." He waved for the waiter. "I think this calls for ouzo." Andros agreed rather reluctantly, did he really want to hear what Nicos had to say about Paris?

"Close your eyes Andros, picture Paris in your mind, then listen." Nicos paused and sighed.

"I see a beautiful panther, moving her graceful legs slowly but purposefully. She walks rather manly but yet so delicately, her long legs move so smoothly, she glides.

Her eyes move constantly, taking in all around her, they are her minds cameras, her notebooks. Their deep amber changes with what she sees, they flash with excitement at spotting something or someone new. They calm when she is listening and when she is making love, they shine as gold." Andros stiffened in his chair, he felt the urge to hit him once again, but instead kept his eyes tightly shut.

"Her skin is like silk, it shines as she moves, glistens as the suns rays highlight her body. A body so wonderful it could have been chipped from marble, she could be a Grecian goddess come to life, and she smells of woman.

Her hair is like a fire. It burns red and gold in the sunlight, a halo around her beautiful face. A face with features so deftly defined, so wonderful. I see a woman in control, happy in her skin. Confident in her work." Nicos stopped and looked across at Andros. "That is what I saw, but now I see a woman who is broken. Her eyes are dull; her skin no longer shines quite the same. She walks too fast, her mind on other things. Do you want me to go on?" Andros shook his head slowly and opened his eyes; he had been fascinated by what Nicos could see. He had never even noticed her eyes, yet this man who had known her for such a short while had described them to perfection.

"I have brought her a ring." He said enthusiastically. "Here. I have it with me now" He took the little velvet box from his shirt pocket and opened it. "It matches with her hair."

"A big mistake Andros. Paris has red hair now, but what happens in a few years time. She will look at it and remember how it used to be. She will look in the mirror and see her hair fading, but the stone will still shine brightly. It will make her feel so old and she will come to hate it. Believe me." He waved for the bill. "Come with me I want to show you something."

They walked through the maze of little shops and entered the Gallery.

"You want to say sorry to her, that is correct?" Andros nodded "You want to say you love her?" Nicos walked around the shop staring at the photographs on the wall. "Here we are. Perfect" He took a frame from the wall. "Sit down and tell me what you see."

Andros stared at the picture. It was of two children, a boy and girl on a beach. She was standing with her back to the boy gazing out to sea. The wind was blowing her hair to one side and he could see her face was sad. The little boy was walking towards her; behind his back he held a twig from an olive tree. His face showed concern.

"Nicos you are a genius. It will speak for me. I will give it to her tonight." Andros was excited the picture was perfect. It said everything he wanted to say.

245

"Wait until you part Andros. If you give it to her too soon she will feel obliged to stay even if she is ready to leave. Let her stand to leave and then give it to her."

"But I had hoped for us to be together tonight." Andros frowned as he looked at him.

"You must wait. Give her time. Let her come to you my friend. No, tonight you will entertain her, make her laugh. Be gentle and listen to what she has to say. Don't go rushing in and expect every thing to be as it was just because she has agreed to meet you. Tell me why do you think she has chosen that particular taverna?"

"Because she likes fish I suppose." Andros replied with a shrug of his shoulders.

"You need many lessons in women my friend. No she has chosen that one because of where it is. She is frightened of you; she wants to be in a public place. That taverna is by the walkway and tonight, as with every night many people will be strolling past. If she feels threatened she can leave and you cannot stop her. There will be too many people about for you to stop her." Nicos paused "Tell me why is she frightened of you? What have you done to her?"

Andros told him, disgusted to hear his own words. Nicos shook his head as he listened.

"What time are you meeting her?" he asked eventually.

"8 o'clock" came the reply.

"You see again. No Greek eats at that time. It is still far too hot, but it is the time the English eat. She is making you do, as she wants. She is showing you she is her own woman."

Andros was amazed. He really had no idea.

"Now what will you wear?" Nicos asked.

"What on earth has that got to do with anything?"

"It means a lot to a woman. Now let me think. You must look relaxed but smart. You must not look threatening not too business like. Do you understand?"

Andros shook his head in bewilderment. He always dressed well, he had wardrobes full of lovely things, but he had never really given them much thought. A suit for a meal out, trousers and jacket for more informal evenings, but how on earth could clothes look threatening?

"Right." Nicos could not believe how little Andros knew. "Have a very close shave, shower and cover you body in cream, don't put on too much aftershave, you want to smell her, not yourself. Dry your hair with your fingers like this." He ran his fingers through his own. "Casual trousers and shirt open one button only. So now you look smart, but at ease.

Have your money in your shirt pocket not in your trousers or you will have to stand over her to pay the bill. It will make her feel unequal. If she wants to contribute to the bill, then allow her." Andros was shocked. He had never allowed a woman in his company to pay for anything. "It will help her regain some of her confidence and she won't feel as if you have bought her." Nicos continued. "You have to tread very carefully Andros. Listen to what I have said and learn."

Andros watched as Nicos wrapped the picture. He took time to place a thin gold ribbon around and curled the ends with some scissors.

"There you are. Perfect. It is in our own paper so she will see you have been here, and the ribbon will show her you stayed for a while. Obviously if you do not have a black eye, then we have not fought." He added laughing.

"Nicos a few days ago I wanted to kill you, but now I want to thank you. How much do I owe?"

Andros reached for his wallet, fumbling in his back pocket.

"I think you have paid an exorbitant price for this already." Nicos replied, "Never before have you listened to me, today you did. That is payment enough as far as I am concerned. I hope this evening goes as you wish." The two men shook hands.

"Thank you." Andros was emotional. It had been quite a morning.

Back at the beach Andros decided to swim before lunch, the sea here was perfect. The surrounding hills sheltered the bay from any winds, allowing the waves to be calm and the shallow water to warm as it moved gently with the tide. He noticed it cooled rapidly as it deepened.

He swam quickly out over the waves, the strength of his muscles pulling him through the water. He remembered what Vanni had said. Yes I remember when we were young, he thought, and how I had always wanted to win, had to win in fact. How he had laughed as Nicos always came last. Now it was Nicos showing him how to win, win back Paris. How the tables had been turned.

Returning to the shore he let the sun dry his skin before dressing for lunch.

Young Eleni was already serving drinks and Tomas the food. He could hear Sofia moving pans in the kitchen and thought how contented they all looked.

Perhaps that was his problem. Never content. He always had to be best at everything, have the best things, and earn the most money. Always striving to do better. Well that would change; if Paris would allow him back into her life he would put her first. Travel with her, help her. The business could be run from anywhere in the world with his laptop. He knew Vanni did much of his work here on the beach, so what was to stop him? His sister's fortune was managing itself and paying her an allowance. So why should he worry? He would change definitely change.

As usual the others gathered around the little table when the customers had been served. Sofia produced a superb array of dishes and Eleni poured the drinks.

"How did this morning go Andros? Did you get what you wanted?" She asked.

"I was a very interesting morning thank you, and yes I got a lovely gift for Paris." He felt no need to tell them anything else.

"Oh Can I see?" Eleni looked excited

"No. It is all wrapped up so no." He could see she was disappointed so he added, "I bought her a picture from Nicos's gallery. He was very helpful" Vanni's expression was one of utter shock.

"Pardon. You have been to see Nicos?" He managed to ask.

"Yes I have." Andros replied and returned to eating, signaling an end to this conversation.

The little group covered many topics as they ate but the underlying subject was Andros and Nicos. Everyone wanted to know more but Andros stayed quiet.

He retired to his room after lunch to try and chose his clothes for the evening. It took some time and the room looked like a bomb had hit it with all of his things scattered around, not that he had brought that many, it was just the way he had thrown them over the bed and sofa. Eventually he made his decision.

He took his time in the shower and in his mind could hear Nicos telling him what to do. It was very strange.

Eventually he was ready. Nervous, even a little scared, but ready.

"How do I look?" He asked Eleni before leaving.

"You look superb." she replied. "Different somehow but I can't put my finger on it. Trendy with your hair like that. It suits you. Makes you look younger."

Andros had taken note of everything Nicos had said and followed it to the letter. He had to admit, he felt good. His skin had drunk in the cream he had pinched earlier from Eleni, and his hair looked so casual, yet smart. Yes he felt good.

Clutching his parcel he walked over to the waiting taxi. Nicos was right yet again, it was far too hot to eat, but if that was what she wanted, so be it.

His shirt stuck to his shoulders as the car took him into the town; it was a good job he was not going by the bus. He would have felt even more scruffy and dirty at the end of his journey if he had. Andros could not believe how nervous he felt as he walked along the harbor towards the taverna. His heart was beating fast and his fist was clenched.

"Good you have arrived in plenty of time." It was Nicos. "Now let's have a look at you." He turned Andros round looking up and down. "Well done, that is perfect. Now go and pick a table in the shade, the sun is still too hot to sit in. Go for one in the middle, so when night comes she will not feel chilly. Don't go too far back as she may feel trapped. Right off you go and remember, be gentle, listen, make her laugh. OK"

"Ok boss." Andros laughed he felt like a child going off to school. How on earth did Nicos know all of these things he thought as he walked away, and how had he gone through life not knowing. It was then he realised his mother had told the truth. She knew just how good Alexi and Nicos were, and how easy it would have been for Paris to fall into his trap. He couldn't even blame Nicos now after the way he had described her, who could resist such a woman. A lovely panther, he was right, she was just that.

He chose a table carefully and sat to wait, fidgeting as he looked time and time again at his watch. His drink arrived and amused himself watching as holidaymakers slowly strolled past. He tried to see them as Nicos would. Looking at the sun reflecting on golden hair, watching the way everyone moved, all so differently he noticed. It took some time but gradually he became accustomed to seeing below the surface.

"Hello Andros." Paris had arrived silently at his table. He stood quickly and helped her to sit.

"You look wonderful." He said taking in her outfit, a well fitting linen dress and pretty sandals. "That colour really suits you. It goes with your eyes." Steady he thought to himself, go steady. He was not saying anything that was untrue; the creamy gold of her dress did suit her eyes. He was angry with himself for not noticing them before. What did Nicos say about them? Flashing, glowing. He looked into her lovely face and saw fear in them.

Oh God what had he done to this marvelous woman.

He ordered her drink and asked about her work, his words sounding stiff and unfriendly, but slowly the drinks, and the warm evening helped him to relax.

He could see Paris settling herself further into her chair and hoped it was a sign that she too was feeling slightly more at ease.

She spoke softly, telling him about her plans. It was almost as if they were strangers he thought.

He learned that she was going to Kefalonia with his mother in a couple of days; and they were going to visit the village where she had been born. They hoped to go to the school and Paris named a host of other places the visit might include. Aunt Eleni had said she wanted to see everything, learn everything, feel Marco, Paris told him excitedly.

He wanted to go with them and asked politely.

"I would love to see where my father was born. Love to see the places in the photographs. In fact I could fly you both over. If you would like that?" He gazed at her longingly.

She could see he was trying, he had made such an effort, she agreed he could come with them. On one condition though, they went where his mother wanted to go.

"Anything you say. I will carry your note books and sharpen your pencils if you like." She laughed at his comment. Good, Nicos had said make her laugh. In his mind he was ticking off the things he had been told to do, that was another one done.

"Would you like to order now?" The waiter was at their side.

"Are you ready Paris? Have you chosen?" He waited for her to order first.

They spent a wonderful evening talking and laughing. It felt so good to be in her company, but he remembered he had to be gentle.

As the time went by her eyes shone, he could see that much of the fear had now gone. He hoped never to see that look in her eyes ever again. It had made him feel like an animal.

They sat drinking coffee and he could see by her movements she was ready to leave. He called for the bill and reached for his money, in his shirt pocket as ordered, it actually did feel much easier. He had learned so much today.

As she reached inside her bag he felt slightly uncomfortable but let her throw some notes on the table anyway.

How he must have hurt her. Nicos was right yet again.

She stood and held out her hand; suddenly he didn't care, no way in this world was he going to shake her hand so he took it and kissed it gently.

"Thank you for a lovely evening Paris. I am looking forward to our little trip and will see you soon." He reached under the table and held out his parcel. He could see from her reaction to the paper and ribbon she was pleased. "Its just a little token to say sorry." His words were inadequate he knew, but touching her skin had emptied his brain almost. He wanted to hold her, stroke her, make better the wrong he had done.

"Thank you" She looked into his eyes "Thank you." He wanted her to open it there and then, but instead she held it in her hands as she walked away.

"Go on follow. But keep your distance." Nicos was at his side. "You have done well so far but the next step is to find out where she lives, then come straight back here. OK"

"OK"

Andros walked behind slowly, easily able to follow her and for the first time he noticed how she seemed to float as she walked, her long legs almost fluid as she moved. She stood to look at the goods on a pavement stall and he turned quickly in fear of being seen.

He watched as she opened the door of a small harbor side house. He had asked Tomas where she was staying, but the reply meant nothing until now. He waited for a few moments just staring at the building. He noticed a light come on in one of the upstairs rooms and saw her reach to close the shutters. He slowly returned to Nicos.

"Right so tomorrow you must be the first thing that she sees. When she opens those shutters you must be sitting on the wall. Do not look up. Just be there, make sure you are early, about 7 I would think. When you can sense she is coming down, run into a shop. Any shop, but don't be there when she comes through that door. Right"

"Right, but what will that do?" Andros was puzzled

"When she opens the shutters and sees you she will come to ask why you are there. It's a woman thing, she won't be able not to. If you are gone when she reaches to door she will wonder all day where you are. What you are doing. Believe me you will be on her mind constantly. Eventually she will give in and phone you. Probably about 6 ish."

"Nicos how do you know all of this?"

"Years of practice my friend, years of practice." He patted Andros's back as they laughed together.

"What shall I say if she phones?"

"Oh Andros. Do I have to do everything for you? Right. It is when not if. You tell her you enjoyed your evening so much you could not stop thinking about her, you could not sleep, and you just wanted to be near her, make out you have been there all night. When she asks why you ran away, tell her you were worried she would be angry. Next you are going to ask why she will phone at 6 o'clock." Andros nodded "It is the right time for you to ask her to go out with you again. Time enough to get ready, and not too late for you to come into the town. It is the time when she knows you will be resting after your day. If you don't ask her out, then it gives her chance to make other arrangements. See how clever I am?" Nicos bewildered Andros; he seemed to know so much it was incredible. "Here" Nicos spoke again "Have my mobile number and you can let me know, in fact let me have yours whilst we are at it."

They concentrated whilst they swapped numbers, their heads close together.

"There, now you are in my phone." Nicos said proudly, and it truly did mean so much to him. "Go home Andros, you have an early start tomorrow, don't forget you will have to take the bus, no taxi's will be running at that time." Andros pulled a face; the last place he wanted to be was on that bus again.

The following morning he was pleased to see the bus was empty as he climbed on board yawning. Unfortunately it did not stay that way for long. Locals on their way to work in the town soon had it brimming full, but at least this time the sweet sickly smell of sun oil was not present.

Andros did as Nicos had told him and sat on the harbor wall. Once or twice he glanced up at Paris's window, but daring only the quickest of peeks. He felt his skin prickle as her heard her open the shutters. He could feel her wonderful eyes looking down upon him; he just sat and gazed out to sea.

He sensed that she had left the window and ran swiftly into the maze of shops.

Hell fire, Nicos had forgotten they would all be closed. He looked round panicking, where could he hide?

"Quick this way." He heard Nicos call. Andros ran into the open door of the Gallery. "Sorry it was not until I was in bed last night that I realized you would have no where to run. I wish you could have seen your face. Oh how I wish I had had my camera, you looked petrified for a moment." They collapsed in laughter. "Come on I will take you back in my car, it is just around the corner."

Vanni and Eleni were just entering the woods with some workmen as the car pulled up. She was amazed to see Andros and Nicos together, and laughing so much.

"Are you going to let us in on the joke?" She called and waved to them

"Not yet little one." Nicos replied, wiping tears from his eyes. "Perhaps one day."

The two men walked together across the sand.

"Come Nicos I owe you a coffee." Andros was still giggling as he spoke.

Tomas too was astonished to see them together, his sister had told him the full story in her phone call the previous night.

Sitting at the little table they discussed the mornings events, laughing now and again like children. It did them so much good. When Eleni and

Vanni came to join them she was angry that they would not tell her, and the fact they still kept laughing made her worse.

Eventually Nicos rose to leave.

"Have a good day my friend." He held his hand out to Andros. "I hope everything works out. Don't forget to phone me later."

"I will I promise." Andros replied shaking his hand. "Bye."

"Bye everyone." Nicos called as he ran back to his car.

"Right what are you planning for today Andros?" Vanni asked.

"Nothing much why?" Came the reply.

"Well I will bring you my laptop and you can get cracking on some work. We have a lot of business to discuss with the builders, and it would help me out no end."

"Ok. Fetch it down and I will work here. It will do me good to do something, help pass the time. I will just phone mama while you go, Eleni do you want to speak to her too?" She nodded eagerly.

Vanni emerged with the slim computer and placed it in front of Andros, who was still talking to his mother. It was the usual parent child conversation.

"Yes mama, with Nicos would you believe, pause, yes that's right", pause. "OK then", pause" No", pause "No", pause "Yes see you tomorrow. Bye, Oh Eleni wants a word." he passed the phone to his sister gladly. His mother was still angry with him but had been pleased he had mentioned Nicos in a friendly way.

"Vanni." Sofia called. "Have you had your breakfast. Don't go working in the sun without food."

Andros looked at Vanni.

"Mothers!" they said in unison.

Eleni and Vanni went off to discuss their project with the workmen further and Andros sat at the little table tapping away on the laptop. It was easy to check Richards shares, as he still thought of them, transfer money from one account to another, and catch up in some stray goods not yet arrived at the warehouse in Athens. He spent some time ordering more goods and decided to have a look at Kefalonia on the Internet. He desperately wanted to make a good impression when they all went over.

He tried to memorise some of the villages' names and came across the one where his mother and father were born. It was huge. The little village of Lassi was now a large tourist area. He hoped his mother would not be too disappointed.

After shutting down the connection and closing the case he began to think once again about Paris. How could he have hurt such a wonderful being? Nicos had painted a marvelous picture with his words, and Andros felt sick to the stomach over his actions. Why did he not see all of the things Nicos had until now, when it could possibly be too late?

He took the little computer back to Vanni's room and changed into his trunks. Looking around he laughed to himself. Here he was one of the richest men in the world, sharing a bedroom with his cousin. He could be in one of the best hotels on the island, but no he was sleeping on a sofa. Why? Because it is where my family is, he thought to himself. Now he understood why young Eleni wanted to live here. She felt safe, felt comfortable. Her security people must be in heaven, they would have to stay as long as she did. What a job.

Once again he swam out as far as he could, the exertion helping to relax his tight shoulder muscles. He felt so nervous, what if Paris didn't phone. What then.

He returned to the beach and fell on to an empty sun bed, one of many today. The season was beginning to slow now autumn was under way. The days were still hot, but the nights just beginning to feel chilly at times. Skiathos would soon be getting ready for winter.

He had spent so long on the computer, and in the sea he was surprised to see that it was already 4 o'clock when he returned to his room. His stomach gave a slight growl, reminding him he had not eaten, but he dare not. Just the thoughts of food made him feel sick, so tight were his muscles.

He looked at his phone and gasped. The battery was flat. Stupid man. Now where was his adapter?

He searched through his things throwing them all over the floor in a state of panic and gasped with relief as the little black box came to the surface. Quickly he plugged it in and watched as the battery light flashed. Andros prayed for there not to be a power cut. It would be just his luck. His phone needed a few hours to recharge fully, but the couple it was going to get now would have to do.

He paced the room watching his phone flashing as life was pumped back into it. How could he have forgotten? Every night for years he had made sure it was plugged in, but last night was so different, he would probably not even remembered his own name had he been asked.

He lay on the bed and waited. Deciding that the phone had got enough power for now he unplugged it and placed it on the pillow by his side. He just stared wishing for it to ring.

He almost fell off the bed in surprise as it sprang to life. "Paris" it flashed. He hardly dare answer. It rang and rang as he stared at her name. Taking a deep breath, so deep he felt dizzy, he pushed the button to answer.

"Hello." was all he could croak. Just as Nicos had said she asked about this morning. He remembered what he could and made a few things up himself as the conversation lengthened.

"I have someone I would like you to meet if you are free tonight," she asked huskily from the little gold phone. "We are eating at the same taverna as last night. You could join us for coffee if you want."

"I would love to come, as long as you are sure." Don't go too fast. Nicos's words rang in his mind. Tread carefully. "But I don't want to intrude."

"No its fine. We will see you about 10 then. Bye"

We. Who was it? Surely she had not got another man this quickly. He jumped as his phone rang once more. "Nicos" the screen flashed this time.

"Well was I right?" He almost shouted. "Has she phoned?"

"Yes she has just a few minutes ago. She has asked me to join her and someone else for coffee tonight. But I haven't a clue who it is."

"Great. It must be another woman or she would not have asked. Perhaps someone who has heard of you. I bet she hasn't said a word to them about what has happened or you would not have been invited. You watch she will greet you as if nothing has occurred."

"Nicos you never cease to amaze me." Andros said in slight shock

"Tell you what I will join you. I will just saunter by and see you. Say hello and speak to Paris. She will see we are friends if you ask me to join you. It will put her mind at ease, then I can talk to this other person and you can carry on being nice to Paris. See you later." Click. He was gone.

"But you haven't told me what to wear." Andros shouted at the dead phone and then laughed at himself for being so silly.

Andros showered and creamed his body. He must buy Eleni some more of this he thought slapping on yet another large blob. He chose his clothes carefully, not threatening, just like Nicos had taught him. Dried his hair with his fingers and was ready. No present to take tonight, his hands felt empty. He would get something when he reached town, anything just to stop his fingers from twitching as they were.

He decided to have a sandwich and sat at the little table by the bar. Eleni was busy serving the customers who were there, but she found time to talk for a while.

"Only a week ago it was crowded, but now only a handful of tourists remain, what a change and so suddenly," Eleni said sighing. "Never mind it will soon be Christmas," she added with a smile. "My first Christmas on Eleni Beach. I wonder if it will snow?"

"I doubt it little one, but you never know. Anyway why don't you all come over to Athens? We could have a family Christmas it would be wonderful."

"That sounds great Andros. I will ask Vanni. By all of us do you mean Tomas and Sofia as well?"

"Of course I mean everyone." He reeled the names off one by one.

"You have forgotten Paris," she said gently.

"I will ask, but I'm not too hopeful. But I will ask one day."

The evening went slowly as he looked yet again at his watch. Blast it I will go now, he thought. It was only 9 o'clock but he could walk through the shops until later. He picked up his phone and rang for a taxi. It came in minutes, the driver too feeling the lack of the tourist trade, he moaned all the way into Skiathos town.

Andros sauntered slowly through the streets, spotted a perfume shop and entered. A pretty young girl came and asked what he was looking for. He remembered Eleni's cream and asked for that, and then seeing that the girl was eager to help he asked her to find a certain perfume for him. Sorry he didn't know the name.

"Tell me about the lady it is for." she asked quite concerned.

He described Paris as Nicos had.

"Ah she has a perfume that is light and lasting, it has a touch of musk yet it is not overpowering. This lady is strong, confident, yet wants to be looked upon as a delicate woman." Andros nodded. "Then I think it will be this." The girl sprayed some mist into the air. "Or perhaps this." Another spray of mist. Andros closed his eyes and took a deep breath. It was as if Paris was standing at his side.

"Yes that is it, the second one."

"Envy."

"Pardon"

"Envy, that is its name. Gucci Envy. Shall I wrap it for you?"

"Please. And thank you so much for your time and effort. What perfume do you wear?"

"None in particular I like most of them" she replied "I don't have to wear any certain one as I try a different one each day. They are a little too expensive for me to buy so I have free sprays." She giggled.

"Then pick your favourite and wrap that one for me too." He smiled at her.

She gave him the two little parcels, one of which he returned immediately.

"This is for you and thank you again." He said still grinning.

She was a little embarrassed and surprised. She had chosen a rather expensive perfume thinking it was for his lady again, but to have it given to her was so kind of him.

He left the shop feeling very pleased with himself; at last he was learning, and enjoying it too. Walking through the shops he stopped outside of a jewellers and gazed at the fabulous gold trinkets on display. He looked closely at the trays of rings and thought perhaps Nicos was right. The red stone might not be right for Paris, but a glorious diamond certainly would be.

He heard the church clock strike 10 and ran through the streets. Turning the corner by the taverna he scoured the faces at the tables. For a moment he thought he was too late and then he heard her laugh, he stood and listened. It was a wonderful sound.

"Andros come and join us." Nicos was already sitting with Paris and her friend. Blast he had hoped for some time with her before Nicos appeared.

"Oh this is Andros is it?" A strangers voice said, "I have heard so much about you. When are you going to make an honest woman of my sister?" It was obvious this person had no idea they had fallen out, a good sign surely that Paris had not mentioned anything to her.

"Andros meet Sky, my little sister." Paris was blushing slightly.

"Sky, hello." He never knew she had a sister. "And the answer to your question is when your sister says yes." They all laughed.

"Don't you think that is the most wonderful name. Sky. It conjures up such a lovely picture." Nicos was staring at the girl. Here he goes again, thought Andros.

"Our parents were a little quirky, 60s hippies no less." She said "They named us after the places where they thought we were conceived" she showed no embarrassment at all "Paris is obvious, but me well I'm lucky not to be called mile high." The joke took a few seconds to register and then they all burst out laughing. "Only they got it slightly wrong" She nodded towards a pair of metal crutches leaning against the wall.

"Sky finds it hard to walk well." Paris said softly

"You mean I can't walk with out those." She nodded towards them again "Something to do with tablets mum took when she was expecting me. They were supposed to stop her throwing up in the mornings, but they did this instead." She was so honest, bright and fresh her comments drew no pity from the others, there was no need.

Nicos waved for the waiter and ordered coffee and brandy for them all.

"Are you trying to get me legless?" Sky asked him quite seriously.

"I never get my girls drunk on a first date." Nicos replied and could have cut his tongue off "But if they want to then that's OK by me." The words came from his mouth quickly.

"Have you brought Paris another present?" Sky asked spotting Andros's parcels.

"I have actually. Her favourite perfume." He handed the bag over "And some cream for my sister. If I had known you were here I would have brought something nice for you too."

"Well you can buy me something another day if you feel that guilty about it but I warn you I have very expensive tastes." Sky replied with a giggle.

"Thank you Andros that was a lovely thought" Paris was surprised he knew what she liked. "And thank you for that marvelous picture. It is breath taking." She smiled into his eyes and he knew she had understood its contents.

The conversation gradually split between Andros and Paris, Nicos and Sky as they all relaxed, only occasionally were all four involved.

Andros asked a few questions about their trip the following day and surprised Paris with his knowledge of Kefalonia, but she supposed as it was his parents home he was bound to know.

Nicos was on another planet. Never before had he met anyone like Sky.

She was beautiful he could see that. Facially like Paris, but she had long pale auburn hair, her skin was so pale it was almost white and flecked with hundreds of tiny freckles. Her eyes were a darker shade of amber than her sisters, but they flashed in a similar way as she spoke.

It was only when he looked below the table he could see the big difference. Whilst Paris had long, lean strong legs, Sky's were much shorter, with one slightly twisted at the ankle. It was obvious that this way the cause of her disability.

She reminded him of a lion cub that had been injured in a fight. She needed to be looked after, loved and helped to grow strong, yet he could see she was filled with inner strength. He felt his heart melt. Surely he was not falling for this girl, he thought. But he already knew the answer; he wanted to look after her now and forever. How many times had he thought that in the past? How many women had heard him speak words of love? How many times had he promised things just to get them into bed? Promise the world and they were his.

This was different and he knew it. All of his past conquests paled into insignificance as he listened to her speak.

"I suppose you'll be off now then." She said as he emptied his coffee cup

"Why do you say that?"

"Well you must have better things to do than sit here talking to a cripple. I bet you have some gorgeous woman locked away waiting for you to return."

"No to both. Any way why can't I sit and enjoy your company. And don't ever let me hear you say you are a cripple again. You are a beautiful young lady, just remember that."

"But I am" she said sadly. "Just look at my leg."

Nicos peered down and could see it was more twisted than he had first thought.

"Listen to me. That was an accident."

"Yeah right. A bottle of pills type accident."

"No an accident by the angels." Paris and Andros stopped talking to listen to him speak, they both knew he was about to tell one of his picture stories.

"Look at it like this" He began "When you were first born, high up in heaven, your angel mother was ecstatic, you were so beautiful, so delicate, but your wings had not quite grown enough. So instead of flying around the clouds you had to be carried. It would only be for a short while as it was a common problem with baby angels in those days." Sky giggled and flapped her arms. "Well one day when your angel parents were taking you for a trip around a huge white puffy cloud you suddenly wriggled and slipped from your mother's arms. How your angel parents cried as you fell through the air, twisting and turning as you gathered speed, heading for the earth, your wings still far too small to help.

Just as you fell this plane flew across the skies, you plunged right through its roof injuring your leg, and straight into your earth mothers womb." Sky giggled again.

"When you were born again some time later, your wings had disappeared; you would not need them on earth. You were still as beautiful, but your leg had not mended. So you see it really was an accident you are actually a little angel."

They were all silent. What a fabulous story it had been. Paris looked at her sisters glowing face and could see tears of happiness welling up in her eyes.

"What would have happened if I had missed the plane and landed in the sea? Would I have grown flippers?" Sky managed to ask.

Nicos looked at her seriously.

"No you would have become a mermaid. The most beautiful mermaid in the Aegean." He said softly

"Why the Aegean, surely it would have been The English Channel near to where I was born for the second time."

"The best mermaids are always found in the seas off Greece, we pride ourselves in having only the most beautiful ones in the universe." He smiled into her eyes. "And now I will give you my arm and walk you back to your room."

"Sky is staying with me so she will be coming with us tomorrow." Paris explained to Andros. "I though it might do her good to spend some time over here. Good fresh food and things, since I am stopping for the next 9 months she can stay as long as she likes."

Nicos stood and held out his arm.

"Madam shall we stroll?" He passed her one of the crutches and carried the other one himself. It took them a few shaky steps to walk in time, but soon they were strolling off down the harbor road. Andros paid the bill and walked slowly behind with Paris, so pleased that she took his arm without hesitating.

"Paris tells me you are an artist?" Sky said after a few moments "Will you paint me?"

"Oh I don't paint, I use a camera. I will show you some of my work when we get back from Kefalonia."

"Are you coming too then? I didn't know that"

"Nor did I until just now. I am going because you are. I want to be with you to be your crutch. It feels nice." He smiled down at her and she lost her rhythm slightly. He stopped and let her sit on the harbor wall. "And I will take a lovely picture. I will show you that you really are an angel."

"Or I could have been a mermaid" she said excitedly.

"Yes an angel mermaid, both rolled into one."

"Nicos" she said seriously "You have made me feel very special tonight, I know it's a load of twaddle, but thank you." She struggled to stand and kissed his cheek.

"What is this twaddle? I'm sorry I don't understand" He had never heard the word before in his life. She explained.

"I am hurt that you don't believe me, but tomorrow I will show you it is true." He put on a sad face. Sky laughed.

"I hope you do." she said smiling "Andros, Nicos is coming with us tomorrow isn't that great." Andros just grinned; he was getting a little tired of Nicos appearing everywhere he went. He still had this urge to punch him, but knew without his knowledge he would probably not be with Paris now.

"I only have room for four in the plane. How will you get there?" He asked, hoping that would put Nicos off.

"On the dolphin "Nicos replied. "The dolphin is the fast water taxi," he explained to Sky. "The early one. I shall probably be there before you so I can meet you at the airport." He added looking into her eyes.

"I think I shall have to make two journeys," Andros said thinking out loud "There's Paris, Sky, Mama, Richard, Eleni, Vanni."

"Can I go with you?" Sky asked, "I have never been on this dolphin you mentioned, it would be so exciting." Her eyes shone like a flame. "Pretty please."

Nicos looked to Paris to decide.

"Only if you behave and if Nicos agrees." She replied to his unasked question. "What time do you want her?"

"It leaves here about 7.30" He said, "Do you think you can be ready for that time?"

"You bet I can. Nicos is going to take my photograph tomorrow Paris, I can't wait" Sky was so excited.

"What time do you want me ready for Andros?" Paris asked.

"Mama and Richard are coming on the 10 o'clock boat, so 10.30 should do. Here in the harbor and we can get taxi's to the airport." He said, now pleased Nicos was going too. With Sky out of the way he would have Paris to himself for a while.

"Ok then. Lets all go to bed and see we'll see you tomorrow." She added, bending to help Sky stand but Nicos beat her to it. He held her arm and walked her across the road.

"See you tomorrow Jack." she said laughing

"Jack. Who is this Jack?" he frowned

"When we were younger we used to watch a TV programme called Jackanory. Someone would read a story and there were lots of nice pictures, so from now on I will call you Jack. I think it fits you perfectly. Night night." She reached up and kissed his cheek again. "Jack" she giggled.

Andros nervously kissed Paris goodnight, his body aching to take her in his arms and stay with her. It was so hard for him, but he knew he had to tread very carefully.

When Nicos returned they decided to go for one last drink.

"Water for me thanks." Andros ordered from the waiter "If I'm flying tomorrow better have water."

"Well I need something stronger." Nicos sighed "What a girl that Sky is?"

They both laughed at the thought of the unusual young girl.

# Chapter 24

It was a beautiful morning as Nicos helped Sky on to the dolphin shaped boat. The sun was still low in the sky and a slight wisp of mist hung over the cypress trees that stood by the harbor entrance.

Swallows swooped low over the sea catching their food before it became too hot for them to do anything other than shelter from the suns rays.

The fishing boats were unloading their catch and there was an air of excitement as the fisherman called to each other. A faint smell of their catch mingled with the sea air, which was fresh and invigorating.

Sky was enchanted as they walked across the little wooden bridge to the boat.

"This is fab" she said gazing around "So much better than London. All I can see from my room is buildings." She took a deep breath "Umm. Lovely if you like fish," she laughed.

Nicos found them two empty seats together and sat her down by the window. He carefully placed his camera bag and rucksack in the locker above them. Then sat down himself, her crutches between his knees.

"I will try to point a few things out to you as we go, but the boat travels very fast so don't be too disappointed if all you can see is spray."

"OK"

"Tell me what do you do in London?" He wanted to know everything about this girl.

"I work for Paris. She tells me where her next interview or whatever is and I sort out her tickets, hotels and everything really. So I know every time she goes to see Andros," she winked and giggled "I find out what the people she is going to see like, what they don't like, what they eat or don't eat. You know that sort of thing. Its no good her wearing red if the person she is seeing hates red, or taking them a box of chocolates if they hate chocolate. Mind you they must be mad not to like chockie. I love it."

Nicos made a mental note.

"It sounds interesting work," he said smiling at her. "Where do you find all of these things out from?"

"I do it all over the internet. It gets a bit boring sometimes though especially in winter and she is off somewhere hot. I always want to go with her, but can't. So this is great. She is staying put for once so I can have a holiday too."

The engines roared into life and the boat began to move. It wobbled as it left the moorings and Sky quickly grabbed his hand.

Nicos was pleased; he held her hand between his as they gathered speed, enjoying the feel of her soft warm skin. A stupid grin lit his face.

"Oh no." he said suddenly making her jump, "I have ordered a motor bike for the other end, I forgot, sorry."

"That's OK. I've never been on one of those either, so that will be two new things in one day. I'm glad Paris isn't with us she would have a fit. At least you haven't booked a stupid sports car; I can get in them but not out. Well not without looking like a right idiot." She giggled. "Oh what a smashing day and it's only just begun. Jack you are brilliant!"

Nicos gulped. His lovely car called stupid, but he could well imagine the trouble she would have trying to get out of the low seats.

As he had promised, he was able to point things out until the boat got up to speed, and then all they could see was spray. Sky seemed to enjoy that though just as much and the journey passed quickly as they chatted.

Her stomach felt as if it was floating as the boat neared Kefalonia and slowed down. Making its way through the narrow channel towards the harbor, the waves, although slight, made it wobble from side to side as gradually it came to a stop.

"Ugh. I don't like that bit much," she said rubbing her tummy and sticking her tongue out. "It's a bit sickey."

Nicos laughed, it was true the floating sensation did make you feel a little queasy until you got used to it. Once again he was able to point out things to her now the spray had stopped flying quite to high.

"Argostoli" He pointed to the town "The village the others are going to is just over that hill, and the airport is that way, but we have got hours before they get here."

"Good" she said "Will you take me for a spin round before Paris sees me on a bike."

"Well I have arranged a photo shoot so we will have to go there first. I will take you later I promise."

"Where are we going to do the photos?" Sky had forgotten her queasy tummy in her excitement. "Come on spill the beans"

Nicos was not too sure what she meant. Some of her words he had never heard before.

"I am going to make you an angel but you must trust me. I can only do this if you trust me 100%."

"You mean I'm going to be naked," she gasped. "Great. That's three new things!"

"No not quite. Anyway stop asking questions, just wait." He was embarrassed.

The boat unloaded is passengers on to the pretty harbor at Argostoli, similar in many ways to that on Skiathos, only much larger and busier.

Here the fishermen had already sold their catch and were busy mending nets, swilling down decks and getting the boats ready for the coming nights work. It was busy yet relaxed, and in the usual Greek way rather noisy.

Nicos held Sky as she negotiated the little wooden bridge once more.

"That was hard work," she puffed as they stepped on to the tarmac. "Not easy with these at all" The heat and effort left a fine shiny film on her forehead.

Damn thought Nicos he had completely forgotten about her crutches when he had ordered the bike earlier that morning. Sky read his thoughts as he walked over to the bike hire office.

"Don't worry. We can leave them here. You will have to be my crutch, you said last night you would be."

Nicos was a bit unsure, but it was the only way, other than to hire a car but he knew she would be so disappointed if he did. The lady in the office agreed to keep the crutches safe and handed over the bikes keys to Nicos. He signed the papers and waited for a mechanic to bring the bike.

Sky whooped with joy as she spotted a big black motorbike being wheeled towards them.

"Paris will have nightmares for weeks" she cried "Come on let's go."

Nicos watched as she shuffled across the floor. Quickly he grabbed her arm and held her straight. "Ta. That's better," she said walking much easier.

They sped out of the town towards the hills. Nicos could hear her shouting with excitement and hoped she remembered his instructions to hold on tight and lean into bends, but he doubted it and slowed down.

"Spoilsport I was enjoying that." She yelled in his ear and then whooped again as he overtook a rusty old van that trundled slowly along the road.

They weaved their way along the narrow bendy coast road past tiny villages and old ruined buildings. Goats fed in fields of poppies, cornflowers and patchy grass, or sheltered from the sun under ancient olive trees. Lizards watched them pass as they peeked out from cracks in old stonewalls, and huge black bees flew in pursuit of nectar. Sky loved every second of it.

Nicos waved his arm and pointed, his shouted words were lost on the wind, but Sky realised from his actions that this was where they were heading.

It was so typically Greek. Tiny white houses many with bright blue shutters at their windows. Tubs of red geraniums stood in courtyards where grape vines sheltered old wooden tables.

The streets were narrow and cobbled making Nicos slow almost to walking pace as he inched the large bike down towards the beach road.

"Right" He said parking the bike "We have to go just up there. Here hold in to me." He put on his rucksack and hung the camera case around his neck. Lifting Sky gently from the bike he helped her steady herself before they set off towards what looked like a souvenir shop.

"You're not serious." Sky said in a disappointed voice. "You're not taking my photo here." They had stopped by a little kiosk.

"Don't be silly, not here. Under here" He pointed to the ground. "Now just wait and see."

He greeted the man behind the tiny glass window speaking rapidly in Greek. Sky didn't understand one word of the exchange.

"Well what was that all about?" She asked.

"Sorry I forgot you haven't learned Greek yet. I will teach you during the long dark winter nights." He assumed she would let him anyway. "Come on this way." He helped her walk up a steep slope towards an old wooden door. "In we go."

He opened the door slowly and shouted. "Kalimera Costas. It is me, Nicos." An old man appeared out of the darkness.

"Kalimera Nicos, this way." He nodded to Sky and led them down the dark cool passage. He waved his arm beckoning them to follow. "Everything is ready for you my friend. Come. Come"

The tunnel like passage opened up to reveal a most breath taking sight. An under ground lake, its water dark at the edges, but brilliant blue in the center as a ray of sun shone through a large hole in the rock above. Water trickled down the roughly hewn black stone of the cavern and tinkled as it ran into the lake.

Nicos turned to Sky, her eyes wide with amazement.

"Now you must do exactly as I say. This water is very cold and very deep so once you are in the boat stay as still as you can. OK"

"OK" she replied. She found it difficult to speak she was so enchanted by the sight before her.

"Now I want you to put this on around your waist." He handed her a life belt.

"Oh so glam" she said as it slid to her hips.

"Right in you go and sit in the middle" He helped her on the a little rowing boat, which wobbled as they scrambled to the center. "Right get yourself comfy" he ordered, "Now take off your top and bra." Sky giggled but did as she was told. Nicos had a different light in his eyes, now he was a professional, now he was serious.

He folded her clothes and placed them at her side. He parted her lovely long hair at the back and draped it over her naked breasts, fanning it out towards the ends. Leaning back slightly he stared at her.

"Perfect. Now let me put this over you." He took a large piece of white muslin and draped it over her shoulders. "Hold the corners," he ordered "And when I tell you slowly bring your arms above your head, like this." He moved her arms up high. "Yes, yes. Very good. Now I am going to leave you but don't worry, I won't be far away. You may not be able to see me, but I will talk so you will know I am still here." Sky nodded. "I am going to tell you the story of the lake and I want you to listen and keep still. The story will help you to get in the right mood for the photograph. Every photograph I take has a story behind it."

Nicos slowly left the boat trying hard not to make it rock too much.

"OK Costas." he called into the darkness "Slowly please. Very slowly."

The tiny boat began to slide across the water and Sky let out a little scream, it echoed around the cavern.

"Stay still Sky. I am here. You are quite safe" Nicos took his camera from the case and began to fiddle with its tiny switches. Occasionally he put it to his eye, only to take it away and fiddle some more. He held up light monitors and studied their readings, for now he was lost in his work. Eventually he was happy. Looking across the water he could see that Sky had not yet reached the center of the lake.

He walked along the thin rocky ledge that ran around the lake until he was level with the little boat.

"You said you would talk." Sky's voice trembled a little.

"And I will" He replied. "Now can you see me?"

"Only just." She said peering through the dim light.

"Now for the story. Ready?"

"Yes Jack, tell me all."

"Many, many years ago, so the legend says" he began "A beautiful Greek princess fell in love with a common farm hand. Her name was Melissani. She was so beautiful and her father so rich, and her lover so handsome, but so poor.

They loved each other on first sight and met whenever they could, wherever they could. They just wanted to be in each other's arms.

Her father found out and was outraged, he banned her from seeing him ever again. The boy was not good enough, not rich enough for his daughter. She was heartbroken and refused to eat, she didn't care about his lack of wealth, she loved him.

Occasionally she managed to sneak out during the night and meet with her lover when they would kiss and make love in the poppy fields." Nicos spoke softly "Her father followed her one night and threatened to kill the boy if she disobeyed him again.

He arranged for her to marry one of his cousins, a man who she hated upon sight. He was old and ugly, but could provide a huge dowry, which her lover could not. Her father was a greedy man who cared little about her happiness.

He told her that if she did not do as he wished and marry the old man then she would never be allowed to marry anyone.

The princess managed to get a message to her young lover and they met for one last time. Up there on the cliffs." Nicos pointed to the roof. "They kissed and vowed their love for each other. They wanted to stay together forever and swore never to be parted. They planned to run away, but knew her father would find them eventually and bring her back. They were distraught as they cried in each other's arms. What were they going to do? There was no way she would marry this cousin, she wanted to be with her young lover.

As they wept a large hole appeared in the rock. They took it as a sign from the Gods, and, holding hands jumped into the darkness.

They both drowned here in the lake. The water swallowed them both, their bodies were never found.

Every day the sun God looks for them just like he is doing now." The boat had reached the center of the lake where a narrow shaft of sunlight shone directly on Sky's head. "Right slowly raise your arms like I showed you."

Sky held the muslin and put her arms high. She lifted her face towards the brilliant ray of sunshine and Nicos could see the glint of tears on her face, as it lit the gold in her hair. The gentle movement of the boat caused the muslin to waft behind her slightly, giving the effect of wings. Nicos clicked away with his camera.

It was the most stunning set of photographs he had ever taken. She really did look like an angel.

"Ok Sky that's it. Slowly bring your arms down and we will pull you back to the shore." Nicos wiped away his own tears, tears of joy in creating such a masterpiece. "Costas, slowly back to the boat station please."

By the time he had packed his camera away and walked around the rock ledge Costas had almost pulled Sky back. She sat stock still as the boat bumped against the rock. Nicos jumped on board and wiggled his way towards her.

"That was superb." Nicos said hugging her close, feeling her cool skin and hard nipples through his shirt. "Absolutely superb" He kissed her nose.

"Can I get dressed now?" she asked rather timidly "I've gone a little cold."

"Of course. Sorry I forgot. Here." He passed her clothes over. "Let's get you out into that sunshine it will soon warm you up." He rubbed her arms with his hands before helping her out of the boat and on to the rock.

"Costas, thank you" He passed the old man a note "Have a drink my friend." The old man smiled and nodded his thanks.

The brilliance of the sun made them both squint as they passed through the old door.

"I loved your story" Sky said still a little emotional "Do you have a story for everything?"

"That one is true, or so they tell me." He smiled down at her as she shuffled her way along "That is why it is called Melissani Lake."

"Did I really look like an angel Jack?" She looked at him seriously.

"You certainly did, a beautiful angel. I told you you would. Don't you ever believe a word I say young lady?" Nicos raised his eyes to the sky "One day you will" he laughed." Right, now time for that spin round. And don't keep yelling in my ear OK."

"Ok."

## CHAPTER 25

Aunt Eleni stood on the cliff edge and sighed. It had been such an emotional morning she felt drained. Coming back to Kefalonia for the first time in all these years, seeing her home now a pile of rubble, and talking to Paris had taken it's toll.

Andros had loved every minute of the trip. He had taken in all that she had said as she pointed out the places of her youth. He had asked almost as many questions as Paris in his quest for knowledge of his father.

She showed him Marco's old home, sadly like hers now a ruin, and watched as he put a small piece of the stone in his pocket.

They had visited the old goat shed and she pointed out her route to school. She showed them where they had swam as children, and where they had played.

Now she stood in the very place where all those years ago she had waved goodbye to her lover. It felt as if she could see her former life before her. The village slightly below, the road to Argostoli and the old school, and she could see the sea stretching out towards the horizon.

It was a very sad morning.

Lassi had changed, but up here on the hillside looking around, it was as if time had stood still. The craggy rocks stood exactly where she could remember, the sights from the cliff, still the same.

"I'm glad we are alone," Eleni said as she watched Paris and Andros walk down the narrow dusty lane towards the village. "I wanted to feel the place for myself again" She looked over towards Richard." I hope they didn't mind me asking them to leave me for a while?"

"I think they understood my love. Do you want me to go too?" He asked quietly.

"No come and join me." She pointed to a wooden seat "This is new. We had nothing like this when I was young." The cliff now boasted two picnic tables with little wooden benches at their sides.

"Well I have come back at last. It's so strange; nothing has changed; yet everything has changed. The village has grown, but we used to live up here, so looking down it is almost the same. I feel so confused, I had always wanted to return to the cellar to start again, but now I have come back I don't feel any different." Eleni felt her age, the heat and dust not helping her in any way. She felt weepy.

"Come my love. Let us stay for a while" Richard held her hand as they sat together. "I'm sorry you are disappointed" He wondered if she was thinking of Marco.

"Oh it's not that it's just so strange"

"Do you still miss him?" He asked tenderly.

"I do in a way, because we were all such good friends, but not as a lover anymore. Please don't upset yourself. It's you I love" She leaned over and kissed him "You mean everything to me."

Richard bent over and picked a bright red poppy, which grew in the grass by the bench.

"This is for you." He said "It is the flower of your youth, and now the flower of our future."

She took the bloom from him and smiled.

"Richard you are so lovely. Thank you. Come on lets us join them for lunch, a very very late lunch" Eleni gazed around as she spoke but didn't make a move.

It was true, they had taken much longer than expected to see the places Paris was interested in. She not only asked many questions, but also spent quite some time scribbling down notes.

She had been pleased when young Eleni had decided not to "tag along" as she put it, saying she preferred to visit with Vanni another day. Her childlike enthusiasm would have worn the older woman out much quicker, and it was lucky Tomas had not to come with them either, it would surely have taken all day if he had started to tell his stories Eleni thought. She loved her brother dearly, but when he began to talk about their youth he tended to get carried away. She remembered her mother once saying, "That boy could talk for Greece!" and smiled to herself.

Fond memories of the woman who had locked her away and then banished her, yet she now felt love towards her. She could almost hear her mother singing as she swept the floor of their kitchen, or washed their clothes in the nearby stream.

She remembered her father, so big and strong striding out across the fields to his work. The times when he held her close and told her lovely stories of the island.

The wonderful man whose great love for his daughter had cost him his life, a life he gladly gave in order to keep her safe.

Wouldn't she have done exactly that for her own son if need be? Of course she would.

They had acted out of love, now she could at last see that.

A strong feeling burned in her aching heart. Yes she loved them both, her mother and father, and now she realised just how much. The hate had gone; it had been replaced at long last.

"They really loved me didn't they?" It was a statement not a question, now she knew the truth. "They were only trying to protect me," She said to Richard. "Coming back has helped me understand" She began to cry.

Crying for her mother, father, her friends, her son who would never meet his own father, but mostly for herself and the wasted years.

He held her whilst the tears fell, stroking her hair and rocking her in his arms until the sobs began to subside. He gently held her face in his hands and looked into her watery eyes.

"Come on let us go and eat," He said eventually. "The past is now behind you." She smiled and nodded.

They walked slowly down the little lane hand in hand, just like young lovers.

"Eleni, would you do something for me?" he asked seriously. She stopped and looked at him.

"Anything you know that"

"I would like to go back to my home in England, I need to try and understand like you have today. Would you come with me?" Richard looked sad.

"Of course I will, I am your wife and where you go I go. Afterwards we can really look to the future, our future for as long as we live"

They kissed gently.

"Thank you my love," he said softly "What would I do without you in my life."

"What a fantastic morning." Andros said as they entered the pretty taverna. "Let's find a nice table and then I'll give Nicos a call. I wonder where they are now, and what he is up to?" he laughed and raised his eyebrows.

The taverna was built in a series of stone steps that led down to the bar and kitchens. Little tables with bench seats had been placed on each step and were sectioned from each other by lush grape vines giving the effect of seclusion.

"Sky is quite safe I imagine, she's not his type." Paris took a couple of steps down "Here this one is nice." Paris slid along to the middle of the seat. "You sit that side," she pointed to the bench opposite.

Andros had wanted to sit next to her, but if she preferred him to be across the table then that was where he would go. He had done everything she had asked this morning and had eventually been rewarded with a kiss on his cheek. It was going to be a long time before he held her in his arms as his lover again, but he knew it would be well worth the wait. He slid along the bench and looked across at her, yes, he thought, well worth the wait.

He ordered their drinks and took his phone from his pocket.

They both looked up as a motorcycle screeched to a halt.

Sky had been whooping in his ear yet again as they sped along the windy roads and Nicos was positive he would be deaf by the end of the day. He didn't want to go this fast really, but as he had arranged to meet Andros at the taverna in Lassi and time was getting on, he really had no choice.

They had spent longer than he had planned at the lake but he was more than pleased with the outcome. Those photographs would be fabulous. His father would be very impressed everyone would be impressed.

After he had taken her to the pretty village of Fiskado where Sky had needed to rest for a while, and then on to Scala in the hope of seeing some turtles. Now here they were hurtling through the luckily quiet village.

He spotted the taverna at the end of the road and brought the bike to a screeching halt outside.

"Good they're not here yet," Nicos said looking towards the bar as he helped Sky from the bike "You OK?" she nodded.

"Paris would go mad if she saw me on this." Sky laughed "But it has been fantastic" She kissed his cheek. "Come on let's find a table and wait."

Sky chose the table nearest the road; she did not want the hassle of shuffling down the steps. Her legs were aching as it was and she knew she would pay for today in more ways than one. Her face was tight from the effects of the sun and dust, her eyes sore, and her hair a mess, her body ached from effort, but boy was she happy.

They sat opposite each other grinning at the sights they saw.

"Jack, you look as much of a mess as I feel." She said looking into his dusty face, his hair scuffed up by the wind.

"Thanks a lot cheeky." He replied laughing.

The waiter came and Nicos ordered hardly glancing up as he spoke.

"Those photographs are going to be fantastic, you're mother is going to love them." He said enthusiastically "I shall give her a print of the best one and I bet she puts it on the wall."

"I doubt that very much" Sky's voice was scathing "I haven't got a mother, nor a father. Well I have but God knows where they are."

"I'm sorry?" Nicos said softly not really understanding her meaning.

"It's just me and Paris." Sky could see Nicos wanted to hear more. "Remember I told you they were hippies" He nodded "Well when Paris was 21 and I was 17 they decided they had done enough for us and buggered off." Nicos was unsure of her words again "Ran away in other words. They just came out with it one day at breakfast. They said they had signed over everything to us and they were going in search of inner peace. That was it. We haven't seen them since. I suppose we should be grateful they left us their money." She shrugged her shoulders. "Ten years ago and not even one postcard, a letter, nothing. I hope they found whatever they were looking for, and I hope it was worth abandoning their children for. I know we were not babies, but it hurt just the same. I think Paris felt it more though, you see now she had me to look after." She tried to lighten her voice.

"Paris has always looked after me, we share a home and everything. We have a lady come in every day to clean and cook, and she stays over at night when Paris is on one of her trips.

We have never heard from our parents since the day they left and I'm sure that's why she does the job she does. It means she can travel all over the world, I'm sure she is looking for them really." Sky took a long drink and then let her finger trace the rim of her glass.

"Paris is so good to me you know. I recon I'm the reason she's never married Andros, well one of the reasons. If she didn't have me to look after she would have gone years ago I bet. I hope she doesn't hate me, thinks I'm holding her back or anything. I would feel so much better if she did marry him I know she wants to because she told me.

The trouble is with those too they are always so busy. Personally I think it is just a poor excuse. They both look so in control, but deep down they are very insecure. Neither of them wants to make a decision, silly really. Its convenient if he doesn't ask, then she can't say yes or no and they still get to bonk no matter what. If they love each other why wait to be together?" Sky shrugged her shoulders again.

"Whilst Paris still has me to look after then she can put it to the back of her mind and Andros just gets on with his work. A right pair of dipsticks if you ask me they want their heads knocking together.

She would like his babies, so she says, but time is running out she's getting a bit old. Mind you so am I." She giggled and a huge grin on her face lit her dusty face.

"Anyway back to today. It's been the best day of my life thanks. One I'll look back on when I'm old and tell my children and grandchildren. That was the day I went on a motorbike and took my shirt off sitting in a boat. That was the day I got to spend with the most handsome man in the world and he made me look like an angel." Sky sat back and gulped, she had hardly stopped to draw breath.

Nicos laughed.

"I think you are exaggerating a bit. Second most handsome perhaps." Now they both laughed. "So you want children then?" He was so interested in her and wanted to know everything.

"Yep. Two." She smiled "How you fixed?"

"You never know you're luck" came the reply.

"I won't hold you to that" she said seriously.

"Well you better had, anyway what's a dipstick?" he replied "and what does bonk mean?"

Sky burst out laughing.

At the table just behind them, hidden by the grape vines Paris and Andros sat staring at each other. They had heard all of Sky's rather disjointed little speech.

Andros had no idea about Paris and her parents, and up until last night he didn't even know she had a sister. He realised he had never even asked, never made time to ask. He felt ashamed.

Paris felt slightly embarrassed. She had told Sky she wanted to marry Andros, but hearing what her sister had said made her think.

They both realised Sky had been right. They had been making excuses for far too long.

Andros reached for her hand. He spoke very quietly but a shocked Sky and Nicos could just about hear. They both giggled as they eavesdropped, realising their own conversation must have been overheard.

"I hope one day you will forgive me and I hope I can forgive myself. I love you so much I feel physical pain when I think about what I have done. Do you think you can, is there hope for us?"

"I hope you can forgive me too Andros" Paris replied. "What you did was unpleasant to say the least but I know how angry you must have felt." Her eyes were full of tears. "Let us start again. Let us cut that night out of our lives and go back to loving each other."

Andros pulled the little ring box from his shirt pocket.

"I have carried this since New York. I had plans to ask you to marry me and then it all went wrong. I had planned to ask you on the cliffs up there. Nothing has worked out as I had wanted, but still that is life."

He slid from the bench and knelt at her side.

"Paris will you please accept this ring, and agree to be my wife? I will wait for as long as you wish just as long as one day we can be together."

Paris stared at the fabulous red stone that shone from the center of the ring.

"Oh Andros it's beautiful, look it goes with my hair. Thank you what a lovely thought" she paused and looked directly into his eyes. "Yes I will marry you but we are waiting no longer. My sister is right, why wait?"

He slid the ring on her finger and kissed her hands. He could hardly control his emotions. At last she would be his.

He stared at the ring, Nicos had been so wrong this time, it was perfect for her.

They both jumped as Sky cheered.

"Well done Andros, at last, a wedding at last. Yuppiee!! Can I be bridesmaid?" She was so excited she clapped her hands wildly. She stood to embrace her sister and fell to the ground in a heap.

"You'll be going no where if you hurt yourself" Nicos was first to kneel at her side. "And what about our babies then eh?"

"Jack do you really mean that?" she asked forgetting about her grazed knees.

"I do. Let's keep up the family tradition and name them something really really unusual." Sky giggled understanding his naughty suggestion immediately.

This time Nicos meant it with every fiber if his soul, his life would mean nothing without this crazy girl by his side and he now understood the meaning of true love. It may mean he would be deaf at an early age, but that was a small price to pay he thought.

"I will even sell my stupid sports car," he added kissing her again to stifle her giggles.

"What is going on?" Richard and Eleni stood at the entrance laughing. It was a very strange sight that had met them.

Andros was kneeling at Paris's feet and Nicos was kissing some girl who was lying on the ground.

"Mama meet my wife to be the beautiful Paris" Andros said rising slowly "And her naughty little sister Sky."

"Oh Andros, Paris I am so happy for you both" Eleni kissed and hugged them, tears streaming from her eyes." I have waited so long to hear you say those words, I thought you would never get round to it. I am so happy it has made me cry."

Paris and Andros looked at each other, another one who obviously thought they had wasted time.

"And this is the lady who will be the mother of my children, when she learns to behave" Nicos said hauling Sky to her feet and dusting her clothes down. "If you can call her a lady."

"Only if you promise to make an honest woman of me, and don't make me wait as long as he has" she laughed and nodded towards Andros." Anyway I'm no lady, I'm an angel, oh, and what happened to the mermaid bit?"

"I've kept that for another day" he kissed her gently.

Paris interrupted doing her best to look angry.

"I want a word with you young lady. What's this about a motorbike, and taking your shirt off?"

"I'll tell you later" Sky replied laughing. "Come here, give me a hug and let me see that ring."

The sisters embraced warmly, both of them crying and laughing at the same time.

"Oh happy day" Sky sang "Oh happy day."

"I think we had better phone Tomas and ask him to put the champagne on ice" Eleni said her tiredness now gone "It looks as if we are in for a party when we get back."

She turned and took Richards hand.

"Today is the start of many things. Thanks to you I have put many ghosts to rest. No more living in the past, thinking of the past. The future holds so much for all of us. Sky is right. It is a happy day." She said softly.

Eleni looked down at her poppy, and speaking in her mind said goodbye to Marco for the last time. She thanked him for her son and also for sending young Eleni, because without her she would never have met Richard, and she knew deep down in her soul that is why Zeus had put her on this earth.

# About the Author

Elizabeth was born in the lovely old town of Stamford, Lincolnshire. She moved to Uttoxeter, Staffordshire with her parents in 1969 where she met and married Peter in 1979.

She recently retired after 32 years working as a bank clerk and now has time to concentrate on her lifetime ambition of becoming an author.

Greece and her lovely islands are her favourite holiday destinations, and she loves the stories surrounding the Greek Gods of Mount Olympus.